RROOOFFF?

I can hear the officer's dog. He says, *ARROOOF ARROOFF, respect. I used to be in your territory when I was a puppy, I remember you!*

Oh yes. I can smell him properly now. I remember too! When he was a little puppy, he was with a Pack near where I live. He was a very nice, friendly puppy, lots of fur, pointy ears, very very big paws. I held his nose in my mouth, to show who's bigger. He did a Wet Message on the ground to show respect, I did one on the wall to show I am Senior. He did puppy-bounces and licked my face. We played running-around and chasing games. He is a Friend called Rebel!

ARRF ARRRF.

I remember. *Hi there, Junior NotMyPack Friend Rebel.*

ALSO AVAILABLE:

I, JACK

Jack and Rebel,
the Police Dog

by Jack the Dog

as told to
Patricia Finney

illustrated by
Peter Bailey

▟ HarperTrophy®

An Imprint of HarperCollinsPublishers

Harper Trophy® is a registered trademark of HarperCollins Publishers.

Jack and Rebel, the Police Dog
Text copyright © 2002 by Patricia Finney
Illustrations copyright © 2002 by Peter Bailey
A paperback edition of this book was published in the United Kingdom
in 2002 by Corgi Yearling Books.

Library of Congress Cataloging-in-Publication Data
Finney, Patricia, date.
  Jack and Rebel, the police dog / by Jack the dog, as told to Patricia
Finney ; illustrated by Peter Bailey. —1st U.S. ed.
    p. cm.
  Summary: Jack the dog returns to tell a tale of his adventures with his
new friend Rebel, a police dog.
  ISBN 978-0-06-088052-1
  I. Bailey, Peter, date., ill. II. Title.

2006036322
CIP
AC

❖

First Harper Trophy edition, 2008

To my walkies leash!!! YIPPEE!

CONTENTS

INTERPRETER'S NOTE

Speaking as Jack's real Pack Lady and interpreter, I would like to make certain things clear.

First, although most of the animals are real, ALL OF THE PEOPLE ARE INVENTED AND SO IS THE STORY ITSELF.

There is no such place as South Cornwall, nobody is trying to build a highway through it, and there are no such people as the Stopes family—although there may be accidental resemblances to some of Jack's Packmembers. I'm afraid the Pack Lady in the story is a lot smaller, slimmer, and more patient than me.

Jack is a Real Dog and has certainly helped me with this book, by clumsying all the computer cables and eating my snail mail.

The Cats are real and just as superior: their full names are Remillard (Remy), Amazon (Maisie), and Musketeer (Muskie).

Police Dog Rebel is named after a real police dog that Jack's real Packleader met in the course of his work. Two of the incidents mentioned about him actually happened, although the original Rebel has probably retired by now. I would like to thank PC

Dave Bulley and the Police Dog Unit in Cornwall for their kind help in explaining what police dogs do and how they do it, and if I have made mistakes when I write about PD Rebel and his (fictional) Packleader, I hope they'll let me off this time. Also I'd like to make it clear that Police Dog Rebel is a made-up character, and the police dogs I met while I was researching the book are proper working dogs who would never be such wallies.

Thanks to my test readers—the real Caroline Burley, Martin Fenton, and my daughter, Alex. If I've forgotten anyone, thanks and please forgive me.

Patricia Finney

Jack and Rebel,
the Police Dog

Hi There, Friend!

Hi! HI THERE! HI FRIEND, HOW LOVELY TO SMELL YOUR FRIENDLY SMELL AGAIN, HI HI HI!
HAPPY DOG, HAPPY! HAPPY!

AROOOOF. I remember you! Can I smell your . . . ?

Oh. Sorry.

I am JACK, old–fashioned yellow Labrador who is Very Thick. I have a Great Big apedog Packleader called Tom Stopes and also Dad, and a Fierce ape-dog Pack Lady called Charlotte and also Mom, and I have three ape-puppies called Terri and Pete and Mikey. Apedogs are funny. They stand on their back

1

legs and they have no tails. (POOR POOR APEDOGS,
I will lick it better. . . . Oh, sorry).

I love everyone in my apedog Pack. Almost as
much as STEAK.

Then there are the dog-puppies who happened
to my Junior Pack Lady, Petra. Everything is different now. Petra's Pack Lady went away, the one who
didn't like dogs, so Petra and her puppies went to
live with her apedog Packleader next door. I am a
bit Sad Dog because it was nice being with Petra,
but a bit Not-too-sad Dog because the puppies kept
chewing my ears and my tail. We all go for Walkies

sometimes as a Big Pack.

My Pack is bigger than your Pack, look!

Oh. Okay.

(Also we have funny-looking normal-walking dogs[1] with hidden claws. They tell me things.)

This story is about me and my friend Police Dog Rebel. He is a Big Fierce Dog, lots of dark fur, big teeth, pointy ears, big swooshy tail. Well, he is a bit fierce. Fiercer than me, anyway.

BUT we are FRIENDS (SO WATCH OUT, GARAGE DOG, ONE DAY WE WILL COME AND MAKE YOU INTO MEAT. . . . GRRRR).

Also it is about me and a Car.

And a rabbit hole.

And nice tasty mature bones.

---

[1] Unfortunately the Big Yellow Stupid is still too thick to realize that, actually, we are Cats. To be precise: Very Large Striped He Who Owns the Radiator, known to the apecats as Remy; Smaller but Fierce Black with a Bit of White She Who Owns the Sofa, known to the apecats as Maisie; and Large but Dim White with Black Spots Who Can Have a Small Armchair if He's Good, known to the apecats as Muskie. Could we get on with the story now, please?

VROOM! Also, CHIPS!

A Car is a big kennel made of metal. It has paws, and it can move, but the paws turn into round things when it stops. It has a short tail that makes horrible whooshy-head smells and smoke. My Packleader's car makes lots of smoke. Lots and lots. More than yours.

Apedogs get in the car to go on the Big Hunt. I can go in the car too. I am not like the Cats. I do not go *Awvooooo, yow, gurrroooomiaaaaaooooowwwww* like the Cats when I am in the car.[1]

Here we are! It's time to go in the car and do

---

[1] This wicked libel is the Big Yellow Stupid's misunderstanding of our dignified and restrained protests when put in a horrible barred box and taken to the evil Whitecoat Apecat in the whooshy car.

some Hunting in town and then get the ape-puppies from the Running Around and Shouting Place.[2]

Oh wow! This is GREAT! Can I come too, please, Great Packleader, much respect, lick lick, please, I want to come too. Please, paws up, can I? CAN I?

OH GREAT! He has my LEASH! WALKIES! Happy HAPPY HAPPY DOG! Much bouncy. Bring him a potato chip packet (any inside? No. Sad Dog).

My Packleader makes the car's tail end open wide. It sticks a bit and creaks. "Hup, Jack, in you go."

It is not so comfy as the backseat. Are you sure, Great Packleader?

"Hup, Jack, hup!"

Are you sure?

"In!"

Oh. Okay. Hup, scrabble. Turn around, clatter, knock over a metal thing, turn around, scrunch, turn around, tinkle, push a big bag of glass things out of the way, turn around. Lie down. That's better. But a bit hard and not so comfy. Also the interesting papers and bits of sandwich are in the comfy bit.

---

2 A place to keep ape-kittens during the day so We can sleep. Apparently they learn useless things like how to make marks on white Cat bedding called paper.

I have found all the good eating stuff in the back. Okay, Packleader, you can shut the funny upswinging door.

"I've got to recycle those bottles," says Packleader.

GREAT. I like recycling. Big garbage cans with so many interesting and complex smells, mature pasta sauce, mature mayonnaise, mature ketchup ... Yum.

"I'll do it tomorrow," says Packleader.

Sad. That means never. Or until Pack Lady notices.

Now Packleader sits in the front bit where the big round thing and the interesting sticks are. He does something with his clever paws. The car goes, *Grrrvvrrr chur chur chur.*

Packleader says bad words. He does the clever thing again. *Grrvvrrr harooo chur chur chur.*

The car doesn't want to wake up. Why not?

Packleader barks at the car. I sit up and bark too. RUFF RUFF, BAD CAR!

"Shuddup, Jack," growls Packleader.

Why? I was only agreeing with you.

Grrrrvvrrrr grrrvrrrachur vrrschchck-chck . . . The car does a Smoke Message out of its tail and goes, *VRRRROOOM*.

See? I was helping you wake up the car, Great Packleader.

Packleader stops barking. He plays with the interesting sticks and makes the wheel go around. The light-trees start moving past, so does the road and the NotMyPack apedog dens. Once the things are moving past, Packleader is stuck where he is until they stop. He can bark, and it's true he has a very LOUD DEEP BARK, but he can't stop me doing what I want.

Hup. I jump over onto the backseat, which is much more comfy to lie on. Also Mikey has left a pile of chips under his little seat and there is a bag with Pete's removable furs in it, a T-shirt and short leg-coverings and very splendidly strong-smelling paw-coverings, all covered in Pete-smell and mud. AAAAAHHHH. Lovely.

"Jack, go in the back. You BAD DOG."

I do not understand, Great Packleader. Why am I a Bad Dog for sitting in the comfy bit?

Packleader growls, "I've gotta get a dog grill for this car."

Hi, Great Packleader, this is FUN, look at the light-trees whizzing past. All the other cars are barking at us and going *vroom* past us. Car barking is LOUD AND IMPRESSIVE, they go BEEP **BEEEP BEEEEEEEP.** Packleader growls and barks back. This is FUN! I put my nose out of the window, very very windy out there, makes my nose tickle so I sneeze.

Tree tree treetretre . . . Boring. I go to sleep with a Pete paw-covering in my mouth.

Garage Dog! GRRRRR

Whooshy feeling stops. Here we are. Great Packleader does some more stuff with the interesting sticks and the car goes to sleep. I open an eye. Are we going WALKIES?

No. We are in a place with Big Food Dens and Removable-Fur Dens and Flicker-Box Dens and lots and lots of apedogs walking about and cars and two-wheels-go-fast-with-roars. Usually, Packleader doesn't like to take me Walkies in the Lots of Dens Together place, unless it's very sunny. But it isn't. It's normal cold and gray weather. Oh well. Never mind. I like saying hello to everyone too.

Packleader opens two windows so the other dogs and apedogs can hear me bark and off he goes. I sit up and watch. He's going into a big den with nothing in it except apedogs behind a glass wall who play with bits of colored paper. I have been there and smelled it. It is a strange boring place with easy-to-knock-over things full of paper. All the apedogs look sad and the colored paper game doesn't look like much fun. Packleader is always grouchy when he goes there, especially if the clicky-clacky Flicker Box stuck in the wall eats his Plastic Biscuit.[1]

Anyway, my Packleader is sensible: He gives all his colored paper to Food Den apedogs and they give him FOOD.

---

[1] This is a flat thing made of hard inedible plastic with shiny bits. Apecats become absurdly huffy when they lose them or the Big Stupid eats them up.

There are lots of apedogs going past the car. *Hi, hi there. ARROOOF. I see you, Suki, and your Pack Lady, respect, respect, much respect, how nice to see you.* . . .

Suki is a Senior NotMyPack Friend girl dog who lives near my Pack's den.

Hi there, Jack, she says, *we have been to get MEAT. This is a very interesting-smelling car, may I leave a Wet Message? Respect, respect.*

ARROOOF! I say. *I am sad I can't respectfully smell your very nice Wet Message, Suki. Maybe later.*

There are Bad Dogs too. OH NO, there is Garage Dog! GRRRRR ROWF ROOOF, ARRROOF GRRRRR, RUFF RUOWF. . . . I hate Garage Dog. . . .

Garage Dog yips back. He stands up on his leash and goes, *Yip yip yarp, riifff yip! I'm very Fierce, I can tear out your tum and your throat and your tail end, yip yip.*

He has an old apedog Pack Lady on his leash. She is the garage apedog's Pack Lady. She is trying to pull Garage Dog away.

GRRROOWF GRRROWF. *I'll get you, Garage Dog. . . .*

I jump into the front bit of the car to go on barking. Put my paws and tummy on the round bit so I'm

TALLER.

BEEEEEEP!

What?

BEEEEP!

OH WOW! The car barked with me! The car hates Garage Dog too! We are a Pack!

ARFF ARFF BEEEEP ARRFFF ARRRFF ARROOOF! BEEEEEEEP!

BEEEP! BEEEP! VERY LOUD BARK. VERY GOOD.

See, Bad Garage Dog, the car is in my Pack too. It is barking at you too, ARRRRRF!

Garage Dog does a Wet Message on the car's wheel, hiding Suki's friendly one.

OH NO! HOW DISRESPECTFUL. *You*

are BAD BAD *BAD!* I jump to the back again, over the interesting sticks.

Garage Dog stands on his back legs (but he's still pretty small) and he goes, *Yip yip, yarp, I'll get you, I'll bite you and make you into meat, yip yip!*

I jump in the front again, try to get the Bad Garage Dog. My paw catches on one of the interesting sticks, ouch, hurt, pull pull, bite, pull . . .

Something goes clunk under the floor. *ARROOOF ARROOOFF ARROOOOF! I'll get my Pack Lady Petra, who is very Fierce and has her own den next to mine, and we'll come and make you into meat, BAD BAD BAD! GRROOOF BAD! . . . ARROOOOFFF!*

What? What's happening?

Oh, how FUNNY! The car isn't going *vrrroomm chuchchug* like it usually does when it wakes up. It sounds still asleep. But the light-trees are moving again.

And all the big dens are moving.

OH WOW! I'm making everything go. The whole world is moving for ME!

OH WOW WOW WOW, THIS IS GREAT!

I DRIVE A CAR

Look at me, Garage Dog, pretty soon I'll bash you with my car and make you into squashed gluey meat like a hedgehog ... ARRRF ARRF! That'll teach Garage Dog to come near my car!

ARROOOF, ARF, WOW WOW WOW!

Hi there, look at me, Suki, I am Very Thick, I am driving a car! This is greeeeeeat! I am like my Packleader now! Oh wow wow wow! Bye now!

I know how to drive, it's easy.[1] You put your paws on the round thing ...

---

[1] Possibly, though not for Big Stupids.

BEEEP! BEEEEP! WHEEEEE
ARF ARRRF WOOF ARROOOOF!
GRROOOOF! ROOOOOFFFF! Very windy
again outside.

All the apedogs are barking at me, and running
away. One of them is pointing a lightning box at
me. An apedog in dark removable furs with a Bad
Headthing[2] on his head is running up the hill.

WOOOWWOWWWOWW ARRF ARRF!
This is GREAT. There is wind. We are going
FAST.

---

2 For some reason the Big Yellow Stupid hates hats.

CRUNCH! Whoops. Broke some wood with stuff on it. Oh dear. Never mind. THIS IS FUN!

Hi there, apedogs! See, I can drive too. ARR–OOOOFFF!

A tree in the middle of the Big Round Place is getting bigger and bigger. It has a fence around it to make Wet Messages harder. Suddenly it jumps in front of me.

Hi, tree, let's be Friends, can I leave a Wet—?

CRUNCH TWang

cRUNch!!

KERLANG

TINKLE

tinkle

tinkle.

OH NO! HELP!

OWCH! YOWCH! There was a HUGE BUMP! Some car fell on my nose! The car is all different! The front bit to look through is all full of big spiderwebs. So is the back. The bit with the interesting sticks is all bent. I bumped myself on something. A Wet Message happened by accident on the front seat, which is Bad Dog.

Oh dear.[1]

OH WOOW! I don't like this! Where is my car! What happened? Who did the Wet Message on the front seat?

Oh no! I am a saaaaad loooonely pupppy . . .

---

[1] You see? We were right. Cars are bad, dangerous, evil things that might suddenly move at any time, especially when Cats are sleeping on the nice, warm top part.

ARROOOOO ARROOOOO!

Help, help yelp! Packleader, help arroooooooooOOOO! I can put my nose out of the window and smell Packleader and bark for him. ROOWF ROWF ARR-OOOOO!

I can smell him, he is upset and worried, he is galloping down the hill from the boring Colored Paper Den.

Whew. Packleader will save me from the strange bad cobweb car. He is very Big and Loud, though he runs funny from when he hurt his leg after he fell down in the Old Mill and I helped him.

Arrooo! I have a hurty, Packleader, quick, come

and lick it better! Hi there, Packleader, please SAVE ME! RRROOOF!

"Oh my GOSH!" *Pant pant. Gasp.* "What happened?" *Pant.* "What on earth happened? Are you Okay, Jack? Oh lord, look at the car. Poor Jack, is your nose sore?"

Yes, Packleader, very sore, and I think there is Jackblood too. Oh dear. ARROOOOO! Help help, Pack Lady, come and lick my nose! ARROOOO!

Packleader gets the door handle and tries to open it, rattles it hard, pulls hard, but no. It's stuck. Oh no, I'm TRAPPED. Even great big strong Packleader can't let me out, oh dear OH DEAR ARROOOOOO!

ARROOOOF ARROOOOOF

ARRRRRRRRRROOOOOO

OOOOOOOOOOO!

Now a Bad-Headthing apedog with dark removable furs is talking to my Packleader. My Packleader's body says: *Tense, might be trouble, big apedog here, be respectful.*

He says, "No, officer, I'm absolutely certain I left

the handbrake on. . . . I guess the cable might have snapped. . . ."

Suki's Pack Lady comes up. Her body says: *I know all about it, I'm very clever, listen.*

"Yes, officer, I saw the whole thing. Hello, Mr. Stopes."

"Hi, Mrs. MacNally."

"You see, Mr. Stopes's lovely dog Jack . . . yes, yes, Jack, poor chap, soon get you out . . . Oh, is the door stuck? Never mind, poor poor Jack."

Hi, Suki's Pack Lady, respect, pleased to smell you again, sorry I can't smell you properly . . .

"Well, anyway, he was barking at the Jack Russell over there—just barking—and the Jack Russell was barking back—you know how they are, don't you . . ."

This particular officer apedog has a dog too. I can smell him, despite my sore nose. In fact, he smells familiar. Sniffff snortle sniffff snortle.

Yes, I have definitely smelled him before. Hmm. I wonder when? He's Big, lots and lots of fur . . .

". . . dreadful little dogs, Jack Russells, never liked them, they all think they're rottweilers and a good thing they're not, the way they go for other dogs. . . . Oh yes. Well, Jack was a bit excited and he jumped over to the front seat and back again and I think his paw must have got stuck in the brake handle because I'm quite sure I heard a *clunk* and then off he went, of course. . . . Yes, yes, poor poor Jack."

Now Packleader is doing his angry face at me. Oh dear. Why? I am a sad, sorry puppy, what did I do?

"I don't believe it. You just wrote off my ruddy car, Jack."

What is "wrote off"?

The officer's body says: *Wait till I tell my Pack about this, this has cheered me up.* "Well, sir, I may need to arrest Jack for stealing a car and driving while disqualified on account of being a dog."

My Packleader makes "Ha ha ha" sounds. His body says: *Not very funny, this is a disaster, better laugh, though.* "Yeah, he's never passed a test either."

22

"Really. Tut tut, Jack."

Why, what did I do? What is "test"? Help, yelp! Packleader, the Jackblood may have stopped, but I don't like being in this funny car. ARRROOOO!

Packleader reaches in and pats my head. "Okay, poor Jack." He sighs a lot. His body says: *Sad, sad, sad Packleader.*

"Still, sir, I expect the insurance will cover it."

"I doubt it'll cover this."

Now the officer is being sympathetic. "That's bad luck."

"You're not kidding. And I'm due in London tomorrow."

ARROOOF ARROOOF!!! Stop barking, Packleader, get me out of here and lick my nose better!

OH WOW! SMELL! IT'S REBEL!

Packleader tries to get the other car doors open, but they are all stuck. He pulls hard, and so does the officer apedog, but the Bad squished car won't let them. Not even the upswinging back bit will open.

Oh no! I'M TRAPPED. ARROOOF ARRROO-OOO–OOO–OOOOOOO!

"Shut up, Jack!"

How can I shut up, Packleader? I am trapped in the scary funny car and my nose is sore.

I know, I will headbutt my way out. Okay, get back and bang with my head. No. Try getting back a bit more, sticks in the way, bang. No, try again.

Why is my head hurting?

The officer goes and gets something from his funny-shaped car. Oh, his dog is there, I can smell him. I know him.

RROOOFFF?

I can hear the officer's dog. He says, *ARROOOF ARROOFF, respect. I used to be in your territory when I was a puppy, I remember you!*

Oh yes. I can smell him properly now. I remember too! When he was a little puppy, he was with a Pack near where I live. He was a very nice, friendly puppy, lots of fur, pointy ears, very very big paws. I held his nose in my mouth, to show who's bigger. He did a Wet Message on the ground to show respect, I did one on the wall to show I am Senior. He did puppy-bounces and licked my face. We played running-around and chasing games. He is a Friend called Rebel!

ARRF ARRRF.

I remember. *Hi there, Junior NotMyPack Friend Rebel.*

My Packleader will help you, Senior NotMyPack Friend Jack, he says.

The officer apedog brings a metal thing and he

25

and my Packleader try to break the car. But the metal is all bent and it doesn't work properly.

I will help. I will summon all my Pack by howling and barking extra loud. ARRRF ARRF, ARR-OOOOF, ARROOOOOO!

Packleader is talking on his talkbone and the officer apedog is talking on his talkbone. When will you get me out of this funny car? . . . AROO-OOOO!

ARROOOOFFF ARRROFFF ARRROO-OOOO!

Garage Dog comes past with his old apedog Pack Lady. *Yip yip yarp, yer Big Nelly, can't get out, can't get out, but I can do a Wet Message saying Big Nelly on your car, yip yip.*

I hate you, Garage Dog, ARRRF ARROO-OOF, *ARRF!*

EEEEOOOOO MONSTER!

Packleader is talking to Garage Dog's Pack Lady and waving his talkbone next to his ear. I can hear Garage Dog's Packleader in the talkbone. Then my Packleader talks to the officer apedog. "Look, I've got to go get the kids from school, it's not far. . . . Would you keep an eye on Jack until the guys from the garage get here?"

"Glad to," said the officer apedog. His body says: *Good, I like dogs.* [1]

I like you too, officer apedog. I will help you get that Bad Headthing off your head as soon as I can,

---

[1] Why?

don't worry, I won't let it sit there scarily. . . . OH NO! My Packleader is GOING AWAY. Don't leave me, Packleader, please. I am a scared puppy, yelp yelp help!

ARRROOO
OOO
OOOOOOOOOOOOOOOOOOO
OOOOOOOOOOOOOOOO

Junior NotMyPack Friend Rebel in the officer's car is helping too. *Arrooof. Arrooooofff!* he says, helpfully. *ARRF ARRF.* We are making a Very Loud helpful noise.

"Quiet, Rebel!" barks the officer apedog.

We bark even more.

Here come some NotMyPack garage apedogs wearing removable furs all covered in carblood and carjuice. They have lots of metal things that smell of lightning and carblood.

Oh dear. Scared puppy. I can smell that this is Garage Dog's Packleader!

OH NO. IT'S A HORRIBLE EVIL MONSTER THAT GOES EEEEEOOOOOO!

Oh no, Wet Message happens again, I am a scared puppy, help help help. Dig a hole in the seat, hide in it, bits of spongy stuff everywhere, bite the seat, oh dear oh dear oh dear, EEEEOOOOO MONSTER COMING TO GET ME!

Officer apedog is on the other side where the window is a bit open. He has a biscuit.

Oh YUM, I like biscuits, thank you, thank you.

Whooops. Now he's holding my collar in his clever paw. He smells a bit scared, his body says: *Careful, Jack might bite, but got to hold him anyway. I like dogs, I will make sure he is safe.*

It's Okay, officer apedog, I won't bite you. If you say Garage Dog's **EEEEOOOO** monster has to eat me, I suppose it's Okay.

ARRRF ARRF, scared puppy, **EEEEOOOO MONSTER** IS BITING THE CAR, OH WOOOOOO!

Thank you, I like chewy sticks, they are very soothing when your tummy is frightened. . . .

More?

Ham sandwich. Yum. Spit out the apefood leaves. CRUNCH! CREAK. *SCREEELLL . . . !*

Oh woof! WOOF?

Now the door is open. Whew. I can escape.

Whew!

Pull really quick away from officer apedog, jump out of the car.

GRRR, it's Garage Dog's Packleader from the garage, talking to his Pack Lady and Bad Bad Garage Dog. . . . GRRRRR. . . . He can't catch me, lots and lots of apedogs here, run round and round, officer apedog trying to catch me.

Oh great! Chasing game! Hi there. Let's play. Puppy-bow, puppy-bow we can play catch!

Run run run . . . *Hi there, Junior NotMyPack Friend Rebel! Respect.*

My friend is sticking his nose through the window of his funny-shaped car. *Hi there, Senior NotMyPack Friend Jack.. I remember you, respect! Respect! Much respect! ARRF ARROOOF!*

Roooof! I remember you, Rebel, how nice to smell your friendly smell again. Can I come in your nice comfy car and cuddle up, because I am a Scared (but Senior) Dog and I would like a cuddle.

I bark, Rebel barks. Rebel's Packleader opens the door. Rebel paws at the inside cage bit. At last his Packleader understands. Opens it. I jump in, smell Rebel's tail end—he eats Chappie and mixer, not too much, and marrowbone Bonios. He smells

my tail end, licks my face to say *Respect*.

Whew. Lie down next to each other where we can feel nice warm fur, whew. It's quite squashed because this is a narrow nest inside the funny car. But that's okay. More cozy. Pant pant. That's better. Rebel is giving my sore nose a nice respectful lick. Happy Happy Dog. I notice Rebel has a torn ear. Poor Rebel. I will give it a nice lick. We take turns licking hurties. Groan. So cozy. Everything is okay now.

Oh look. There's a car all bent, squashed up against a tree, how funny. I wonder why? [1]

Rebel's officer Packleader scratches his head. Then he pats Rebel's head and my head. "I wonder if you really are the softest dog on the force, Rebel," he says.

Yes, Rebel's Packleader, Rebel is very nice and soft and furry. This is much better.

---

[1] The Big Yellow Stupid's boneheadedness sometimes surprises even Us.

My Pack Comes Back

Now my own Packleader is there with the ape-puppies, who are all talking at once.

"I'd never have believed it," says Rebel's Packleader. "They're friends. Look at them."

"Aaahh, look at Jack, Mikey, he's being friends with the big police-dog puppy." Terri smiles at me and my friend Rebel.

"Oh. Is that an Action Man Brave Hero Dog?"

"Yeah, that's right. Police dogs have to arrest criminals and track down bombs and all kinds of stuff like that. . . ."

"Not all at once, Pete." Terri is doing her

I-am-nearly-grown-up voice.
"They have special tracker
dogs for bombs. There was
a program about it after
you went to bed and . . ."

"Well, I bet this police
dog does tracker-dog
stuff when there's escaped
convicts. Look how big he
is, he's huge."

Mikey is holding his Packleader's hand. "He's an Action
Man Brave Hero Dog, isn't he, Dad?"

"Yeah, I expect he is. But he's being nice to Jack
at the moment."

"CanIyava Action Man Brave Hero Dog? With
a sled? And skis and a big gun that fires rockets and
lasers for the Brave Hero Dog, can I, Dad?"

"No, Mikey, not for the foreseeable future."

Terri is smiling at Rebel. "He must be a really
cool dog. Usually big male dogs are fierce to Jack
and growl at him and climb on his back and stuff."

The officer apedog smiles back. "Well, Rebel is
a big softie, but . . ."

"Rebel?" barks my Packleader. "Hang on, is that

little puppy Rebel? With the soup plate paws? Was he puppywalked by a retired couple in Trenever?"

My Packleader is strangely stupid about this. Why did he need to ask? We used to meet Rebel a lot when he was a puppy. Can't he smell who Rebel is? [1]

"That's right. Police Dog Rebel now."

"*Rebel!*" says Terri. "Wow, you've grown. He's grown, hasn't he, Dad? He's caught up with his paws."

"Wow. I can't believe it," says Pete. "Wow. Look at him. That's Rebel. Look, Mikey, that's puppy-dog Rebel. He used to lick your face clean when it was all covered in chocolate."

"No, Pete, it's Action Man Brave Hero Dog."

"Mikey won't remember, Pete, he was only a baby himself."

Rebel has smelled my Packleader, of course. He jumps out of the van, does much respect for him.

"Well, hi there, big guy, how are you doing as a police dog?"

Rebel does paws-up for my Packleader and Packleader pats his tummy. "Boy, he's big, isn't he?"

"He's certainly the biggest police dog in the

---

[1] After extensive research, the feline primatologists working on this problem have concluded that apecats are, for all intents and purposes, noseblind. This terrible condition accounts for a lot of their peculiar behavior, such as feeding Us food that is clearly Not Freshly Killed!

force," says Rebel's Packleader. His body says: *Not too pleased with Rebel at the moment, even though I love my Junior Dog.*

Terri sees Rebel's hurty ear. "Oh, poor puppy, what happened to his ear?"

The officer apedog sighs. His body says: *Embarrassed, about to look silly here, don't really want to tell Terri what happened.* "Bit of an accident."

"It's a bad tear," says my Packleader, checking out Rebel's ear. "Did he get in a fight?"

"You could put it that way."

"Wow? Really? A dogfight? What happened?"

"His ear got bitten, Pete."

"I can see that. Who by, a rottweiler? Rhodesian ridgeback? Pit bull?"

"Much worse."

"Dinosaur?"

"Er . . . no, Mikey. Human."

"Huh?"

Rebel's officer Packleader sighs. "He was supposed to help arrest some brawlers down at the Feathered Serpent by the quay. Big fight, couple of the lads that started it were off down an alley, so I warned them, then I let Rebel go."

"Uh-huh?"

"Rebel brought the ringleader down all right, he's big enough. He was pinning him in place, like he'd been trained. And then the bad guy grabbed his neck and somehow bit his ear."

My Packleader looks at Rebel and then at Rebel's Packleader and then back at Rebel. All the ape-puppies have their mouths open, showing their teeth; only Mikey is scowling.

"The *guy* bit *his* ear?" Packleader's body says: *I don't believe it.*

"Nasty bite too . . . Oh all right. I know. I'll

never hear the last of it, either. Rebel yelped and ran away, and one of my mates and I had to grab the bloke."

"Mm-hm." Packleader's body says: *I'm desperate to laugh, but I mustn't, shouldn't make officer apedog lose face, oh dear, VERY MUCH WANT TO LAUGH.* "Well, poor Rebel, how shocking."

I don't know why my Packleader thinks it's funny. At least the ape-puppies are properly sympathetic.

Rebel's officer Packleader says, "Not much of a Brave Hero Dog, I'm afraid, Mikey."

Wow, I say to my friend Rebel. *Mikey bit me on the tummy once, but that was when he was a very little puppy and he didn't understand. I didn't know apedogs did stuff like that after they got big.*

I didn't either, says Rebel. *It was awful. Something to do with Falling Over Juice,*[2] *from the smell.*

I lick his ear for him again.

I was very frightened, says Rebel. *It is hard being a police dog, you have to be Fierce to Big NotMyPack Enemy apedogs and often they are Fierce back and bark at you and they might hit you or kick you if you don't run away. And you have to do this hard head stuff as well. But I do not like Fierce apedogs, especially when they bite.*

---

2 Poison that apecats like to drink. It makes them act like Big Stupids—or worse!

I keep on licking his sore ear. Poor Rebel. It must be terrible, having to be Fierce so much and do Thinking too.

Mikey is still scowling. He takes his thumb out of his mouth. "No. You're wrong. Rebel is Action Man Brave Hero Dog."

We Find a Mature BONE!

Today is so exciting. So much happening. Meeting my friend Rebel! And then we got a NEW PACKMEMBER.

Another car with a NotMyPack apedog in it came to take Packleader and the ape-puppies home. Then Rebel's Packleader took me and Rebel in the back of his van. When we got home the two Packleaders did stuff with paper and snail-trail sticks, and my Packleader talked to lots of ape-dogs in the talkbone.

Rebel and I and all the ape-puppies played in the Outside, doing chasing games and jumping games and pawball. Petra was in her own Outside and we said *hi* through the fence. Her puppies have gone to be with other apedog packs now. Rebel was very respectful  because she is a Pack Lady. She smelled his Wet Message but she still preferred mine!

After Petra's Packleader called her inside, we did more running around. It was GREAT. Rebel said he was sure there was something buried in the ground-with-NotGrass, and so we had a nice dig, and Mikey helped with his spade, and we found a Bone I lost ages ago, which was all green and nicely mature so Rebel and I lay down to enjoy it.[1]

Packleader came out to get the ape-puppies for their tea and found us and he yelped. Lots. "Oh no,

---

[1] One of the things that most clearly demonstrates the stupidity of Big Stupids is their addiction to extremely Unfresh Food. This can sometimes be useful if the Food for the Cats is a whole day old and therefore unpleasant to eat. Given the chance, the Big Yellow Stupid will eat it up and then We can convince the big Tom apecat to open another hard-shelled Food for Us. Care must be taken that the queen apecat does not notice because she is, unfortunately, not so easy to fool and will callously allow Us to starve for the night. Then We have to make the strenuous journey down the road to one of Our other apecat territories.

Charlie's flowers! She'll really kill me now! You morons, why'd you do that?"

I think it is somehow Bad Dog, digging big holes in the ground-with-NotGrass. Packleader was yelping lots and saying "Bad Bad Bad" and trying to put some of the green stuff back in the hole.

"Rebel, you're useless," said Rebel's Packleader, laughing because it wasn't his NotGrass that got dug up. "You're supposed to stop crime, not assist it."

So Rebel brought him the interesting Bone as a present to calm him down and dropped it on his foot, and then both Packleaders were barking lots. It seems nice fragrant complex-smelling green Bones don't make apedogs feel calm.[2]

OH NO, Sad Dog. Rebel had to go home. It was Very Very Sad. Terri and Pete patted him and Mikey put his arms around his neck. "No. He's *my* Action Man Brave Hero Dog."

Rebel licked Mikey's face and Mikey licked Rebel's nose, but Rebel had to go with his Packleader, of course. Mikey was doing apedog water-howling when Pack Lady got home.

Pack Lady was mad.

Oh dear. Pack Lady is VERY MAD INDEED.

Pack Lady is barking at me lots. I am a Bad Dog.

---

2 Not surprising, in view of the stench.

I am AN IDIOT. BAD BAD BAD.

Oh dear.

I have made a hole in her flowerbed and ruined all her flowers.

What is "flowerbed"?

I totaled the car.

When? What's that?

She and Packleader are going on a Big Hunt in London and SHE DOES NOT NEED THIS EXTRA NUISANCE!

What's "London"? Maybe a very very very Big Huge Food place. Can I come?

Packleader did paws-up voice for her, and got her to go into the den to relax.

Oh dear. She fell over the nice mature bone in the Sitting Room.

Oh dear oh dear. SAD DOG. What a waste! She put it in the trash!

Sigh.

Now she has to go off again. Packleader offers to go because she's tired. "You can't," she says to

43

Packleader. "You're not allowed to drive the company car because it's against the firm's policy. And we can't drive it to London either for the same reason, so now we'll have to get the train. I'll try and get tickets when I pick up Auntie Zoo."

What is an "Auntie Zoo"?

Welcome, New Packmembers!

Pack Lady is back again.

Hi there, Pack Lady, so glad you came back. Hi hi, wow, OH WOW, WHO'S THAT WITH YOU?

Sniff snortle snifff snortle . . .

How interesting. This is a Senior apedog related to my own Pack Lady. She is the same height as Pack Lady but her hair has stripes in it and she is a lot wider. She smells like she is a Pack Lady too, but maybe a long time ago. She has a big long bag over her shoulder and two plastic Food Hunt bags full of things.

Terri and Pete give her big hugs and kisses. "Gosh, Auntie Zoo, are you going to look after us again? Really? Wow!"

Pete looks at Terri and Terri looks at Pete and they giggle.

Mikey is hiding be-hind his Pack Lady with his thumb in his mouth.

"Come on," says Pack Lady. "Auntie Zoo won't eat you, Mikey."

"She's a witch," says Mikey. "Like on the telly."

"Shhh," says Terri. "That's rude. She looked after me and Pete when Mom was having you."

"Which witch is that?" asks Auntie Zoo.

"The one in *One Hundred and One Dalmatians*."

"Cruella? I don't think so. I would never ever wear fur, you know. But I am a witch, in fact, Mikey, that's very clever of you. I can make spells and charms too."

Pete's mouth is open. Terri smiles in a grown–up way. "Oh really? How fascinating."

Auntie Zoo smiles back at her. "Isn't it? Do you still like the Spice Girls?"

Terri smells embarrassed and Pete and Mikey both laugh lots.

My Pack Lady leads Auntie Zoo into the den and she comes but then she stops. "Wait a minute. We can't leave Lulu in your mom's car."

"Lulu?" Packleader is looking worried. I don't think he likes Auntie Zoo very much.

Auntie Zoo puts down her bags and lopes back to the car. She has very long legs and plastic shoes that smell very interesting and complex. She opens the back and gets a big cage out. Pack Lady coughs and looks a little embarrassed.

"Lulu?" says Packleader again. His body says: *Oh dear.*

Oh wow! How interesting. WHAT AN INTERESTING SMELL! Snnifff snortle sniff. WOW! A FLY-ING FEATHERY?

Can I see?

"Catch Jack, Terri," shouts Pack Lady, and Terri puts her clever paw on my collar.

Back comes Auntie Zoo holding the cage up high. "Here she is."

It *is* a Flying Feathery. Very Big. HUGE. AS BIG AS A CROW! With a huge curved beak. It sees me and it says, **"Arrk Arrk. Bad Dog! Arrk."**

What? I'm not a Bad Dog.

A Flying Feathery SAID APEDOG WORDS!

Oh no. Scared Puppy. Run away. . . .

"Stop him," shouts Packleader, but Terri isn't strong enough to hold me when I really want to run away, and I DO. This is TOO SCARY FOR ME! You can't have Flying Featheries saying APEDOG WORDS.[1]

RUN RUN

RUN RUN.

Out the front gate,
d o d g e,
run,
down
the
road . . .

RUN AWAY QUICK!

Phew. I'm tired. Pant pant. Sniff. . . . Snortle. Snortle. Maybe there are some chips at the bus stop.

Hi there, Packleader. Are you scared of the evil

---

[1] Of course not. They are Food.

Feathery too? It's Bad. Shall we go find a den somewhere else? Oh, Okay, you can put my leash on.

Oh dear. I think Packleader is somehow mad
at me. Much barking. What is "menace"? What is
"dummy"? Do we have to go back to our den?
Oh well. If you say so, I suppose it's Okay.

Maybe the Flying Feathery Who Talks Apedog
has gone by now.

No. I can smell it in the den. Oh dear. Oh dear.

Flying Feathery!

Auntie Zoo has put the big cage on the table in the kitchen. The Scary Flying Feathery is sitting in the corner of it, biting some banana.[1] Remy is asleep on his radiator. Maisie and Muskie are not here yet. Remy opens one eye to look at the Flying Feathery, shuts it again.

"Arrk."

"Yes, I brought Lulu on the train," Auntie Zoo is saying to Pete. "In the guard's car. No reason why not, and I sat with her so she wouldn't get lonely."

"Gosh."

---

[1] This is an OUTRAGE.

"Why not a car?" asks Mikey. *"Vroom."*

"Cars are the great evil of our age, Mikey."

"Eh?" says Pete. "What, even ones with catalytic converters?"

"Even them. They still contribute to global warming."

Packleader coughs. "Speaking of which, I'm afraid Jack totaled the car and . . ."

"I know, Charlie was telling me. No problem, we'll get the bus."

Boring ape-talk. About stoves. And central heatings (what is "central heating"?[2]). And trash cans. And shops. And buses. And stuff. Boring. Sniff snortle. Wander around the kitchen.

Hi there, Flying Feathery. Er . . . can I smell your . . . ?

"Arrk. Push off."

WHUFF. Jump backward, bash into a bag, sit on it. Oh dear. Squashy grapes.

Auntie Zoo laughs, washes

<hr />

[2] A noble and wondrous thing, inspired by Cats, which renders the cold, damp apecat lairs a little more hospitable for Us. The apecats do not keep the heat high enough, however, despite being asked politely.

them, and puts them in a bowl. Then she pats my ears and my side. She has a nice *I-like-you* smell.

"Arrrk arrk push off push off push off . . . wuzzock."

How rude.

Lots of ape-barking. "Take no notice, Jack, she's just jealous."

Auntie Zoo strokes the Flying Feathery with her other finger. She is very strange.

Oh, here is Muskie coming to see when he can eat the Flying Feathery.

"Arrk arrk ARRK ARRK NEENAW NEENAW WUZZOCK PUSH OFF.**"**

And Auntie Zoo stops stroking me and strokes Muskie. Why? I want stroking too. ME. You have to stroke ME! Push my head under her hand.

"Ah . . . yeah, I was going to ask about the cats . . ." says Packleader. His body says: *She's crazy.*

"No problem. Lulu's used to cats. I have four of them, after all. They're all friends."

"Right," says Packleader, but his body says: *Oh boy, I bet the cats eat that bird.*[3]

Muskie sits down and looks at the Flying Feathery, licks his paw.

"Arrk," says Lulu. **"Arrrk. NEENAW."**

The strange Flying Feathery sounds like a whirly-whirly-light car. *If you try to eat me, I will bite your ears off*, Lulu says with her body.

Um. Okay. I can wait, says Muskie with his body.

Oh dear. Oh dear. What can I do? Cats eat Flying Featheries. But this Pack Lady Auntie Zoo has a Flying Feathery for a Packmember. Cats can't eat Packmembers.[4] Oh dear oh dear. My head hurts.

Maisie comes in from the other room. She sits down and looks at the cage with interest.

"Arrk ARRRK. NEENAW WUZZOCK." *Bite your ears off too*, says Lulu with her body.

Hm, says Maisie with hers. *An interesting problem. The cage must open. But how?*

"Push off PUSH OFF PUSH OFF. ARRk!"

Hm, says Maisie, stepping a little closer and looking up, making chitter-chatter noises with her teeth. This means *I'm going to eat you* in cat.

Oh dear oh dear. Packmembers must not eat Packmembers. Oh dear. I will interpose myself. . . .

---

[3] Occasionally, generally by pure chance, even apecats get things right.
[4] Yes we can. We just don't always choose to.

Whoops. I bumped the table and the cage slid....[5]

Zoo grabs for it. Pack Lady grabs for it. Pack-leader grabs for it. They get tangled up. I try to help and Auntie Zoo falls over me. Pete yells. Mikey jumps up and down. Terri starts laughing. The cage door opens with a clang, and there are lots of feathers as Lulu flies right up and Maisie jumps at her.[6]

OH NO OH NO OH NO. BLOOD!

Gosh. Maisie got scratched on her nose by Lulu.[7] Oh dear.

Arrf arrf arrrrrrf. WOOF AROOF. You can't scratch my Packmember Maisie.[8]

Remy opens his eye and shuts it again.

Auntie Zoo has picked herself up off the floor and caught Maisie by her scruff.[9] She hisses at her. An apedog speaks cat! She says, *Hisssschhheeees-wwwwshshshs.*

---

[5] Bull's-eye! The good thing about the Big Yellow Stupid is that he is pathetically easy to control.

[6] A mere trial run, of course. Practicing.

[7] The prey accidentally got lucky.

[8] That's right, Big Yellow Stupid! Fetch! Kill!

[9] Outrageously disrespectful behavior, in any apecat.

I don't speak cat so well, but it sounds very rude.[10]

Auntie Zoo taps Maisie on the nose twice.[11] Throws her down onto the floor again.[12]

Maisie is very very embarrassed.[13] Much washing.[14] Muskie is still staring because he doesn't know what to do.[15]

Maisie goes and hits Muskie on the head with her paw and Muskie runs away.

All the apedogs laugh lots.[16]

"Arrk," says Auntie Zoo, holding up her hand, and the Flying Feathery flies down and lands on her hand. She picks up the cage and puts all the food dishes and bottles and dangly things straight and then she puts Lulu back in.

Remy turns on his other side and twitches his tail.

"Are you sure about this, Zoe?" asks Packleader, who is doing tooth-showing friendly face a lot. His body says: *I wish I could stay here and watch the fun.*

"Absolutely. You go off to London and give them all what-for at the Inquiry. Especially you, Tom—the nerve of it, trying to demolish the Old Mill on the sly to get it out of the way of the

---

[10] Extremely rude.

[11] Even ruder.

[12] Who does she think she is? We must devise a method of killing her and eating her Flying Feathery.

[13] Simply appalled at the elderly apecat's lack of manners and good breeding.

[14] One must keep oneself clean, of course.

[15] Stupid boy.

[16] Traitors! There will be a reckoning.

developers. And now they want to cut down Pencerriog Wood and put the road through there. It's outrageous. I'll do anything I can to stop those awful planet-wreckers!"

Oh NO! BAD Carry-boxes!

FOOD TIME. The Cats say I do not have to explain about this even though it is a very Happy Time, best time of day.
Then going Outside to do Wet Messages. The Flying Feathery Packmember Lulu is in the room where the clicky-clacky Flicker Box lives, and the sofa bed has suddenly turned into a nice nest. For me?

Oh, sorry. For new Senior extra Pack Lady Auntie Zoo.

"He can sleep with me if he's used to it," says Auntie Zoo.

Yes please. Please? I like sleeping all cuddled up and cozy in a nest. Yes?

"Do you have any idea how much that dog snores?" says Pack Lady.

Terri is helping with putting nice soft blankets in the nest for me and she nods seriously. "We don't let Jack on beds because he not only snores and makes horrible smells, he takes up all the space and you fall out."

Auntie Zoo laughs even more and pats my head. Ohhh lovely, I love you too.

Sleep time now, but in my own nest. Muskie comes and lies on my head. Maisie is busy Outside, having cat-type fun. We have inter-esting dreams where I sit on

Lulu's cage and squash it so it breaks and the Cats can get at her.

Very very early in the morning. Still dark. So early, my tummy is only a little bit HUNGRY. Packleader and Pack Lady are coming *pad pad pad* quietly down the stairs. Shhh.

OH WOW! Hi, Packleader! Hi, Pack Lady! How lovely to see you! ARRRF. ARROOF. ROOF. LISTEN TO MY HAPPY MORNING BARK. "Erro! ERRO!"

"Shuddup, Jack," growls Packleader. He looks very sad, even though he is wearing his not-yet-smelly new leg-coverings.

Pack Lady staggers into the kitchen to make Hot Brown drinks. "Oh NO! You bad cats!"

Oh dear. She has trodden on a small Flying Feathery that Maisie made into meat last night. Pack Lady does much ape-barking, but quietly, mostly about how she hates cats.

Does she? Why does she let Maisie and Muskie upstairs and not me?[1]

She picks up the feathery meat and puts it in the trash, washes her hands, sighs. She is a Sad Pack Lady.

Time for a dog to make her feel better. I lean against her legs to cheer her up, so she nearly falls

---

[1] Because she recognizes that We actually own the lair and allow her to stay while she is useful to Us (for obtaining and opening hard-shelled Foods, mostly).

over. Hi, Pack Lady, I love you.
  Food? FOOD?
  It's breakfast! YIPPEE! MY FAVORITE.
  Pack Lady opens the hard-shelled Food thing.
  SLURP SLURP SLURP, GULP, CRUNCH, YUM YUM.
  Erp.
  More?
  Remy comes down from his radiator. Maisie
and Muskie come through the cat door. They all go
Mrrup merrryow at the Pack Lady and wind around
her feet so she trips. All the cats get breakfast,
though Pack Lady says they do not deserve it.

  Oh Okay, I'll go Outside. Pad pad. Wet Message,
Hard Message. Enemy Tomcat came yesterday.
Another Cat, one of Maisie's littermates. Another
Cat. Lots of Cats.[2]

---

[2] Naturally, the invasion of our territory by that revolting parrot occasioned
great interest among other Cats in the neighborhood. It was necessary
to make it clear that We have the right to eat it first.

"Do you think they'll be Okay?" says Pack-leader to Pack Lady.

"Of course they will," says Pack Lady. "Auntie Zoo used to look after me when I was a kid."

"Jeez, what was she like?"

"Exactly the same, only much younger and skinnier. She was my mom's baby sister, and she was into the Rolling Stones, and we thought she was great. And who else are we going to get to look after three kids, a dog, and three psychopathic cats on this short notice? For nothing?"

"Okay, Okay."

Pad out into hall. What?

There are Bad square boxes with handles for carrying removable furs. This is Very Bad. This means Packleader and Pack Lady are GOING AWAY.[3]

Quick. Bark at the Bad carry-boxes, frighten them off. ARRRF. ARROOOOF. WOOF. ARROOO-OOOF.

Pring on the doorbell. It is a NotMyPack apedog, with a smoky stick. ARRRF ARRF ARRF. ROOOF. RUFF. Go away, you can't come here.

---

[3] Sometimes this is Bad for Cats because We are put in the barred box and taken to a horrible place with cages. Other times it is Good because an ape-kitten from another Pride comes to give us Food and We can do what We like in Our den.

But instead of helping me to see him off, Pack-leader and Pack Lady get the square boxes and start to follow the NotMyPack apedog.

Oh dear oh dear oh dear. Does this mean I am the Packleader while they go on a Very Big Hunt? I am not as Big as Great Packleader, but I will do my best. Maybe it's too hard. *Don't go, Packleader, I love you.*

Eeoo eeoo eeooo. Sad puppy whines. Sadness.

Packleader and Pack Lady pat my tummy. "See you soon, Jack," says Packleader.

Oh dear. What is "soon"?

Auntie Zoo is up. "Bye, Charlotte, bye, Tom," she says. "Good luck."

♥ BACON SANDWICH! ♥

Very interesting morning time. Breakfast is all different. The ape-puppies have to eat up fast and get ready because they are going ON THE BUS.

Pete and Mikey get excited. Terri hates mornings and she goes on the bus anyway. Poor Terri.

Auntie Zoo calls me and she PUTS MY LEASH ON! OH WOW OH WOW, GREAT, HAPPY HAPPY HAPPY. WALKIES. I LOVE WALKIES. OH WOW. Come on, Packmembers, hurry up, happy happy, let's go, QUICK!

WALK, walk along the hard road, sniff snortle. Suki has already had her walk. Bad Garage Dog has left a Wet Message. I do one on top and higher. *Grrrr. I hate you, Garage Dog.*

Stand at the bus stop. Chips? No. Sad Dog.

Here comes a HUGE GREAT ENORMOUS KENNEL-THAT-MOVES WITH LOTS OF WINDOWS. Arrf, arrf.

"It's Okay, Jack, it's only a bus."

Terri goes on the first bus, full of ape-puppies shouting and pushing each other and young male apedogs being threatening at each other. Scary. We get the next one. ME and Auntie Zoo and Pete and Mikey.

SO EXCITING. Oh wow! I can smell something good. I can smell . . . OH WOW! Snifff snortle sniff snortle . . . Yum. Somebody has left a bacon sandwich. MINE NOW!

Slurp.

I like buses.

Vroom   chuggga chugggaa. Whooshy feeling. Tummy turning around. Oh dear. Maybe buses aren't so good. Lie down on my tummy to stop it turning around. Gulp gulp.

"Look!" says Mikey. "I'm driving the bus. *Vrrooom. Beep beep.*"

No good. I have to unswallow. *Ugga ugga glerp.*

"Yuck, Jack," groans Pete.

Feel better now. Oh look, someone left some nice prechewed bacon sandwich right by my nose. Yum. Slurp, lick lick.

"Oh yuck, that's *so* horrible," says Pete.

Auntie Zoo is looking out the window, didn't see.

Head between paws, sigh. Don't like the whooshy feeling. Sleep now.

REBEL! Again!

Running Around and Shouting Place is here. Quick quick, let's get off the whooshy bus. Pete and Mikey say good-bye and run in being NEEEOWW things. Auntie Zoo gets my leash and off we go, boring hard road.

Walk walk. This is great. Here is a soft road, full of interesting news, lots and lots of other dog friends I don't know yet. Girl dogs. A Fierce Brown Small dog-type person eating a rabbit. Lots of Flying Featheries. Lots of Wet Messages and some Hard Messages. I leave plenty of Jack Messages so they know I've been here.

I wonder where we're going, Auntie Zoo. I know our Pack's den is that way. Why are we going this way? I can feel it's not quite the right direction. Aren't we going to get a car or a bus? You can walk from the Running Around and Shouting Place to our Pack's den, but it's a very very long way. Packleader and I did it once when the car was sick and Packleader gave up waiting for the bus back. It took all morning and we met some very fierce-looking cows.

Oh Okay. Walkies. LONG Walkies. GREAT. I can go off the leash? Oh WOW. *Sniff,* snortle, *sniff,* snortle. We  are going down a soft road at the back of some dens. Lots of interesting things here.

I know that smell! A very Big Strong (quite Fierce) dog left a Wet Message here. He was very happy and excited. I know him!

It's Rebel! Junior NotMyPack Friend Rebel! ARROOOF? Arrf ARRF?

We are going along some fences now and the lovely friendly Rebel smell is very strong. Here he is! This is Rebel's pack territory! Sniffff.

ARROOOF?

Somebody big says, *ARRRRF ARRF* ARRF!

Yes, Rebel has smelled me through the fence, which has a little door in it, locked. I put my paws up, look.

WOW! Rebel has his own den! He has a kennel and some running-around-Outside inside his Pack's Outside. There he is! ARROOOOF! ARRF!

Rebel's Packleader is there, opening Rebel's door for him.

Hi there, Junior NotMyPack Friend Rebel. How lovely to smell you, respect for your territory, here I will leave a respectful Wet Message for you to smell.

Rebel has smelled me too. *Hi there, Senior*

NotMyPack Friend Jack, lovely to smell you too, I will smell your very friendly Wet Message later because my Packleader and I are going out Hunting now and it's VERY EXCITING!

"What's so interesting, Jack?" says Auntie Zoo. "Oh, a police dog. Are you friends?"

"Morning," says Rebel's officer Packleader.

"Good morning, officer," says Auntie Zoo.

Rebel's Packleader smiles, his body says: *I know the dog, but who are you?* "Is that Jack there?"

"Yes. Tom told me about Jack's adventures—that must be Rebel and you must be Officer Janner."

"Crashed any more cars, Jack?"

What? I do not understand Rebel's officer Packleader, much respect.

He pats my head and Rebel comes to sniff. Rebel's Packleader and Auntie Zoo do ape-barking about how she's looking after the Stopes children and so on. She laughs quite a lot about it. "Um . . . I wonder, if I keep going this way, will I come to Moonshadow Farm?"

"Eh? Oh, you mean the old Chybrynog place? Yes . . . just along the footpath, couple of miles, not very far. They've got a lot of people staying there at the moment, you know."

"Oh yes, I know. Friends of mine."

"Are they? Fancy that. Well, be seeing you. Bye there, Jack."

Bye bye, Junior NotMyPack Friend Rebel, smell you later.

Smell you, Senior NotMyPack Friend Jack. I am going Hunting with my Packleader now.

Walk walk walk. Sniff snortle, sniff snortle. This is quite a LONG WALKIES.

Soft Apedog Dens; Ape-puppies

We come out between two hedges, where there is a square wooden board on a stick with boring ape-dog smears on it. There is a large field with some Cow Messages in it.

Oh! Lots of interesting and complex smells. Many apedogs, many cars. Carblood, carjuice. Dogs. Small movable apedog dens made of cloth and some of plastic and some big ones with wheels. NotMyPack dogs come to smell me. Lots. Oh dear. They smell quite fierce and a bit like Garage Dog.

They smell my face and my tail end. Some of them growl and bark.

Er . . . hi, NotMyPack dogs, I am respectful, I am not fierce, I do not want any of your food.

Make quite small, low tail.

One of them growls. He is their Packleader.

Oh dear. Hide behind Auntie Zoo. She pats me, puts on my leash. That doesn't help, Senior extra Pack Lady. What if I have to run away from all these fierce-smelling dogs? I don't think you can run as fast as me and it's hard to drag a whole grown-up apedog.

"Karl! Karl, are you there?" shouts Auntie Zoo, hauling me back when I pull her into a big cow-pat. "Stoppit, Jack, you great dummy."

One of the Junior Pack Ladies with a big tummy sees us and comes over. She smells interesting and

complex and . . . sniff . . . snortle . . .
How interesting! She is Special.
Respect, Special Pack Lady.

"Hello," she says. "What a
beautiful dog."

Pat pat. Hi there, apedog
Pack Lady. Can I smell how
Special you are? Snifff. You
are very lovely-smelling.

"Jack, stop it! Is Karl in
the camp yet?"

The Pack Lady smiles
but she smells nervous. "Who wants him?"

Auntie Zoo smiles back. "His mother."

"Oh." She looks at Auntie Zoo. Her body says:
Gosh what a shock, his mom, wow! "He was over at
Pencerriog Wood, but they got evicted." Off she
runs.

Here comes a new apedog. He is quite big and
very thin, and he has long brown tails on his head,
stuck together. They smell very strong and interesting. He has metal in his face: metal in his nose,
metal in his ears, metal in his lip. Poor POOR apedog, how did that happen? It must be dreadfully
hurty, let me lick it for you . . .

"Down, Jack."

Oh sorry. Yes, Auntie Zoo, this is your ape-puppy, I can smell that.

"Mom!" says the new apedog called Karl. "Great to see you, how are you?" Oh. How funny! His face says, *Happy*, his voice says, *Happy*, but his body says: *Oh dear, oh no, complicated, how can I get rid of her?*

Grrrr. I don't like it when apedogs say one thing in their voice and another thing in their body. It's scary. It makes my head hurt.

"Stop it, Jack. I'm very well, thank you, Karl."

Quick ape-barking. They're here because they got chased away from another place. The field with Cow Messages belongs to apedogs who like them and hate roads, so they can stay as long as they want. More come out of the soft dens and do ape-barking. All around are lots of apedogs and most of them have bits of metal in their faces. Some have metal in their tummies. It's terrible. Who did it to them?

A small girl ape-puppy comes. She is interesting to smell as well. She has a biscuit for me and she  throws it. Ulp. Yum. I like you, girl puppy, even though you have metal stuck in your poor ears too. Your Pack Lady must be very neglectful, not licking them better. Paws up. Show tummy. She pats my tummy. She smells the same age as Pete but I haven't seen her at the Running Around and Shouting Place.

Auntie Zoo sees her. "What's your name, dear?"

"Caroline Burley."

"Is your mom called Bud?"

"Yes. Are you Zoe? She said to tell you she's coming in a minute when she's done the washing up."

"Yes, I'm Zoe. Caroline, do you think you could look after Jack for me while I say hello to everyone?"

The girl ape-puppy nods. I like her. She is small and thin but strong. Auntie Zoo gives her the leash. OH WOW, WONDERFUL, GREAT! The girl ape-puppy Caroline and I are going to play. YES!

BURGER WRAPPERS!
BAKED BEANS!

She is a very nice girl ape-puppy. She has more biscuits in her removable furs. She throws a ball to play
NotFetch, and when I drop it, she runs and gets it
for me. She holds my leash and I take her down to
the end of the field where the Message Huts are so
I can lift my leg and leave plenty of Jack Messages.

There is a kennel-that-moves, sort of half a bus,
quite short. The window is open . . . sniff, snortle . . .
definitely food. Put my head in through the window . . . ahh! Burgers—wrappings for burger,
proper ground-up-cow burger, yum, slurp. Eat

 them up. I like burgers and wrappers.

We play running up and down. I find a nice Food Dish full of mature baked beans. MINE NOW. Yum yum ulp gulp erp.

Grrrr, says one of the dogs. . . . *Yer Big Soft Thicko, that's my grub, give it back.*

Oh dear oh dear. He's growling at me Very Loud. His fur is up. His tail is up. He looks very VERY MAD.

Oh no, he's showing his teeth. Quick, Caroline girl ape-puppy, quick quick, this way, there's a little path here . . . run run run.

Caroline hangs on to my leash and I pull her away from the bad NotMyPack Enemy dog, down the path, through the bushes, away from the field where the apedogs have their little movable dens. She is squeaking and laughing about how small the other dog is.

But FIERCE!

Nice mushroomy smells here. Let's have a look. Mmm. . . . Trot trot, pad pad. Badgers. Rabbits.

Oh. Suddenly we're on the hard road. Trot trot trot. Wet Message, Hard Message.

Caroline stops and looks.

Why? Oh yes, over there is a van. There are big apedogs sitting in them. They smell quite fierce and scary.

Yes, Caroline, I think you're quite right to hide under a bush. I'll hide too. Move over. They smell very fierce, don't they? Pant pant.

Oh look. Here comes Auntie Zoo's big ape-puppy, Karl. He has got his funny tails in a Bad Headthing. He smells a bit scared, a bit excited, a bit happy. His body says: *No one looking, no one can see me, yes, there they are.* He looks up and down the road, then he quickly sits in the front of the van with them. His body says: *I am being bad and liking it!*

They do ape-barking, quite quiet. It's something about Karl creating a diversion while they do over a village nearby. What is "diversion"? Maybe Food?

Caroline lies very soft, very quiet next to me. She is biting her lip and wrinkling her above-eyes skin. She smells cross.

Now Karl gets out of the van. One of the fierce apedogs leans out. He gives Karl a big, thick brown envelope. Caroline makes a little angry growl in her throat.

Karl smiles, big tooth-showing. "God, I'm sick of hippie tree huggers," he says. "Bye." He puts the envelope inside his shirt, walks away.

I don't want to say hello. I think he's scary.

Caroline waits very soft, very quiet, just like a cat.[1] After Karl has gone and the van has vroomed away, she hisses in my ear, "Did you see that? Karl was getting paid off like a villain. Did you see?"

No, girl ape-puppy, I'm sorry. I don't know what you mean. Lick your poor ear where the metal is.

"Stoppit, Jack. I don't know what to do. If I tell my mom, she'll say I was imagining it. She thinks Karl's great. And Zoe's his mom. What will she say? I can't think what to do."

Poor girl ape-puppy. She smells worried. I lick her other ear.

"Oh stoppit, that tickles."

We get up and go back up the path. Caroline doesn't want to play now. Never mind, sniff snortle, wander wander. Here we are where the soft apedog dens are. There is lots of smell of Food. Is it sausages?

No. Sad Dog. Sort of things-that-look-like-sausages-but-made-of-plant.[2] Still Food, of course,

---

[1] Learn from her, Big Yellow Stupid.

[2] An abomination! Definitely not Cat food.

but not nearly as nice as real sausages.

Caroline wants to talk to Auntie Zoo, but she is busy having an argument with her puppy. "Don't be ridiculous, Karl. I went to antiwar demonstrations when I was pregnant with you. Of course I'm coming tomorrow. I wouldn't miss it for anything."

"Well, I dunno, Mom. Maybe it'll just be a small protest, pretty boring really." Karl's body says: *Bored, tense, got to make her believe me.*

Auntie Zoo smiles and ruffles his brown tails. He winces. "Oh all right. I get it," she says, and her body says: *I love you so much, my puppy.* "You don't want your square old mom spoiling your protest. Okay. I won't wave any banners, I won't march around, I won't get arrested. Is that cool?"

"Groovy, Mom," says Karl, and his body says: *Whew, close one there, my Pack Lady is stupid.* "I'll tell you all about it afterward."

Such disrespect! I growl at him, not too loud in case he hears me.

Caroline gives him a very hard stare as he goes by, but he doesn't notice because she is only a puppy. She puts her head on one side and looks at Auntie Zoo. You can see from her face she is doing the apedog thing called Thinking, when nobody

81

is allowed to bark or howl.

Most of the apedogs are friendly and like me. They pat my tummy and say I am a bit Tubby. This is the same as Good Dog because my Pack Lady says it too. Some of them sit by the warm red Cat God[3] and make interesting and loud noises. They do the apedog Pack howling where you bang tight strings on a roundish box to make d o i o i n g sounds and howl up and down. It's good. Like in Terri's Howling and Banging Box, only not so loud and bangy. I can help, NotMyPack Friend apedogs! I can do howling up and down too! Listen!

ARROOOO ARROOO, AWOWWOW ARROOOOOO.

Caroline hugs me and giggles. I howl even more helpfully. AWWOWOOooo.

The apedogs thank me by throwing sticks and bits of mud and some burned plant-stuff-Not-Sausages at me—ULP GULP—and barking enthusiastically. They even know my Pack's friendly bark: "Shuddup you stupidog." I am so Happy I made them happy.

HAPPY Dog. Sleep now.

Caroline Comes to Our Den

Oh, hi there, Auntie Zoo. And here is another Pack Lady, quite big and round with lots of interesting dangly things on her removable furs. She smells nice too. Oh, I smell she's Caroline's Pack Lady.

Hi, Caroline's Pack Lady, respect, respect, paws up, show tummy. Pat pat pat. AAAAH.

Caroline's Pack Lady, who is called Budleia, and Auntie Zoo are talking. They know each other. They once protested against nuclear weapons together. They are friends.

Oh good. I like friends. Hi, Friend Pack Lady.

It was raining, says Budleia, and their tent fell

down. Caroline's sleeping bag was soaked. She is not very well, has a bit of a chesty cough, can Auntie Zoo help?

"Yes, of course I can," says Auntie Zoo.

It is a warmy comfy feeling to see them. Lean against Auntie Zoo's legs and groan. Let Budleia pat my tummy, say I'm Tubby.

AHHHHH. Happy Dog!

It's all arranged. Caroline goes and gets a spare sleeping bag. OH GREAT! Is she coming to our den? That's GREAT! Hi, Caroline, hi, Caroline's Pack Lady, arf arf.

You know it's time to get the ape-puppies from the Running Around and Shouting Place? ARF. Arf. Don't forget the ape-puppies!

Off we go down the soft path. Caroline is squishing through the mud with her rainboots. She has her backpack. She is talking about her school in London. What is "school"? What is "London"? Never mind, here is Rebel's territory, all full of his lovely friendly smell.

Here he is with his Packleader. Oh wonderful! Happy happy happy dog to smell Junior NotMyPack Friend Rebel again!

Pull away from Auntie Zoo, run up to him. *Hi there, can I smell you? Yes, you smell very strong. I like chocolate drops. You can smell me too.*

Rebel's Packleader lets him off the leash and Rebel does puppy-bows I puppy-bow back. *Let's play.* Bounce bounce, jump jump. Run round and round. *Smell this!* Oh wow, Stripy Face. Whew chiff. A slimy. Bouncy bouncy. *Run that way.* Rabbits!

Hi there, Caroline Puppy, this is my friend Rebel. *Rebel, here is Caroline, she is a NotMyPack Friend of ours.* Sniff sniff. Run round and round.

Caroline throws a stick for him. He gets it AND BRINGS IT BACK. *Wow, Rebel, you are very clever.* It's very hard to remember the bringing-back bit when you run for a stick.

Yes, I can do that stuff, says Rebel. *It is not so hard.*

Caroline is staring at Rebel's Packleader while

he talks about Rebel to Auntie Zoo. "Um . . . ," she says in a small voice. "Um . . ." Nobody hears.

We run ahead, run round and round and round. Sniff snortle, leave Wet Message. Hi Caroline, throw a stick, please, *here you are, this is a good stick!*

Caroline stops looking worried, throws the stick, bouncy bouncy. Rebel and I are a Pack, so you watch out, Garage Dog, we'll come and make you into meat. On we go. Auntie Zoo has said good-bye to Rebel's Packleader and he calls Rebel, so Rebel goes off with him. A bit Sad Dog. It was good to play with Rebel again.

Sniff snortle. Wet Message. Grrr. Garage Dog's relative. Grrr. Wet Message on top and scrape up all the earth.

Oops. Sorry, didn't mean to hit you with some mud.

Here's the Running Around and Shouting Place. Hi, ape-puppies, hi, nice to see you, did you have a lovely day running around and shouting? Why can't I come in and . . . ?

Oh. Sorry.

Auntie Zoo shows them her friend's girl ape-puppy.

Pete and Mikey say hello to Caroline and smile at her. Pete's body says: *Oh no, a girl, I don't like them*

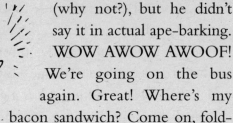

(why not?), but he didn't say it in actual ape-barking. WOW AWOW AWOOF! We're going on the bus again. Great! Where's my bacon sandwich? Come on, folding doors, open up quick quick. . . . Get in the bus quickly. . . . Pull Auntie Zoo to the back, where's my sandwich . . .? Sniff snortle, check under the backseats, quick, snifff . . .

Oh. Sad Dog. No sandwich. Somebody else must have got it first. Sigh. Lie down. Much whooshiness. Ulp gulp. Glerp.

"Oh yuck," say Pete and Caroline; they say it together.

"Honk city," says Caroline, and pretends to unswallow. Pete does it too, a very good pretend. I am hopeful I might get some of his lunch, but no.

Both of them giggle lots.

NEENAW! NEENAW!

Whew, I'm glad to get off the bus now. Home again.

Maisie is sitting by the door to the clicky-clacky Flicker-Box room where Auntie Zoo is staying. She is looking up. Inside, Lulu's cage is lying on its side with the door open. Muskie is

sitting on it, asleep.

Remy is still asleep on his radiator.

"Oh no," barks Auntie Zoo. "Oh no, you bad bad cats. Bad. Bad! Wicked!"[1]

She rushes into the room, Maisie runs away and Muskie wakes up and blinks. His body says: *Eh, what?*[2]

Auntie Zoo picks him up and throws him out of the room. She rushes around calling, "Lulu, Lulu."

I sniff. No blood. No feathers lying around. I don't think Maisie and Muskie actually made the Flying Feathery into meat.[3] In fact . . .

Plop. A Wet Message lands right on my nose.

"Ark, push off, bad bad bad, NEENAW NEENAW."

Auntie Zoo sees Lulu on the light and puts up her hands to catch her. "Come on, darling. Don't worry about those bad cats."

"Wuzzock, push off, wuzzock." Lulu flies around

---

[1] How, pray, is it bad for Us to entertain Ourselves by hunting a nice tasty bird clearly brought into Our den for Our benefit? What else are birds for?

[2] Nobody could call Muskie the sharpest claw on the paw.

[3] We will, of course. But on this occasion We were only having fun.

the room with Auntie Zoo putting her hands up to her. Then she flies out the door, feathers float down, her body says: *Upset, scared, bite the cats.*[4]

"Shut all the windows," shouts Auntie Zoo, rushing after Lulu, but it's too late.

"Ark ark. Wuzzock," shouts Lulu as she flies out the window.

Auntie Zoo rushes out into the back Outside, which is a bit messy, and rushes around it calling for Lulu.

Lulu sits in the apple tree with her head on one side, watching.

The Cats watch Lulu hungrily. Don't they know she is a (very peculiar) Friend?[5]

At last Auntie Zoo comes back in with her striped hair all standing on end. She smells very cross. "Pizza all right for you children?" she asks. She sounds very cross too.

"Can I have a pepperoni feast?"

---

[4] Ha. Ha. Very droll.
[5] No. She is Food for Cats.

"Mine's a pineapple and ham."

"I will have a very big pizza with sausages," says Mikey.

But Auntie Zoo has found pizza in the freezer with no meat on it. She cooks it with more cheese and ape-plant stuff and everybody groans except Caroline, who just looks surprised.

"Are you allowed to eat meat at home?" she says to Pete.

"Yeah, my dad hates vegetables. He'd never eat a pizza with all this muck on it."

"It's a green pepper, Pete," says Auntie Zoo. "Did you read the book about the gentle dragon who only ate vegetables?"

"Well yeah, but it's not very believable, is it? I mean, if they existed, dragons must've evolved, right, and they evolved with sharp carnivorous teeth, right, and so I don't think a dragon could ever want to eat vegetables any more than cats do, right . . . ?"

"That's three 'rights' in one sentence," says Terri,

very Senior Packmember. "You're getting a bad habit."

"Oh yeah? Well you've got a bad habit of being snotty and spotty. . . ."

. Terri kicks Pete under the table and Pete flicks green pepper at her and Mikey spits out his pizza.

ARRF ARRF ARRF, I say, interposing myself. Don't fight, fellow Packmembers. . . . Oh nice for me! A bit of part-chewed pizza, gulp.

Mikey is sad when it's going-to-bed time because he wants his Pack Lady and his Packleader.

Poor Mikey, I will give you cuddles. Here is your blankie, you lie on my tummy and suck your thumb. There. AAAAAH. I love you, Mikey. ♥♥

"Ah, bless you," says Terri.

Auntie Zoo picks up Mikey and carries him up to bed. It's Okay. He could sleep in my basket. It would be cozy and warm, we would be cuddling.

Oh well. Maybe another time.

Caroline is going to put her sleeping bag in Terri's room. Terri is being very nice to her: She is a Senior NotMyPack Friend girl ape-puppy for Caroline. Soon they are doing claw-smearing, which makes funny horrible smells, all swimmy head, and

tastes YUK! Terri
and Pete did it on
me once, made my
paws taste nasty.
Much unswallow-
ing. Pack Lady was
very cross. She said

Halloween was no excuse. What is "Halloween"?
Maybe it is something to do with bags of sweets
and biscuits that you can eat if you find them first.

Later they come down in pajamas to show
Auntie Zoo. They have painted their nails all
slightly different smells. They show her, they are
very proud.

YUK. You know it isn't very nice to eat, ape-
puppies.

Also, when is it suppertime? Oh great! My
favorite. Dog food. . . .

Yum yum slurp
slurp gulp. Erp.

More?

Oh great!
MORE DOG
FOOD! WOW WOW
YES YES.

Yum yum slurp slurp gulp. Erp.

More?

"I don't believe you're still hungry, Jack, you've had two big cans."

Yes I am, Senior extra Pack Lady, Very Very Hungry. STARVING.

"Well, have a biscuit."

Gulp. Yum. Thank you, respect respect.

How Funny!

The Cats say, Leave out all the stuff about night-time and going to sleep. They were in the garden trying to catch the Flying Feathery. Sometimes there was a crashing and a lot of arking and grrooooa-owing.[1]

It was quite exciting. Right in the middle of the night Auntie Zoo went out with a net on a stick she found in the cupboard under the stairs, but Lulu was too high up. Auntie Zoo fell over one of my Hard Messages she hadn't picked up in the morning. She said lots of Packleader-type

---

[1] We were having fun.

words and shouted at Lulu. Lulu said them back. It is Scary that a Flying Feathery can do ape-barking.

Morning time was **GREAT**. I was Very Very Very Very HUNGRY. I got both front paws and a back paw cans of dog food! I LIKE AUNTIE ZOO. SHE IS A GREAT PACK LADY.

Then, after Terri gets her bus, we go on a great bus ride. Caroline comes too—bacon sandwich? Oh. Somebody else ate it. Sad Dog.

Running Around and Shouting Place? Oh, how funny. No ape-puppies? No apedogs? Empty Outside?

Gosh. Wow. We could run around and bark in it!

Pete stares at the place and then he bangs his head with his clever paw. He digs in his bag for putting chocolate and chips and stuff in. He gets some paper from the bottom of it, quite a lot, some with squashed Mars bar on it. Yum, drool. Mine? For me?

Pete smells each paper, wrinkles up his eyes when he finds one. "Oh no, I forgot."

"Forgot what?" Auntie Zoo is tapping her foot and looking very annoyed.

"Um . . . it's an in-service day. Staff training or something. There's no school today. Here's the note."

Auntie Zoo holds the paper by the corner and looks at it as if it has a bad smell, which it doesn't, it's just treeish like all paper. With a bit of mature Mars bar. And some chips. Quite nice in fact. "This is from two weeks ago."

"Um . . . yeah. I forgot. Sorry."

"No school?" asks Mikey. "Why not? I like it."

"Just today," says Pete. "The teachers are learning stuff about being teachers."

Mikey nods. "I could help them."

Auntie Zoo does a big puffing out-of-breath that apedogs do when their puppies have been stupid. "Why didn't you tell your mom?"

"Well . . . I forgot. I meant to give it to Mom, but we played football against Bosdrear and we won two to one and I was telling her and I forgot. I was going to."

"Can we go to Disneyland now?" says Mikey.

"No, we're not doing that. We're going to a sort of . . . well, sort of a party. That's what I'd planned to do today, so that's what we'll do. You'll just have to tag along like Caroline. Make sure you behave yourselves."

"Oh, Okay. What sort of party?"

"A protest against the road builders."

"Wow! Cool! Will there be security guys? And tree people? And riot police?"

"No, there won't, or I wouldn't dream of taking you! This is a *peaceful* protest. Come along. This way."

Off we go down the hard road and then the soft road, and Caroline is telling Pete and Mikey about protests and how she's been on loads with her mom and how you just march up and down shouting stuff and maybe hold a banner and get your picture taken for the paper with a policeman and stuff. Pete smells sad that he hasn't done that.

Oh yes! I can smell where we are. I can smell my pawprints and Wet Messages from yesterday, and Rebel's too. This is GREAT!

Auntie Zoo pats me. I go check if Rebel is here. No, Sad Dog, he's out. I leave a respectful Wet Message for him, find a lovely Hard Message he left under a bush.[2] Very Strong Dog. Likes Chappie. Chocolate drops.

The ape-puppies are very excited about going to a demonstration and run up and down and round and round. ARRF ARRF. Chase. Throw sticks. No, Pete, I don't know what you mean. What is "fetch"? Then Mikey gets tired and has to have a rest. Auntie Zoo gives him a piggyback ride.

When we get to the field with the soft apedog dens, quite a lot of the apedogs are not there. Nice smells of cooking and fires. Caroline's Pack Lady, Budleia, comes to say hello, pats me all over. The Junior Pack Lady who is Special, called Poppy, brings some of that big soft paper with ink smudges that apedogs like to smell at breakfast time.

"Is he the dog in the paper?" asks Poppy. "Look. Driving a car."

"Yeah, Jack did that and busted the car," said

---

2 Aren't Big Yellow Stupids disgusting?

Mikey proudly. "It was all smashed. *Vrooom, crunk peeeyong!* Like that."

Auntie Zoo and Pete and Caroline look.

"Hey," says Pete. "It *is* Jack. Look. That's definitely him all right, he's barking."

" 'Shoppers were running for their lives when Jack the Labrador went for a spin in his master's car ...,' " says Auntie Zoo in a funny voice.

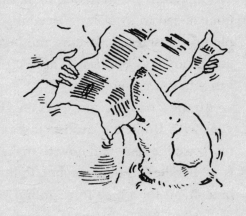

"And there's the car. Crunched. You look cool in your photo, Jack, you look like you were steering with your paws on the wheel," says Pete.

What is Pete talking about? What is "steering"?

He holds the paper under my nose for me to smell—it's got big smudges on it, but is not edible. In fact it smells quite poisonous. Why is it interesting, Junior Packmember? Maybe there is food inside it, like chips? Chomp, snortle ...

"Hey, don't eat it!" Pete pulls it away. "Bad Dog."
Why? I only made a little hole.

Auntie Zoo is asking about her ape-puppy and the other apedog friends.

"It's a nuisance we got evicted from Pencerriog Wood before we were dug in, but there it is. Karl's gone ahead to organize everything, get some people up the trees, make sure the press know what's going on," says Budleia. "The rest of us'll go in the van when it comes back."

Auntie Zoo hangs my leash on a little branch and goes with Budleia. Caroline takes Pete and Mikey off to see the tents and how to make a bender. What is a "bender"? Food maybe? Pull, pull, break the branch, go for a nice sniff around.

YES! IT'S FOOD! Sniff snortle. Yum. Mature macaroni with ketchup. MINE NOW. Slurp, ulp, gulp.

GRRRRRR . . .

Oh dear. Oh no, it's the Bad NotMyPack dogs. They're hackles-up, tail-waving high, growling, tooth-showing. *We will tear out your throat for eating our Food, we are a Pack*, is what they're saying.

Oh dear oh dear oh dear. Run away. Hide behind Auntie Zoo, who is talking to Budleia.

102

"You dummy, Jack. It's only a . . . miniature dachshund crossed with whippet, maybe?"

"Who knows? Gandhi, stop it. That's enough, you bad dog."

Turn you into meat and eat you! WOOOF WOOF, says Gandhi.

He is a Very Bad Dog, but I make little puppy, hide because he is FIERCE like GARAGE DOG. Oh dear. Bud is big, I'll hide behind her.

"Poor Jack, he doesn't seem very popular."

"They're jealous of him getting his picture in the paper," laughs Bud. "Really, Jack, you're four times his size."

Yes, but he's VERY FIERCE.

"No, he's probably eaten their food. You wouldn't

believe how much that dog packs away," says
Auntie Zoo.

"Well, yes I would. He's a Labrador, isn't he?"
asks Bud.

"I don't understand how he can be hungry. He's
already finished all the food Charlotte left for him."

"Mm. You're a softy,
Zoe. Don't you know you
can't feed Labradors on
demand? They get circular.
He's already a bit tubby."

Pant pant. Everybody says
I am Tubby. This is Good. I
am a Good Thick Tubby Dog.

"I was going to leave him here to play with the
other dogs, but that may not be such a good idea,"
Auntie Zoo says.

"No, I wouldn't do that with Gandhi around.
Jack can come with us and help protect Pencerriog
Wood. After all, it's near where the Stopeses live. I
expect he's visited every tree in it at some time. It'll
be a good angle for the *South Cornwall News*—they
always like a nice animal picture if they can get
one. We could put a sign on his back: I CAN'T GO
WALKIES ON A HIGHWAY!"

Walkies? Yes, Walkies! I love Walkies. WHERE? NOW? Oh please, I love Walkies.

Auntie Zoo laughs. "Come on then, Jack, let's get in the van."

Oh wow. A sort of tiny bus. Maybe bacon sandwich? Burger wrappers?

GREAT! Chips! Snortle, chomp, lick, sneeze. I like buses.

Everybody gets in, budges up. Pete and Caroline are sitting next to each other, talking about demonstrations, Mikey is sitting on Auntie Zoo's lap, sucking his thumb. She is telling Bud about the Cats nearly catching Lulu and Lulu escaping.[3]

Caroline is still telling Pete about demonstrations. "My mom took me to a sit-in in the city too. There was a party there. It was wicked."

Lie down under Pete's legs. Slurp lick. Very thirsty now. I wonder why. Oh dear, whooshy feeling. I don't like buses when they go whooshy. *Vroom.* Light-trees and ordinary trees going by. Much bumpiness at first, then it's smooth, then it's bumpy again.

"Hey," says Pete. "I know this road, we're nearly

---

[3] Not so. No mere bird Dinner could really escape Us. We merely let her go so We could have more fun later.

home. This is near our village. Look, there's a sign for Trenever. Great. You can stay the night again, Caroline—can't she, Auntie Zoo?"

Auntie Zoo and Bud look at each other and smell of going-to-laugh, but they don't. "Of course," says Bud.

"Are you stopping them knocking down the Old Mill again?" asks Pete.

"No, that's legally protected now. Thanks to your mom and dad."

"I know. That's why they're up in London. So Dad can be a witness at the inquiry and Mom can do lawyer stuff and give 'em all what-for. That's what Dad said."

"Well, now they're trying another route for the road. The trouble is they're going to fell this beautiful old woodland called Pencerriog to make room for it. . . ."

"Oh, I know Pencerriog. It's not that beautiful. It's only a load of old trees," says Pete. Everybody stares and he goes red and uncomfy, as if he ate something that belonged to the Packleader. "Well, there's lots of trees around, aren't there?"

"Some of them are quite rare and there's the wildlife—rare amphibians and a couple of rare species of butterfly," says Bud in that I'm-quite-cross-but-trying-to-sound-friendly voice that Senior NotMyPack Ladies often have.

"Oh. Right," says Pete, nodding a lot. His body says: *Oops, embarrassed in front of a girl ape-puppy.*

The other apedogs start talking again, about the time when they went to support the tunnel diggers and the time when they all hugged trees. . . .

"You've got to remember," whispers Caroline to Pete. "Trees are good, roads are bad."

"Why?"

She stares at him. "They just are. It's not something you argue about."

"Why not?"

"You just don't. It's ecology."

"Oh. Mom says there isn't anything you can't argue about, except not with her in the morning or no TV."

"Well, you can't argue about trees. It's like not eating meat."

"What?"

"Eating meat is wrong. You can't eat meat because it's wrong."

"Why?"

"It just is. You wouldn't want to eat a little fluffy lamb."

" 'Course I would." Caroline gasps. Pete frowns. "I like lamb, specially with garlic and rosemary. Dad does this really great roast[4] with potatoes and stuff and . . ."

"Ugh."

"It's not ugh, it's nice. Anyway, you don't eat them when they're little and fluffy, you eat them when they're a bit bigger, right? And they wouldn't be there at all if we didn't eat them. You can't keep sheep as pets, they're too stupid."

"It's just wrong because animals are people too. . . ."

"No they're not. Have you ever tried talking to

---

4 Roasting is an appalling apecat custom: they put delicious food for Cats in a very hot cupboard and burn it until it is unrecognizable, and then they put plants with it and eat it all up and give the Cats hardly any, no matter how politely We ask, so We have to wait until there are no apecats about and the Big Yellow Stupid is near enough to take the blame.

a sheep? Even Jack's brighter than a sheep. They're not people."

"Well, they're like people."

"But they're not."

"And it's disgusting to eat carrion, dead things."

"Why? You eat dead plants. Have you ever actually tried any meat?"

"I'm not allowed. . . . Except the hot dog I had once at a demonstration, which wasn't really proper meat. My mom says I mustn't. I have to eat loads and loads of lentils and tofu and stuff instead."

"Ugh . . . lentils! I hate them."

"So do I."

"But that sounds awful. So you've never eaten a ham sandwich or a burger?"

"I had a hot dog. That's like it."

"It's nothing like it. Never?"

"Never." Caroline shakes her head.

Pete holds her paw with his clever paw. "Well, I say that's terrible. Tell you what. I'll get you some proper food so you can try it yourself. Then you'll know if you like it or not."

Caroline frowns at him but she doesn't smell annoyed, she smells pleased. Her face looks like it's doing that ape-thing called thinking. "When my mom's not looking."

"'Course. I'm not stupid."

"Okay then. I'll try it."

"Great. Do you like soccer?"

They stop talking about food, which is interesting, and talk about football, which is boring. I like playing football, though: the ape-puppies kick a big ball to each other and you bark at it and chase it and paw it and bite it and turn it into a rag and play rag with it.

FUN!

Sleep now.

Oh Dear. Scary Fierce Male Apedogs

Here we are, off we get. Sniff snortle, sniff sniff. Oh!
I KNOW THIS PLACE. It's full of lovely Jack-smells. This
is the Special Good Walkies Place when Packleader
is tired of marching around the house drinking Hot
Brown Stuff. It's a HAPPY HAPPY place. Lots
of nice trees for Wet Messages and bushes to hide
Hard Messages, and humps and bumps in the earth
to run up and down and mushroomy smells and a
stream with mud for making your tummy feel tickly
and interesting NotFurries in the water and lots of
good Messages from all my NotMyPack Friends.

WOW! WHAT BRILLIANT WALKIES!

It's GREAT here, only not the badgers because they're Fierce and might bite.

Sniff snortle. I can smell dug-up earth. The apedogs have been digging a lot. Maybe they could smell bones! Can I have some? I like mature bones!

All the apedogs are milling around, ape-barking. Some of them are young male apedogs, smelling

very aggressive and fierce. They are in a pack. Then there are older male apedogs and female apedogs. Not many ape-puppies. Some of them have flappy things on sticks with paint on and old nest-coverings with paint.

ROOF ROOOF ARROOOF. There are apedogs climbing in some of the trees, just like Cats.[1] It's so clever. I tried it once and I got stuck

---

[1] Mostly done by ape-kittens. It shows they really are basically monkeys, as anyone with half a nose can easily smell. However, they are not nearly as good at it or as graceful as Cats. Big Stupids are unable to climb even the simplest of trees and fall entertainingly into brambles if they try, pulling the Tom apecat down with them.

and Packleader had to come and get me down on a ladder. He says I nearly crippled him.

Over in another field are some cars and big trucks. There are more apedogs there, another pack. They have got Big SCARY RRRRRR things for cutting trees. Then there are apedogs in between. They are wearing dark removable furs and Bad Headthings like Rebel's Packleader. Some more apedogs come with boxes on their shoulders and start talking to the boxes. NotAnybody'sPack.

This is all very interesting. Is there Food anywhere? Sniff snortle.

Auntie Zoo sees the young male apedogs and frowns. "What are they doing here?"

Bud looks, frowns, and her body goes: *hate you!* "Oh, not again." She starts to smell scared-fierce, like all Pack Ladies do when their ape-puppies might be in danger. "Karl promised me he wouldn't tell them about this. . . ."

"*Karl* invited them?" says Auntie Zoo. She puts my leash on a tree branch and marches over to where Karl is talking to some young apedogs with no hair who have come in another van.

Sniff, snortle. Squirrel in this tree. Yum (but very Fierce, with Big Teeth). Wet Message. Oh, George

and Fido III have been here recently. Hard Message
for them as well.

Auntie Zoo is talking to her grown-up puppy.
I can't hear what they say very well, but their bodies say:

Auntie Zoo: *Angry,
you bad puppy!*
Karl: *Angry, not your
puppy anymore, what
are you doing here?
Disrespect.*
Auntie Zoo: *You bad
bad puppy, this is bad,
those male apedogs are
bad.*

Karl: *My Pack, they're Okay. We are going to do
fighting. I like fighting. Not your puppy anymore.*

Auntie Zoo: *Bad puppy, what about the ape-
puppies over there and Jack?*

Karl: *Not your puppy. Oh no, why are they here?
Oh no.*

Now I can hear them because they're both
shouting.

"I told you not to flipping bring them, Mom. I
told you, why can't you just once believe . . . ?"

"Why should I believe you when you lie to me? You told me you wouldn't get mixed up with that group again. This isn't a peaceful protest against a road anymore. Your friends are here for a fight. You silly boy, do you think you're going to keep the press on our side . . . ?"

"Oh come on, Mom, can't you? Remember your antiwar demonstrations? You've bored me about them often enough. Violence is a necessary tool of political protest. . . ."

"No it isn't. It doesn't work. And what about the kids?"

"Do what you like with them. I told you not to come. It's your fault for bringing them."

Auntie Zoo goes and talks to Budleia, and she gets mad too. *She* goes and talks to Karl and Karl is very disrespectful to her. All the Senior Pack Ladies talk to each other, but not the Junior Pack Ladies, who are admiring the male apedogs and talking to them.

Then Budleia goes and barks at Poppy, the Junior Pack Lady who is Special, and Poppy looks angry. Her body says: *No, I won't, not your puppy. I'll stay here with all these nice young male apedogs.*

Caroline and Pete and Mikey have found some red unripe blackberries and are talking about whether you can eat them yet. No you can't, ape-puppies. Can't you smell that? Push them away from the Bad Food with my nose.

Pete has seen the young male apedogs with no hair. "Wow, look. Don't they look cool?"

"Oh, them," says Caroline. "They think they're so big and strong. My mom says they're just stupid hoodlums. They don't really care about the environment or anything except a good punch-up."

What is "punch-up"? Food?

"Great. I've always wanted to see a real punch-up." Pete's body says: *Uh-oh, might be scary.*

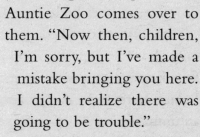

Auntie Zoo comes over to them. "Now then, children, I'm sorry, but I've made a mistake bringing you here. I didn't realize there was going to be trouble."

"Right," says Pete, looking very excited. "Like a big riot?"

117

"No, not a big riot. But it might get nasty."

"Wow. Cool!"

"Can I get my light saber?"

"No, Mikey, you're not going to be here. Caroline and Pete are going to take you and Jack straight home."

"Owww."

"What, now? Just when something might happen?" Pete is disappointed.

"Don't argue."

"Can I come back when I've taken Mikey home?"

"Certainly not. You have to stay with Mikey and look after him, you and Caroline. Understand?"

"But I've never been in a real riot. . . ."

"And that's how it's going to stay."

"Are we going by ourselves, without you?" says Caroline, and her body says: *Thinking lots*.

"It's Okay," says Pete, very Packleaderish. "It's only about ten minutes' walk and there aren't any four-lane highways or busy roads, not like London. I came here every day to get horse chestnuts last autumn."

"Oh." Caroline looks impressed.

Auntie Zoo says, "Now, you've got to be responsible, Pete. I'd come with you if I had a car, but

I daren't leave yet in case Bud and I can head off the trouble. Bud certainly won't go until she's got that silly girl Poppy away from here. So here's the front door key. Off you go. Straight home, no detours."

"What about you?" asks Pete.

"I'll be along as soon as I can."

Special Poppy is with Karl, giving him a cuddle. Oh wow! Karl is her Packleader! Wow! How interesting. Like with me and Petra.

"Can you manage that, Pete?"

"But I . . ."

"Or I'll just have to come with you and then Poppy might get caught up in whatever happens and she might get hurt and so might her baby."

Pete makes *tsk-tsk* noises. He looks very sad. His voice is sad. But his body says: *Whew, maybe a real fight with those big male apedogs in it might be too scary*.

"Oh Okay," he says, lots of whining in his voice, but now his body says: *Hey, we can do naughty stuff now, great!* "Can I have some money to . . . to get comics at the shop?"

The apedogs with RRRR things are starting to move this way. Auntie Zoo looks worried. She really wants to get rid of the ape-puppies. "Yes, all right. Here's a five. And I want the change. I'll join you at the house just as soon as I've talked some sense into these silly kids."

"Okay." Pete gets my leash. "Come on, Jack, let's go."

Oh NO! Stranger!

Okay, Pete, as I am Senior Packmember, sort of Packleader, I will go first. (Get away quicker from all those fierce-smelling apedogs. I didn't know apedogs did fighting like that. It's scary. They're Very Big.)

Pete holds my leash. Caroline holds Mikey's hand. We go down a little path that Pete knows and I know from coming here with Packleader. I can smell my old trail from last week, it's easy. Off we go. To the shop. GREAT!

There is some loud barking from the apedogs,

all together. It's scary. Let's run, ape-puppies, quick, this way.

Look here, ape-puppies, what a lovely deep-smelling mud wallow. Big Furries with clip-clop paws have left Hard Messages here. Isn't it delicious? Come on. Let's lie in it and wear the nice fragrance, so the Bad apedogs can't smell us.

"No! No, Jack, don't go in the . . ."

SPLASH! WALLOW

SLURP, AAAHHH . . . Lovely cool tickly mud on my tummy. **Ahhh.**

". . . mud. Oh no."

"Jack did it again, Pete," says Mikey. "Look, he likes it. Shall we try it?"

"No way, Mikey. You wouldn't like the smell."

"Chocolate-coated labrador." Caroline laughs again. "Phew. He stinks."

"We'll have to hose him down when we get home."

We come out of the path and onto the hard boring road. There is the shop. I like it. It's a Big Food Place where they have MEAT. But I can't go in. I don't know why. I would be very good at getting all the Food. YUM.

Pete puts my leash on the railing. He and Caroline and Mikey go in. They are a very LOOONG time. Yawn. Boring. There is a strange van over there. With NotMyPack apedogs in it, talking and eating smoky-sticks. They smell nervous.

Ruff ruff.

Oh, here is a Senior NotMyPack Friend girl dog. *Hello, Suki, did you have a nice walk?*

Yes, thank you, Jack, I smell you found somewhere interesting to lie down.

Yes, it's that way, isn't it complex and delightful?

Mmm, yes. Horse Message and some Rabbit Message too, I think. With overtones of blackberries.

123

And dead leaves, of course, Suki, you can't beat dead leaves for that earthy undernote.

Very true. Here is a respectful Wet Message for you, Jack, I have to go with my Pack Lady now, respect.

Sniff snortle, lovely, she has given you Steak, I smell, how lucky you are to have such a generous Pack Lady, respect.

Bye, Jack, smell you later.

Here come the ape-puppies. They are talking and smelling very excited. They have a bag of FOOD. FOR ME? Thank you, thank you, ape-puppies, clever, strong ape-pupies, all by yourselves you have hunted me lots of splendid MEAT!

"We were lucky there was so much in the cut-price basket. Now you can try all of them," says Pete. "No, not for you Jack, down."

Why not?

Off we go now. Pete lets me off the leash because he doesn't like the nice mud wallow fragrance.

I run ahead to our Pack's den. . . .

STOP!
BADNESS!

What is this?

Sniff snortle, sniff SNIFFF.

GRRRRR. A Stranger Smell! There is a NotMyPack apedog in Our Den! He is picking up stuff and carrying it to the door, which is open.

GRRRRR. You can't have Our Den, NotMyPack enemy apedog. GRRRRR,

I am a Big (quite Fierce) Smelly Dog, I will BITE YOU . . . GRRRRRR. Stand between my ape-puppies and the den. Hackles up. Make myself EVEN BIGGER. Little slitty eyes. GRRRRRR.

Pete and Mikey and Caroline stop because I am in the way. They try and push past. I stand on my back legs and push them back. No, no, ape-puppies, you can't go there, BADNESS! It's a NotMyPack Enemy apedog in

OUR DEN!

They start getting cross with me. Then they see that the Flicker Box is outside on the ground and the front door is open. They stare openmouthed while I growl. Caroline says, "Quick, hide."

Pete gets my collar and drags me backward and we duck down behind the hedge. The NotMyPack Enemy apedog comes out with Terri's Howling and Banging Box and puts it down. Pete puts his hand around my nose so I can't bark at him. Why? Next door there is another Enemy apedog, putting things on the front step.

OH WOW!
WHAT'S HAPPENING?

"Wow," says Pete. "Burglars!"

"I know him! And him! They were giving money to Karl yesterday. Like I told you last night," says Caroline.

"They must be doing the whole village at once while the police are busy with the protest."

"Won't more cops come?"

"Not in time. Not all the way from Liskeard, they can't. My mom was telling my dad she'd heard about this gang that specialize in tying up all the local police with an accident or a pub brawl or something, so they can't come when the burglar alarms go off, and then they rob every house in the nearest village as quick as they can; they make a fortune."

"Ohh. What if somebody's there?"

"They knock 'em down and do it anyway. They're a nasty lot, my mom says."

Pete and Caroline look at each other and then grab Mikey, who is going toward Our Den scowling and waving his fists and shouting, "You can't have my telly!"

"No, Mikey. Come on, run."

Very good thinking, Pete, run away from the Bad Enemy apedogs.

Pete and Caroline and Mikey run back to the

shop. They forget to put my leash on the rail. I can hear them saying stuff, their voices all sharp and excited. Makes my hackles go up. The man in the shop has a talkbone, he is talking to it. I guard the door. Grrrrrrrr. You can't come in, this is my territory, I am guarding my ape-puppies.

The van with the Enemy apedogs in it goes down our road and stops. Another Enemy apedog puts our Flicker Box in the back. What are they doing? Caroline comes outside, stares hard at the back of the van, and goes in again, muttering.

Why are we waiting, ape-puppies? I don't think we've run far enough, apedogs can run quite fast (though not as fast as me) and we could be miles away by now, which would be good, I think. ARRRF ARRF. Shall we run away a bit more?

Hunting with Rebel!

<small>ROOOF</small> ROOOF ARROOF
GRRRRROWF.

Here comes another van, very
fast around the corner. I smell . . .

OH WOW!
OH GREAT!
It's Rebel! And his

Packleader! JUNIOR NOTMY-PACK FRIEND REBEL!

Hi there! ARRRROOOF ARRRF GRRROOOF! *Shall we play, Rebel?* ARRRF?

Rebel smells very excited and strong. He is doing serious stuff. He is Hunting with his Packleader. He does one serious WOOF so I know what's happening.

Rebel's van goes down our road. Then the Enemy apedogs' van vrooms out of it very fast, goes around *s c r e e e e e l* the corner and vrooooms away. The back is still open and a Flicker Box falls out onto the road and smashes.

Where are all the little dogs and apedogs in the Flicker Box? It is just metal string and glass and stuff. How funny. Where did they go?[1]

Here comes Lulu, Auntie Zoo's Flying Feathery. She is flying around going, *"NEENAW NEENAW."*

---

[1] Obviously you weren't quick enough to catch them, Big Yellow Stupid. What a pity We weren't there. Feline primatologists have long wondered if the very small apecats inside the Flicker Box would be fun to play with and tasty to eat.

ARRF! Don't mess up Friend Rebel's Hunting!

I can hear Rebel's Packleader. He says very loudly, "This is the police with a dog. You have one minute to come out or the dog will be sent in to find you."

Two enemy apedogs come over the fence at the back of Our Den and see Rebel! He looks FIERCE. They start running down the road to the path. Rebel is after them! Rebel is Hunting! Arroof. ARRRF? *Can I help your Hunting, Rebel? Did you know there are many Bad apedogs?*

ROOF, says Rebel as he runs past on a very long leash with his Packleader running behind. It means, *Okay, you can hunt with my Pack.* I run after Rebel.

Lulu says, "NEENAW NEENAW," and flies round and round in circles.

I can hear my ape-puppies shouting at me, but I'm too excited to listen because I AM HELPING MY FRIEND REBEL CATCH THE BAD APEDOGS WHO WENT IN OUR DEN! ARRRF! ARRRF!

Run run run run after the Bad apedogs, so exciting, so happy, hunting with my Friend Rebel. . . .

Round the corner. Where are the Bad Enemy ape-dogs? Sniff snortle sniff snortle. Rebel is smelling for them too.

"Jack? It was *your* house. Go home, boy."

Sorry, Rebel's Packleader, but you are not *my* Packleader and I am helping Rebel. Sniff snortle. Whoops. No, you can't get my collar. I know about clever paws. Dodge, run. Sniff snortle.

Ah yes, frightened fierce mature male apedog smell in the air, foot smell on squashed grass with

many other feet. . . . Rebel can smell them too. He growls. Goes down the path. I go with him. Pad pad now, following the exciting smell. Here it is, smells very strong. They stopped running here. Splashed through the delicious mud wallow, went on. They smell not-so-scared. They think they've hidden their scent.

Very very strong male apedog smells in the air: double. Hmm. Interesting. I wonder why. . . . Ah. Maybe they came this way before. I think they did.

There is old Bad apedog smell here too. They came from over there. . . .

A Big Furry with clip-clop paws came. Female. Sniff snortle, snifff snortle. *Smell the Big Furry. Rebel, can you smell her?*

Yes, I can, says Rebel, *but we mustn't get distracted. We must follow the Bad ape-dogs. This way.*

My Friend Rebel is Very Clever. It is hard to keep on thinking about one thing.

His Packleader is saying nice encouraging things to him. But "Go home, Jack," he says to me.

But he is not my Packleader, so I don't have to do it. And he is busy helping Rebel hunt the Bad apedogs so he hasn't got time to catch me.

I can hear that Pete and Caroline and Mikey are also following, quite a ways back because they don't want anybody to know they're there. They hide behind bushes and whisper. They are being a Pack too.

OH! THEY ARE OPENING A MEAT-SKIN. YUM. Ham, I like ham. Pig with smoke on it. Go back, follow the lovely smell, round the corner, into the bushes.

Hello, ape-puppies, can I have some MEAT? PLEASE?

"Go away, Jack," whispers Pete.

Sorry, Pete, I do not understand. Maybe it would help if you gave me some MEAT.

Caroline is munching it with a thoughtful expression. "Very salty," she says.

"Shhh," says Pete. He gives me some ham.

Mikey pats me. "You go help the Action Man Brave Hero Dog," he says. "Go on."

More Food? Oh, thank you, Mikey.

Okay, let's see what Rebel has found. Hi there, Rebel's Packleader. *Hi, Junior NotMyPack Friend Rebel.* . . .

You smell good, says Rebel. He licks my chops and I burp for him. His

Packleader reminds him about Hunting.

Oh, the trail stops. Where did they go? Sniff snortle this way. Sniff snortle that way.

Smell, says Rebel, very happy. *They went that way, then they came back and went this way. Down this little path here. They doubled back.*

How clever of you, Rebel, respect for Junior Dog. That was puzzling for me.

This is a very little path. Rebel goes ahead much faster because the smell is so strong. His Packleader is running behind him, I am running.

Whew, it's a bit pant-making, running like this. Rebel's Packleader is very strong. He is not as big as my Packleader but my Packleader would be going *hur hur hur* by now and coughing.

The path comes to the wood. Oh dear. One Bad apedog went that way. One Bad apedog went the other way. Many ways. My head feels tight with all the hard thinky stuff.

Rebel stops, points with his nose. *Would you follow that apedog and bite him if you catch him, Senior NotMyPack Friend Jack?* he says, very respectfully.

Oh dear. I've never bitten an apedog. What if he is Fierce? What if he bites my ear?

Oh dear.

But I can't let Rebel think I'm not as brave as

136

he is, especially when I'm not.

Okay. Sniff snortle sniff snortle. Follow the other trail, even though my tummy is going whirly whirly.

The Bad apedog is going right through the wood toward where all the apedogs in the trees and the other apedogs with RRRRR things are barking at each other. Oh, I smell. He is one of the apedogs that Karl talked to yesterday in the van. He is a Friend of Karl's. He is going this way, very clear strong smell in the air, fierce male apedog. . . . Now not so scared, he thinks he will be safe.

Ha, Bad apedog. Not with Me on your trail, I will (probably) bite you and anyway I can

BARK VERY VERY LOUD. ARRF.

What's that?

wooof WOOOF WOOOOOOF.

I can hear Rebel's deep bark. He is angry and scared. There is ape-barking and thumping.

Oh dear. Very confusing. Which do I do? Go

after the Bad apedog or see why Rebel's scared?

Oh dear. Hard head stuff. Um. Bubble in my head. Pop!

Go help Rebel, he is a Junior Dog. Also, he is closer to my ape-puppies. I can always find the Bad apedog later. Rebel and I can do it together. Anyway, there is lots of scary shouting and yelling from all the apedogs on the other side of the wood.

Rabbits?

"NEENAW NEENAW."
Push off wuzzock. THIS IS THE POLICE.
WE'RE COMING IN."

It's Auntie Zoo's Feathery! She's flying round and round barking.

Turn, run back. Sniff snortle, sniff snortle. Where are Rebel and his Packleader? And the Bad apedog? Find Rebel's trail, sniff snortle . . . around this bush, past these trees (quick Wet Message, hide one of Garage Dog's). Past this heap of big stones . . .

Oh. How funny. The smells of Rebel and his Packleader and the Bad apedog are there but . . .

Nobody. Just a hole in the earth under some more rocks.

Lulu sits on the rock. **"Arrk, arrk. Wuzzock, wuzzock. Bad bad."**

Smell . . . Sniff snortle . . .

Gosh. They went in the hole. Wow. Dark in there. Scary. Oh dear. Maybe very big rabbits. Or badgers. Or foxes. Or ALL OF THEM.

And a Bad Enemy apedog who might be Fierce and bite my ear.

Maybe if I bark very loudly and helpfully outside, Rebel and his Packleader will hear and come out.

RRROOOOF, ROOOF, RRRROOOOF, ARRRF, ARRRROOOOF!

Smell. Rebel's Packleader and the Enemy apedog are fighting! They are struggling! Phew. Chiff. Very very strong smell of angry mature male apedogs.

Maybe a bit too scary to go in there.

My ape-puppies are hiding in another bush, eating some ROAST BEEF. I think I'll go and . . . Oh. They finished it too quick.

Sad Dog.

ARRROOOF! ARRRF!

Here is Rebel coming out of the hole. All his fur is up, he is scared.

Hello, Rebel, what have you got there?

Hi, Jack, it is a bit too scary for me in the dark.

Well that's true. *But what about helping your Packleader fight the Bad Enemy apedog, Rebel?*

Um . . . scared puppy . . . Might bite my ear. Also, smell what I found!

Oh. A nice very MATURE BONE, long and thin. Hmm. Sniff.

Grrrr, says Rebel. He thinks I might take his bone.

All right, Friend Rebel, it's your bone. Maybe I'll go and smell if I can find a bone too.

Okay, plenty for you too, says Rebel.

Go in the hole under the rocks where Rebel found the bone.

SMELL BONE! FOR ME!

The earth is fresh, the hole has only been here a short time. Very dark. Much apedog grunting and panting. They are wrestling. Shall I bite the Enemy apedog?

Maybe not. I don't know how. I have never ever bitten an apedog.

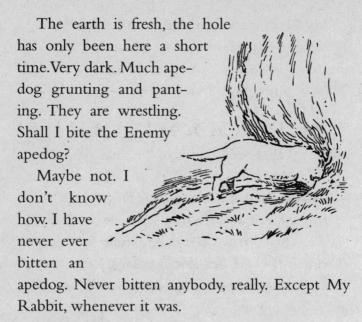

Never bitten anybody, really. Except My Rabbit, whenever it was.

Oh dear.

Snifff sniff . . . Yes. MATURE BONES that way. Carefully go around Rebel's Packleader and the Bad apedog. Clinky stuff, sharp and breakable. Bowls and cups made of that burned earth my Packleader makes sometimes. Metal things under a rock. The kind of metal my Pack Lady wears in her ears. Smell only a bit of metal. Lots of stuff.

But also NICE MATURE BONES. Sniff sniff. Here's a big round one. MINE NOW!

Oh NO! Rebel's Packleader and the Bad apedog

have bumped into the bit of wood next to the hole where we came in.

Pitter patter ... ARRRF!
scumble thud thud. Pitter patter
The earth FELL DOWN!
THERE IS NO HOLE.

Oh dear. Oh dear. No more air moving, smell of fresh earth. Oh dear!

Pant gasp, says Rebel's Packleader. Loud clicks. "Now stay still!"

Sudden bright light. Makes my eyes wrinkly and sore. Blink blink. Whine. It's Rebel's Pack-leader with his carrying-light. He has got the Bad apedog by an arm. The Bad apedog has his clever paws held behind his back by a metal thing. He is panting and gasping too and all covered in mud. Rebel's Packleader is nicely covered too. He smells very fine.

He is THE WINNER.

ARRRF! I bark respectfully. You are **THE WINNER,** Rebel's Packleader. All by yourself you fought and won against another **FIERCE MALE APE– DOG.** You are very **BIG AND STRONG AND FIERCE.** Much much respect.

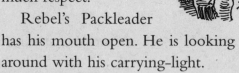

Rebel's Packleader has his mouth open. He is looking around with his carrying-light.

We are in a little room made of rock with swirly patterns like water on the walls. There is a rock with mature bones and metal things under it, burned–earth things around it. Where the hole was is a lot of earth and a rock fallen down. There are some Flicker Boxes and Howling and Banging boxes next to it, piled up.

"Good . . . heavens!" says Rebel's Packleader. "What the . . . ?" He points his carrying-light at the mature bones and all the other old apedog stuff. "This must be incredibly old." He sounds pleased about the mature bones too. Oh dear. I hope there will be enough.

Outside I can hear that Rebel is barking at the place where the hole isn't. He is barking loudly. He is scared. Me too. It's only a little room made of rock. How do I get out? Oh dear!

I bark too. ARRRRF ARRRF ARRRRF. Help! PACKLEADER, QUICK. PACKMEMBERS, QUICK. ARRRF ARRRF ARROOOOF ARROOOOOO! I am a poor scared puppy dog. Get me out of this little room made of rock.... ARRROOOOOOO!

Rebel's Packleader sees that the hole isn't there anymore, smells scared as well as interested.

"Rebel! You there, boy?"

Rebel barks back. ARRF WOOOOF WOOOF WOOOF.

"Watch, Rebel," shouts his Packleader. "Watch!"

Rebel barks even more helpfully. ARROOO! ARRROOO!

The Bad apedog suddenly sits down on the ground and starts doing the apedog howly thing with water in his eyes. Oh dear. Poor apedog, have you got a hurty?

Maybe I should lick you, make you feel better.

I bring the round bone over so I don't lose it. Then I go and lick the howling apedog's face, make him feel better. . . . He howls more.

It must be a bad hurty. Even though you are a Bad apedog, I will help you. Lick lick. Dribble, lick lick lick.

"Gerrimoffme!" he howls encouragingly. More licking.

146

"Down, Jack," says Rebel's Packleader, not very loudly or very firmly. His body says: *This is funny, I don't really mean it.*

The Bad apedog isn't happier. He is still howling. Okay. Go find my nice round bone.

"What the . . . ?" says Rebel's Packleader. "What have you got there, Jack?"

Oh, all right. Since you are Rebel's Packleader and you just won a fight with a Bad apedog. You are probably a bit hungry. You can have my bone.

Sigh.

Rebel's Packleader gets my round bone and points his shiny bright carrying-light at it. It looks a bit apedoggish but it's too old to smell what sort of animal it was.

"Holy . . . wow. Jack, do you know what you found?"

Yes, Rebel's Packleader. It is a round bone, like a ball. Can I have it back now?

Rebel's Packleader has the big eyes and mouth of a surprised apedog. The Bad apedog makes more water in his eyes. "Oh, that's horrible, is it . . . ooorgh . . . sniff."

" 'Alas, poor Yorick!' . . . I'm afraid I can't let you chew this skull, Jack. It might be evidence."

Oh, all right. You can put it up on a rock for later. Yes, there are more bones over there. You can go and smell them.

Rebel's Packleader doesn't smell them, but he puts the shiny light on them and all around them. His voice gets more and more excited. "I know what this is. This is . . . a burial chamber. Good Lord. What a find!" He turns to his beaten enemy. "You. How did you find this place?"

The Bad ape-dog is wrinkling his face, staring at the ground. Are you feeling poorly again, Not–MyPack vanquished apedog? Let me clean your face some more. Lick. Dribble. Slurp.

"Ow ow, oooorrrggh. Gerrimoffme!" The Bad apedog is still doing howling with water, despite my helpful licking. "We didn't know about all that stuff. We thought it was just badgers . . ."

"This?"

"We were keeping . . . things in it."

"Stolen goods?"

"Yeah." The Bad apedog is just doing puppy whines now. "I'm scared. We might die. What if it all falls down?"

Rebel's Packleader looks up at the rock roof.

I look up, sniff sniff. There's a bit of air coming in from somewhere, but not much. Oh dear. I think that might be bad.

ARRRF ARRRF ARRRF. Rebel is still barking helpfully outside.

"You thought *badgers* did this? How big do you think they are?"

"Karl said it was just an old mine working. He said we could keep the stuff here and hide here if we had to."

"So he knew you boys were robbing the village?"

"He said all the cops would be too busy keeping him and his tree huggers away from the developers—we'd be in and out easy, like at Oldchester last month. I don't wanna die . . . !"

The apedog makes more water in his eyes. Rebel's Packleader is smelling much-thinking as well as scared.

Oh dear oh dear. My tummy is frightened. I don't like being in this funny cave even though Rebel's Packleader is with me. Sniff the rock walls. Sniff the ground. Aha! Here is his Bad Headthing. Grrrrr . . . *You Bad Headthing, you*

*can't sit on apedog heads and look scary,
I will get you. . . . Pounce. Bite.*

"Oh no, Jack, no, not my hat!"

GRRRRRRRR. . . . Bite, chew,

SHAKE…GRRRRRrrr.

"Oh, you idiot."

GRROWF GRRRRRR GRRROWF.

Shake shake bite,

stand

on it,

r r r r r i p.

Good. I made it into meat. Well, not meat, maybe—sort of bits of removable fur and shoe-stuff and bits of metal. Apedog Bad Headthings are quite complicated. Interesting smell of Rebel's Packleader's hair: he washes it with stuff that smells of trees.

"You've ripped it to shreds. Why? What harm has my hat ever done you, Jack?"

It's all safe now, Rebel's Packleader, the Bad Headthing won't sit on your head and be scary any more.[1] Whew. That's better. One less thing to worry about.

I come and sit on Rebel's Packleader's feet. He pats me. Ohh ahhh . . . so nice. Paws up, you can pat my tummy. Grooooaaan. Lovely. Scratch scratch.

The Bad apedog watches. "Is he yours?"

"No, he's just a big softie, aren't you, Jack."

I still don't like it here. There aren't any more Bad Headthings to chew up, are there? Oh. Smell. Lulu is out there, going *ark ark*. I can hear her very well. Pad pad. Quick lick of the Bad apedog. Round the back of the stone with the mature bones. Oh, that's where the air is coming. Aha. A badger hole. Snifff snortle. Push my head in. That's the way out.

---

[1] The Big Yellow Stupid has always hated hats. We find they make perfectly acceptable Cat bedding if well pawed down and squashed, but otherwise they are completely pointless.

Come on, Rebel's Packleader and vanquished ape-dog. This way.

Rebel's Packleader looks, shakes his head. This is apedog bodytalk for: *Oh dear.*

Well, it is a bit small, but ... Push into the hole. Push. My tummy is a bit round for it, but I can push a bit more. There is rock all around. **Push. Ouch. Hurty tum. Push push, scrabble, scrape.**

YES! Outside on the other side of the hump with trees in. Great! Now, where are my Packmembers?

DOUGHNUT! FOR ME! ♥

Rebel is still barking, I can hear him. But my Packmembers can't hear him because of all the apedog shouting at the edge of the wood. They are hiding in some bushes because they are scared Auntie Zoo will find them and be cross. I can smell that they are scared.

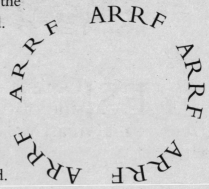

Run round and round barking.

Nobody can hear.

Oh dear.

RRROWF ROWF ARRRF ARROOOF. I

wonder why I am barking? There is something scary about Rebel's Packleader but I can't remember what it is. Where is he? *Rebel, hi there, where is your Packleader?*

I'm not sure, I think he is eating my bones, but I have to bark now: WOOOF ARRROOOF!

Oh dear. Pad pad, run run. Back to the other place. Sniff snortle. Hi there, Rebel's Packleader. How did you get in a rabbit hole?

"Go get help, Jack," says Rebel's Packleader. "Go on. Some more stones fell down. Fetch, boy."

WHAT? There are no sticks? You have lovely mature

bones there, Rebel's Packleader, why is your tummy tense? Is it being in a dark rabbit hole?

Here is a stick for you.

"Not that. Fetch people. Get Pete and Mikey! And Auntie Zoo! Okay?"

No, Rebel's Packleader, I'm very sorry, I do not know what you want. It is making my head hurt lots, especially with all the shouting from the ape-dogs. Here is another nice stick for you to chew. There. Happy now?

"Boy, are you thick, Jack. You're even thicker than Rebel. You make him look like a genius."

Thank you, thank you, Rebel's Packleader, I am

Thick. Thick is Good. I am the THICKEST DOG IN THE WORLD! Proud dog! Rebel's Packleader says I am Thick. Thicker than Rebel.

PROUD DOG!

ARRRF. ARRRF.

I am Hungry. Oh look. A van. It's a different van, not the same smell as the one the Bad apedogs were in. I wonder where the Food is. . . .

Sniff snortle, snifff . . .

156

Yes! The window is open! Yes! I can get through, even with my round tummy, if I hup and kick and scrabble with my back legs. OOooff.

Yum. The food is there, but where? It is a doughnut. I know it is. Yum yum! I like doughnuts!

Sniff snortle, sniff. Smell the seats. Smell under the seats. Apedog stuff—I don't like apple cores. Where is my doughnut? Snnnnniffff.

It's near here. Where the interesting sticks and the big round thing for holding are. Better be a bit careful. Bad things happen where there are big round things and interesting sticks. Not sure what, but Bad.

Doughnut?

Snifff . . . Aha. I found it. It's on the little shelf there. Get it with my nose. Snifff. Yum. I like doughnut. Sit on the seat, put my paws on the round thing, put my nose where the doughnut is stuck.

BEEEEP!

What?

Try again.

BEEEEP!

BEEEEP!

BEEEEEEEEEEEEEP!

Why is the van barking? There are no Enemy dogs. It is hard to get my doughnut. I have to lean my tummy on the round thing and push with my nose and lick lick lick . . .

BEEEEP!

BEEEEEEEEEEEEEEEEEEE
EEEEEEEEEEEEEEEEEP!

Yes! Got it! Yum yum snortle gulp erp.

Maybe sleep now on a comfy seat?

DIG! DIG!

"Jack! What are you doing in there?"

It's Caroline and Mikey and Pete. My Pack-members.

Well, you can't have my doughnut, Pack-members, sorry, but it's mine. Slurp, lick, gulp. Never mind the paper, eat all of it. Yum yum. I like doughnuts even if they make my teeth feel funny.

ARRRF. Poke my head out of the window.

They open the back and I get out easier. My poor tummy is a bit sore and very covered in mud.

"Where's Rebel and Officer Janner? What happened to your tummy?"

Who? Oh, I know where Rebel is. Can't you hear him barking? He is puzzled and scared because he has lost his Packleader.

Something about Rebel's Packleader is worrying me, but I don't know what. Let's go home? Oh Okay, put my leash on. Here's Rebel.

WOOOF WOOF, WOOF.

Hi, Rebel, nice to smell you.

Hi, Jack, but this is my bone, you can't have my bone.

Oh yes, I remember now. There are good bones in this rabbit hole. Come on, Pete, I'll show you some lovely mature bones. Yum. Here is the rabbit hole where the rocks are. Smell. Lovely mature bones and . . .

Rebel's Packleader! And the Bad apedog!

ARROOOOF! Hi, Rebel's Packleader, how lovely to smell you again!

"Help!" shouts Rebel's Packleader. "Can you hear us!"

"Help!" shouts the Bad apedog.

Caroline and Pete look around to find where

the shouting is from. They look up in the trees.

Mikey goes to the rabbit hole and leans in. "Are you rabbits?" he asks.

"Hi there, Mikey," says Rebel's Packleader. "Can you get your auntie?"

"Are you stuck like Winnie the Pooh?"

"Yes."

"Oh wow," shouts Pete. "Look, it's Officer Janner and somebody else. Look. They're down there. How did you get there?"

"Long story, Pete. Can you get help? We can't get out and I'm worried the roof is unstable."

"Oh wow. Right. Okay. Right."

"Go get your Auntie Zoo."

"Er . . . but . . . um . . . well, Okay."

Pete and Caroline look at each other and at Mikey. They look over where the shouting and RRRRR things are.

"Auntie Zoo will flip out if she sees me," says Pete.

"So will my mom," says Caroline.

"How about if I say Jack got away and came here."

"Hm. We've got to tell her something."

"Oh dear."

ARRRF. I can smell that Rebel's Packleader is getting frightened. Some bits of earth fell down in the rabbit hole. He is scared in case the rocks fall down. "Kids, can you get a move on?"

ARRRF ARRRF ARRRF. I will bark at the Bad rabbit hole. ARRROOOOFF!

"I will stay here and look after Jack," says Mikey. "You and Caroline can tell Auntie Zoo."

Caroline and Pete look at each other. They hold hands. Off they go to where the apedogs are shouting.

ARROOOF! Bad rabbit hole, let Rebel's Packleader come out. ARROOOO ARROO–

OOO, YIP YIP ARRROO-OOOOO!

"I told you to go straight home, no detours, and you come straight back here and you bring Mikey as well. . . . I told you this is no place for kids and you ignored me. . . . When your mom and dad get home . . ."

It's Auntie Zoo! ARRRF ARRF
ARROOO
ARRROOOOOF.

"Help!" shout Rebel's Packleader and the Bad apedog. "Get us out of here!"

Auntie Zoo is too busy being cross to hear them, and Pete can't get a word in either.

ARRRF
ARRRF
ARROOF.

"And you brought Jack back with you as well when you know . . . ?"

ARRRF! Stop barking at the ape-puppies, and

smell! I get her removable fur very softly in my teeth and pull her to where the rabbit hole is.

"Jack, stoppit, I can see there's a rabbit hole and I'm really not interested in ..."

"HELP!" shout Rebel's Pack-leader and the Bad apedog together.

"What?" Auntie Zoo looks all over.

Pitter patter, more earth. Rebel's Packleader very scared now. "Can you hear me! I'm down here!"

At last she smells him. Why are apedogs so slow?[1] "Good lord, Officer Janner. What are you doing down there?"

"Hoping I don't get buried alive."

ARRRF ARRRF.

"How did you ... ?"

"This is some kind of old burial chamber, but the entrance has fallen in. We need digging out. Quickly."

"Who's with you?"

"Huh, him," says Caroline. "That's one of Karl's mates."

---

[1] A fascinating question to which there is no easy answer.

Lots of quick ape-barking. Auntie Zoo runs off. I can see her going to where all the apedogs are shouting at each other. She pushes to the front. She shouts at everybody.

Then Lulu flies over to her, barking and shouting ape-barking.

"ARRK ARK. WAZZUCK. PUSHOFF. Bad DOG.

THIS IS THE POLICE WITH DOGS, WE'RE COMING IN!

NEEENAW   NEEENAW   NEEENAW"

Lots of things happen. Very complicated to smell and hear. The young male ape-dog Pack suddenly stop pushing and shoving and shouting. They stop wanting to fight. The ape-dogs with RRRRR things stop wanting to fight. The apedogs with dark removable furs and Bad Headthings stop wanting to fight. They all turn and listen to Auntie Zoo.

More barking between them. She waves her arms. Suddenly, everything changes.

Soon lots of apedogs are here, being a quick Pack. They bark at each other. Some of them were miners once. They all talk very quick, too quick and too complicated to understand. They push a bit of pipe down through the earth so more air goes in. They dig with digging sticks. The apedogs with RRRR things get a Big Huge Kennel-that-moves with big knobbly wheels, very scary.

Rebel is scared, barks and barks, ARRRRF **ARRRF GRR-RROOOOF.**

One of the officer ape-dogs with a Bad Head-thing comes along. His body says he is impor-tant, like a Packleader. He goes to Rebel and tries to get his collar.

Rebel thinks he is trying to get his nice mature bone. Rebel growls at him, *Stay away, mine now.*

The officer Packleader doesn't understand. He doesn't even have dog smell on his removable furs. He smells important and he thinks Rebel will know it. "Come on," he says. "Leave it, boy. Come this way."

Rebel doesn't want to leave the earthy bit where his Packleader went in. GRRRRRR, he says. *I don't like you, you can't have my bone, you can't go near my Packleader. . . .*

GRRRRRR . . .

Oh dear. Rebel is going to fight the officer apedog. Oh no. He jumps up, showing teeth, and when the officer apedog turns to run away, he BITES HIS TAIL END! Wow!

Mikey laughs lots. The officer apedog falls over and bumps himself. He is barking lots. ARRRF.

He leaves Rebel alone now. That would be best. Nobody is happy when his Packleader is lost. Also, Rebel has a bone.

Now the apedogs with digging sticks are digging

hard. They are digging out the earthy bit. They use some of the stones lying around to hold it up. Some of them have bits of flat wood ready.

ARRRF! That's right, dig that way. Lots of nice mature bones there.

Oh, and Rebel's Packleader and the Bad apedog. Probably they have chewed up the nice bones by now, what with being nervous and having whirly tummies from being stuck in a rabbit hole.

The apedogs who carry boxes and furry sticks around are here and pointing their boxes at the apedogs who are digging. Mikey is with Pete and Caroline talking to the apedog who is holding a sort of stick with a fat bit on top. Is it a chewy thing?

Hi there, are you a Friend? You smell nice, you have eaten lots of fish. Can I smell your . . . ?

Sorry.

"This is Jack, my dog," says Pete. "He's really cool. He told us where Officer Janner was. He made the horn on the van beep so we could hear, and he barked at the hole. He's a hero!"

The apedogs point their boxes at me. Oh dear. They have a long furry thing on a stick. What is it? It must be a chewy thing. Why is it on a stick?

ARRRF ARRRF ARRRF!
Jump up. Bite. Crunch. Bite,
SHAKE. It falls to bits.

The apedogs are all barking at me now. Pete and
Mikey and Caroline are giggling because I ate the
sound-boom. What is a "sound-boom"?

It doesn't taste very nice.

ARRRRRRF!

The Huge Kennel-that-moves with big wheels
has got a rope on, going to the rock that fell down.

Now it goes backward. Pull pull . . . Dig dig. Lots of hard work. The apedogs are digging as if they are all in one Pack.

Only Auntie Zoo's ape-puppy isn't there. Karl has gone away now. When everybody else was busy digging for the mature bones, and Rebel's Pack-leader and the Bad apedog, he ran very quickly, very quietly, and got in the van where my dough-nut was, and he drove away with the other Bad apedog I had to stop chasing. I wonder why.

The apedogs with boxes bark excitedly at the boxes. Rebel barks back at them. We both bark. We are A PACK. We have little slitty eyes. GRRRR, we

don't like you apedogs with chewy furry things on sticks. . . .

All the apedogs bark very excitedly. They are helping Rebel's Packleader and the Bad apedog out of the hole they made, all barking at each other at once. The apedogs with boxes stop barking at me and Rebel and point their boxes at the hole where they can see the rocks and the mature bones.

No, you can't have those bones, those are MY BONES and REBEL'S BONES, YOU CAN'T HAVE THEM. GRRRRRRR.

Here comes Rebel's Packleader and the Bad apedog, all covered with interesting-smelling mud and smelling very happy and relieved.

Rebel jumps up and puppy-bounces, he is VERY VERY HAPPY. SO HAPPY.

I am happy too, Rebel! HAPPY HAPPY HAPPY Dog.

Rebel and his Packleader do big cuddles while the apedogs with whirring boxes and lightning boxes point at him and bark. His Packleader talks to the officer apedog that Rebel bit. He sounds a bit sad. Rebel growls at the officer apedog again.

"That's enough, Rebel. You've done it now," says Rebel's Packleader. "Why on earth did you bite the chief inspector?"

GRRRRRRR, says Rebel. *I still don't like him.*

"I'm very sorry about that, sir. I think he was frightened and upset about me being in that old burial chamber," says Rebel's Packleader. His voice is paws-up for a Senior apedog Packleader but also trying not to laugh.

Then Rebel's Packleader pats me and says I am a Good Dog. Rebel whines a little bit, but then he comes over and we do Wet Messages to show respect.

Pete and Mikey and Caroline are cuddling me now while the apedogs with boxes talk. Ohhhh ahhhh groan . . . lovely. I like this. It's great to have so much cuddling. Pat pat pat.

Happy ♥ Dog. ♥

Paws up, pat tummy. Lots of lightning boxes. Lots of apedogs talking. The people with the lightning boxes and whirring boxes on shoulders want me to sit next to Rebel's Packleader. Everybody is too excited to do any more angry barking or fighting and any-way, nobody can find Karl or his pack of young male apedogs. They have all gone away.

Auntie Zoo is sad about that, but she isn't say-ing anything. Lulu sits on her shoulder saying **"NEENAW"** sometimes.

All the apedogs from the soft dens are there, cheering and waving their arms, Pat pat pat the dog, me! Happy Dog.

Rebel's Packleader says to the Pack Lady with the fat furry stick: "Police Dog Rebel tracked the burglar and found the entrance to the place where they were going to hide their stolen goods—down there in the burial chamber. I think  they must have found the place when they were digging a tunnel. I made the arrest. Jack came in to keep me company. Then, when the tunnel col-lapsed, Jack got out through that little hole there to get help. He fetched Caroline Burley and Pete and Mikey Stopes, and they acted very sensibly and fetched their aunt, who organized the rescue. Nobody could hear Rebel barking because of all the shouting. It was Jack who raised the alarm by honking the horn of the escape van."

Oh. Did I?

Is that "Good Dog"?

STEAK?

I GET STEAK!

The Cats said I should jump over a suppertime and a sleeptime.

In the night I heard Auntie Zoo talking on the talkbone. Her voice was angry and sad. "Never mind how I know. I know what you were up to with those thieves and your nasty friends."

Then I could hear her ape-puppy Karl in the talkbone. He was making whining paws-up voice for her, but she interrupted. "I'm so ashamed of you, Karl. How could you use people like that?"

Next he was barking. I came and leaned on her and growled a little, so she knew I was On Her

Side. She patted me sadly. "I know a lot of people. Either you give yourself up to the police or I'll tell everyone I can what your game is, which will put a stop to it because you won't be welcome at any protest site. Understand? No, I won't inform on you. You have to do it."

More barking from Karl. Grrrr. You are bad to your Pack Lady. You should have more respect. GRRRRR.

"Good-bye, Karl," says Auntie Zoo, and puts the talkbone back softly. She smells terribly sad. Poor poor Pack Lady. Let me lick your face, there there, cuddle.

I have a lovely sleep on her bed until she pushes me out in the middle of the night because she says I am too loud.

How am I loud? I don't think I'm loud even when I'm chasing exciting rabbits in the sleepy place.

More jumping over: breakfast time and a lovely bus ride, Walkies and coming back on the bus (CHIPS!), and spending the day doing bark- ing games with Lulu.

"ARRF ARRF," she says, sitting in her cage. "ARRF ARRRF ARRROOOF!"

"ARRF ARRF ARRRF ARRRRRF," I bark back. She is doing dog-barking![1] It's great. She is my Friend. Auntie Zoo has a headache. A NotMy-Pack apedog Friend Pack Lady brought back Pete and Mikey and she gave me big patting and cuddles too because I saved Pencerriog Wood. Is that a Good Dog? Oh great. Steak?

Oh. Auntie Zoo talked to the talkbone for a long time when we got home. She still sounded

---

[1] Horrible abomination! Outrageous wicked evil terrible anti-Cat behavior! How can We hunt and kill the Flying Feathery Food when it barks like a dog so We have to run away? We are actively researching better apecat lairs where Cats are decently treated.

upset and sad. I could hear my Packleader in the talkbone.

ARRF ARRF! I said. ARROOOF. Pant pant. *Hi, Great Packleader, how lovely to hear you, where are you? Can I cuddle . . . ?*

Oh. Sad Puppy. Where is he?

It's funny when apedogs are in the talkbone. You can hear them but you can't see them and you can't smell them.[2]

Auntie Zoo said what happened and did paws-up voice for my Pack Lady. Pack Lady was only a little bit mad about it. She laughed lots in the talkbone when Auntie Zoo explained about me making the van bark and said she was sure Food was involved somehow.

Now Pete and Mikey are jumping up and down because they are going to be on the television. A TV person came to school today and talked to them about finding the Iron Age site in Pencerriog Wood. They are Famous and I am too.

What is "television"? What is "famous"?

Terri is in her room listening to her Howling and Banging box. She is very mad that she

---

2 Feline primatologists are working hard on the telephone problem. Apecats use them all the time, and it's true that they are not edible. If you knock one over, it makes pleasant purring sounds until an apecat starts to speak and then there is a nasty wailing noise. We have decided to ignore them mercilessly until they become more Cat-friendly.

wasn't there when Rebel and I found the mature bones and isn't going to be on the TV.

Where is my STEAK? No steak. Sigh. Doze.

What's that? I can hear happy-footsteps. Pack-leader is back! Pack Lady is back! Here they are, coming through the door.

OH HAPPY HAPPY HAPPY JOYFUL HAPPY DOG!!!★★★Wag

Hi, arrrf arrrf . . . Jump, hop, dance dance. Puppy dance! You have been GONE FOR SO LONG!

Did you get any GOOD FOOD? Where is my STEAK? Snifff. Something nice in Packleader's bag. Mmm.

HAPPY HAPPY. Puppy-bow, Wag wag, ARRRF ARRRF ARRF ARRF, Packleader, welcome, Pack Lady, can I smell your . . . ?

Sorry.

Pat pat. Can I have Food now, Great Packleader?

Okay, the puppies can have a cuddle.

The Flicker Box is on. Pete and Mikey are pointing at bits in it. Terri is watching too; her body says: *Huh, unfair.*

There is barking. GREAT! I can hear my friend Rebel. ARRRRF! *Hi, Rebel, come in!*

How funny. I can hear him in the Flicker Box, but I can't smell him. Another dog is barking. Oh dear. He sounds Big and Loud and Scary.

ARRROOOF. ARRROOOF. ARR– ROOF.

Lots of ape-barking and laughing. Some NotMy-Pack apedog Friends have come. They are all talking at once and drinking Falling Over Juice made from bad grapes. Trot out to the hall, sniff snortle snifff snortle. Removable-fur boxes. Hm. No one there. Lurk. Pull. Yum yum.

"Pencerriog Wood might be one of the most important Iron Age sites in the West Country," says Packleader. "I was talking to one of the archaeology experts at the Inquiry and he said that there's no way they'll build a road there now, not when they've got real burial chambers to investigate and all the artifacts to study. Some of the ceramics were damaged and they think a fox or even a wolf might have had a go at some of the bones, but . . ."

They all cheer and point at the Flicker Box.

More dog-barking. Maybe he isn't so Big and Scary. He sounds a bit familiar. All the apedogs say, "Wahoo," and I am getting lots of pats and cuddles.

Pack Lady is talking to another Pack Lady. "They'll probably build over the old Second World War aerodrome, which is where they were supposed to do it in the first place," says Pack Lady. "It's the obvious sensible route. And it's all thanks to Jack. Ooops. I nearly forgot! Where's Jack's present, Tom?"

"It's in my bag."

Pack Lady goes and looks. Um.

Oh dear.

Maybe this is Bad Dog. It was a very delicious-smelling Steak, Pack Lady, and there was a little teeny hole in the bag and I couldn't help it . . .

"JACK! YOU GREEDY PIG!"

Oh dear.

"It's all right," says Packleader, coming out with more Falling Over Juice for Pack Lady. "It was his steak in the first ... OH JACK! YOU GREEDY PIG!"

"Belgian chocolates!" wails Pack Lady in a terribly sad voice.

Yes, Pack Lady. I like chocolate too.

And STEAK. I love STEAK. MORE? ERP.

Jackspeak: English

B

Bad Headthing	hat
between-ears face	forehead
Big Furry-with-hard- 　clip-clop paws	horse
Big Hunt	supermarket shopping
Big White Water Dish	toilet
brown tails	dreadlocks
burned earth	ceramic

C

Cats' God	fire
carblood	oil
carjuice	gasoline
carry-boxes	suitcases
carrying-light	flashlight
claw-smearing	nail polishing
clicky-clacky Flicker Box	computer
Cold Cupboard	fridge
colored paper	money

D

Den	where Jack lives, house
Den That Moves	moving van/bus
digging stick	spade

F   Falling Over Juice   wine

fat stick   microphone

flappy things on sticks   placards

Flicker Box   television

Flying Featheries   birds

food-skin   packaging

Funny Pricklies   hedgehogs

G   ground-with-NotGrass   flowerbed

H   Hard Message   poo

hard-shelled food   can

hot brown drink   coffee

Howling and Banging box   portable stereo

Huge Great Food Place   superstore

I   interesting sticks   gearshift and hand brake

K   Kennel That Moves   car

L   leg-coverings   trousers

lightning box   camera

light-tree   lamppost

| Little Crawlies | insects |
| Lots of Dens Together place | town |

M making into meat — killing

meat-skin — package

Medium Eatable Furries with Long Ears — rabbits

message huts — portable toilets

mouth-happy-squeaky-thing — squeaky plastic hedgehog toy

N NEEEOOWWW things — jet planes

nest — bed

nest-coverings — bedspreads

NotFetch — you fetch the stick and then forget to bring it back

O Outside — yard

Outside Outside — everywhere else

P pawball — good game involving ape-puppies kicking

	a ball, Jack pawing it, and then Jack biting it until it turns into a rag
paw-coverings	shoes/boots/socks
piled-up bread	sandwich
plastic biscuit	bank card
prechewed cow-meat	ground beef

R

Ready	in season
removable furs	clothes
roaring-sucky-tube	vacuum cleaner
round thing	steering wheel
round tick-tick thing	clock
RRRR-thing	chainsaw (any mechanical cutter)

S

shoe stuff	leather
singed bread	toast
Slimys	frogs
Small Fierce Brown Wild Dog	fox
Smaller Fierce Stripy Face	badger
Small Furries	mice, voles, hamsters, etc.
Smoke Message	exhaust fumes

smoky-sticks	cigarettes
snail-trail stick	pen
soft apedog dens	tents
soft paper with ink smudges	newspapers
Special	pregnant
Special Messages	puppies

T

tail end	bottom
talkbone	telephone
things-that-look-like-sausages-but-made-of-plant	vegetarian sausages
two-wheel-go-fast thing	bike

U

unswallow	vomit

W

water-howling	crying
Water NotFurries	fish
water-running	swimming
weeaweeaw cars	police cars/ambulance
Wet Message	pee
Whitecoat apedog	vet

ABOUT THE AUTHOR

Jack Perry was born near Plymouth on April 7, 1993, the only pup in his litter. After a brief time with someone else, he was adopted (at great expense) by the Perry Pack and their Owner, Remy.[1] Jack has moved dens twice and went to obedience school in Camborne, where he was not at all obedient and far too friendly. His interests include eating, walking, food, swimming, breakfast, playing pawball with his Pack, supper, playing NotFetch and, of course, food theft. He is an accomplished cereal killer, dustbin desperado, and birthday-cake bandit. Apart from this, however, he is mostly a Good Dog and is very gentle with everyone.

Since *I, Jack* was published, Jack has become an

---

[1] Nobody asked ME.

accomplished Media Dog. He has pawed books in bookshops, had his picture in the local newspaper, and given barks to primary school children. Pack Lady comes along to interpret and is often quite mean with the dog-biscuit royalties. Jack is available [2] for author appearances so long as he doesn't have to travel too far and is provided with a bowl of water and some Outside for Wet Messages.

[2] We, however, do not stoop to such vulgar crowd-pleasing and would in any case be extremely expensive.

ABOUT THE INTERPRETER

Patricia Finney is Jack's real Pack Lady. She spends a lot of time running around after Jack, the Cats, her three children, and the Packleader. When she can, she writes all kinds of things, including historical and contemporary novels, scripts, and articles for newspapers (winning the David Higham Award for her first novel), despite the Cats' constant attempts to stop her by marching across the clicky-clacky Flicker Box's keyboard and making it

crash
hhhh<>%^$£★&^

hhhh<>%^$£★&^

P9-CQV-178

Study Guide to Accompany

Abrams' Clinical Drug Therapy

RATIONALES FOR NURSING PRACTICE

EIGHTH EDITION

Mary Jo Kirkpatrick, MSN, RN
Assistant Professor and Chair
Department of Associate Degree Nursing
College of Nursing and Speech Language Pathology
Mississippi University for Women
Columbus, Mississippi

Lippincott Williams & Wilkins
a Wolters Kluwer business
Philadelphia · Baltimore · New York · London
Buenos Aires · Hong Kong · Sydney · Tokyo

Senior Acquisitions Editor: Margaret Zuccarini
Managing Editor: Doris Wray
Editorial Assistant: Delema Caldwell-Jordan
Senior Production Editor: Sandra Cherrey Scheinin
Senior Production Manager: Helen Ewan
Senior Managing Editor/Production: Erika Kors
Creative Director: Doug Smock
Manufacturing Coordinator: Karin Duffield
Compositor: TechBooks
Printer: Victor Graphics

Eighth Edition

9 8 7 6 5 4 3 2 1

ISBN: 0-7817-7582-5

Care has been taken to confirm the accuracy of the information presented and to describe generally accepted practices. However, the author, editors, and publisher are not responsible for errors or omissions or for any consequences from application of the information in this book and make no warranty, express or implied, with respect to the content of the publication.

The author, editors, and publisher have exerted every effort to ensure that drug selection and dosage set forth in this text are in accordance with the current recommendations and practice at the time of publication. However, in view of ongoing research, changes in government regulations, and the constant flow of information relating to drug therapy and drug reactions, the reader is urged to check the package insert for each drug for any change in indications and dosage and for added warnings and precautions. This is particularly important when the recommended agent is a new or infrequently employed drug.

Some drugs and medical devices presented in this publication have Food and Drug Administration (FDA) clearance for limited use in restricted research settings. It is the responsibility of the health care provider to ascertain the FDA status of each drug or device planned for use in his or her clinical practice.

Introduction

The Study Guide to Accompany Abrams' Clinical Drug Therapy: Rationales for Nursing Practice, eighth edition, has been developed to complement Anne Abrams' text. It provides a wealth of learning opportunities to reinforce content that students learned from the text, and it promotes their ability to apply this information in the patient-care setting.

Pharmacology is a tough and demanding science, fraught with seemingly endless detail about an ever-growing number of drugs. Helping students learn its principles as applied to nursing practice to foster safe and effective management of drug therapy is perhaps one of the most challenging tasks surrounding nursing education today.

This study guide offers a variety of activities and exercises that accommodate many student-learning styles and increase the appeal of learning. These activities and exercises will help students establish a connection between how a drug works and why it is used for a particular disorder.

This *Study Guide to Accompany Abrams' Clinical Drug Therapy* will help prepare students in the following ways:

- **Prepare for *NCLEX* test taking.** NCLEX-style multiple choice and alternate format questions in every chapter give students an opportunity to practice their test-taking skills.
- **Develop *critical thinking* skills.** Applying Your Knowledge exercises challenge students to develop their critical thinking skills and help them explore how to apply those skills in clinical situations.
- **Develop *insight about client teaching needs*.** Mastering the Information exercises are aimed at expanding students' knowledge base and understanding of drug therapy and increasing their comprehension of what clients should know to maximize drug therapy.
- **Receive *immediate reinforcement* of learning.** Answers for multiple choice and alternate format questions, and all other exercises, are provided in the back of this guide, allowing for immediate feedback.
- **Expand *personal understanding* of drug therapy.** Completing the activities and working through the exercises provide valuable learning opportunities for students to immediately enhance learning effectiveness and build on classroom lectures and textbook reading and reflection.

Mary Jo Kirkpatrick
Author

Contents

CHAPTER 1

Introduction to Pharmacology

■ Mastering the Information

MATCHING

Match the terms in Column I with a definition, example, or related statement from Column II.

COLUMN I

1. _____ prototypes

2. _____ biotechnology

3. _____ pharmacology

4. _____ over-the-counter (OTC) drugs

5. _____ Food and Drug Administration (FDA)

6. _____ generic drug name

7. _____ medications

8. _____ U.S. Drug Enforcement Administration (DEA)

9. _____ trade drug name

10. _____ drug therapy

COLUMN II

a. charged with enforcing the Controlled Substances Act

b. drugs that can be purchased without a prescription

c. individual drugs that represent groups of drugs

d. related to the chemical or official name and is independent of the manufacturer

e. the study of drugs (chemicals)

f. drugs given for therapeutic purposes

g. designated and patented by a manufacturer

h. charged with enforcing laws concerning drugs

i. use of drugs to prevent; diagnose; or treat signs, symptoms, and disease processes

j. the process of manipulating deoxyribonucleic acid (DNA) and ribonucleic acid (RNA) in the development of drugs

TRUE OR FALSE

Indicate if the following statements are true or false.

_____ 1. Most drugs are given for their local effects.

_____ 2. Synthetic drugs are less likely to produce allergic reactions.

_____ 3. A nurse practitioner may prescribe a medication.

_____ 4. The Controlled Substances Act regulates the manufacture and distribution of antibiotics.

_____ 5. Nurses are not allowed to administer Schedule II drugs.

_____ 6. Most drugs used today are synthetic chemical compounds manufactured in laboratories.

_____ 7. Generic drugs are required to be therapeutically equivalent to trade name drugs and are much less expensive.

_____ 8. Internet sites are the best source of information for beginning students of pharmacology.

_____ 9. Schedule V drugs may be dispensed by a pharmacist without a physician's prescription but with some restrictions.

_____ 10. The testing process and clinical trials for new drugs begin with human studies to determine potential uses and effects.

SHORT ANSWER

Answer the following:

1. Explain the advantages of synthetic drugs in relation to pure-form drugs.

_____

_____

_____

2. Discuss pharmacoeconomics.

_____

_____

_____

3. Compare the two routes of access to therapeutic drugs.

_____

_____

_____

4. Distinguish between trade names and generic names of drugs.

_____

_____

_____

5. How are drugs classified?

_____

_____

_____

■ Applying Your Knowledge

Using this text and a drug handbook or the *Physicians' Desk Reference* (PDR), look up the following drugs: meperidine and diazepam. Indicate the controlled substance category for each drug. From the information you obtained in researching the drug, reflect on why each drug was placed in the assigned category. How did the resources you used differ in the organization and depth of information provided about drugs?

_____

_____

_____

_____

_____

_____

_____

■ Practicing for NCLEX

MULTIPLE-CHOICE QUESTIONS

1. Which of the following deals with how drugs are used in the prevention, diagnosis, and treatment of disease?
   a. pharmacokinetics   c. pharmacogenetics
   b. pharmacotherapy   d. pharmacodynamics

2. Which law established official standards and requirements for accurate labeling of drugs?
   a. Pure Food and Drug Act of 1906
   b. Food, Drug and Cosmetic Act of 1938
   c. Kefauver-Harris Amendment of 1962
   d. Sherley Amendment

3. The physician has ordered phentermine, an appetite suppressant, for a client. In explaining the potential for abuse, the nurse is aware that this drug is categorized as a
   a. Schedule II drug   c. Schedule IV drug
   b. Schedule III drug   d. Schedule V drug

4. New drugs are categorized according to
    a. half-life and bioavailability
    b. side effects and contraindications
    c. cost and availability
    d. review priority and therapeutic potential

5. Most drugs are prescribed for
    a. local effects   c. immediate effects
    b. systemic effects   d. long-term effects

6. Penicillin is the standard by which other antibacterial drugs are compared and is considered a/an
    a. regulatory drug
    b. experimental drug
    c. prototype drug
    d. placebo-controlled drug

7. Testing of new drugs usually will continue if
    a. there are excessive side and toxic effects
    b. there is evidence of safety and therapeutic potential
    c. human subjects will participate in a clinical trial
    d. there is an increased number of people who need the drug

8. Which of the following is an advantage of using OTC drugs?
    a. self-diagnosis of an illness
    b. delay in having to seek treatment from a health care provider
    c. faster and easier access to effective treatment
    d. insurance coverage for OTC drugs

9. A nurse would know that Schedule II controlled drugs
    a. are not approved for medical use
    b. may be sold over the counter
    c. may be refilled once with a new prescription
    d. have high abuse potentials

10. In studying pharmacology, the most important strategy is to
    a. focus on therapeutic classifications and their prototypes
    b. memorize all drugs and their side effects
    c. not worry about the therapeutic effects
    d. use only the *Physicians' Desk Reference* as a source for drug information

ALTERNATE FORMAT QUESTIONS

1. The Food, Drug, and Cosmetic Act of 1938 is important because of drug regulation concerning the following. (Select all that apply.)
    a. _____ advertising
    b. _____ distribution
    c. _____ labeling
    d. _____ manufacturing
    e. _____ marketing
    f. _____ research

2. Pharmacoeconomics is concerned with the costs of drug therapy. This would include the following. (Select all that apply.)
    a. _____ salaries of nurses
    b. _____ cost of supplies
    c. _____ laboratory tests ordered by health care providers
    d. _____ length of hospitalization by client
    e. _____ the number of health care providers prescribing drugs

CHAPTER 2

Basic Concepts and Processes

■ Mastering the Information

MATCHING

Match the terms in Column I with a definition, example, or related statement from Column II.

COLUMN I

1. _____ pharmacokinetics

2. _____ absorption

3. _____ distribution

4. _____ metabolism

5. _____ excretion

6. _____ serum half-life

7. _____ pharmacodynamics

8. _____ agonists

9. _____ antagonists

10. _____ drug tolerance

COLUMN II

1. Drugs that inhibit cell function

2. Involves drug movement through the body to sites of action

3. The method by which drugs are inactivated or detoxified by the body

4. Refers to elimination of a drug from the body

5. Drugs that produce effects similar to those produced by naturally occurring substances

6. The process that occurs between the time a drug enters the body and the time it enters the bloodstream to be circulated

7. Occurs when the body becomes accustomed to a drug over time so that a larger dose is required to produce the same effect

8. Involves the transport of drug molecules within the body

9. The time required for the blood concentration of a drug to decrease by 50%

10. Involves drug actions on target cells

TRUE OR FALSE

Indicate if the following statements are true or false.

_____ 1. Carcinogenicity is the ability of a substance, when taken by pregnant women, to cause abnormal fetal development.

_____ 2. The most common mechanism involving movement of a drug from an area of higher concentration to one of lower concentration is passive diffusion.

_____ 3. Protoplasm constitutes the external environment of body cells and is composed of water, electrolytes, proteins, lipids, and carbohydrates.

_____ 4. Carbohydrates play a major role in cell nutrition.

_____ 5. The antidote for warfarin (Coumadin) is vitamin K.

_____ 6. Absorption of a drug is impaired by increased blood flow to sites of administration.

_____ 7. Sepsis-induced alterations in cardiovascular function can accelerate drug metabolism.

_____ 8. Central nervous system disorders may affect pharmacokinetics and cause acid-base imbalances.

_____ 9. Naloxone (Narcan) is the antidote for opioid analgesics.

_____ 10. Most drug information has been derived from clinical drug trials using African American men.

SHORT ANSWER

Answer the following:

1. List factors influencing drug action.

_____

_____

_____

2. List the mechanisms that can cause drug fever.

_____

_____

_____

3. List goals of treatment for a poisoned client.

_____

_____

_____

4. Describe the concept of drug displacement and give an example.

_____

_____

_____

5. How does drug tolerance contribute to cross tolerance of other drugs?

_____

_____

_____

■ Applying Your Knowledge

A client has a drug level of 100 units/mL. The drug's half-life is 1 hour. If concentrations above 25 units/mL are toxic and no more drug is given, how long will it take for the blood level to reach the nontoxic range?

_____

_____

_____

_____

_____

_____

_____

_____

■ Practicing for NCLEX

MULTIPLE-CHOICE QUESTIONS

1. When caring for the elderly, the nurse is aware that the effect of aging on the liver results in
   a. reduced intensity of drug effects
   b. reduced incidence of toxicity
   c. prolonged drug effects
   d. inadequate blood levels of a drug

2. Vistaril, given in combination with Talwin, counteracts the side effects of nausea caused by the Talwin. The drug–drug interaction responsible for the desired effect is
   a. addition   c. synergism
   b. antagonism   d. potentiation

3. On the 2 A.M. round, the nurse finds a client restless and unable to sleep. A sedative-hypnotic is administered. Two hours later, the nurse finds the client irritable and restless. This is characteristic of
   a. an allergic reaction
   b. a teratogenic effect
   c. a tachyphylactic reaction
   d. an idiosyncratic response

4. A client is receiving an antibiotic for an infection. The nurse teaches the client that taking most drugs with food will

   a. have no effect on the physiological action of the drug

   b. increase the rate of absorption of the drug

   c. decrease the amount of drug being absorbed

   d. increase appetite

5. A client is experiencing extrapyramidal symptoms associated with a phenothiazine antipsychotic. The nurse will expect to administer which of the following drugs to relieve the side effects?

   a. protamine sulfate

   b. acetylcysteine (Mucomyst)

   c. naloxone (Narcan)

   d. diphenhydramine (Benadryl)

6. A motor vehicle accident client is admitted to the intensive care unit. Mechanical ventilation is ordered. The nurse is aware that respiratory impairment can interfere with which of the following pharmacokinetic activities?

   a. absorption   c. metabolism

   b. distribution   d. excretion

7. Which of the following clients will a nurse expect to experience alterations in drug metabolism?

   a. a 52-year-old male with cirrhosis of the liver

   b. a 35-year-old female with ulcerative colitis

   c. a 41-year-old male with cancer of the stomach

   d. a 60-year-old female with acute renal failure

8. A client has been taking a medication for several months for chronic back pain. He tells you that the medication is no longer relieving the pain. In discussing this with the client, the nurse explains the possibility of

   a. drug fever   c. drug tolerance

   b. diffusion   d. hypersensitivity

9. The nurse is caring for a client with cirrhosis. The nurse is aware that this disease may impair all pharmacokinetic activities. However, the nurse will be most concerned about

   a. absorption   c. metabolism

   b. distribution   d. excretion

10. A client has nephritis. The nurse would question the order for which of the following drugs:

   a. acetaminophen (Tylenol)

   b. phenytoin (Dilantin)

   c. gentamicin sulfate (Garamycin)

   d. isoniazid, INH (Nydrazid)

ALTERNATE FORMAT QUESTIONS

1. In clinical practice the nurse acknowledges that monitoring serum drug levels is helpful in the following situations. (Select all that apply.)

   a. _____ A drug overdose is suspected.

   b. _____ Drugs are given that have narrow margins of safety.

   c. _____ Multiple health care providers are administering medications.

   d. _____ The client is taking more than five medications.

   e. _____ Documentation is needed concerning possible adverse effects.

   f. _____ Unexpected responses to drugs occur.

2. The emergency room nurse has just received a client, brought in by family members, who has overdosed on drugs. Arrange the following actions in the order the nurse should perform them.

   a. _____ Establish an intravenous line.

   b. _____ Assess the level of consciousness and vital signs.

   c. _____ Administer an antidote if indicated.

   d. _____ Ask family members if they know what drugs the client took.

CHAPTER 3

Administering Medications

■ Mastering the Information

MATCHING

Match the terms in Column I with a definition, example, or related statement from Column II.

COLUMN I

1. _____ parenteral
2. _____ vials
3. _____ IV push
4. _____ controlled-release tablets
5. _____ medications
6. _____ gt
7. _____ enteric-coated tablets
8. _____ pc
9. _____ ampule
10. _____ unit-dose system

COLUMN II

a. coated with a substance that is insoluble in stomach acid
b. after meals
c. direct injection of a medication into a vein
d. drugs given for therapeutic purposes
e. drugs dispensed in single-dose containers for individual clients
f. contains high amounts of drug intended to be absorbed slowly and act over an extended period of time
g. refers to any route other than gastrointestinal
h. closed glass or plastic containers with rubber stoppers through which a needle can be inserted to withdraw medication
i. drop
j. sealed glass containers that have to have the tops broken off to allow insertion of a needle to withdraw medication

Match the abbreviations with the appropriate terms.

COLUMN I

1. _____ cubic centimeter
2. _____ before meals
3. _____ right eye
4. _____ by mouth
5. _____ drops
6. _____ immediately
7. _____ when needed
8. _____ after meals
9. _____ daily
10. _____ every 4 hours
11. _____ left eye
12. _____ bedtime
13. _____ twice daily
14. _____ as desired
15. _____ four times daily

COLUMN II

a. OS   i. stat
b. PRN   j. OD
c. pc   k. hs
d. qd   l. bid
e. PO   m. ac
f. q 4h   n. qid
g. cc   o. gtt
h. ad lib

TRUE OR FALSE

Indicate if the following statements are true or false.

_____ 1. A nurse should never question a physician if a drug order is unclear.

_____ 2. When calculating a child's drug dosage, always ask a pharmacist or another nurse to do the calculation also and compare the results.

_____ 3. A nurse is not legally responsible for actions delegated to other health care personnel.

_____ 4. Only the nurse is responsible for getting medication to a client.

_____ 5. Unit-dose wrappings of oral drugs should be left with the medication until the nurse is in the presence of the client and is ready to administer the drug.

_____ 6. Nurses may take verbal or telephone orders from physicians.

_____ 7. Some drugs are available in one-dosage form only.

_____ 8. The metric system is the most commonly used system of measurement.

_____ 9. Units express the ionic activity of a drug.

_____ 10. A 22-gauge, 1-½–inch needle is used for subcutaneous injections.

SHORT ANSWER

Answer the following:

1. List the "seven rights."

_____

_____

_____

2. Explain why the nurse is legally responsible for safe and accurate administration of medication.

_____

_____

_____

3. List all the components of a medication order.

_____

_____

_____

4. Interpret the following medication order:

Mylanta 30 mL ac and hs

_____

_____

_____

5. Explain why controlled-released tablets and capsules should never be broken or crushed.

_____

_____

_____

Fill in the blank with the approximate equivalent.

1. 1 kg = _____ lb

2. 1 g = _____ mg

3. 60 mg = _____ gr

4. 1 mL = _____ cc

5. 1 cc = _____ minims

6. 1 cup = _____ mL

7. 1 mg = _____ mcg

8. 30 mL = _____ oz

9. 1 dram = _____ mL

10. 15 gtt = _____ mL

Convert each item to the equivalent.

1. 30 drops = _____ minims

2. 50 lb = _____ kg

3. 2 drams = _____ mL

4. 3500 mg = _____ g

5. 2.5 tsp = _____ mL

6. 15 mL = _____ cc

7. 2 L = _____ mL

8. 32 minims = _____ cc

9. 500 mL = _____ cups

10. 2.5 mg = _____ mcg

Calculate the following drug dosages.

1. Order: Carbamazepine (Tegretol) 800 mg/d
   Label: Carbamazepine (Tegretol) 200 mg/tablet
   How many tablets will the client take each day?
   _____

2. Order: Diphenhydramine hydrochloride
   (Benadryl) elixir 25 mg
   Label: Diphenhydramine hydrochloride
   (Benadryl) elixir 12.5 mg per 5 mL
   How many milliliters will the client receive?
   _____

3. Order: KCL 40 mEq PO
   Label: KCL 10 mEq/15 mL
   How many milliliters will the client receive?
   _____

4. Order: Heparin 1500 units IV
   Label: Heparin 1000 units/mL
   How many milliliters will the client receive?
   _____

5. Order: Levothyroxine sodium (Synthroid) 50
   mcg PO daily
   Label: Levothyroxine sodium (Synthroid) 0.025
   mg/tablet
   How many tablets will the client receive?
   _____

6. Guaifenesin (Robitussin) cough syrup 600 mg in
   1 oz is available. The order is for 225 mg. How
   many cc should the nurse administer?
   _____

7. Cephalexin (Keflex) is available in 250-mg
   capsules. Cephalexin (Keflex) 0.5 gm PO is ordered.
   How many capsules should the nurse administer?
   _____

8. Prepare penicillin G benzathine 600,000 units
   for intramuscular (IM) injection. Penicillin G
   benzathine 1,200,000 units/mL is available. How
   many milliliters will the nurse administer?
   _____

9. Meperidine hydrochloride (Demerol) 50 mg/mL
   is available. The order is for meperidine
   hydrochloride (Demerol) 100 mg. How many
   milliliters will the nurse administer?
   _____

10. Loperamide (Maalox) ½ oz is ordered. How
    many cc will the nurse administer?
    _____

■ Applying Your Knowledge

Your client has a nasogastric feeding tube in place.
You will be administering morning medications,
including four tablets, one capsule, and 10 cc of an
elixir. Describe how you will safely administer
medications through a feeding tube to this client.

_____

_____

_____

_____

_____

_____

_____

_____

▪ Practicing for NCLEX

MULTIPLE-CHOICE QUESTIONS

1. The client is to receive ampicillin 500 mg PO tid ac. Which of the following reflects proper scheduling?
   a. 4 A.M., 12 noon, 8 P.M.
   b. 7 A.M., 11 A.M., 6 P.M.
   c. 7 A.M., 1 P.M., 8 P.M.
   d. 8 A.M., 12 noon, 4 P.M., 8 P.M.

2. A client asks the nurse whether he can divide his enteric-coated tablet in half. The nurse tells him not to because dividing the tablet will
   a. make the drug less potent
   b. cause severe abdominal cramps
   c. alter the drug's absorption
   d. produce no therapeutic effect

3. The client is a 4-year-old who has a temperature of 103° F and is vomiting. The physician has ordered Tylenol for the fever. The nurse would administer the Tylenol in which of the following forms?
   a. liquid   c. tablet
   b. lozenge   d. suppository

4. The nurse is assigned to administer medication to 10 clients. Which of the following would be the initial action of the nurse before preparing the medications?
   a. Identify the clients by asking them to state their names.
   b. Wash his hands.
   c. Explain the action of the medication to each client.
   d. Record the administration of the medication.

5. The nurse is to administer an IM injection. Which of the following statements best describes the reason why the nurse will aspirate before injecting medication into the muscle?
   a. to determine whether the needle is in the correct muscle
   b. to decrease discomfort
   c. to avoid major nerves in the area
   d. to avoid injecting the medication into a blood vessel

6. The client is 15 months old and is hospitalized for pneumonia. The nurse will administer an intramuscular injection in which of the following muscles?
   a. deltoid   c. ventrogluteal
   b. dorsogluteal   d. vastus lateralis

7. The nurse is to administer a drug intravenously over a 30-minute period. Which of the following indicates this action?
   a. a loading dose
   b. an IVP (push)
   c. a peripheral IV infusion
   d. an IVPB (piggyback)

8. A nurse is to administer a medication to a 22-year-old male by the intramuscular route. Which of the following best describes the proper placement of the needle during the administration?
   a. below the greater trochanter and posterior iliac spine
   b. above and inside a diagonal line drawn from the greater trochanter of the femur to the anterior superior iliac crest
   c. below the anterior superior iliac spine and above the greater trochanter
   d. above and outside a diagonal line drawn from the greater trochanter of the femur to the posterior superior iliac spine

9. Which of the following best describes administration of medication by the oral route?
   a. It is convenient and relatively inexpensive.
   b. Oral administration causes the fastest drug action.
   c. Gastrointestinal upset rarely occurs.
   d. Water given with medication retards drug absorption.

10. A nurse is to administer medication to a female client who is 5' 7" tall and weighs 175 lb. The nurse has chosen the ventrogluteal area. Which size needle will the nurse use?
    a. 18-gauge, 1-inch needle
    b. 20-gauge, 3-inch needle
    c. 22-gauge, 1- to 1.5-inch needle
    d. 25-gauge, 3-inch needle

ALTERNATE FORMAT QUESTIONS

1. What are the "rights" to medication administration? (Select all that apply.)

   a. _____ Right medication administration report (MAR)

   b. _____ Right medication

   c. _____ Right drug manufacturer

   d. _____ Right client

   e. _____ Right time

   f. _____ Right dose

   g. _____ Right route

2. The nurse is to administer an IM injection in the ventrogluteal area. Identify the correct placement of the needle by marking an X on the following diagram:

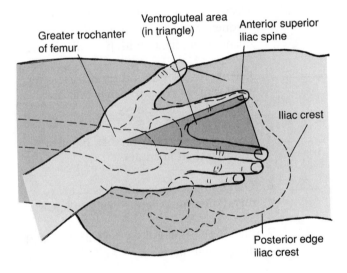

CHAPTER 4

Nursing Process in Drug Therapy

■ Mastering the Information

MATCHING

Match the terms in Column I with a definition, example, or related statement from Column II.

COLUMN I

1. _____ application of heat or cold
2. _____ chondroitin
3. _____ relief of acute pain after administration of an analgesic
4. _____ Saint John's wort
5. _____ self-administer drugs safely
6. _____ Risk for Injury Related to Adverse Drug Effects
7. _____ valerian
8. _____ critical pathways
9. _____ an allergic reaction to a drug
10. _____ black cohosh

COLUMN II

a. a nursing diagnosis
b. an herbal/dietary supplement used to relieve menopausal symptoms
c. an herbal/dietary supplement used to promote sleep
d. evaluation of medication administration
e. guidelines for the care of clients with particular conditions
f. assessment information
g. an herbal/dietary supplement used to treat depression
h. a client goal
i. a nursing intervention
j. an herbal/dietary supplement used to treat arthritis

TRUE OR FALSE

Indicate if the following statements are true or false.

_____ 1. The goal of drug therapy should be to minimize beneficial effects and maximize adverse effects.

_____ 2. Few variables influence a drug's effect on the body.

_____ 3. Decreasing the number of drugs and the frequency of administration increases the client's compliance with prescribed drugs.

_____ 4. Clients with severe kidney disease often need smaller doses of drugs that are excreted by the kidneys.

_____ 5. Drug therapy is less predictable in children than in adults.

_____ 6. Older adults are usually less likely to metabolize and excrete drugs efficiently.

_____ 7. Liver impairment does not interfere with drug metabolism.

_____ 8. Alcohol is toxic to the liver and increases the risk of hepatotoxicity.

_____ 9. The dosage should be reduced for drugs that are extensively metabolized in the liver because toxicity can occur in clients with hepatic disease.

_____ 10. For a critically ill client, therapeutic drug effects may be increased.

SHORT ANSWER

Answer the following:

1. List five areas of nursing intervention in relation to drug therapy.

   _____

   _____

   _____

2. Explain why client teaching related to drug therapy is important.

   _____

   _____

   _____

3. Why do nurses have difficulties in evaluating outcomes of drug therapy?

   _____

   _____

   _____

4. List major components of critical paths.

   _____

   _____

   _____

5. What are the two major concerns that health care providers have concerning the use of herbal and dietary supplements?

   _____

   _____

■ Applying Your Knowledge

You are assigned to care for a low-birth-weight infant, who has been started on digoxin to treat congenital heart problems until corrective surgery can be performed. The digoxin dosage seems very low to you. What factors might you consider before questioning the physician regarding the dosage that was ordered?

_____

_____

_____

_____

_____

_____

_____

■ Practicing for NCLEX

MULTIPLE-CHOICE QUESTIONS

1. A client is being discharged on an antibiotic and has little knowledge concerning the drug. Which of the following best reflects an expected goal of client teaching related to the antibiotic?

   a. The client will be able to interpret a culture and sensitivity test.

   b. Family members will understand the physiological action of the antibiotic.

   c. The client will exercise three times a week.

   d. The client will be able to identify two adverse effects of the antibiotic.

2. The nurse has just administered a sedative to a 65-year old client who was admitted to the hospital because of chest pain. Which of the following would be an appropriate nursing diagnosis for this client?

   a. Deficient Knowledge: Safe and Effective Self-administration of Medication

   b. Risk for Injury Related to Adverse Drug Effects

   c. Deficient Knowledge: Unfamiliar with Ordered Drug

   d. Noncompliance: Overuse of Drug

3. A client is in the cardiac care unit following a mild cardiac infarction. She is on multiple drug therapy, including three intramuscular (IM) injections per day. Which of the following would be an appropriate nursing diagnosis related to the administration of the IM injections?

a. Altered Nutrition: More than Body Requirements Related to Overeating

b. Anxiety Related to Three IM Injections Each Day

c. Impaired Social Interaction Related to Being in the Cardiac Care Unit

d. Noncompliance Related to Overuse of Medication

4. Which statement by a client with heart disease would indicate that health teaching related to a medication was ineffective?

a. "It's best to take my medication as the doctor ordered."

b. "It shouldn't matter that I skip a couple of doses now and then."

c. "I will call the clinic if I experience any side effects from my medications."

d. "I will get all of my medications at the same pharmacy."

5. During drug therapy, clients with liver disease are monitored for which of the following?

a. dizziness   c. headache

b. jaundice   d. constipation

6. The goal of drug therapy in critically ill clients is to

a. support vital functions

b. decrease medication use

c. disregard laboratory tests related to the client's physiological condition

d. increase or decrease dietary intake depending on the weight of the client

7. Which of the following herbal/dietary supplements could increase the potential for bleeding when taking aspirin?

a. melatonin   c. ginseng

b. saw palmetto   d. chondroitin

8. When implementing medication therapy for a client, the nurse is responsible for which of the following actions?

a. changing the drug dosage if side effects occur

b. discontinuing the drug if the client does not want to take it

c. sharing information concerning therapeutic value of the drug in other clients

d. checking for the correct dosage of the drug prior to administration

9. Which phase of the nursing process requires the nurse to formulate a client outcome related to the administration of medication?

a. assessment   c. implementation

b. planning   d. evaluation

10. In gathering assessment data from a medication history, which of the following would be most helpful to the nurse in planning client care?

a. the name of the pharmacist the client talks to regarding his or her medication

b. a list of all prescribed and over-the-counter medications and herbal and dietary supplements the client takes

c. the medication history of the client's mother

d. dietary intake for 1 day

ALTERNATE FORMAT QUESTIONS

1. A nurse is working with clients in a pain clinic. Arrange the following expected outcomes of drug therapy in order of priority.

a. _____ Verbalize essential drug information.

b. _____ Experience relief of pain.

c. _____ Self-administer drugs safely and accurately.

d. _____ Take drugs as prescribed.

e. _____ Avoid preventable adverse drug effects.

f. _____ Keep follow-up appointments for monitoring.

2. Drug therapy in children requires special consideration. Which of the following pharmacokinetics consequences is related to drug administration in children?

a. _____ increased excretion of drugs eliminated by the kidneys

b. _____ increased absorption of topical drugs

c. _____ increased distribution of drugs into the central nervous system

d. _____ decreased volume of distribution of drugs

e. _____ increased or decreased biotransformation of drugs

CHAPTER 5

Physiology of the Central Nervous System

■ Mastering the Information

MATCHING

Match the terms in Column I with a definition, example, or related statement from Column II.

COLUMN I

1. _____ synapse
2. _____ myelin cover
3. _____ gamma-aminobutyric acid (GABA)
4. _____ serotonin
5. _____ receptors
6. _____ glutamate
7. _____ neurons
8. _____ amino acids
9. _____ acetylcholine
10. _____ neurotransmitters

COLUMN II

a. protects and insulates the axon
b. chemical substances that carry messages from one neuron to another
c. proteins embedded in the cell membranes of neurons
d. basic functional unit of the central nervous system (CNS)
e. neurotransmitter in the cholinergic system
f. a site for receiving stimuli or messages
g. thought to produce sleep by inhibiting CNS activity and arousal
h. an important excitatory neurotransmitter in the CNS that may be involved in the pathogensis of epilepsy
i. major inhibitory transmitter in the CNS
j. can serve as structural components for protein synthesis and transmitters

TRUE OR FALSE

Indicate if the following statements are true or false.

_____ 1. Mild CNS depression is characterized by drowsiness or sleep and a decreased perception of pain, heat, and cold.

_____ 2. The basal ganglia coordinate muscular activity.

_____ 3. The reticular activating system receives impulses from all parts of the body and evaluates the significance of the impulses.

_____ 4. The entry of sodium ions is required for neurotransmitter release from storage sites.

_____ 5. Neurotransmitters are derived from body proteins.

_____ 6. Synapses may be electrical or chemical.

_____ 7. The noradrenergic system uses serotonin as its neurotransmitter.

_____ 8. Decreased acetylcholine is a characteristic of Alzheimer's disease.

_____ 9. The cerebral cortex is involved in all conscious processes.

_____ 10. Serotonin is thought to produce sleep by stimulating CNS activity.

SHORT ANSWER

Answer the following:

1. List characteristics of CNS depression.

_____

_____

_____

2. List characteristics of CNS stimulation.

_____

_____

_____

3. Explain characteristics that allow neurons to communicate with other cells.

_____

_____

_____

4. List three mechanisms by which free neurotransmitter molecules are removed from the synapse.

_____

_____

_____

5. List four factors that affect the availability and function of neurotransmitters.

_____

_____

_____

■ Practicing for NCLEX

MULTIPLE-CHOICE QUESTIONS

1. The area of the brain responsible for helping maintain homeostasis is the
   a. cerebellum   c. cerebrum
   b. limbic system   d. hypothalamus

2. Normal function of skeletal muscle is influenced by
   a. acetylcholine   c. glutamate
   b. dopamine   d. serotonin

3. A client has Alzheimer's disease. The nurse is aware that in this condition there is a decrease in
   a. acetylcholine   c. serotonin
   b. aspartate   d. glycine

4. Neurons that carry messages to the central nervous system are called
   a. efferent neurons   c. afferent neurons
   b. glia neurons   d. motor neurons

5. Which of the following is an energy source for brain cells?
   a. thiamin   c. oxygen
   b. glucose   d. oxytocin

6. A client has had a cerebrovascular accident (CVA, or stroke) and is having difficulty in speaking. The nurse is aware that, most likely, the CVA involved which of the following areas in the brain?
   a. cerebral cortex   c. hypothalamus
   b. thalamus   d. medulla oblongata

7. A client is experiencing CNS depression. Which of the following would a nurse observe in the client?
   a. increased muscle tone
   b. hyperactive reflexes
   c. short attention span
   d. increased perception of cold sensations

8. Which of the following plays an important role in blood coagulation?
   a. tryptophan   c. aspartate
   b. glycine   d. serotonin

9. The hypothalamus regulates the production of oxytocin, which
   a. regulates body temperature
   b. initiates uterine contractions
   c. regulates arterial blood pressure
   d. decides which impulses to transmit to the cerebral cortex

10. A client has a head injury. The physician explains that most of the trauma was located in the cerebellum area of the brain. The nurse would expect the client to
    a. have a hard time maintaining balance and posture
    b. exhibit rigidity and increased muscle tone
    c. exhibit decreased mental alertness
    d. have frequent periods of crying

ALTERNATE FORMAT QUESTION

Identify the following areas on the drawing.

Receptor sites

Neurotransmitters

Presynaptic nerve terminal

Presynaptic nerve cell membrane

Postsynaptic nerve terminal

Synapse

Release site

Postsynaptic nerve cell membrane

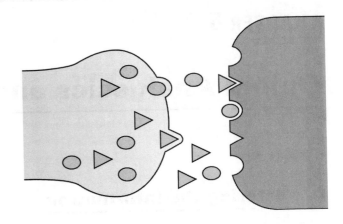

CHAPTER 6

Opioid Analgesics and Opioid Antagonists

■ Mastering the Information

MATCHING

Match the terms in Column I with a definition, example, or related statement from Column II.

COLUMN I

1. _____ thalamus
2. _____ patient-controlled analgesia
3. _____ nociceptors
4. _____ visceral pain
5. _____ opioid peptides
6. _____ chronic pain
7. _____ bradykinin
8. _____ neuropathic pain
9. _____ acute pain
10. _____ somatic pain

COLUMN II

a. pain-producing substance
b. pain originating from abdominal and thoracic organs
c. pain lasting 3 to 6 months
d. delay station for incoming stimuli
e. pain originating from injury of peripheral pain receptors, nerves, or the central nervous system (CNS)
f. pain described as sharp, lancing, or cutting
g. interact with opiate receptors to inhibit pain transmission
h. free nerve endings
i. pain originating in structural tissues, such as bone, muscle, and soft tissue
j. allow for self-administration of medication

TRUE OR FALSE

Indicate if the following statements are true or false.

_____ 1. Opioid antagonists reverse respiratory depression caused by all CNS depressants.

_____ 2. Morphine given in combination with cimetidine (Tagamet) may increase CNS and respiratory depression.

_____ 3. An opioid analgesic, given in combination with an antihypertensive drug may cause hypertension.

_____ 4. Clients taking naltrexone (ReVia) do not respond to opioid analgesics if pain control is needed.

_____ 5. The drug of choice in treatment of opioid overdose is naloxone (Narcan).

_____ 6. Use of a narcotic analgesic for acute pain is likely to lead to addiction.

_____ 7. Crushing or chewing a long-acting tablet of an opioid analgesic delays the release of the drug.

_____ 8. Referred pain is pain occurring from tissue damage in one area of the body but felt in another area.

_____ 9. Opioid analgesics are not indicated for long-term use in chronic pain associated with osteoarthritis.

_____ 10. Opioid analgesics are commonly used to manage pain associated with disease processes and invasive diagnostic and therapeutic procedures.

SHORT ANSWER

Answer the following:

1. Explain the physiological action of an opioid analgesic.

   _____

   _____

   _____

2. List pharmacological effects of opioid analgesics.

   _____

   _____

   _____

3. Why would opioid analgesics be contraindicated in a client with chronic lung disease?

   _____

   _____

   _____

4. Describe the physiological action of opioid antagonists.

   _____

   _____

   _____

5. Why does a dose of an oral opioid analgesic need to be larger than an injected dose?

   _____

   _____

   _____

■ Applying Your Knowledge

Mr. George Reyes had major abdominal surgery yesterday. His pain is being controlled with morphine delivered via a patient-controlled analgesia (PCA) infusion pump set on a basal rate. During the night it delivered a continuous infusion of morphine to relieve his pain. When you try to wake him up at 8 A.M., he is groggy but he does not complain of pain. His vital signs are BP 130/72, pulse 74, and respiratory rate 8 and shallow. Naloxone (Narcan) has been ordered for a respiratory rate below 8. How should you proceed?

_____

_____

_____

_____

_____

_____

■ Practicing for NCLEX

MULTIPLE-CHOICE QUESTIONS

1. It may be necessary to repeat doses of naloxone (Narcan) to a client who has had too much morphine because the opioid antagonist

   a. has less strength in each dose than do individual doses of morphine

   b. has a shorter half-life than does morphine

   c. combined with morphine, increases the physiological action of the morphine

   d. causes the respiratory rate to decrease

2. Which of the following would indicate a therapeutic effect of an opioid analgesic for a client who has been experiencing severe pain?

   a. restlessness during the night hours

   b. increased participation in A.M. care activities

   c. shorter intervals between medication administration

   d. increased facial grimacing during movement

3. Before administering an opioid analgesic, the initial action of the nurse would be to

   a. check the apical pulse and compare it with the radial pulse

   b. check blood pressure while the client is lying and standing

   c. check the client's temperature

   d. check the rate, depth, and rhythm of the client's respirations

4. It's Friday night and a nurse is working in the emergency department at the local hospital. The nurse's first client is a 17-year-old high school soccer player who is complaining of severe muscle spasms in her left leg. The nurse would classify her pain as

   a. acute pain   c. neuropathic pain

   b. chronic pain   d. somatic pain

5. A postoperative client will be receiving hydromorphone (Dilaudid) via PCA and is having second thoughts about administering his own medication for fear of overdosing himself. An appropriate nursing diagnosis for this client would be

   a. Knowledge Deficient Related to the Use of PCA

   b. Impaired Gas Exchange Related to the Surgery

   c. Anxiety Related to Surgical Procedure

   d. Impaired Judgment Related to Increased Dosage of Medication

6. The client is to receive propoxyphene (Darvon) as needed for pain. Which of the following would be an appropriate medication order for your client?

   a. 390 mg qid IM

   b. 65 mg q 4h PRN PO

   c. 65 mg bid PRN PO

   d. 100 mg q 2h PO

7. The nurse has just administered an IM injection of meperidine (Demerol) to the client. The most important nursing measure the nurse should perform before leaving the room should be to

   a. close the draperies

   b. make sure the side rails are up

   c. ask all the visitors to leave the room

   d. offer your client something to drink

8. Which of the following medication orders should a nurse question?

   a. oxycodone (Oxycontin) PO 10 mg q 4h PRN for a 6-year-old, 8 hours after surgery

   b. meperidine (Demerol) IM 50 mg q 2–4h for four doses for a 23-year-old woman in labor

   c. fentanyl (Sublimaze) IM 0.1 mg 60 minutes before surgery for a 35-year-old male

   d. tramadol (Ultram) PO 100 mg q 4–6h PRN for a 65-year-old female with fibromyalgia pain

9. The nurse suspects that a neonate being received in the newborn intensive care unit may be experiencing opioid withdrawal. The nurse will most likely see signs and symptoms that include

   a. tremors   c. constipation

   b. decreased muscle tone   d. bradycardia

10. An automatic "stop order" for opioids is usually between

    a. 24 and 36 hours   c. 60 and 96 hours

    b. 48 and 72 hours   d. 72 and 130 hours

ALTERNATE FORMAT QUESTIONS

1. A 5-year-old female is to receive meperidine (Demerol) PO 1.5 mg/kg q 3–4h after a tonsillectomy. Her weight is 42 pounds. How many milligrams will the client receive with each dose?

2. The nurse has just administered an opioid analgesic and will observe the client for adverse effects. Arrange the following adverse effects in order of intervention priority.

   a. _____ nausea and vomiting

   b. _____ excessive sedation

   c. _____ respiratory depression

   d. _____ constipation

   e. _____ hypotension

CHAPTER 7

Analgesic-Antipyretic-Anti-inflammatory and Related Drugs

■ Mastering the Information

MATCHING

Match the terms in Column I with a definition, example, or related statement from Column II.

COLUMN I

1. _____ pyrogens

2. _____ acetaminophen

3. _____ aspirin

4. _____ prostaglandins

5. _____ osteoarthritis

6. _____ glucosamine

7. _____ rheumatoid arthritis

8. _____ Reye's syndrome

9. _____ inflammation

10. _____ bursitis

COLUMN II

a. a normal body response to tissue damage

b. inflammation of a cavity in connective tissue that contains synovial fluid

c. drug of choice for pain or fever in children

d. chemical mediators found in most body tissue

e. effective in low to moderate pain involving the skin, muscles, joints, and other connective tissue

f. a disease that affects the cartilage of weight-bearing joints

g. an essential structural component of joint connective tissue

h. a chronic, painful, inflammatory disorder that affects joints and has systemic effects

i. fever-producing agent

j. a disease seen in children under 15 associated with use of aspirin

TRUE OR FALSE

Indicate if the following statements are true or false.

_____ 1. The first drug of choice for osteoarthritis is acetaminophen.

_____ 2. Aspirin is the drug of choice for pain or fever in children.

_____ 3. Acetaminophen must be taken with food.

_____ 4. If one nonsteroidal anti-inflammatory drug (NSAID) is not effective, another one may produce therapeutic effects.

_____ 5. Over-the-counter (OTC) ibuprofen is the same medication as prescription Motrin.

_____ 6. Anticoagulants decrease the effects of indomethacin (Indocin).

_____ 7. Acetylcysteine (Mucomyst) is the antidote for acetaminophen poisoning.

_____ 8. Celecoxib (Celebrex) should be taken with food.

_____ 9. Aspirin toxicity occurs at levels above 500 mcg/mL.

_____ 10. In older adults, long-term use of NSAIDs can increase the risk of serious gastrointestinal bleeding.

SHORT ANSWER

Answer the following:

1. List conditions in which aspirin, NSAIDs, and acetaminophen are used.

_____

_____

_____

2. List signs and symptoms of salicylism.

_____

_____

_____

3. What are the two major advantages of using acetaminophen over aspirin?

_____

_____

_____

4. Why should aspirin be avoided for 1 to 2 weeks before and after surgery?

_____

_____

_____

5. Describe the physiological action of cyclooxygenase-2 (COX-2) inhibitors?

_____

_____

_____

■ Applying Your Knowledge

Mrs. Whynn, a 73-year-old widow, has severe osteoarthritis. To control the pain, she takes 400 mg of ibuprofen every 4 hours while awake and 5 mg of prednisone daily. Also, she swims and uses moist heat to decrease stiffness and discomfort. Lately, she has been feeling weak and tired. She has also experienced dizziness when getting up from bed, and today she fainted. She asks you if this could be related to the medications she is taking and what she should do.

_____

_____

_____

_____

_____

■ Practicing for NCLEX

MULTIPLE-CHOICE QUESTIONS

1. The client is 9 years old and has symptoms of influenza. Her mother explains that her fever has been between 102° F and 103° F for the last 2 days. Which medication would the nurse suggest for her?

   a. acetaminophen   c. naproxen

   b. aspirin   d. nabumetone

2. The client has been diagnosed with rheumatoid arthritis. He has been placed on celecoxib (Celebrex) 100 mg tid. The nurse will provide the client with the following information about this drug:

   a. Expect heart palpitations to occur.

   b. Take with food to decrease gastric irritation.

   c. Increase the dosage if the prescribed dosage does not provide relief.

   d. Wear sunscreen when outside because of hypersensitivity to sunlight.

3. The emergency department nurse is expecting a client to be brought in who is exhibiting signs and symptoms of acetaminophen poisoning. The nurse will have the following drug available for administration when the client arrives:

   a. oxaprozin (Daypro)

   b. vitamin K

   c. acetylcysteine (Mucomyst)

   d. naloxone (Narcan)

4. The client has been on naproxen (Naprosyn) for some time. When evaluating him on his return visits to the clinic, the nurse will monitor which of the following?

   a. low-density lipoprotein levels

   b. serum amylase level

   c. blood glucose level

   d. bleeding time

5. The client is to begin colchicine therapy for acute gout. The nurse informs him that, with oral therapy, he should have pain relief within

   a. 2 to 4 hours   c. 12 to 20 hours

   b. 6 to 12 hours   d. 24 to 48 hours

6. The client has a history of migraines. She has just been given a prescription for sumatriptan (Imitrex). Which symptoms would the nurse tell her to report to her physician immediately?

    a. decreased appetite   c. slight weight gain

    b. chest pain   d. fatigue

7. Which of the following statements by a client reveals a potential problem with NSAID therapy?

    a. "I take my medication with a full glass of water."

    b. "I can still have my glass of wine every night."

    c. "I should make sure my doctor checks for blood in my stool."

    d. "I have problems with swallowing, but I do not crush my tablets."

8. The client is on an antigout drug. The nurse's teaching plan concerning this drug in preventing the formation of uric acid kidney stones would involve which of the following?

    a. Walk at least 2 miles, three times a week.

    b. Take the drug on an empty stomach.

    c. Avoid exposure to sunlight.

    d. Drink 2 to 3 quarts of water daily.

9. A 72-year-old man has been taking a baby aspirin every day for the last 5 years. He is scheduled for major dental work in 1 month. It will be important for this man to

    a. double the amount of aspirin he is taking

    b. avoid aspirin for 2 weeks prior to the dental procedure

    c. increase his fluid intake by 1000 cc per day 1 week prior to the dental work

    d. expect complications following the dental work

10. A 65-year-old client has recently been diagnosed with osteoarthritis of the hands and feet and has begun medication therapy. She reveals to the nurse that she does not have an appetite and is nauseated all the time. Which of the following would be an appropriate nursing diagnosis related to her complaint?

    a. Risk of Injury Related to Adverse Drug Effects

    b. Activity Intolerance Related to Pain

    c. Knowledge Deficient Related to Medical Diagnosis

    d. Altered Nutrition Related to Medication

ALTERNATE FORMAT QUESTIONS

1. The nurse has to administer pain medication to four clients in the clinic. Arrange the following in the order in which the nurse will administer the medication.

    a. _____ Imitrex 6 mg administered subcutaneously (sc) to a 21-year-old female complaining of a migraine

    b. _____ choline salicylate (Arthropan) 50 mg PO (orally) to a 17-year-old female for dysmenorrhea

    c. _____ indomethacin (Indocin) 75 mg PO to a 68-year-old male for bursitis

    d. _____ ketorolac (Toradol) 60 mg IM to a 31-year-old male experiencing a kidney stone

2. The nurse will teach the following to the client regarding NSAID therapy. (Select all that apply.)

    a. _____ Do not take an antacid with NSAIDs.

    b. _____ Drink 1–2 pints of fluid daily.

    c. _____ Take NSAIDs with a full glass of water.

    d. _____ Never take NSAIDs with food.

    e. _____ Report signs of bleeding to the health care provider.

    f. _____ Avoid alcoholic beverages.

CHAPTER 8

Antianxiety and Sedative-Hypnotic Drugs

■ Mastering the Information

MATCHING

Match the terms in Column I with a definition, example, or related statement from Column II.

COLUMN I

1. _____ clonazepam (Klonopin)

2. _____ alprazolam (Xanax)

3. _____ kava

4. _____ midazolam (Versed)

5. _____ oxazepam (Serax)

6. _____ dexmedetomidine (Precedex)

7. _____ flumazenil (Romazicon)

8. _____ zaleplon (Sonata)

9. _____ diazepam (Valium)

10. _____ sertraline (Zoloft)

COLUMN II

a. herbal/dietary supplement that suppresses emotional excitability

b. antidote for benzodiazepines

c. prototype benzodiazepine

d. a benzodiazepine used in acute alcohol withdrawal

e. used for sedating intubated and mechanically ventilated clients in intensive care settings

f. an oral, nonbenzodiazepine, Schedule-IV controlled substance used for short-term treatment of insomnia

g. prescribed for obsessive-compulsive disorder

h. a benzodiazepine used for seizure disorders

i. preoperative sedation used for short-term treatment of anxiety

j. a benzodiazepine used for panic disorder

TRUE OR FALSE

Indicate if the following statements are true or false.

_____ 1. Midazolam (Versed) may be mixed in the same syringe with morphine sulfate.

_____ 2. At bedtime, food should be taken with zolpidem (Ambien).

_____ 3. Cimetidine (Tagamet) decreases the effects of zaleplon (Sonata).

_____ 4. Opioid analgesics increase the effects of antianxiety and sedative-hypnotic drugs.

_____ 5. Diazepam (Valium) is physically incompatible with other drugs.

_____ 6. Benzodiazepines can be given intramuscularly in the deltoid muscle.

_____ 7. Adverse effects of antianxiety and sedative-hypnotic drugs are caused by central nervous system depression.

_____ 8. Excessive drowsiness is more likely to occur when drug therapy begins.

_____ 9. Alprazolam (Xanax) is the most commonly prescribed benzodiazepine.

_____ 10. To prevent withdrawal symptoms, doses of benzodiazepines should be tapered and gradually discontinued.

SHORT ANSWER

Answer the following:

1. List major clinical uses of benzodiazepines.

_____

_____

_____

2. Explain the pharmacokinetics of benzodiazepines.

_____

_____

_____

3. List contraindications to benzodiazepines.

_____

_____

_____

4. Compare buspirone and benzodiazepines.

_____

_____

_____

5. What is the goal for use of antianxiety agents?

_____

_____

_____

■ Applying Your Knowledge

Georgia Summers is admitted to your unit for elective surgery. During your admission assessment, she states she has been taking 1 mg of alprazolam (Xanax) tid and hs for the last 3 years. She claims to be a social drinker, consuming two to three drinks every evening. During the interview she appears nervous and asks you at least five times whether the doctor will order her Xanax while she is in the hospital. Discuss your interpretation of these assessment data and how it will affect your plan of care for Ms. Summers.

_____

_____

_____

_____

■ Practicing for NCLEX

MULTIPLE-CHOICE QUESTIONS

1. A client describes having feelings of fear and impending doom. The client states that she has palpitations, shortness of breath, and sometimes dizziness and nausea. The nurse's assessment indicates that the client is having panic attacks. The most appropriate drug for the client is
   a. hydroxyzine (Vistaril)
   b. buspirone (BuSpar)
   c. alprazolam (Xanax)
   d. lorazepam (Ativan)

2. Which of the following statement by a client indicates his understanding of his new drug, buspirone (BuSpar)?
   a. "My muscles are so relaxed after I take my medication."
   b. "BuSpar will cause me to go to sleep after I take each dose."
   c. "BuSpar gave me immediate relief the first day I took it."
   d. "It will probably take 3 to 4 weeks for my new medication to make me feel better."

3. Which of the following nondrug measures would the nurse implement to enhance the effectiveness of an antianxiety drug?
   a. Turn out bright lights and decrease the temperature.
   b. Do not worry the client with details concerning his or her care.
   c. Spend at least 30 minutes explaining how his antianxiety drug will decrease his anxiety.
   d. Withhold all other medications.

4. A client is drowsy and his speech is slow. He appears to have difficulty concentrating. The nurse suspects that he is experiencing
   a. a panic attack
   b. sleep deprivation
   c. obsessive-compulsive disorder
   d. hyperactivity

5. Which of the following drugs will decrease the effects of an antianxiety agent?
   a. nicotine   c. cimetidine
   b. alcohol   d. oral contraceptives

6. A client is to receive a hypnotic for the first time. The nurse will tell the client to expect drowsiness within
   a. 10 minutes   c. 30 minutes
   b. 15 minutes   d. 60 minutes

7. What nursing action is high priority after administering a sedative or hypnotic to a client who is hospitalized?
   a. check the armband for identification
   b. call the client by name
   c. raise all bed rails
   d. place the call light within client's reach

8. When administering a sedative, the nurse encourages the client to drink a full glass of water. When the client questions the nurse about the amount of water, the following response would be most appropriate
   a. "The water is necessary to dilute the drug."
   b. "The water increases dissolution and absorption of the drug for a faster onset of action."
   c. "The more fluid you drink, the faster the elimination of the drug from the body."
   d. "The fluid helps decrease the irritation to the body tissues."

9. If a client is excessively sedated at the time of the next sedative dose, the nurse should
   a. omit the dose and record the reason
   b. withhold the dose for 30 minutes
   c. administer flumazenil
   d. have the physician discontinue the drug

10. A client has cirrhosis. Which of the following antianxiety agents would be appropriate for the client?
   a. temazepam (Restoril)   c. buspirone (BuSpar)
   b. lorazepam (Ativan)   d. zaleplon (Sonata)

ALTERNATE FORMAT QUESTIONS

1. The nurse is caring for a hospitalized client who has been taking a sedative-hypnotic drug. In evaluating the effectiveness of the drug, the nurse will consider which of the following? (Select all that apply.)
   a. _____ Sedative-hypnotics should not be taken every night.
   b. _____ Most benzodiazepines lose their effectiveness in producing sleep after 4 weeks of daily use.
   c. _____ To restore the sleep-producing effect, administration of a hypnotic drug must be interrupted for 1 to 2 weeks.
   d. _____ It is not helpful to switch from one drug to another because of cross-tolerance.

2. It has been determined that a benzodiazepine is the best drug choice for a client. The nurse is aware that the physician may prescribe which of the following drugs for the client? (Select all that apply.)
   a. _____ lorazepam (Ativan)
   b. _____ zaleplon (Sonata)
   c. _____ buspirone (BuSpar)
   d. _____ alprazolam (Xanax)
   e. _____ clorazepate (Tranxene)
   f. _____ oxazepam (Serax)

CHAPTER 9

Antipsychotic Drugs

■ Mastering the Information

MATCHING

Match the terms in Column I with a definition, example, or related statement from Column II.

COLUMN I

1. _____ hallucinations
2. _____ risperidone (Risperdal)
3. _____ thioridazine (Mellaril)
4. _____ clozapine (Clozaril)
5. _____ psychosis
6. _____ aripiprazole (Abilify)
7. _____ olanzapine (Zyprexa)
8. _____ haloperidol (Haldol)
9. _____ chlorpromazine (Thorazine)
10. _____ delusions

COLUMN II

a. the first drug to effectively treat psychotic disorders
b. an atypical antipsychotic agent that is more likely to cause extrapyramidal side effects
c. sensory perceptions of people or objects that are not present in the external environment
d. an atypical antipsychotic agent that may cause life-threatening agranulocytosis
e. a frequently prescribed, atypical, first-choice antipsychotic agent
f. false beliefs that persist in the absence of reason or evidence
g. the newest atypical antipsychotic agent approved for the treatment of schizophrenia
h. a formerly used drug that is now indicated only when other drugs are ineffective because of its association with serious cardiac dysrhythmias
i. an antipsychotic drug that produces a low incidence of hypotension and sedation but a higher incidence of extrapyramidal effects
j. a severe mental disorder characterized by disordered thought processes

TRUE OR FALSE

Indicate if the following statements are true or false.

_____ 1. Antipsychotic drugs are frequently used in clients who are critically ill.

_____ 2. African Americans experience a higher incidence of adverse effects from antipsychotic drugs.

_____ 3. Tardive dyskinesia may occur with long-term use of typical antipsychotic drugs.

_____ 4. Haloperidol (Haldol) may be used in children from ages 2 to 12 years old.

_____ 5. Extrapyramidal effects are more likely to occur with newer atypical agents.

_____ 6. Intramuscular injections of antipsychotic drugs require double the dose of oral dosages.

_____ 7. Aripiprazole (Abilify) may be taken with or without food.

_____ 8. Weight gain is more likely with ziprasidone (Geodon) than other antipsychotic drugs.

_____ 9. Quetiapine (Seroquel) relieves both positive and negative symptoms of psychosis.

_____ 10. Clozapine (Clozaril) is indicated for clients with schizophrenia, including those that have exhibited recurrent suicidal behavior.

SHORT ANSWER

Answer the following:

1. List positive symptoms of schizophrenia.

_____

_____

_____

2. List negative symptoms of schizophrenia.

_____

_____

_____

3. Describe the difference between "typical" antipsychotics and "atypical" antipsychotics.

_____

_____

_____

4. List clinical indications for phenothiazines, other than psychiatric illnesses.

_____

_____

_____

5. Why is clozapine (Clozaril) considered a second-line drug?

_____

_____

_____

■ Applying Your Knowledge

You are assigned to care for John Chou, hospitalized 2 weeks ago and started on fluphenazine hydrochloride (Prolixin) to treat acute psychotic symptoms. During your assessment, John appears restless, unable to sit still, and uncoordinated. He also has a fine hand tremor. How would you interpret these data?

_____

_____

_____

_____

_____

■ Practicing for NCLEX

MULTIPLE-CHOICE QUESTIONS

1. A client is a newly diagnosed schizophrenic. Which of the following drugs will his physician most likely prescribe for him?
   a. pimozide (Orap)
   b. risperidone (Risperdal)
   c. sotalol (Betapace)
   d. thioridazine hydrochloride (Mellaril)

2. Which of the following clients would be more likely to experience tardive dyskinesia?
   a. a 32-year-old African-American male
   b. a 24-year-old Asian female who has taken haloperidol (Haldol) for 2 weeks
   c. an 18-year-old Caucasian male who has just started loxapine (Loxitane) therapy
   d. a 50-year-old Hispanic female who has taken ziprasidone (Geodon) for 2 years

3. A 28-year-old male was hospitalized 1 week ago for acute psychotic symptoms. He is taking 6 mg of fluphenazine hydrochloride (Prolixin) daily. He will least likely experience
   a. extrapyramidal reactions   c. hypertension
   b. hypotension   d. sedation

4. The nurse is talking to the mother of a 19-year-old boy who is exhibiting hostility and hyperactivity and is very combative. The physician explained that her son is probably experiencing an acute psychosis and will be started on an antipsychotic drug. She asks the nurse how long his agitated behavior will last. The following would be an appropriate response:

   a. "It will be several weeks before he calms down."

   b. "He will always appear agitated."

   c. "I'm not sure. It's really hard to tell."

   d. "Your son should become less agitated a few hours after the drug therapy is started."

5. A client has been taking an antacid for 2 months. Her physician prescribes loxapine (Loxitane) for acute psychosis. The nurse understands that the dosage of Loxitane will likely be

   a. 10 mg tid PO (by mouth)

   b. decreased because she is taking an antacid

   c. 250 mg/day because of the antacid

   d. increased because of the interaction with the antacid

6. The nurse has just given a client 5 mg of haloperidol (Haldol) intramuscularly (IM). The nurse tells him that he should lie down for at least 30 minutes. This will help

   a. prevent orthostatic hypotension

   b. prevent tissue irritation

   c. increase distribution of the drug

   d. prevent delay of the medication reaching the neurotransmitters

7. A client has been diagnosed with an acute psychosis. Aripiprazole (Abilify) has been ordered. The nurse is aware that she should assess for which of the following conditions before drug therapy is started?

   a. cardiac dysrhythmias   c. seizure disorder

   b. anemia   d. diabetes

8. A client is a newly diagnosed schizophrenic and has been started on risperidone (Risperdal). Which of the following could contribute to noncompliance with his drug therapy?

   a. multiple daily doses of risperidone

   b. the high cost of his medication

   c. an unpleasant odor of the medication

   d. nausea that occurs after each dose of the medication

9. A client is on chlorpromazine (Thorazine). For the last 2 days his blood pressure has been 100/60. He has complained of dizziness and weakness and has not wanted to get out of bed. Which of the following would be an appropriate nursing diagnosis for him?

   a. Impaired Physical Mobility Related to Sedation

   b. Risk of Injury Related to Excessive Sedation

   c. Altered Tissue Perfusion Related to Hypotension

   d. Self-care Deficit Related to Psychosis

10. Which of the following adverse effects would the nurse look for in a client who is taking ziprasidone (Geodon)?

    a. constipation   c. agitation

    b. hypertension   d. diarrhea

ALTERNATE FORMAT QUESTIONS

1. In planning the care for a client starting antipsychotic medication, the nurse identifies the following goals. Arrange the goals in order of priority.

   a. _____ Prevent acute episodes of psychotic behavior.

   b. _____ Decrease symptoms of aggression, agitation, and hostility.

   c. _____ Increase the client's ability to cope with the environment.

   d. _____ Increase the client's ability for self-care.

   e. _____ Increase the client's socialization.

2. Which of the following should be included in a teaching plan for the caregiver of a newly diagnosed schizophrenic? (Select all that apply.)

   a. _____ Minimize exposure to sunlight.

   b. _____ Avoid exposure to excessive cold.

   c. _____ Practice good oral hygiene.

   d. _____ Take an antacid with the antipsychotic if heartburn is present.

   e. _____ Take the antipsychotic at bedtime.

   f. _____ Do not drive a car or operate machinery when drowsy from an antipsychotic.

CHAPTER 10

Antidepressants and Mood Stabilizers

■ Mastering the Information

MATCHING

Match the terms in Column I with a definition, example, or related statement from Column II.

COLUMN I

1. _____ bupropion (Wellbutrin)

2. _____ nefazodone (Serzone)

3. _____ fluoxetine (Prozac)

4. _____ paroxetine (Paxil)

5. _____ isocarboxazid (Marplan)

6. _____ imipramine (Tofranil)

7. _____ mirtazapine (Remeron)

8. _____ sertraline (Zoloft)

9. _____ clomipramine (Anafranil)

10. _____ lithium carbonate (Eskalith)

COLUMN II

a. may be useful in clients with severe insomnia, anxiety, and agitation

b. used to treat social anxiety disorder

c. antidepressant that can cause seizure activity

d. used to treat post-traumatic stress disorder

e. prototype for tricyclic antidepressants

f. a selective serotonin reuptake inhibitor (SSRI)

g. a monoamine oxidase inhibitor (MAO)

h. an antidepressant that decreases migraine headaches as well as depression

i. used to treat bipolar disorder

j. used to treat obsessive-compulsive disorder

TRUE OR FALSE

Indicate if the following statements are true or false.

_____ 1. Imipramine (Tofranil) is used to treat childhood enuresis.

_____ 2. Nefazodone (Serzone) can be taken with an MAO inhibitor.

_____ 3. Depression is thought to result from a deficiency of norepinephrine and/or serotonin.

_____ 4. MAO inhibitors are considered third-line drugs because of their potential for serious interactions with certain foods.

_____ 5. An SSRI and an MAO inhibitor can be given concurrently.

_____ 6. Bupropion (Wellbutrin) can cause sexual dysfunction.

_____ 7. A sodium deficit causes more lithium to be reabsorbed and increases the risk of lithium toxicity.

_____ 8. St. John's wort should not be combined with alcohol or antidepressant drugs.

_____ 9. Cimetidine (Tagamet) may increase the effects of SSRIs.

_____ 10. Most SSRIs should be taken at night before going to bed.

SHORT ANSWER

Answer the following:

1. Define monoamine neurotransmitter dysfunction associated with depression.

2. Explain the mechanism of action for antidepressant drugs.

3. Why are SSRIs considered first-choice drugs?

4. Why should clients be given only a 5- to 7-day supply of antidepressants?

5. Describe a tricyclic antidepressant (TCA) overdose.

■ Applying Your Knowledge

Ms. Jordon started taking fluoxetine (Prozac) for depression 1 week ago. When she returns to the clinic, she states she is still depressed and requests that the dosage of Prozac be increased. She also complains that she is having trouble sleeping. What teaching is appropriate for Ms. Jordon?

■ Practicing for NCLEX

MULTIPLE-CHOICE QUESTIONS

1. A client comes to the clinic complaining of a metallic taste in his mouth, blurred vision, tinnitus, and hand tremors. The nurse questions him about taking which of the following drugs?
   a. propranolol (Inderal)
   b. furosemide (Lasix)
   c. lithium carbonate (Eskalith)
   d. sertraline (Zoloft)

2. The nurse is aware that his client has been depressed and is on medication. The client has tachycardia and increased respirations and is sweating. The nurse concludes that the client is experiencing
   a. a lithium overdose   c. a MAO overdose
   b. a TCA overdose   d. an SSRI overdose

3. The lithium dose has been decreased for a client. The nurse tells the client he should have serum levels checked every
   a. month   c. 3 months
   b. 6 weeks   d. 6 months

4. The client has been taking citalopram (Celexa) and complaining of dizziness, nausea, and a headache. Before talking with the client, the nurse suspects that the client has

   a. increased her dosage to 40 mg daily

   b. either omitted doses or stopped taking the drug

   c. had a drug–drug interaction

   d. been smoking

5. A client is taking isocarboxazid (Marplan). The nurse cautions the client about eating

   a. eggs   c. onions

   b. aged cheeses   d. strawberries

6. The client is being treated for a mood disorder. She is taking nefazodone (Serzone). The nurse stresses the importance of reporting which of the following?

   a. headache   c. dark urine

   b. dizziness   d. fatigue

7. Which of the following anticonvulsants is used in mood disorders?

   a. diazepam (Valium)

   b. phenytoin (Dilantin)

   c. lorazepam (Ativan)

   d. carbamazepine (Tegretol)

8. When a client appears depressed, the nurse should assess for which of the following first?

   a. suicidal thoughts   c. social skills

   b. blood pressure   d. habits

9. A client comes to the clinic explaining that her husband wants her to stop taking fluoxetine (Prozac). The nurse suspects that she is experiencing which adverse effect?

   a. headache   c. sexual dysfunction

   b. dizziness   d. heavy sedation

10. The nurse is taking care of a 70-year-old woman who is depressed and is on an SSRI. Which of the following will the nurse monitor over the next 3 months?

    a. smoking   c. visual disturbances

    b. weight loss   d. blood glucose levels

ALTERNATE FORMAT QUESTIONS

1. The nurse is evaluating the effects of an antidepressant medication a client has been receiving for 4 weeks. Which of the following indicates the client is experiencing a desired effect from the medication? (Select all that apply.) The client

   a. _____ states he is less depressed

   b. _____ has decreased appetite

   c. _____ has increased physical activity

   d. _____ has decreased interest in what is happening to him

   e. _____ has improved sleep patterns

   f. _____ has improved appearance

2. A client has started lithium therapy. Which of the following will the nurse include in a teaching plan for this client? (Select all that apply.)

   a. _____ Take medication with food or milk or soon after a meal.

   b. _____ Decrease salt intake.

   c. _____ Drink 8–12 glasses of fluids daily.

   d. _____ Avoid excessive intake of caffeine.

   e. _____ Minimize activities that cause excessive perspiration.

CHAPTER 11

Antiseizure Drugs

■ Mastering the Information

MATCHING

Match the terms in Column I with a definition, example, or related statement from Column II.

COLUMN I

1. _____ epilepsy

2. _____ lorazepam (Ativan)

3. _____ phenobarbital

4. _____ generalized seizures

5. _____ valproic acid

6. _____ ethosuximide (Zarontin)

7. _____ gabapentin (Neurontin)

8. _____ status epilepticus

9. _____ phenytoin

10. _____ partial seizures

COLUMN II

a. reduces the effects of cardiovascular drugs

b. characterized by generalized tonic–clonic convulsions lasting for several minutes or occurring at close intervals, during which the client does not gain consciousness

c. characterized by abnormal and excessive electrical discharges of nerve cells

d. drug of choice for absence seizures

e. begin in a specific area of the brain

f. long-acting barbiturate used to treat seizures

g. used to treat partial seizures and post-therapeutic neuralgia

h. used to treat seizures and manic reactions in bipolar disorder and to prevent migraine headaches

i. have no discernible point of origin

j. drug of choice for status epilepticus

TRUE OR FALSE

Indicate if the following statements are true or false.

_____ 1. Alcohol increases the effect of carbamazepine (Tegretol).

_____ 2. Hypercalcemia may occur when antiseizure drugs are taken in high doses and over long periods.

_____ 3. The occurrence of nystagmus indicates phenytoin toxicity.

_____ 4. Most antiepileptic drugs (AEDs) are metabolized in the liver.

_____ 5. Carbamazepine decreases the effects of oral contraceptives.

_____ 6. For routine monitoring of AEDs, blood samples should be obtained in the afternoon after the noon meal.

_____ 7. In 20% to 30% of clients, two or more AEDs are required.

_____ 8. Kidney stones can be an adverse effect of topiramate (Topamax).

_____ 9. Phenytoin is contraindicated in clients with sinus bradycardia or heart block.

_____ 10. The injectable solution of phenytoin is highly recommended.

SHORT ANSWER

Answer the following:

1. List the most common adverse effects of phenytoin.

_____

_____

_____

2. Why is lamotrigine (Lamictal) not given to children younger than 16 years of age?

_____

_____

_____

3. Why is the first dose of gabapentin (Neurontin) given at night?

_____

_____

_____

4. Explain why levetiracetam (Keppra) has a low potential for drug interactions?

_____

_____

_____

5. Why should clients not switch between generic and trade name formulations of phenytoin?

_____

_____

_____

■ Applying Your Knowledge

You are a nurse working in a clinic. Mr. Eng, an epileptic for the last 10 years, comes into the clinic complaining of problems with poor coordination and fatigue. His speech also seems somewhat slurred. His seizures have been well controlled on phenytoin (Dilantin) 300 mg hs. His Dilantin level is drawn and is 19 mcg/mL. How should you proceed?

_____

_____

_____

_____

_____

■ Practicing for NCLEX

MULTIPLE-CHOICE QUESTIONS

1. In teaching a client the importance of taking her antiseizure drug at the same time each day, the nurse explains that this will
   a. decrease expected side effects of the drug
   b. help maintain therapeutic blood levels of the drug
   c. prevent further seizures
   d. make it easier for her to remember to take the medication

2. A client has begun phenytoin therapy. He asks the nurse how long it will take for the drug to work. This would be an appropriate response:
   a. "Approximately 7 to 10 days after phenytoin is started, therapeutic blood levels should occur."
   b. "After a maximum of 3 weeks, benefits will be evident."
   c. "There is really no way to know how long it will take the drug to work."
   d. "There should be a decrease in seizure activity."

3. Gabapentin (Neurontin) is prescribed for a client. In a discussion about this drug, the nurse would explain that
   a. the client should stop taking the drug if she experiences dizziness
   b. the client should take the medication on an empty stomach
   c. hypertension will occur
   d. if the client has to take an antacid, she should wait at least 2 hours after the gabapentin dose.

4. A client is starting carbamazepine (Tegretol) for a seizure disorder. Which of the following groups of drugs should the nurse caution the client about concerning a possible fatal reaction?
   a. benzodiazepines
   b. monoamine oxidase inhibitors (MAOs)
   c. antibiotics
   d. opioid analgesics

5. In assessing a client who is to start zonisamide (Zonegran) for generalized seizures, the nurse should question him concerning
   a. episodes of dizziness
   b. his diet
   c. a history of kidney stones
   d. chronic fatigue

6. In a child 6 years old and younger, an oral antiseizure drug is rapidly absorbed and has a short half-life. This explains why
   a. the rate of metabolism in children is decreased
   b. therapeutic blood levels are reached earlier in children than in adults
   c. children need lower doses of antiseizure drugs per kilogram of body weight than do adults
   d. excessive sedation is not a concern

7. A client is taking oxcarbazepine (Trileptal). Which of the following lab tests should have been done before drug therapy was started?
   a. cholesterol
   b. partial thromboplastin time (PTT)
   c. creatinine clearance
   d. follicle-stimulating hormone (FSH)

8. The most important goal for a client experiencing seizures is to
   a. take medication as prescribed
   b. experience control over seizures
   c. avoid serious adverse drug effects
   d. keep follow-up appointments with the health care provider

9. A 42-year-old client who has diabetes mellitus has just been diagnosed with a seizure disorder. She is started on phenytoin (Dilantin) therapy. Which of the following should the nurse instruct the client to do?
   a. Decrease fat and sodium intake.
   b. Weigh daily and record her weight.
   c. Check blood sugar more often.
   d. Decrease the amount of insulin taken daily.

10. The nurse's assessment reveals that a client does not take his antiseizure medication as it is prescribed. He stated that not only did the medication make him "sleepy all the time," but it was also expensive. An appropriate nursing diagnosis would be
    a. Ineffective Coping related to denial of seizure disorder
    b. Knowledge Deficit: Drug effects
    c. Noncompliance: Inappropriate use of medication related to adverse effects and loss
    d. Risk for Injury: dizziness related to drug therapy

ALTERNATE FORMAT QUESTIONS

1. A client is brought into the emergency department via ambulance with a diagnosis of status epilepticus. Lorazepam 0.1mg/kg at 2 mg/minute is ordered. The client weighs 180 pounds. How many total milligrams will the client receive over a 30-minute period?

2. A nurse is instructing a client who has recently been diagnosed with a seizure disorder. When discussing precipitating factors for seizures, the nurse will include which of the following? (Select all that apply.)
   a. _____ diet high in fat
   b. _____ ingestion of alcohol
   c. _____ emotional and physical stress
   d. _____ high blood pressure
   e. _____ flashing lights

CHAPTER 12

Antiparkinson Drugs

■ Mastering the Information

MATCHING

Match the terms in Column I with a definition, example, or related statement from Column II.

COLUMN I

1. _____ dopamine

2. _____ levodopa/carbidopa (Sinemet)

3. _____ levodopa (Larodopa, Dopar)

4. _____ amantadine (Symmetrel)

5. _____ selegiline (Eldepryl)

6. _____ carbidopa (Lodosyn)

7. _____ tolcapone (Tasmar)

8. _____ entacapone (Comtan)

9. _____ bromocriptine (Parlodel)

10. _____ ropinirole (Requip)

COLUMN II

a. an antiviral agent used to increase dopamine levels

b. increases dopamine in the brain by inhibiting its metabolism with monoamine oxidase (MAO)

c. an antiparkinson drug used to decreased the peripheral breakdown of levodopa

d. ninety percent excreted through the biliary tract

e. form of levodopa/carbidopa combination

f. an antiparkinson drug that is contraindicated in clients with liver disease

g. the most effective drug in treating Parkinson's disease

h. a neurotransmitter

i. used to treat amenorrhea associated with hyperprolactinemia

j. renal failure does not appear to alter effects

TRUE OR FALSE

Indicate if the following statements are true or false.

_____ 1. Parkinson's disease occurs in both men and women between 50 and 80 years of age.

_____ 2. People with Parkinson's disease have an increase in dopamine and a decrease in acetylcholine.

_____ 3. Several drug combinations may be used before the start of levodopa therapy.

_____ 4. Clients with Parkinson's disease may become depressed, isolated, and withdrawn.

_____ 5. Iron increases absorption of levodopa.

_____ 6. When dopaminergic drugs are discontinued, the dosage should be tapered over 1 week.

_____ 7. The optimal dose of an antiparkinson drug is the largest one that allows the client to function.

_____ 8. A dopamine agonist is given with levodopa/carbidopa to help relieve symptoms of Parkinson's disease.

_____ 9. Levodopa becomes more effective after 5 to 7 years of use.

_____ 10. Central activity anticholinergic drugs given for Parkinson's disease may cause confusion, agitation, and hallucinations.

SHORT ANSWER

Answer the following:

1. What causes Parkinson's disease?

_____

_____

_____

2. Discuss the goal of antiparkinson drug therapy.

_____

_____

_____

3. List two advantages of antiparkinson combination therapy.

_____

_____

_____

4. What effect do antihistamines have on a client who is taking an anticholinergic drug for Parkinson's disease?

_____

_____

_____

5. List side effects of levodopa.

_____

_____

_____

■ Applying Your Knowledge

Mr. Simmons has had Parkinson's disease for 4 years, and despite treatment with Sinemet, his functional abilities continue to decline. His physician prescribes a tricyclic antidepressant. He comes to the clinic 3 weeks later complaining of constipation and difficulty voiding. Are these symptoms related to his medications?

_____

_____

_____

_____

_____

■ Practicing For NCLEX

MULTIPLE-CHOICE QUESTIONS

1. A client has been diagnosed with Parkinson's disease but is unable to take levodopa. Which of the following drugs may be used in her treatment plan?
   a. antipsychotic drugs
   b. anticholinergic drugs
   c. antiadrenergic drugs
   d. antiemetic drugs

2. When assessing a client who will probably be placed on levodopa, which of the following would concern the nurse most?
   a. narrow-angle glaucoma
   b. urinary retention
   c. dilated pupils
   d. hallucinations

3. To prevent or reduce nausea and vomiting, the nurse would encourage the client to take Sinemet
   a. without regard to meals
   b. at bedtime
   c. during or right after a meal
   d. 2 hours prior to the noon meal

4. A client is taking amantadine. Which of the following would be an appropriate nursing diagnosis?

   a. Risk for Injury: Hypotension Related to Adverse Effects of Amantadine

   b. Risk for Injury: Ataxia and Dizziness Related to Adverse Effects of Antiparkinson Drug

   c. Alteration in Nutrition: Vomiting Related to Adverse Effects of Amantadine

   d. Alteration in Nutrition: Anorexia Related to Adverse Effects of an Anticholinergic Drug

5. A nurse is working in a neurological clinic and will see clients who have Parkinson's disease. When the nurse observes clients who exhibit restlessness, agitation, and confusion, the nurse suspects that

   a. most are on levodopa/carbidopa combination drug therapy

   b. they are on levodopa therapy

   c. they are not taking the prescribed drugs

   d. they need to be reevaluated for drug therapy

6. Which of the following statements would indicate that the client understands levodopa therapy?

   a. "I will have to cut liver out of my diet."

   b. "If I don't feel better in 2 weeks, I will discontinue the levodopa."

   c. "I will take my medication at night."

   d. "I take an over-the-counter drug when I get a sinus infection."

7. Which instructions should the nurse give an older client who is taking trihexyphenidyl?

   a. "You must adhere to a strict low-sodium diet."

   b. "Avoid extreme heat. Stay inside as much as possible during the summer."

   c. "Adverse effects will be greatly reduced if taken at night."

   d. "Diarrhea is a likely adverse effect."

8. Which of the following would be an expected outcome of levodopa (Larodopa) in a client with Parkinson's disease?

   a. decrease in salivation

   b. decrease in tremors

   c. decrease in sweating

   d. decrease in rigidity

9. A client is taking pramipexole (Mirapex). Which of the following adverse effects will the nurse most likely observe for?

   a. hypertension   c. orthostatic hypotension

   b. constipation   d. blurred vision

10. The nurse is teaching a client about his new drug, benztropine (Cogentin). The nurse will stress that he should avoid which of the following?

    a. antihistamines

    b. alcohol

    c. antiemetics

    d. antipsychotics

ALTERNATE FORMAT QUESTIONS

1. The nurse has been assigned a client who has had Parkinson's disease for some time. The client has been taking an anticholinergic drug to decrease salivation, spasticity and tremors. The client informs the nurse that his symptoms are getting worse and that he is having difficulty with his speech and is having difficulty walking. The nurse suspects the physician will discontinue the current drug therapy and prescribe levodopa. Which of the following will the nurse question the client about during the initial assessment? (Select all that apply.)

   a. _____ skin disorders

   b. _____ hypertension

   c. _____ narrow-angle glaucoma

   d. _____ myasthenia gravis

   e. _____ angina

2. A client is taking 25 mg of carbidopa/100 mg of levodopa three times daily. Entacapone (Comtan) is also ordered. How many total milligrams of entacapone will be taken daily?

CHAPTER 13

Skeletal Muscle Relaxants

■ Mastering the Information

MATCHING

Match the terms in Column I with a definition, example, or related statement from Column II.

COLUMN I

1. _____ carisoprodol (Soma)

2. _____ methocarbamol (Robaxin)

3. _____ diazepam (Valium)

4. _____ metaxalone (Skelaxin)

5. _____ spasm

6. _____ tizanidine (Zanaflex)

7. _____ dantrolene (Dantrium)

8. _____ baclofen (Lioresal)

9. _____ orphenadrine (Norflex)

10. _____ cyclobenzaprine (Flexeril)

11. _____ spasticity

COLUMN II

a. contraindicated in clients with anemia

b. must be used cautiously in clients with renal impairment

c. may be used to treat tetanus

d. contraindicated in clients with cardiovascular disorders

e. should be used cautiously in clients with cardiovascular disease

f. used to relieve discomfort from acute, painful musculoskeletal disorders

g. parenteral administration relieves pain associated with acute musculoskeletal trauma but is uncertain whether oral administration has any beneficial effect

h. inhibits the release of calcium in skeletal muscle cells, which decreases the strength of muscle contraction

i. increased muscle tone or contraction and stiff, awkward movements

j. may cause psychotic symptoms, including hallucinations

k. sudden, involuntary, painful muscle contraction

TRUE OR FALSE

Indicate if the following statements are true or false.

_____ 1. Dantrolene (Dantrium) is a central-acting skeletal muscle relaxant.

_____ 2. Cyclobenzaprine (Flexeril) can be used safely for up to 6 months.

_____ 3. Fatal hepatitis is a serious adverse effect of dantrolene (Dantrium).

_____ 4. Carisoprodol (Soma) can safely be given to children under age 10.

_____ 5. Skeletal muscle relaxants should be taken with milk or food.

_____ 6. Antihypertensive agents may decrease the effects of skeletal muscle relaxants.

_____ 7. Corticosteroids are used to treat multiple sclerosis.

_____ 8. A common side effect of cyclobenzaprine (Flexeril) is dry mouth.

_____ 9. The oral form of methocarbamol (Robaxin) is contraindicated in clients with renal impairment.

_____ 10. Skeletal muscle relaxants may be stopped abruptly with no adverse effects.

SHORT ANSWER

Answer the following:

1. Describe conditions that skeletal muscle relaxants are used to treat.

_____

_____

_____

2. Discuss contraindications for the use of skeletal muscle relaxants.

_____

_____

_____

3. What is the goal of treatment when skeletal muscle relaxants are used?

_____

_____

_____

4. List common side effects of cyclobenzaprine (Flexeril).

_____

_____

_____

5. Formulate two nursing diagnoses related to skeletal muscle relaxants.

_____

_____

_____

■ Applying Your Knowledge

Sarah Johnson is experiencing severe muscle spasms. Her physician orders 50 mg of Valium to be given intravenously (IV) stat. Your stock supply has 10 mg of Valium in a 2-cc vial. Discuss how you will safely administer this medication.

_____

_____

_____

_____

_____

■ Practicing for NCLEX

MULTIPLE-CHOICE QUESTIONS

1. A client is a 15-year-old male who has cerebral palsy. Which of the following skeletal muscle relaxants would he take for spasticity?
   a. orphenadrine (Norflex)
   b. methocarbamol (Robaxin)
   c. tizanidine (Zanaflex)
   d. metaxalone (Skelaxin)

2. Which of the following statements by a client indicates that he has an understanding of baclofen (Lioresal) therapy?
   a. "I will not take the drug if I develop a rash."
   b. "It takes at least 3 hours to feel the effects of my medication."
   c. "That drug is giving me diarrhea."
   d. "I would rather get my medication in an injection than take it by mouth."

3. A client is experiencing muscle spasms from a four-wheeler accident. He is receiving 10 mg of cyclobenzaprine (Flexeril) tid. The nurse's teaching plan should include which of the following instructions?
   a. Do not take the medication with food.
   b. Do not drive or operate heavy machinery for the first week.
   c. Increase the dosage if needed.
   d. Stop the drug if dizziness occurs.

4. A client is scheduled for surgery in the morning for a herniated spinal disk. He has been experiencing severe muscle spasms for the last 2 weeks. He will more than likely take which of the following skeletal muscle relaxants?

   a. metaxalone (Skelaxin)

   b. baclofen (Lioresal)

   c. dantrolene (Dantrium)

   d. tizanidine (Zanaflex)

5. A client is taking tizanidine (Zanaflex). Which of the following adverse effects may be significant for a client taking this drug?

   a. drowsiness   c. hypotension

   b. dry mouth   d. constipation

6. Which of the following clients would have the highest risk for hepatotoxicity from taking dantrolene (Dantrium) for 2 months?

   a. a 71-year-old female who is taking a cardiac glycoside and a diuretic

   b. a 53-old-year-old female who is on hormone replacement therapy

   c. a 22-year-old male who is taking a monoamine oxidase inhibitor

   d. a 56-year-old male who is receiving an antihypertensive agent

7. Which of the following is the most common adverse effect of cyclobenzaprine (Flexeril)?

   a. dry mouth   c. agitation

   b. bradycardia   d. insomnia

8. A client has muscle spasms associated with multiple sclerosis. She is taking baclofen (Lioresal). At times, she needs help with activities. Her 10-year-old daughter has been helping her dress and comb her hair. However, the nurse's main concern at this time is her drug therapy. An appropriate goal for the client would be

   a. to experience improved motor function

   b. to take medication as prescribed

   c. to experience relief from pain

   d. to increase self-care in daily living activities

9. When a skeletal muscle relaxant is given for acute muscle spasms, which of the following would indicate the best therapeutic effect?

   a. decreased tenderness

   b. increased mobility

   c. decreased mobility

   d. decreased ability to maintain posture and balance

10. A client is receiving 30 mg of dantrolene (Dantrium) daily PO (orally). Which of the following would be most important to monitor periodically?

   a. blood pressure   c. liver function

   b. red blood count   d. blood sugar

ALTERNATE FORMAT QUESTIONS

1. An 8-year-old child is receiving 2 mg/kg of dantrolene (Dantrium) four times daily to relieve spasticity associated with multiple sclerosis. How many milligrams does the child receive for one dose? The child weighs 66 pounds.

2. A client has been taking baclofen (Lioresal) for 2 weeks. Which of the following is the most common adverse effects of this drug? (Select all that apply.)

   a. _____ drowsiness

   b. _____ constipation

   c. _____ headache

   d. _____ dizziness

   e. _____ confusion

CHAPTER 14

Substance Abuse Disorders

■ Mastering the Information

MATCHING

Match the terms in Column I with a definition, example, or related statement from Column II.

COLUMN I

1. _____ naloxone (Narcan)
2. _____ acetone
3. _____ gamma-hydroxybutyric acid (GHB)
4. _____ amphetamines
5. _____ flumazenil (Romazicon)
6. _____ heroin
7. _____ LSD
8. _____ "crack"
9. _____ dronabinol (Marinol)
10. _____ 3,4-methylenedioxymethamphetamine (MDMA)

COLUMN II

a. antidote for benzodiazepines
b. referred to as "ecstasy"
c. hallucinogen derived from lysergic acid
d. a legal cannabis preparation
e. a very potent, widely used form of cocaine
f. a volatile solvent
g. therapeutically used for narcolepsy
h. a semisynthetic derivative of morphine
i. a date-rape drug
j. used for an opiate overdose

TRUE OR FALSE

Indicate if the following statements are true or false.

_____ 1. Nurses can prevent abuse by promoting the use of nondrug measures when indicated.

_____ 2. Volatile solvents are most often abused by men over the age of 40.

_____ 3. Phencyclidine (PCP) produces intoxication similar to that of alcohol.

_____ 4. It is difficult to predict the effects of marijuana.

_____ 5. Mental alertness is associated with nicotine dependence.

_____ 6. A person who abuses one drug will probably abuse others.

_____ 7. Substance abusers are quick to seek health care.

_____ 8. Alcohol enhances the effects of hypoglycemia.

_____ 9. Benzodiazepine agents are the drugs of choice for treating alcohol withdrawal syndrome.

_____ 10. There is no antidote for barbiturate overdose.

SHORT ANSWER

Answer the following:

1. Define substance abuse.

_____

_____

_____

2. Define drug dependence.

_____

_____

_____

3. Define psychological dependence.

_____

_____

_____

4. Define physical dependence.

_____

_____

_____

5. Define tolerance.

_____

_____

_____

■ Applying Your Knowledge

Your daughter brings her college roommate home for a weekend visit. She tells you she has tried to quit smoking many times before but this time she is determined. She went to her physician for a prescription for "the patch," and she even bought some nicotine gum at the drugstore in case the cravings get really bad. You notice a patch on her right upper arm and her left upper arm. Because you are an RN, as well as the mother of a friend, what advice can you give her regarding smoking cessation?

_____

_____

_____

_____

■ Practicing for NCLEX

MULTIPLE-CHOICE QUESTIONS

1. A client is admitted to the emergency room with multiple lacerations from a motor vehicle accident. The nurse is aware that the accident was caused by alcohol ingestion. In obtaining a health history from a family member, the nurse learns that the client is an alcoholic and that he is on an anticoagulant. Which of the following would concern the nurse most regarding this client?

   a. decreased urinary output

   b. hypertension

   c. increased bleeding

   d. hypoglycemia

2. The nurse works in a detoxification unit in a large hospital. The nurse is assigned to work with clients experiencing alcohol withdrawal. Which of the following drugs would the nurse administer in the treatment of the clients?

   a. benzodiazepines   c. amphetamines

   b. barbiturates   d. nicotine

3. A client is receiving disulfiram (Antabuse) and complains of fatigue, headache, and dizziness. The nurse explains that

   a. she will ask the doctor to decrease the dosage

   b. after about 2 weeks of treatment, the adverse effects usually subside

   c. some people experience less-pleasant adverse effects than he has

   d. the adverse effects will continue as long as he is taking the medication

4. Which of the following drugs would a nurse administer to reduce symptoms of hyperactivity associated with alcohol withdrawal?

   a. naltrexone (ReVia)

   b. clonidine (Catapres)

   c. metyrosine (Demser)

   d. disulfiram (Antabuse)

5. A nurse suspects a client is abusing benzodiazepines. Which of the following might indicate that the nurse is correct?

   a. seizures

   b. memory impairment

   c. mental confusion

   d. poor motor coordination

6. A nurse is caring for a client who has abused alprazolam (Xanax) for 5 years. She wants to stop taking the drug. Which of the following will the nurse include when discussing withdrawal from this drug?

   a. Withdrawal symptoms usually begin 12 to 24 hours after the last dose.

   b. There will be no noticeable adverse effects.

   c. She may experience a seizure.

   d. She will be given methadone to help decrease withdrawal symptoms.

7. A nurse is assisting with a client who was diagnosed as having an opiate overdose. Naloxone (Narcan) is administered. There is no response to the opioid antagonist. The nurse suspects

   a. an incorrect amount of naloxone was administered

   b. mechanical ventilation will be needed

   c. clonidine should have been administered

   d. the overdose could have been caused by another depressant drug

8. A nurse is caring for a client who abuses cocaine. Which of the following vital signs would the nurse expect to find when assessing the client?

   a. blood pressure (BP): 98/50, pulse (P): 120, respirations (R): 40

   b. BP: 130/88, P: 92, R: 28

   c. BP: 150/90, P: 80, R: 16

   d. BP: 170/98, P: 110, R: 20

9. Even though marijuana is illegal and not used for therapeutic purposes in the United States, it is useful in treating nausea and vomiting associated with anticancer drugs and in decreasing

   a. intraocular pressure

   b. hypotension

   c. urinary output

   d. blood glucose levels

10. Assessment of an emergency room client reveals an elevated blood pressure, heart rate, and temperature; dilated pupils; and delusional thought processes. These symptoms indicate ingestion of

    a. an opiate

    b. an amphetamine

    c. a hallucinogen

    d. a cannabinoid

ALTERNATE FORMAT QUESTIONS

1. A client comes to the clinic asking for help to quit smoking. She has a 21-year history of the habit and is worried about developing lung cancer. In discussing the cessation plan, the nurse will include which of the following signs and symptoms of nicotine withdrawal? (Select all that apply.)

   a. _____ weight loss

   b. _____ anxiety

   c. _____ headache

   d. _____ irritability

   e. _____ decreased appetite

2. A nurse is working in the emergency department and is assigned to a client brought in by family members. The family thinks that the client is on a methamphetamine. Which of the following will the nurse assess for in this client? (Select all that apply.)

   a. _____ hyperactivity

   b. _____ agitation

   c. _____ decreased heart rate

   d. _____ increased heart rate

   e. _____ increased body temperature

CHAPTER 15

Central Nervous System Stimulants

■ Mastering the Information

MATCHING

Match the terms in Column I with a definition, example, or related statement from Column II.

COLUMN I

1. _____ modafinil (Provigil)

2. _____ atomoxetine (Strattera)

3. _____ caffeine

4. _____ dexmethylphenidate (Focalin)

5. _____ guarana

6. _____ theophylline

7. _____ NoDoz

8. _____ xanthines

9. _____ methylphenidate (Ritalin)

10. _____ doxapram (Dopram)

COLUMN II

a. an herbal/dietary supplement that may cause excessive nervousness and insomnia

b. an amphetamine-related drug used only for attention deficit hyperactivity disorder (ADHD)

c. central nervous system (CNS) stimulation is considered an adverse effect of this drug

d. has psychoactive and euphoric effects and is used to treat narcolepsy

e. is not a stimulant but is used to treat ADHD

f. a frequently consumed CNS stimulant worldwide

g. stimulates the cerebral cortex, which increases mental alertness and decreases drowsiness and fatigue

h. the most commonly used CNS stimulant provided for children

i. an analeptic that may be used by anesthesiologists as a respiratory stimulant

j. an over-the-counter antisleep product

TRUE OR FALSE

Indicate if the following statements are true or false.

_____ 1. Methylphenidate (Ritalin) has become a drug of abuse.

_____ 2. When a CNS stimulant is prescribed, the largest dose should be given.

_____ 3. Signs of CNS stimulant toxicity include high body temperature.

_____ 4. Methylphenidate (Ritalin) will decrease the effects of phenytoin (Dilantin).

_____ 5. Administer CNS stimulants at least 6 hours before bedtime.

_____ 6. Atomoxetine (Strattera) may be given with or without food.

_____ 7. Carbamazepine (Tegretol) increases the effects of modafinil (Provigil).

_____ 8. Oral contraceptives increase the effects of caffeine.

_____ 9. Most CNS stimulants act by facilitating initiation and transmission of nerve impulses.

_____ 10. Amphetamines decrease the amounts of norepinephrine, dopamine, and possibly serotonin in the brain, which produces increased mental alertness and euphoria and prolongs wakefulness.

SHORT ANSWER

Answer the following:

1. Why could chewing a long-acting form of methylphenidate (Ritalin) cause an overdose.

_____

_____

_____

2. List three therapeutic effects from CNS stimulants.

_____

_____

_____

3. Why are amphetamines and methylphenidate (Ritalin) given to children 30 minutes before meals?

_____

_____

_____

4. Why should CNS stimulants be taken as prescribed?

_____

_____

_____

5. Why are drug holidays encouraged with the use of CNS stimulants in children?

_____

_____

_____

■ Practicing for NCLEX

MULTIPLE-CHOICE QUESTIONS

1. An adult client is taking methylphenidate (Ritalin) for narcolepsy. He is to receive 40 mg bid. Which of the following times would be best for him to take his medication?

   a. 6 A.M. and 4 P.M.   c. 10 A.M. and 6 P.M.

   b. 8 A.M. and 8 P.M.   d. 10 P.M. and 6 A.M.

2. Which of the following adverse effects of CNS stimulants would indicate a decrease in dosage?

   a. anxiety

   b. excessive nervousness

   c. constipation

   d. diarrhea

3. In teaching a client who ingests several soft drinks a day to decrease caffeine intake, instructions would be to avoid

   a. Coke   c. Pepsi

   b. Mountain Dew   d. Dr. Pepper

4. Which of the following clients could safely use a CNS stimulant?

   a. a 38-year-old Caucasian female with glaucoma

   b. a 65-year-old African-American male who experiences angina

   c. a 50-year-old male who has adult-onset diabetes

   d. a 28-year-old African-American female with hyperthyroidism

5. An 8-year-old is taking 10 mg of methamphetamine (Desoxyn) daily for ADHD. At each clinic visit, the nurses' priority assessment would be

   a. height and weight

   b. vision

   c. temperature

   d. blood pressure

6. A mother of a young client being treated for ADHD is concerned about her child having to take medication. The best response to her would be

   a. "The medication is needed to help your son function in society."

   b. "Without the medication, your son would not be able to go to school."

   c. "We can discuss the adverse effects of his medication if you like."

   d. "Hopefully, the medication can be omitted during the summer when he is out of school."

7. A client is being instructed on the use of modafinil (Provigil) for narcolepsy. Which of the following best reflects an expected goal of client teaching activities related to the drug?
   a. The client will be able to identify two adverse effects of the drug.
   b. Family members will understand why the client must take the drug.
   c. The client will understand the physiological action of modafinil.
   d. Client will exercise three times a week.

8. Which of the following activities would the nurse be responsible for during the evaluation phase of drug therapy for a child receiving methylphenidate (Ritalin) for ADHD?
   a. preparation and administration of the drug
   b. ongoing monitoring of the child for therapeutic effects
   c. establishment of outcome criteria related to the drug therapy
   d. acquisition of data related to a drug history

9. Counseling a mother concerning her 7-year-old daughter's treatment of ADHD would include the importance of
   a. providing well-balanced meals
   b. increasing physical activities
   c. limiting social encounters
   d. using sunscreen when outside

10. A nurse is aware that an antipsychotic agent such as chlorpromazine (Thorazine) may be given to a client receiving an amphetamine. This drug–drug interaction produces which of the following effects?
    a. simple summation
    b. potentiation
    c. synergism
    d. antagonism

ALTERNATE QUESTIONS

1. Doxapram (Dopram), 1.5 mg/kg stat, is given intravenously to a client in the recovery room following surgery. How many milligrams will the client receive? The client weighs 148 pounds.

2. Arrange the following sources of caffeine in order of largest milligrams of caffeine to the smallest amount of caffeine (with number 1 being the largest amount of caffeine):
   a. _____ iced tea
   b. _____ Diet Pepsi
   c. _____ Mountain Dew
   d. _____ Coke
   e. _____ 2 oz of espresso

CHAPTER 16

Physiology of the Autonomic Nervous System

■ Mastering the Information

MATCHING

Match the terms in Column I with a definition, example, or related statement from Column II.

COLUMN I

1. _____ homeostasis
2. _____ desensitization
3. _____ ligands
4. _____ muscarinic receptors
5. _____ somatic nervous system
6. _____ norepinephrine
7. _____ nicotinic receptors
8. _____ hypersensitization
9. _____ acetylcholine
10. _____ autonomic nervous system

COLUMN II

a. controls voluntary activities in the visceral organs of the body
b. increase in beta-adrenergic responsiveness
c. located in most internal organs
d. innervates skeletal muscle and controls voluntary movements
e. main neurotransmitter of the autonomic nervous system
f. located in motor nerves and skeletal muscle
g. neurotransmitters, hormones, or medications that bind to receptors
h. synthesized from the amino acid tyrosine
i. decrease in beta-adrenergic responsiveness
j. constant internal environment

TRUE OR FALSE

Indicate if the following statements are true or false.

_____ 1. The peripheral nervous system includes the brain and spinal cord.

_____ 2. Afferent neurons carry sensory input from the periphery to the central nervous system (CNS).

_____ 3. The somatic nervous system innervates skeletal muscles and controls voluntary movement.

_____ 4. The main neurotransmitter of the autonomic nervous system is serotonin.

_____ 5. Norepinephrine acts on receptors in body organs and tissues to cause parasympathetic effects.

_____ 6. Ligands are neurotransmitters that can bind to receptors in the autonomic nervous system.

_____ 7. The sympathetic nervous system is stimulated by physical or emotional stress.

_____ 8. Epinephrine acts on alpha receptors only.

_____ 9. Parasympathetic stimulation increases heart rate.

_____ 10. Drugs that act on the autonomic nervous system affect the entire body rather than specific organs and tissues.

SHORT ANSWER

Answer the following:

1. _____ neurons carry sensory input from the periphery to the central nervous system.

2. Decreased heart rate is the body's response to _____ stimulation.

3. _____ receptors allow calcium ions to move into the cell and produce muscle contraction.

4. _____ neurons transport motor signals from the central nervous system to the peripheral areas of the body.

5. Increased muscle strength is the body's response to _____ stimulation.

■ Practicing for NCLEX

MULTIPLE-CHOICE QUESTIONS

1. Which term is used to describe a drug that has the same effects on the body as stimulation of the peripheral nervous system?
   a. adrenergic   c. sympathomimetic
   b. cholinergic   d. parasympatholytic

2. The physiological action of nicotine receptors is to
   a. inhibit respiratory response
   b. excite the cardiovascular system
   c. produce muscle contraction
   d. increase intracellular concentration of calcium

3. Adrenergic fibers secrete
   a. epinephrine   c. acetylcholine
   b. norepinephrine   d. dopamine

4. Which adrenergic neurotransmitter is necessary for normal brain function?
   a. acetylcholine   c. dopamine
   b. catecholamine   d. epinephrine

5. Beta$_1$ adrenergic receptors are found in the
   a. blood vessels   c. kidneys
   b. liver   d. heart

6. A specific body response to parasympathetic stimulation is
   a. dilated pupils
   b. increased motility of the gastrointestinal tract
   c. increased heart rate
   d. decreased secretions from sweat glands

7. Parasympathetic nervous system responses are regulated by
   a. dopamine
   b. cyclic adenosine monophosphate (cAMP)
   c. norepinephrine
   d. acetylcholine

8. A specific body response to the "fight-or-flight" reaction is
   a. increased muscle strength
   b. decrease in breakdown of muscle glycogen
   c. decrease in sweating
   d. increase in secretions from the lungs

9. The autonomic nervous system is regulated by centers in the central nervous system, including the
   a. thyroid gland   c. hypothalamus
   b. pituitary gland   d. adrenal medullae

10. A function of alpha$_1$ adrenergic receptors is
    a. relaxation of intestinal smooth muscle
    b. increased heat rate
    c. bronchodilation
    d. aggregation of platelets

ALTERNATE FORMAT QUESTIONS

1. Specific body responses to parasympathetic stimulation include the following. (Select all that apply.)
   a. _____ dilation of blood vessels in the skin
   b. _____ dilation of smooth muscle of bronchi
   c. _____ decreased secretions from glands in the lungs
   d. _____ contraction of smooth muscle in the urinary bladder
   e. _____ decreased heart rate

2. Specific body responses to sympathetic stimulation include the following. (Select all that apply.)
   a. _____ decreased cardiac output
   b. _____ increased blood sugar
   c. _____ increased muscle strength
   d. _____ increased respirations
   e. _____ decreased sweating

CHAPTER 17

Adrenergic Drugs

■ Mastering the Information

MATCHING

Match the terms in Column I with a definition, example, or related statement from Column II.

COLUMN I

1. _____ pseudoephedrine (Sudafed)

2. _____ metaraminol (Aramine)

3. _____ norepinephrine (Levophed)

4. _____ naphazoline hydrochloride (Privine)

5. _____ ephedrine

6. _____ phenylephrine (Neo-Synephrine)

7. _____ dopamine (Intropin)

8. _____ epinephrine (Adrenalin)

9. _____ oxymetazoline hydrochloride (Afrin)

10. _____ tetrahydrozoline hydrochloride (Visine)

COLUMN II

a. vasoconstriction in the eye

b. gout

c. cardiac stimulation

d. hyperglycemia

e. nasal decongestion

f. ophthalmic conditions

g. hypotension and shock

h. hypertension

i. diuresis

j. bronchodilation

TRUE OR FALSE

Indicate if the following statements are true or false.

_____ 1. Topical decongestants can be used for 10 days.

_____ 2. Many over-the-counter preparations contain adrenergic drugs.

_____ 3. Adrenergic drugs are given to decrease blood pressure.

_____ 4. Antihistamines may increase the effects of adrenergic drugs.

_____ 5. Acute bronchospasm is most often relieved within 5 minutes of administration of epinephrine.

_____ 6. A tuberculin syringe is not aspirated when giving epinephrine.

_____ 7. The use of an adrenergic drug in a critically ill client may result in hyperglycemia.

_____ 8. Liver disease is a contraindication to use of adrenergic drugs.

_____ 9. The most common use of epinephrine in children is for the treatment of asthma.

_____ 10. Pseudoephedrine toxicity occurs with doses four to five times greater than the normal dose.

SHORT ANSWER

Answer the following:

1. List three examples of direct-acting adrenergic drugs.

_____

_____

_____

2. What is the predominant effect on the body in response to beta₁ receptors?

_____

_____

_____

3. What is the predominant effect of the activation of beta₂ receptors in the body?

_____

_____

_____

4. Why are adrenergic drugs often referred to as emergency drugs?

_____

_____

_____

5. List five contraindications to using adrenergic drugs?

_____

_____

_____

■ Applying Your Knowledge

Jack Newton, a healthy 46-year-old, develops seasonal allergies. He medicates his allergy symptoms with over-the-counter ephedrine (Bronkaid) for approximately 4 weeks before going to his physician. When the nurse takes his vital signs, he is surprised that his blood pressure is 160/92 and his pulse is 102. How does ephedrine, an adrenergic agent, relieve allergy symptoms? What side effects are common?

_____

_____

_____

_____

■ Practicing for NCLEX

MULTIPLE-CHOICE QUESTIONS

1. When discussing nasal decongestants with a client in the allergy clinic, the nurse will impart information regarding
   a. rebound congestion
   b. foods to be avoided
   c. compliance with allergy injections
   d. environmental factors

2. A client is to have surgery and will have a general anesthetic. The nurse will question her concerning the use of adrenergic drugs because of increased risk of
   a. bronchial relaxation
   b. mydriasis
   c. cardiac dysrhythmias
   d. emotional disturbances

3. Which of the following drugs would be contraindicated for use with adrenergic drugs because of a potentially fatal outcome?
   a. doxapram (Dopram)
   b. isocarboxazid (Marplan)
   c. amitriptyline (Elavil)
   d. methylphenidate (Ritalin)

4. The nurse has administered 1 gt of tetrahydrozoline hydrochloride (Visine) OU (in each eye). An expected outcome would be
   a. decreased redness
   b. pupil constriction
   c. decreased tear activity
   d. improved accommodation

5. A nurse in the critical care unit has an order for epinephrine by intravenous (IV) injection. Before the drug is administered, a priority nursing action will be to
   a. measure urine output
   b. check the last blood sugar level
   c. check the IV injection site
   d. turn client to his or her left side

6. The client is experiencing a serious allergic reaction to a bee sting. Epinephrine is administered to relieve

   a. pain and swelling around the sting site

   b. itching of skin around the site

   c. anxiety

   d. acute bronchospasm and laryngeal edema

7. A client has been taking pseudoephedrine (Sudafed) for sinusitis. Which of the following adverse effects may be experienced?

   a. bradycardia

   b. hypertension

   c. hypoglycemia

   d. hypothyroidism

8. A client is a diabetic and is on insulin therapy. During treatment of acute asthmatic bronchitis, the nurse should assess

   a. partial thromboplastin time level

   b. blood glucose level

   c. blood pressure

   d. urinary output

9. When teaching a client about the use of tetrahydrozoline hydrochloride (Visine), the nurse should include which of the following as most important?

   a. Keep the eyes closed for at least 1 hour after use.

   b. Wear sun glasses when outdoors.

   c. Do not wear soft contact lenses while using the drug.

   d. Rest the eyes at least once every 2 to 3 hours after use.

10. The nurse has administered isoproterenol (Isuprel) to a client who is in shock. Which of the following would be an expected outcome?

    a. decreased pulse

    b. decreased blood pressure

    c. increased blood pressure

    d. increased body temperature

ALTERNATE FORMAT QUESTIONS

1. When administering epinephrine, the nurse is aware that the drug can be administered by which of the following routes? (Select all that apply.)

   a. _____ oral

   b. _____ subcutaneous

   c. _____ intramuscular

   d. _____ inhalation

   e. _____ intravenous

2. Before administration of an adrenergic drug, a nurse will assess for other drugs. Which of the following drugs increase the effects of adrenergic drugs? (Select all that apply.)

   a. _____ antihistamines

   b. _____ ergot alkaloids

   c. _____ digitalis (Digoxin)

   d. _____ Synthroid

   e. _____ haloperidol (Haldol)

CHAPTER 18

Antiadrenergic Drugs

■ Mastering the Information

MATCHING

Match the terms in Column I with a definition, example, or related statement from Column II.

COLUMN I

1. _____ prazosin (Minipress)

2. _____ guanfacine (Tenex)

3. _____ tolazoline (Priscoline)

4. _____ acebutolol (Sectral)

5. _____ tamsulosin (Flomax)

6. _____ carvedilol (Coreg)

7. _____ clonidine (Catapres)

8. _____ propranolol (Inderal)

9. _____ alfuzosin (Uroxatral)

10. _____ methyldopa (Aldomet)

COLUMN II

a. reduces blood pressure within 1 hour

b. alpha$_1$ adrenergic antagonist prototype

c. a beta blocker that is well tolerated in older adults

d. a cardioselective beta-blocker

e. can cause hemolytic anemia and hepatotoxicity

f. the first alpha$_1$ antagonist designed specifically to treat benign prostatic hyperplasia (BPH)

g. used to treat vasospastic disorders in adults and persistent pulmonary hypertension in newborns

h. prototype of the beta-adrenergic blocking drugs

i. an alpha$_2$ adrenergic agonist that is given once daily

j. the newest alpha$_1$ blocking drug indicated for BPH

TRUE OR FALSE

Indicate if the following statements are true or false.

_____ 1. Antiadrenergic drugs decrease or block the effects of sympathetic nerve stimulation, epinephrine, and adrenergic drugs.

_____ 2. Beta$_1$ blockers increase heart rate and blood pressure.

_____ 3. Chronic use of beta-blockers causes a potential risk for clients with cardiovascular disease.

_____ 4. Beta blockers may be used alone or with a diuretic.

_____ 5. Sotalol (Betapace) is a beta-blocker that exerts an antiarrhythmic effect by blocking potassium channels in cell membranes.

_____ 6. Beta blocker monotherapy is more effective in African Americans than in Whites.

_____ 7. Beta blockers increase myocardial contractility, cardiac output, heart rate, and blood pressure in clients with angina.

_____ 8. Alpha-adrenergic blocking agents are contraindicated in angina pectoris, myocardial infarction, heart failure, and stroke.

_____ 9. Propranolol (Inderal) is useful in the prevention of migraine headaches.

_____ 10. It is thought that in myocardial infarction, beta blockers prevent or decrease the incidence of catecholamine-induced dysrhythmias.

SHORT ANSWER

Answer the following:

1. Why are alpha$_1$ blocking agents used in BPH?

_____

_____

_____

2. List five effects on the body caused by beta-adrenergic blocking agents.

_____

_____

_____

3. What is the goal of antiadrenergic drug therapy?

_____

_____

_____

4. Describe the blocking effects of antiadrenergic drugs?

_____

_____

_____

5. What is the physiological action of alpha$_2$ agonist drugs?

_____

_____

_____

■ Applying Your Knowledge

Mrs. Viola Green, 36 years of age, was prescribed propranolol (Inderal) to treat a newly diagnosed mitral valve prolapse. She has been healthy except for multiple allergies and asthma. Ms. Green calls the consulting nurse to report that her asthma has deteriorated since she started on the Inderal, and she wonders if she might be allergic to this new medication. How would you advise her?

_____

_____

_____

_____

_____

■ Practicing for NCLEX

MULTIPLE-CHOICE QUESTIONS

1. The home health nurse is caring for a diabetic client who is taking metipranolol (OptiPranolol) for glaucoma. She will observe for
   a. weight gain
   c. headaches
   b. hypoglycemia
   d. hyperglycemia

2. Clients who have received beta blockers after a myocardial infarction should be monitored for
   a. hypertension and respiratory distress
   b. hypotension and heart failure
   c. hypertension and hyperthyroidism
   d. hyponatremia and kidney failure

3. A client has cirrhosis and is taking tamsulosin (Flomax) for BPH. The nurse anticipates that the client will receive
   a. a lower-than-usual dose of the drug
   b. twice as much as the usual dose
   c. a combination dose
   d. a normal adult dose

4. Early administration of a beta blocker after an acute myocardial infarction can decrease the occurrence of
   a. renal failure
   c. ventricular dysrhythmias
   b. heart block
   d. respiratory depression

5. Which of the following beta blockers is most frequently used in children?

   a. propranolol (Inderal)

   b. sotalol (Betapace)

   c. pindolol (Visken)

   d. nadolol (Corgard)

6. A client is starting methyldopa (Aldomet) for hypertension. The nurse would instruct the client to take the medication

   a. on an empty stomach

   b. first thing in the morning

   c. with food

   d. at bedtime

7. An expected outcome for a client with BPH who is on an alpha-blocking agent would be

   a. increased blood pressure

   b. improved urination

   c. decreased blood glucose

   d. decreased sex drive

8. An adverse effect of propranolol (Inderal) that should be discussed with a client is

   a. dizziness with activity

   b. excessive sleeping

   c. increased anxiety in crowds

   d. rapid weight loss

9. A client is taking methyldopa (Aldomet). The nurse would question her concerning her use of

   a. steroids   c. oral contraceptives

   b. vitamins   d. sedatives

10. A client is leaving the hospital on a beta blocker. He has had a history of angina in the past, but there are no major cardiac concerns at this time. Which of the following should the nurse tell him to report to his physician?

    a. a weight gain of more than 2 pounds a week

    b. excessive energy

    c. decreased appetite

    d. insomnia

ALTERNATE FORMAT QUESTIONS

1. Beta-adrenergic blocking agents prevent epinephrine and norepinephrine from occupying receptor sites on cell membranes. Indicate on the accompanying drawing the adrenergic blocking drug cells by marking an X on each cell.

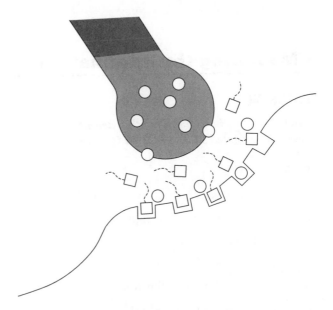

2. A client has started taking a beta-blocking agent for hypertension. The nurse should include which of the following when discussing general considerations of the drug with the client? (Select all that apply.)

   a. _____ Take the medication at the same time each day.

   b. _____ The drug may be taken with or without food.

   c. _____ Report weight loss of more than 2 pounds a week.

   d. _____ Count the pulse daily and report to the health care provider if it is under 50 for several days in a row.

   e. _____ Do not take over-the-counter medications without the health care provider's knowledge.

CHAPTER 19

Cholinergic Drugs

■ Mastering the Information

MATCHING

Match the terms in Column I with a definition, example, or related statement from Column II.

COLUMN I

1. _____ physostigmine salicylate (Antilirium)
2. _____ neostigmine (Prostigmin)
3. _____ donepezil (Aricept)
4. _____ tacrine (Cognex)
5. _____ edrophonium (Tensilon)
6. _____ rivastigmine (Exelon)
7. _____ pyaridostigmine (Mestinon)
8. _____ galantamine (Reminyl)
9. _____ bethanechol (Urecholine)
10. _____ ambenonium (Mytelase)

COLUMN II

a. used to treat urinary retention and postoperative abdominal distention caused by paralytic ileus

b. used to treat Alzheimer's disease; delays progression of the disease for up to 55 weeks

c. the only anticholinesterase capable of crossing the blood-brain barrier; has potential for serious adverse effects

d. a prototype anticholinesterase and antidote for tubocurarine

e. the maintenance drug of choice for clients with myasthenia gravis

f. has potential for hepatotoxicity

g. used to differentiate between myasthenic crises and cholinergic crisis

h. a long-acting, central anticholinesterase drug that may be taken with food to decrease gastrointestinal (GI) upset

i. used with myasthenia gravis clients who are on ventilators

j. the newest long-acting anticholinesterase drug approved for treatment of Alzheimer's disease

TRUE OR FALSE

Indicate if the following statements are true or false.

_____ 1. In a myasthenic crisis, more anticholinesterase drug is required.

_____ 2. All people who have myasthenia gravis require a caregiver to administer their medication.

_____ 3. Myasthenia gravis is an autoimmune disorder.

_____ 4. Cholinergic stimulation results in decreased peristalsis.

_____ 5. Acetylcholine stimulates cholinergic receptors to promote normal urination.

_____ 6. Direct-acting cholinergic drugs decrease respiratory secretions.

_____ 7. Cholinergic drugs are contraindicated in peptic ulcer disease.

_____ 8. Cholinergic drugs produce miosis.

_____ 9. The best route for administration of bethanechol (Urecholine) is the oral route.

_____ 10. Because of its duration of action, rivastigimine (Exelon) can be taken twice a day.

SHORT ANSWER

Answer the following:

1. List adverse reactions for cholinergic drugs.

   _____

   _____

   _____

2. Differentiate between anticholinesterase drugs that are classified as either reversible or irreversible inhibitors of acetylcholinesterase.

   _____

   _____

   _____

3. What is the antidote for cholinergic drugs?

   _____

   _____

   _____

4. List three indicators of therapeutic effects of cholinergic drugs when given for postoperative hypoperistalsis.

   _____

   _____

   _____

5. Describe the mechanism of indirect cholinergic drug action.

   _____

   _____

   _____

■ Applying Your Knowledge

Jill and her boyfriend ate mushrooms they picked while hiking. They were admitted to the hospital later that afternoon with acute cholinergic poisoning. Describe the signs and symptoms that they likely exhibited. What antidote do you think was given and why?

_____

_____

_____

_____

_____

■ Practicing for NCLEX

MULTIPLE-CHOICE QUESTIONS

1. A client has a confirmed diagnosis of myasthenia gravis and is started on pyridostigmine (Mestinon). The nurse is aware of the following adverse effect of pyridostigmine:

   a. dry mouth

   b. nausea

   c. constipation

   d. urinary retention

2. A 73-year-old man has been diagnosed with Alzheimer's disease and is started on tacrine (Cognex). Client instruction would include the following:

   a. Renal function should be monitored for 3 months.

   b. Cardiac enzymes should be monitored indefinitely.

   c. White blood cell count should be checked every month.

   d. Liver function should be monitored for at least 6 months.

3. It would be important to tell a client who has started on neostigmine (Prostigmin) that

   a. he should limit fluids for a few days

   b. the drug could cause constipation

   c. he will take an oral form of the drug once a day for 5 days

   d. the drug acts within 1 hour of administration

4. The client, age 69, has a diagnosis of myasthenia gravis. She is experiencing abdominal cramping, diarrhea, weakness, and difficulty breathing. The nurse suspects cholinergic crisis and prepares which of the following?

   a. atropine 0.6 mg for intravenous (IV) administration

   b. atropine 1.0 mg for intramuscular (IM) injection

   c. atropine 0.4 mg for subcutaneous (sc) injection

   d. atropine 0.5 mg for oral (PO) administration

5. A client's daughter calls the clinic and states that her mother, age 73, appears to be extremely dizzy. After questioning the daughter, you determine that the mother has Alzheimer's disease and is taking donepezil (Aricept). The nurse will be most concerned about the possibility of

   a. headaches during the morning

   b. orthostatic hypotension

   c. injury while ambulating

   d. nausea and vomiting

6. The nurse is working in a women's hospital where she is caring for a new mother who is experiencing postpartum urinary retention. Bethanechol (Urecholine) has been ordered. To prevent nausea and vomiting, the nurse will administer the medication

   a. before meals

   b. during meals

   c. after meals

   d. with a full glass of milk

7. A client has started taking a cholinergic agent for postoperative abdominal distention caused by a paralytic ileus. The nurse would be most concerned if the client was taking which of the following?

   a. corticosteroids

   b. aminoglycoside antibiotics

   c. antihyperglycemics

   d. antihistamines

8. A client has myasthenia gravis and is receiving pyridostigmine (Mestinon). She is complaining of nausea and vomiting. An appropriate response to her would be the following:

   a. "I'm so sorry, but that is to be expected."

   b. "Try taking your medication with food."

   c. "I'll talk to your doctor about decreasing the dose."

   d. "Make sure you get plenty fluids during the day."

9. Which of the following could determine if a client could or could not take tacrine (Cognex)?

   a. a bilirubin level greater than 3 mg/dL

   b. a blood glucose level less than 100 mg/dL

   c. a creatinine level greater than 0.6 mg/dL

   d. a serum amylase level less than 110 U/L

10. When neostigmine (Prostigmin) is given for postoperative distention, which of the following would indicate increased GI muscle tone and motility?

    a. absence of flatus through the rectum

    b. increased urination

    c. presence of bowel sounds

    d. absence of bowel movements

ALTERNATE FORMAT QUESTIONS

1. A 9-year-old child who weighs 66 pounds is to receive an IM injection of edrophonium (Tensilon). How many milligrams will the child receive?

2. A nurse is discussing adverse effects of a cholinergic drug with a client. Which of the following will be included in the discussion? (Select all that apply.)

   a. _____ decreased frequency of urination

   b. _____ dizziness

   c. _____ increased respiratory excretions

   d. _____ hypertension

   e. _____ drowsiness

CHAPTER 20

Anticholinergic Drugs

■ Mastering the Information

MATCHING

Match the terms in Column I with a definition, example, or related statement from Column II.

COLUMN I

1. _____ ipratropium (Atrovent)

2. _____ trihexyphenidyl (Trihexy)

3. _____ benztropine (Cogentin)

4. _____ atropine

5. _____ flavoxate (Urispas)

6. _____ oxybutynin (Ditropan)

7. _____ tolterodine (Detrol)

8. _____ belladonna tincture

9. _____ scopolamine

10. _____ homatropine hydrobromide (Homapin)

COLUMN II

a. used in the treatment of parkinsonism and extrapyramidal reactions

b. most often used for antispasmodic effects

c. antimuscarinic, anticholinergic agent used to treat urinary frequency and urgency

d. useful in treating rhinorrhea caused by allergies or the common cold

e. used in treatment of overactive bladder

f. useful in treating cystitis

g. used to treat acute dystonic reactions

h. a prototype anticholinergic drug

i. used for motion sickness

j. ocular effects do not last as long as with atropine

TRUE OR FALSE

Indicate if the following statements are true or false.

_____ 1. Anticholinergic drugs act by attaching to receptor sites on target organs innervated by the parasympathetic nervous system.

_____ 2. Anticholinergic drugs produce effects in the ears.

_____ 3. Atropine is the drug of choice for treatment of symptomatic sinus bradycardia.

_____ 4. Diverticulitis is treated with anticholinergic drugs.

_____ 5. Trospium chloride (Sanctura) is used to treat an overactive bladder.

_____ 6. When anticholinergic drugs are used in parkinsonism, large doses are given initially and are gradually decreased.

_____ 7. For gastrointestinal disorders, give most oral anticholinergic drugs immediately after meals and at bedtime.

_____ 8. Tachycardia may occur with a therapeutic dose of an anticholinergic drug because the drug blocks vagal action, which normally slows the heart.

_____ 9. Take tropsium chloride (Sanctura) on an empty stomach.

_____ 10. Anticholinergic drugs decrease respiratory tract secretions.

SHORT ANSWER

Answer the following:

1. List five specific effects of anticholinergic drugs on the body.

   _____

   _____

   _____

2. Why are anticholinergic drugs given prior to surgery?

   _____

   _____

   _____

3. List signs and symptoms of an anticholinergic overdose.

   _____

   _____

   _____

4. Why is the use of cyclopentolate (Cyclogyl) and tropicamide (Mydriacyl) guarded in children?

   _____

   _____

   _____

5. List five adverse effects associated with the use of anticholinergic drugs in the elderly.

   _____

   _____

   _____

■ Applying Your Knowledge

Scott Andrews is scheduled for a bronchoscopy. Before this procedure, you have been ordered to give him Valium and atropine. Explain the rationale of giving an anticholinergic agent as a preoperative medication.

_____

_____

_____

_____

_____

■ Practicing for NCLEX

MULTIPLE-CHOICE QUESTIONS

1. A client is being discharged from the hospital and will be taking dicyclomine (Bentyl) for irritable bowel syndrome. It will be important to instruct the client to
   a. take the medication on an empty stomach
   b. limit intake of red meat
   c. take the drug 30 minutes before meals and at bedtime
   d. avoid drinking caffeinated beverages

2. A nurse in a large eye clinic works in the client education department. He is working with a client who is receiving homatropine (Homapin). It is important to teach the client
   a. to stop the medication and call her physician
   b. that she cannot wear her contacts
   c. that she should rest her eyes two to three times a day
   d. that her visual acuity will decrease with use of the drug

3. Client teaching concerning anticholinergic drugs includes explaining to the client that which of the following can increase the effects of anticholinergic drugs?
   a. cardiac glycosides
   b. antihistamines
   c. anti-inflammatory agents
   d. oral hypoglycemics

4. A client is 68 years old and is planning a cruise to Mexico. In anticipation of "seasickness," he asks the nurse for medication to prevent this. The nurse suggests that his physician may prescribe a scopolamine patch but cautions him concerning

   a. heatstroke
   b. urinary retention
   c. decreased saliva
   d. diarrhea

5. Because of the adverse effect of urinary retention, anticholinergic drugs should not be prescribed for clients with

   a. chronic constipation
   b. increased blood pressure
   c. benign prostatic hypertrophy
   d. urinary tract infections

6. A client is planning a deep-sea fishing trip. He will take Transderm-V to protect him against motion sickness. The nurse instructs him that a dose will provide protection for

   a. 12 hours
   b. 24 hours
   c. 36 hours
   d. 72 hours

7. A client is receiving oxbutynin (Ditropan) for a neurogenic bladder. An expected outcome of this drug is

   a. decreased frequency of voiding
   b. increased frequency of voiding
   c. decreased bladder capacity
   d. increased urgency in voiding

8. A client has been taking glycopyrrolate (Robinul) for adjunctive management of peptic ulcer disease for 3 years. The nurse questions him concerning:

   a. chronic diarrhea
   b. dental hygiene practices
   c. headaches
   d. diet

9. Anticholinergic drugs are contraindicated in which of the following?

   a. diabetes mellitus
   b. rheumatoid arthritis
   c. hyperthyroidism
   d. bradycardia

10. A client has been taking propantheline bromide (Pro-Banthine) for irritable bowel syndrome. She tells the nurse that the medication is making her constipated and confused at times. She states that she has missed doses because the "pills just cost too much." An appropriate nursing diagnosis for the client would be

    a. Constipation Related to Decrease in Gastrointestinal Motility
    b. Disturbed Thought Process: Confusion
    c. Impaired Urinary Elimination: Decreased Bladder Tone and Urine Retention
    d. Noncompliance Related to Adverse Drug Effects and Cost of the Medication

ALTERNATE FORMAT QUESTIONS

1. A nurse is discussing the use of anticholinergic drugs with a client who is 79 years old. Which of the following adverse effects will the nurse include? (Select all that apply.)

   a. _____ constipation
   b. _____ confusion
   c. _____ frequent urination
   d. _____ blurred vision
   e. _____ hallucinations

2. The nurse is formulating nursing diagnoses for a client who is taking an anticholinergic drug. Rank the following in order of priority starting with No. 1.

   a. _____ Risk for Injury Related to Drug-induced Blurred Vision and Photophobia
   b. _____ Constipation Related to Slowed GI Function
   c. _____ Knowledge Deficit: Drug Effects and Accurate Usage
   d. _____ Disturbed Thought Processes: Confusion
   e. _____ Risk for Noncompliance Related to Adverse Drug Effects

CHAPTER 21

Physiology of the Endocrine System

■ Mastering the Information

MATCHING

Match the terms in column I with a definition, example, or related statement from Column II.

COLUMN I

1. _____ progestin
2. _____ cyclic adenosine monophosphate (cAMP)
3. _____ growth hormone
4. _____ mineralocorticoids
5. _____ hormones
6. _____ calcium
7. _____ secretin
8. _____ thyroxine
9. _____ vasopressin
10. _____ adrenocorticotropic hormone (ACTH)

COLUMN II

a. considered a second messenger
b. secreted by the anterior pituitary gland
c. help regulate electrolyte balance
d. a hormone secreted in relation to the 28-day menstrual cycle
e. regulates the metabolic rate of the body and influences growth and development
f. a second messenger for angiotensin II
g. an example of a posterior pituitary hormone
h. a hormone that is secreted in 24-hour cycles
i. a hormone produced by the gastrointestinal mucosa
j. substances that are synthesized and secreted into body fluids by one group of cells and have physiologic effects on other body cells

TRUE OR FALSE

Indicate if the following statements are true or false.

_____ 1. Hormones initiate cellular reactions and functions.

_____ 2. Steroid hormones are water soluble and can easily cross cell membranes.

_____ 3. Most hormones from endocrine glands are secreted into the bloodstream and act on distant organs.

_____ 4. A peptide is a protein-derived hormone.

_____ 5. Water-soluble hormones have a long duration of action.

_____ 6. Some hormones may act as a "first messenger" to cells.

_____ 7. Cyclic AMP is considered a first messenger for some hormones.

_____ 8. Malfunction of an endocrine organ is most often associated with hyposecretion or inappropriate secretion of its hormones.

_____ 9. Drugs are more often given for endocrine gland hypofunction than for hyperfunction.

_____ 10. Malfunction of endocrine organs can cause death.

SHORT ANSWER

Answer the following.

1. List the major organs of the endocrine system.

_____

_____

_____

2. List the body activities that are regulated by the endocrine system.

_____

_____

_____

3. Give an example of how one hormone can affect different body tissues.

_____

_____

_____

4. Describe two mechanisms that eliminate hormones from the body.

_____

_____

_____

5. Differentiate between physiologic use and pharmacologic use of hormonal drugs.

_____

_____

_____

■ Practicing for NCLEX

MULTIPLE-CHOICE QUESTIONS

1. The hormone that stimulates bone marrow to produce red blood cells is
   a. secretin
   b. glucagon
   c. cholecystokinin
   d. erythropoietin

2. Which of the following best describes hormones given for physiologic effects?
   a. small doses of hormones given as a replacement or substitute for the amount of hormone normally secreted
   b. the same amount of hormone given that would normally be secreted
   c. hormones given that have more potent and prolonged effects than naturally occurring hormones
   d. large doses of hormones given for greater effects than the amount normally secreted

3. The connection between the nervous system and the endocrine system is the
   a. thyroid gland
   b. hypothalamus
   c. pancreas
   d. pituitary gland

4. An example of a hormone that affects specific target tissue is
   a. prolactin
   b. peptides
   c. corticotropin
   d. secretin

5. Which of the following is not an effect of ovarian estrogen?
   a. promotion of ovarian follicle maturation
   b. stimulation of the endometrial lining of the uterus to promote its growth and cyclic changes
   c. promotion of uterine contractions during labor
   d. stimulation of breast tissue to promote growth of milk ducts

6. Which of the following statements best describes water-soluble, protein-derived hormones?
   a. have longer duration of action and are bound to plasma proteins
   b. have a short duration of action and are inactivated by enzymes in the liver and kidneys
   c. are conjugated in the liver to inactive forms and excreted in bile or urine
   d. are inactivated by enzymes at receptor sites on target cells

7. Calmodulin is an intracellular regulatory protein that activates protein kinases when bound to
   a. calcium
   b. phospholipids
   c. cAMP
   d. adenyl cyclase

8. Which of the following hormone is secreted in a 24-hour cycle?
   a. epinephrine
   b. growth hormone
   c. progestin
   d. estrogen

9. Receptors in target organs for hormones may be increased or decreased in response to
   a. a hormone binding to receptors
   b. changes in the secretions produced by cells
   c. malfunction of the endocrine organ involved
   d. chronic exposure to abnormal levels of hormones

10. Hypofunction of an endocrine gland can result from
    a. inappropriate response of intracellular metabolic processes
    b. excessive stimulation of the gland
    c. enlargement of the gland
    d. a hormone-producing tumor

ALTERNATE FORMAT QUESTIONS

1. Which of the following body activities are influenced by the endocrine system? (Select all that apply.)
    a. _____ metabolism of nutrients and water
    b. _____ reproduction
    c. _____ growth and development
    d. _____ adaptation to changes in internal and external environments

2. Which of the following are examples of anterior pituitary hormones? (Select all that apply.)
    a. _____ prolactin
    b. _____ follicle-stimulating hormone
    c. _____ somatotropin
    d. _____ oxytocin
    e. _____ cortisol
    f. _____ corticotropin

CHAPTER 22

Hypothalamic and Pituitary Hormones

■ Mastering the Information

MATCH THE FOLLOWING

Match the terms in column I with a definition, example, or related statement from Column II.

COLUMN I

1. _____ corticotropin-releasing hormone

2. _____ hypophyseal stalk

3. _____ anterior pituitary

4. _____ serotonin

5. _____ thyrotropin-releasing hormone

6. _____ somatotropin

7. _____ follicle-stimulating hormone

8. _____ antidiuretic hormone

9. _____ posterior pituitary

10. _____ Cushing's disease

COLUMN II

a. stores and releases hormones synthesized in the hypothalamus

b. neurotransmitters that stimulate the secretion of corticotropin-releasing hormones

c. anatomically connects the hypothalamus and pituitary gland

d. used in diagnostic tests of pituitary function and hyperthyroidism

e. stimulates functions of sex glands

f. stimulates growth of body tissues

g. released in response to stress or threatening stimuli

h. a disorder characterized by excessive cortisol

i. regulates water balance in the body

j. composed of glandular cells that synthesize and secrete hormones

TRUE OR FALSE

Indicate if the following statements are true or false.

_____ 1. Corticotropin-releasing hormone is secreted during the night.

_____ 2. There are many uses for hypothalamic and pituitary hormones.

_____ 3. Vasopressin enables corticotropin-releasing hormone to stimulate adrenocorticotropic hormone (ACTH) secretion.

_____ 4. Most all hormones are administered or taken orally.

_____ 5. Somatostatin inhibits the release of the growth hormone.

_____ 6. Norepinephrine stimulates secretion of corticotropin-releasing hormone.

_____ 7. Hypothalamic hormones are rarely used in most clinical settings.

_____ 8. The growth hormone-releasing hormone is found only in the hypothalamus.

_____ 9. Elevated levels of glucocorticoids decrease or prevent the ability of corticotropin-releasing hormone to stimulate ACTH secretion.

_____ 10. Pituitary hormones are given to replace or supplement naturally occurring hormones.

SHORT ANSWER

Answer the following.

1. Describe an inappropriate use of growth hormone.

_____

_____

_____

2. How is thyrotropin secretion controlled?

_____

_____

_____

3. What is the significance of interstitial cell-stimulating hormone?

_____

_____

_____

4. List adverse effects of high doses or chronic use of growth hormone.

_____

_____

_____

5. Which two hormones produced by the anterior pituitary gland act directly on their target tissues?

_____

_____

_____

■ Applying Your Knowledge

After surgery for a brain tumor, Mr. Willis has excessive, dilute urine output (8000 mL/24 h). The physician diagnoses deficient antidiuretic hormone production and prescribes lypressin (Diapid), a synthetic vasopressin. What assessment data will indicate that this medication is effective?

_____

_____

_____

_____

_____

■ Practicing for NCLEX

MULTIPLE-CHOICE QUESTIONS

1. A client, age 7, has a deficiency of endogenous growth hormone. She is started on 0.03 mg/kg of somatropin (Humatrope) by intramuscular (IM) injection, three times a week. Before the physician administers the first injection, a priority action for the nurse will be to check documentation for which of the following?

   a. evidence of open bone epiphyses

   b. daily urine output

   c. daily fluid input

   d. understanding of drug therapy

2. In teaching parents about growth hormone therapy for their child, a priority instruction that the nurse will include is

   a. reporting the type of exercise the child participates in weekly

   b. monitoring the child's height and weight regularly

   c. recording the food intake daily

   d. administering the medication weekly

3. A mother whose child is taking growth hormone therapy reports that her child is complaining of localized muscle pain. The nurse's response should be as follows:

   a. "Adverse effects are very common."

   b. "The muscle pain will go away. Don't worry about it."

   c. "You may give her Tylenol. If she still experiences pain, let me know."

   d. "You will need to limit her physical activity."

4. A client is starting fertility drug therapy. She asks the nurse how long will it take for her to get pregnant. The nurse's best response should be

   a. "That is hard to say. It could take years for you to become pregnant."

   b. "Typically pregnancy may occur within 4–6 weeks of therapy."

   c. "You should discuss that with your physician."

   d. "Some women may never get pregnant."

5. A client has diabetes insipidus and is receiving desmopressin (DDAVP). During 9 P.M. rounds, the nurse notices that he is confused and lethargic. Upon questioning him, the nurse determines that he has a headache and is nauseated. The nurse suspects he is experiencing

    a. water intoxication

    b. depression

    c. dehydration

    d. an allergic reaction

6. A nurse is working in the postpartum unit. Three of her clients are receiving oxytocin (Pitocin) to control postpartum bleeding. In observing for therapeutic effects in each client, the nurse will expect to find

    a. decreased vaginal bleeding and a firm uterine fundus

    b. intense uterine contractions and decreased vaginal bleeding

    c. a soft, round uterus and moderate vaginal bleeding

    d. cessation of vaginal bleeding and a large, soft uterine fundus

7. A client is taking octreotide (Sandostatin). Which of the following is a common adverse effect of the drug?

    a. nausea

    b. symptoms of gallstones

    c. hypoglycemia

    d. constipation

8. A client has been taking choriogonadotropin alfa (Ovidrel) for several months. Client feelings of grief, disappointment, and failure are evident to the nurse. Which of the following is the most appropriate nursing diagnosis for this client?

    a. Knowledge Deficit: Drug Effects

    b. Anxiety Related to Drug Administration

    c. Ineffective Coping Related to Frustration with Difficulty with Conception

    d. Risk for Injury: Adverse Drug Effects

9. Which of the following would indicate that vasopressin is producing its therapeutic effect in a client diagnosed with diabetes insipidus?

    a. increased signs of dehydration

    b. decreased urine output

    c. decreased urine specific gravity

    d. increased thirst

10. When assessing a client who is taking vasopressin (Pitressin), the nurse will report which of the following?

    a. increased temperature

    b. decreased blood pressure

    c. thirst

    d. sore throat

ALTERNATE FORMAT QUESTIONS

1. Place an X on the area where the anterior pituitary gland is located.

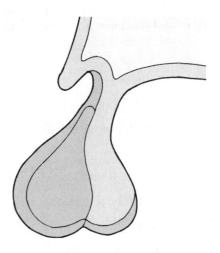

2. A client is receiving a menotropin for infertility. In discussing this drug therapy with the client, the nurse will include which of the following adverse effects? (Select all that apply.)

    a. _____ weight loss

    b. _____ hypotension

    c. _____ abdominal discomfort

    d. _____ oliguria

    e. _____ ascites

CHAPTER 23

Corticosteroids

■ Mastering the Information

MATCH THE FOLLOWING

Match the terms in column I with a definition, example, or related statement from Column II.

COLUMN I

1. _____ dexamethasone

2. _____ budesonide (Entocort EC)

3. _____ methylprednisolone (Medrol)

4. _____ glucocortocoids

5. _____ prednisolone (Delta-Cortef)

6. _____ hydrocortisone (Hydrocortone)

7. _____ aldosterone

8. _____ mometasone (Nasonex)

9. _____ fluticasone (Flonase)

10. _____ prednisone (Deltasone)

COLUMN II

a. a prototype of corticosteroid drugs

b. a corticosteroid given by nasal inhalation that is useful in respiratory disorders

c. used in clients with liver disease

d. the main mineralocorticoid

e. important in metabolic, inflammatory, and immune processes

f. the corticosteroid of choice for cerebral edema associated with head injury or brain tumors

g. a new drug for Crohn's disease given orally

h. causes less growth inhibition when given to children with asthma than beclomethasone (Vanceril)

i. the glucocorticord of choice in nonendocrine disorders

j. a corticosteroid effective in acute spinal cord injury

TRUE OR FALSE

Indicate if the following statements are true or false.

_____ 1. Excessive corticosteroid secretion damages body tissues.

_____ 2. Corticosteroids are secreted directly into the bloodstream.

_____ 3. High plasma levels of cortisol cause excessive corticotropin secretion.

_____ 4. Only a few adrenal corticosteroids are available as drug preparations.

_____ 5. Hydrocortisone and cortisone are most often the drugs of choice for adrenocortical insufficiency.

_____ 6. Corticosteroid therapy for children is calculated according to weight.

_____ 7. During periods of stress, corticosteroid therapy must be increased.

_____ 8. Corticosteroids should be given locally rather than systemically to prevent systemic toxicity.

_____ 9. Parenteral administration of corticosteroids is indicated for all clients.

_____ 10. The body's normal response to critical illness is decreased secretion of cortisol.

SHORT ANSWER

Answer the following.

1. Explain the process that has to occur before corticosteroids are secreted.

_____

_____

_____

2. Why is the use of corticosteroids in children a major concern?

_____

_____

_____

3. Discuss how dietary changes can be helpful in reducing some adverse effects of corticosteroid therapy.

_____

_____

_____

4. Give one example of a corticosteroid whose duration of action lasts 48 hours.

_____

_____

_____

5. Describe alternate-day therapy.

_____

_____

_____

■ Applying Your Knowledge

Kim Wilson, 62 years of age, was admitted for elective abdominal surgery. Her medication history reveals daily use of prednisone. Individualize a postoperative plan for Kim considering her chronic steroid use.

_____

_____

_____

_____

_____

_____

_____

■ Practicing for NCLEX

MULTIPLE-CHOICE QUESTIONS

1. A client is an 81-year-old male who has been on long-term prednisone therapy for rheumatoid arthritis. During the nurse's assessment of him, which of the following signs might she find related to chronic steroid use?

   a. poor vision

   b. thin, easily injured skin

   c. dry, flaky skin

   d. decreased hearing

2. Which of the following would be the most appropriate nursing diagnosis for a client taking steroids?

   a. Imbalanced Nutrition: Less Than Body Requirements

   b. Deficient Fluid Volume

   c. Risk for Infection

   d. Ineffective Breathing Pattern

3. A client has been on an oral corticosteroid for 3 weeks. He tells the nurse that he has missed several doses. An appropriate response to him would be the following:

   a. "Don't worry about it. It will not affect the intended outcome."

   b. "Alteration in administration of the drug can cause complications."

   c. "Next time you miss a dose, take an extra tablet with the next dose."

   d. "You really should be more careful in taking your medication."

4. A client has a diagnosis of adrenocortical insufficiency and is steroid dependent. She has just lost her husband in a motor vehicle accident. During this time of stress, her medication will be

   a. the same   c. increased

   b. decreased   d. discontinued

5. A client is taking flunisolide (Nasalide) for allergic rhinitis. On her recent visit to the allergy clinic, she tells the nurse that she has gained 20 pounds. The nurse will assess for

   a. increased activity   c. sodium intake

   b. potassium intake   d. use of alcohol

6. The nurse will encourage the client to take which of the following medications at a different time rather than with the prescribed corticosteroid?

 a. ampicillin   c. Advil

 b. Mylanta   d. Dramamine

7. A client has Addison's disease and is taking 50 mg of cortisone (Cortone) daily PO (orally). A priority expected outcome of cortisone therapy for the client would be

 a. increased energy level

 b. weight gain

 c. increase in blood pressure

 d. normal bowel function

8. A client, age 53, has severe asthma. She has taken prednisone (Deltasone) for years. Recently, her physician has started her on alternate-day therapy. She tells the nurse she would rather take her medication every day. Which of the following would be the nurse's best response?

 a. "This schedule will be more convenient for you."

 b. "This schedule will enable you to lose weight."

 c. "This schedule will decrease the cost of your medication."

 d. "This schedule allows rest periods so that adverse effects are decreased but the anti-inflammatory effects continue."

9. A client is taking 0.1 mg of fludrocortisone (Florinef) daily PO for chronic adrenocortical insufficiency. Client teaching for him will always include

 a. taking his medication on an empty stomach

 b. promoting a diet high in potassium

 c. discouraging activity

 d. stopping the medication if drowsiness occurs

10. A client is admitted to the emergency room in acute respiratory distress related to severe asthma. Which of the following conditions should the nurse assess for prior to administering methylprednisolone sodium succinate (Solu-Medrol)?

 a. peptic ulcer disease

 b. urinary retention

 c. irritable bowel syndrome

 d. sinus infection

ALTERNATE FORMAT QUESTIONS

1. A nurse is instructing a client on the use of an oral inhalation corticosteroid. Arrange the following instructions in order of usage. (Number one should be the first action.)

 a. _____ Hold breath for 10 seconds or as long as possible.

 b. _____ Exhale completely.

 c. _____ Rinse mouthpiece at least once per day.

 d. _____ Shake canister thoroughly.

 e. _____ Activate canister while taking a slow, deep breath.

 f. _____ Place canister between lips or outside lips.

 g. _____ Wait at least 1 minute before taking additional inhalations.

 h. _____ Rinse mouth after inhalations to decrease the incidence of oral thrush.

2. A client is to receive 0.5 mg/kg of methylprednisolone sodium succinate (Solu-Medrol) IM every 24 hours. The client weighs 25 pounds. How many milligrams will the client receive in a 24-hour period?

CHAPTER 24

Thyroid and Antithyroid Drugs

■ Mastering the Information

MATCHING

Match the terms in column I with a definition, example, or related statement from Column II.

COLUMN I

1. _____ levothyroxine (Synthroid)
2. _____ radioactive iodine
3. _____ propylthiouracil (PTU)
4. _____ liothyronine (Cytomel)
5. _____ methimazole (Tapazole)
6. _____ Lugol's solution
7. _____ sodium iodide I^{131} (Iodotope)
8. _____ propranolol (Inderal)
9. _____ liotrix (Thyrolar)
10. _____ saturated solution of potassium iodide

COLUMN II

a. prototype of the thioamide antithyroid drugs
b. used to treat short-term hyperthyroidism and as an expectorant
c. used to treat symptoms of hyperthyroidism involving stimulation of the sympathetic nervous system
d. a synthetic preparation of T$_3$ that requires frequent administration if used for long-term treatment of hypothyroidism
e. resembles the composition of natural thyroid hormone
f. the drug of choice for long-term treatment of hypothyroidism
g. used to treat thyroid cancer
h. similar to propylthiouracil (PTU); is well absorbed and reaches peak plasma levels quickly
i. used to treat thyrotoxic crisis
j. a safe, effective, inexpensive, and convenient treatment of hyperthyroidism

TRUE OR FALSE

Indicate if the following statements are true or false.

_____ 1. Thyroxine is more potent than triiodothyronine.

_____ 2. The thyroid gland extracts iodine from the circulating blood.

_____ 3. The thyroid-stimulating hormone (TSH) stimulates the thyroid gland to release thyroid hormones into circulation.

_____ 4. Thyroid hormones influence very few cells in the body.

_____ 5. Hypothyroidism and hyperthyroidism produce opposing effects on the body.

_____ 6. Hypothyroidism is characterized by excessive secretion of thyroid hormone.

_____ 7. Simple goiter is the most common thyroid disease.

_____ 8. Iodine preparations and thioamide antithyroid drugs are contraindicated in pregnancy.

_____ 9. Taking levothyroxine on an empty stomach decreases absorption of the drug.

_____ 10. Thyroid replacement therapy in clients with hypothyroidism is lifelong.

SHORT ANSWER

Answer the following:

1. List five drugs that decrease the effects of thyroid hormones.

_____

_____

_____

2. What is the goal of treatment with levothyroxine?

_____

_____

_____

3. Why is an iodine preparation given in a thyroid disorder?

_____

_____

_____

4. Why is replacement therapy required in children with hypothyroidism?

_____

_____

_____

5. Why is radioactive iodine not used in children unless absolutely necessary?

_____

_____

_____

■ Applying Your Knowledge

Mrs. Sanchez has been taking Synthroid for approximately 2 years. She switched to a generic brand of levothyroxine 2 months ago. When she returns to the clinic, she is complaining of fatigue, weight gain, dry skin, and cold intolerance. What do you suggest?

_____

_____

_____

_____

_____

_____

_____

■ Practicing for NCLEX

MULTIPLE-CHOICE QUESTIONS

1. Which of the following is an initial indication that a client has subclinical hyperthyroidism?
   a. serum TSH of 5.2 microunits/L
   b. serum TSH of 0.1 microunits/L
   c. serum TSH of 0.5 microunits/L
   d. serum TSH of 3 microunits/L

2. A client has been diagnosed with hyperthyroidism. The nurse expects that an appropriate nursing diagnosis related to her weight would be
   a. Altered Nutrition: Less Than Body Requirements
   b. Altered Nutrition: More Than Body Requirements
   c. Swallowing: Impaired
   d. Oral Mucous Membranes: Altered

3. An expected outcome for a client who has been on thyroid medication would be
   a. decreased pulse rate
   b. increased blood pressure
   c. increased energy and activity levels
   d. decreased appetite

4. A client has been recently started on levothyroxine (Synthroid). Which of the following would be included in the teaching plan?
   a. Over-the-counter drugs may be taken.
   b. The drug can be stopped within 1 year.
   c. Do not switch from a brand name to a generic form.
   d. Caffeine beverages do not have to be limited.

5. A client is taking levothyroxine (Levothroid) and explains to the nurse that occasionally he has to take an antacid for heartburn. The nurse's response to him should be as follows:
   a. "Take the two medications together."
   b. "You should not take an antacid when taking Levothroid."
   c. "Take your thyroid medication 2 hours before you take the antacid."
   d. "Skip the Levothroid dose when you take the antacid."

6. A client, age 28, has primary hypothyroidism and is taking levothyroxine (Synthroid). She asks the nurse how long she will have to take the medication. The nurse's best response to her would be

a. "Just for a few weeks."

b. "You will take the medication for 1 year, and then your physician will taper your dose for a few months."

c. "Usually, people with hypothyroidism will need to take their medication for the rest of their lives."

d. "Don't worry about that now. We will discuss it later."

7. A client is 25 years old and is on thyroid hormone replacement. She is taking an oral contraceptive. The nurse suspects that her thyroid medication will need to be

a. increased   c. kept the same

b. decreased   d. discontinued

8. Propranolol (Inderal) is given to a client who has been diagnosed with hyperthyroidism. This drug

a. enhances the effects of PTU

b. controls symptoms resulting from excessive stimulation of the sympathetic nervous system

c. converts levothyroxine hormone to liothyronine (T_3)

d. replaces the thyroid hormone from an exogenous source

9. A client has been placed on PTU. The nurse's assessment data reveal that he is on medications for high blood pressure and high cholesterol. Because of the change in the rate of body metabolism from the PTU, the nurse will expect the physician to

a. discontinue the other medications

b. increase the dosage of blood pressure medication

c. keep the dosages of the other two medications the same

d. reduce the dosage of the blood pressure and cholesterol medication

10. A client is taking PTU for hyperthyroidism. Which of the following instructions should be given to him concerning administration of this medication?

a. Take the medication every 8 hours around the clock.

b. Take the medication once daily.

c. If a dose is missed, double the next dose.

d. Take the daily dose at bedtime.

ALTERNATE FORMAT QUESTIONS

1. A nurse discusses thyroid drug therapy with her client. Which of the following outcomes should the client expect? (Select all that apply.)

a. _____ increased constipation

b. _____ increased appetite

c. _____ increased energy

d. _____ increased alertness

e. _____ decreased pulse rate

f. _____ decreased temperature

2. A client is taking an antithyroid. Within 1 to 2 weeks the client should experience which of the following? (Select all that apply.)

a. _____ decreased nervousness

b. _____ decreased tremors

c. _____ improved ability to sleep and rest

d. _____ increased weight gain

e. _____ decreased pulse rate

CHAPTER 25

Hormones that Regulate Calcium and Bone Metabolism

■ Mastering the Information

MATCHING

Match the terms in column I with a definition, example, or related statement from Column II.

COLUMN I

1. _____ raloxifene (Evista)
2. _____ vitamin D
3. _____ zoledronate (Zometa)
4. _____ calcium gluconate
5. _____ teriparatide (Forteo)
6. _____ etidronate (Didronel)
7. _____ calcium carbonate
8. _____ alendronate (Fosamax)
9. _____ sodium chloride
10. _____ calcitonin

COLUMN II

a. used in the treatment of osteoporosis by increasing the number of osteoblasts

b. used to treat hypercalcemia resulting from a malignancy

c. a fat-soluble vitamin that functions as a hormone and is important in calcium and bone metabolism

d. a selective estrogen receptor modulator used for postmenopausal osteoporosis

e. given for asymptomatic, less severe, or chronic hypocalcemia

f. a normal saline injection, which is the treatment of choice for hypercalcemia

g. a bisphosphonate used to treat osteoporosis and Paget's disease

h. a hormone whose secretion is controlled by the concentration of ionized calcium in the blood flowing through the thyroid gland

i. a bisphosphonate that inhibits bone mineralization and may cause osteomalacia

j. given for acute, symptomatic hypocalcemia

TRUE OR FALSE

Indicate if the following statements are true or false.

_____ 1. One 8-oz glass of milk daily will furnish approximately half of the daily calcium requirement.

_____ 2. Oral calcium preparations increase the effects of oral tetracycline by combining with the antibiotic and preventing its absorption.

_____ 3. Hypocalcemia is common in children.

_____ 4. Teriparatide (Forteo) can safely be given to clients who have renal impairment.

_____ 5. Calcitonin should be given or taken at bedtime.

_____ 6. The main action of vitamin D is to increase serum calcium levels by increasing intestinal absorption of calcium and mobilizing calcium from bone.

_____ 7. Bisphosphonates can affect liver function.

_____ 8. Most diets for all ages are thought to be deficient in calcium.

_____ 9. Bisphosphonate must be taken with food.

_____ 10. When the serum level of ionized calcium is increased in the thyroid gland, secretion of calcitonin is decreased.

SHORT ANSWER

Answer the following.

1. List five calcium and bone disorders.

   _____

   _____

   _____

2. Describe the pharmacokinetics of bisphosphonates.

   _____

   _____

   _____

3. How does calcitonin lower serum calcium levels?

   _____

   _____

   _____

4. List five functions of calcium.

   _____

   _____

   _____

5. Why is phosphorus one of the most important elements in normal body function?

   _____

   _____

   _____

■ Applying Your Knowledge

Ms. Sadie Evans had a subtotal thyroidectomy 2 days ago. When you perform your morning assessment, she complains of tingling in her fingers. What additional data should be collected at this time?

_____

_____

_____

_____

_____

_____

_____

_____

_____

■ Practicing for NCLEX

MULTIPLE-CHOICE QUESTIONS

1. A client is taking calcitriol (Rocaltrol) and is complaining of headaches, nausea, drowsiness, and muscle weakness. The nurse suspects that she has

   a. hypocalcemia   c. hypokalemia

   b. hypercalcemia   d. hyperkalemia

2. A client complains that having to sit in an upright position after taking alendronate (Fosamax) is inconvenient. The nurse's explanation to her would include that the upright position

   a. is necessary for proper absorption of the drug

   b. is not necessary

   c. allows for a faster metabolism and excretion of the drug

   d. helps prevent esophageal irritation and stomach upset

3. A client in the emergency room is being treated for hypercalcemia. The physician orders an injection of calcitonin (Calcimar). The nurse is aware that the serum calcium level should decrease in

   a. 30 minutes   c. 2 hours

   b. 1 hour   d. 3 hours

4. Which of the following should be included when instructing a client how to take tetracycline and calcium preparations?

   a. Take the drugs at the same time.

   b. Take the drugs 2 to 3 hours apart.

   c. Do not take calcium supplements when taking tetracycline.

   d. Take the tetracycline 30 minutes after taking the calcium supplement.

5. During an initial assessment of a client, a nurse discovers that she is taking digoxin and a calcium supplement. The nurse should assess for signs of

   a. anemia

   b. digitalis toxicity

   c. hyponatremia

   d. Paget's disease

6. Which of the following drugs used to treat osteoporosis increases bone formation?

   a. vitamin D

   b. raloxifene (Evista)

   c. teriparatide (Forteo)

   d. alendronate (Fosamax)

7. A client has renal impairment and is being treated for osteomalacia. Which of the following drugs is she most likely taking?

   a. calcitriol (Rocaltrol)

   b. alendronate (Fosamax)

   c. risedronate (Actonel)

   d. zoledronate (Zometa)

8. A client is to start treatment for osteoporosis. The nurse learns that she has cirrhosis of the liver. The nurse suspects that she will take

   a. dihydrotachysterol (Hytakerol)

   b. paricalcitol (Zemplar)

   c. calcitriol (Rocaltrol)

   d. teriparatide (Forteo)

9. Hypocalcemia is the diagnosis for a client. Prior to drug therapy, the nurse would expect his serum calcium level to be

   a. below 8.5 mg/dL

   b. between 5.2 and 10 mg/dL

   c. above 12 mg/dL

   d. above 20 mg/dL

10. Which of the following would be an expected outcome for a client taking alendronate (Fosamax) for osteoporosis?

    a. decreased bone mass density

    b. presence of Chvostek's sign

    c. absence of bone fractures

    d. decreased serum calcium level

ALTERNATE FORMAT QUESTIONS

1. Which of the following outcomes would a nurse include when discussing therapeutic effects with a client who is taking a calcium preparation? (Select all that apply.)

   a. _____ serum calcium level between 8.5 and 10.5 mg/dL

   b. _____ absence of Trousseau's sign

   c. _____ presence of Chvostek's sign

   d. _____ increased paresthesias

   e. _____ decrease in muscle spasms

2. A client is taking calcitonin. Which of the following adverse effects will be included in the nurse's teaching plan? (Select all that apply.)

   a. _____ itching and redness at the site of injection

   b. _____ diarrhea

   c. _____ nausea and vomiting

   d. _____ constipation

   e. _____ headache

CHAPTER 26

Antidiabetic Drugs

■ Mastering the Information

MATCHING

Match the terms in Column I with a definition, example, or related statement from Column II.

COLUMN I

1. _____ Apidra

2. _____ DiaBeta

3. _____ insulin

4. _____ metformin (Glucophage)

5. _____ nateglinide (Starlix)

6. _____ Humalog

7. _____ glucosamine

8. _____ acarbose (Precose)

9. _____ pioglitazone (Actos)

10. _____ NovoLog

COLUMN II

a. the newest short-acting insulin analog

b. an alpha-glucosidase inhibitor that delays digestion of carbohydrate foods when acarbose and food are present in the gastrointestinal (GI) tract at the same time

c. an oral antidiabetic agent used with caution in clients at risk of developing congestive heart failure

d. identical to human insulin except for the reversal of two amino acids

e. lowers blood glucose levels by increasing glucose uptake by body cells and by decreasing glucose production in the liver

f. a second-generation sulfonylurea, which is an oral hypoglycemic agent

g. a nonsulfonylurea that lowers blood sugar by stimulating pancreatic secretion of insulin

h. an insulin analog that has a more rapid onset and shorter duration of action than Humalog

i. referred to as an antihyperglycemic rather than a hypoglycemic agent because it does not cause hypoglycemia

j. an herbal/dietary supplement that may cause impaired beta-cell function and insulin secretion similar to that observed in humans with type 2 diabetes

TRUE OR FALSE

Indicate if the following statements are true or false.

_____ 1. Insulin is never given to clients with type 2 diabetes.

_____ 2. Insulin can be given orally.

_____ 3. Insulin can be given with all types of oral antidiabetic drugs.

_____ 4. There are higher levels of insulin in clients with hepatic impairment because less insulin is metabolized.

_____ 5. Insulin is absorbed faster from the upper arm than the abdomen.

_____ 6. Symptoms of hypoglycemia are excess thirst, hunger, and increased urine output.

_____ 7. One-half of the insulin that is secreted reaches systemic circulation.

_____ 8. Epinephrine raises blood glucose levels, which can stimulate insulin secretion.

_____ 9. Glucosuria appears when the blood glucose level is 4 times the normal value.

_____ 10. Omitting or decreasing insulin dosage may lead to ketoacidosis.

SHORT ANSWER

Answer the following.

1. Discuss the three mechanisms that facilitate insulin to lower blood glucose levels.

_____

_____

_____

2. Why is oral glucose more effective in the stimulation of insulin secretion than intravenous glucose?

_____

_____

_____

3. Differentiate between type 1 and type 2 diabetes.

_____

_____

_____

4. What is a contraindication to the use of insulin?

_____

_____

_____

5. What are the goals of treatment for clients needing antidiabetic drugs?

_____

_____

_____

■ Applying Your Knowledge

Your patient is managing his diabetes with the following split-dose insulin regimen:

Thirty-two units of NPH insulin before breakfast (8 A.M.)

Ten units of NPH insulin before dinner (6 P.M.)

Using information in "Drugs at a Glance: Insulins" in the textbook, calculate when this patient is most likely to experience hypoglycemia.

_____

_____

_____

_____

_____

_____

_____

■ Practicing for NCLEX

MULTIPLE-CHOICE QUESTIONS

1. A nurse is teaching a mother of a newly diagnosed diabetic child how to assess for hypoglycemia. Which of the following signs will the nurse include?
   a. increased urine output
   b. increased hunger
   c. shakiness/nervousness
   d. excessive thirst

2. Before a client is started on metformin (Glucophage), he should be assessed for which of the following?
   a. renal disease   c. osteoporosis
   b. anemia   d. hypertension

3. A client has been controlled on 30 U of NPH insulin for several years. Recently, he was place on prednisone for rheumatoid arthritis. The nurse suspects that, because of the prednisone therapy, the NPH dosage may
   a. stay the same
   b. need to be increased
   c. be discontinued for a short period
   d. need to be decreased

4. A client who takes NPH insulin asks a nurse about the use of an insulin pump. In considering her question, the nurse is aware that which of the following insulin products is used in a pump?

    a. NPH
    b. Ultralente
    c. Lente
    d. regular

5. A 38-year-old client is receiving 30 U of NPH insulin and 8 U of regular insulin at 7:30 A.M. She is receiving 25 U of NPH insulin and 5 U of regular insulin at 3:30 P.M. Her blood glucose levels have been elevated by 10:30 A.M. for the last several days. What adjustments should be made in her insulin therapy?

    a. Both morning doses of NPH and regular insulin should be increased.
    b. The morning dose of regular insulin should be increased.
    c. Both afternoon doses should be increased.
    d. The afternoon NPH dose should be increased.

6. A client receives 25 units of NPH insulin at 8 A.M. At what time of day should the nurse be alert for a potential hypoglycemic reaction?

    a. after breakfast
    b. before breakfast
    c. at bedtime
    d. before dinner (evening meal)

7. A client has been on metformin (Glucophage) for 5 years. He is scheduled for major surgery in 2 weeks. The nurse informs him that

    a. his metformin dose will increase
    b. he will be taken off of metformin and placed on insulin therapy during surgery and for some time after surgery
    c. he will take metformin as prescribed during and after surgery
    d. he will not need to take therapy for diabetes during or after surgery

8. A client will be taking insulin lispro (Humalog). What instructions do you need to give to him concerning the administration of this drug?

    a. take 1 hour before meals
    b. take at bedtime only
    c. take 1½ hours after meals
    d. take 15 minutes prior to a meal

9. A client has just been diagnosed with type 1 diabetes and is placed on regular and NPH insulin. When teaching her about self-administration of her medication, the nurse will most likely advise her to

    a. administer medications separately in two syringes
    b. administer both medications in one syringe, drawing up the regular insulin first
    c. administer the regular insulin first, and then check the blood sugar to determine whether NPH is needed
    d. administer both medications together, drawing up the NPH insulin first

10. Which of the following statements from a client indicates a need for further education regarding diabetes therapy?

    a. "I will need more insulin on the days I take my aerobics class."
    b. "I wear a medical alert bracelet at all times, stating that I am diabetic."
    c. "I get a family member to check my syringe and make sure I have drawn up the correct dose of insulin."
    d. "I know that I should eat my meals at regularly scheduled times."

ALTERNATE FORMAT QUESTIONS

1. Select all that apply concerning use of oral antidiabetic drugs.

    a. _____ Take pioglitazone (Actos) and rosiglitazone (Avandia) without regard to meals.
    b. _____ Take metformin (Glucophage XR) with the breakfast meal.
    c. _____ Take acarbose (Precose) after each meal.
    d. _____ Take glipizide (Glucotrol) about 30 minutes before meals.
    e. _____ If a meal is skipped, the dose of repaglinide (Prandin) should be skipped as well.

2. When teaching a client about adverse effects of insulin, a nurse will include which of the following? (Select all that apply.)

    a. _____ perspiration
    b. _____ weakness
    c. _____ weight loss
    d. _____ blurred vision
    e. _____ bradycardia

CHAPTER 27

Estrogens, Progestins, and Hormonal Contraceptives

■ Mastering the Information

MATCHING

Match the terms in Column I with a definition, example, or related statement from Column II.

COLUMN I

1. _____ Preven

2. _____ Estring

3. _____ Premarin

4. _____ estradiol

5. _____ progestins

6. _____ Estraderm

7. _____ Depo-Provera

8. _____ Norplant

9. _____ Cenestin

10. _____ Provera

COLUMN II

a. an estradiol transdermal patch

b. a commonly used oral progestin

c. a naturally occurring, nonconjugated estrogen

d. a commonly used oral estrogen

e. a long-acting progestin contraceptive preparation that lasts for 3 months per injection

f. a contraceptive implant that lasts 5 years

g. approved by the U.S. Food and Drug Administration (FDA) for postcoital contraception

h. a new synthetic conjugated estrogen approved for short-term treatment of hot flashes and sweating

i. used in contraception products and for dysmenorrhea, endometriosis, and uterine bleeding

j. used to treat atrophic vaginitis

TRUE OR FALSE

Indicate if the following statements are true or false.

_____ 1. Estrogens and progestins are synthesized from cholesterol.

_____ 2. Small amounts of estrogens are found in adipose tissue.

_____ 3. Estrone is the major estrogen.

_____ 4. During pregnancy, the placenta produces small amounts of estriol.

_____ 5. When fertilization does not take place, levels of estrogen and progesterone increase.

_____ 6. If an ovum is fertilized, progesterone acts to maintain the pregnancy.

_____ 7. Most hormonal contraceptives are synthetic estrogen and progestin.

_____ 8. Decreased pituitary stimulation of the ovaries may result in estrogen replacement therapy.

_____ 9. Women who take hormones should have a complete physical every 3 years.

_____ 10. Oral contraceptives increase the effects of insulin.

SHORT ANSWER

Answer the following.

1. Describe the main function of estrogen.

   _____

   _____

   _____

2. Why is progestin used in hormone replacement therapy?

   _____

   _____

   _____

3. List five contraindications to hormone therapy.

   _____

   _____

   _____

4. Describe the three mechanisms of hormonal contraception.

   _____

   _____

   _____

5. Why is estrogen contraindicated in pregnancy?

   _____

   _____

   _____

■ Applying Your Knowledge

Jane Smily, an adolescent, called the clinic because she forgot to take her birth control pill yesterday. What effect will this have on the therapeutic effects of the birth control pills? How should you advise her? What teaching can you provide that will help her remember to take her birth control pills regularly?

   _____

   _____

   _____

   _____

   _____

   _____

   _____

■ Practicing for NCLEX

MULTIPLE-CHOICE QUESTIONS

1. A 19-year-old female is seen in the clinic for unprotected sexual intercourse the night before. She is requesting emergency contraception. Which of the following drugs will she be given?

   a. Estraderm   c. Preven

   b. Prempro   d. Cenestin

2. A client has been placed on hormone replacement therapy. Provera has been prescribed for her. She should be instructed that she is at risk for

   a. colon cancer   c. Alzheimer's disease

   b. gallbladder disease d. osteoporosis

3. A client who has been placed on estrogen complains of nausea. The nurse should instruct her to

   a. eat six small meals a day

   b. take her medication before breakfast

   c. drink a full glass of water with each pill

   d. take medication after meals or at bedtime

4. A client will be using estradiol skin patches for hormone replacement therapy. The nurse teaches her that she should apply the patch

   a. to the abdomen   c. in the waistline area

   b. to her breast   d. on the forearm

5. A client has a history of seizures and is taking carbamazepine. Her physician has just prescribed an oral contraceptive for her. The client will be informed that she should

   a. use an additional birth control method

   b. stop taking her seizure medication

   c. ask her neurologist about decreasing her dose of carbamazepine

   d. take her seizure medication at night with her oral contraceptive

6. A client has been placed on 1 mg of Premarin daily. The nurse will advise which of the following in her teaching session with the client:

   a. Take the medication only if nausea occurs.

   b. Report to the emergency room if nausea occurs.

   c. Avoid exercise.

   d. Monitor her weight.

7. A nurse is assessing a client who will be placed on hormone replacement therapy. Which of the following data would cause immediate concern?

   a. walking 2 miles a day

   b. smoking cigarettes

   c. eating large meals

   d. suffering from occasional headaches

8. A client has requested to be placed on hormone replacement therapy for severe hot flashes and fatigue. She has been told that she is not a good candidate for hormone replacement therapy. The nurse suspects she has a history of

   a. kidney disease   c. asthma

   b. liver disease   d. osteoporosis

9. A client has been taking birth control pills for 3 years. She calls the clinic to tell the nurse that she has had a stomach virus and has been unable to take her pills for 2 days. Which of the following responses would be appropriate?

   a. "Take three pills today and continue taking them as prescribed."

   b. "Take two pills now!"

   c. "You need to speak to your physician."

   d. "Take two pills today and two tomorrow; then continue taking them as prescribed."

10. Which of the following would indicate a contraindication to birth control pills?

    a. frequent headaches

    b. calf tenderness

    c. weight loss

    d. dizziness

ALTERNATE FORMAT QUESTIONS

1. A client is taking 2 mg of estradiol (Estrace) daily for menopausal symptoms. How many milligrams will she take each month?

2. Which of the following could be adverse effects of estrogen? (Select all that apply.)

   a. _____ edema and weight gain

   b. _____ cancer

   c. _____ breakthrough bleeding

   d. _____ thrombophlebitis

   e. _____ amenorrhea

CHAPTER 28

Androgens and Anabolic Steroids

■ Mastering the Information

MATCHING

Match the terms in Column I with a definition, example, or related statement from Column II.

COLUMN I

1. _____ oxandrolone (Oxandrin)

2. _____ testosterone

3. _____ androstenedione

4. _____ Testopel

5. _____ danazol (Danocrine)

6. _____ methyltestosterone (Android)

7. _____ Androgel

8. _____ cholesterol

9. _____ calcitonin

10. _____ Androderm

COLUMN II

a. an androgen over-the-counter dietary supplement

b. the most important male sex hormone

c. involved in synthesizing male sex hormones

d. may be used to prevent or treat endometriosis or fibrocystic breast disease in women

e. an anabolic steroid

f. a transdermal form of testosterone that has a rapid onset of action and lasts approximately 24 hours

g. used to treat cryptorchidism

h. testosterone pellets used for delayed puberty and hypogonadism

i. a topical preparation applied to shoulders and upper arms once daily

j. decreases the effects of androgens

TRUE OR FALSE

Indicate if the following statements are true or false.

_____ 1. All synthetic anabolic steroids are weak androgens.

_____ 2. Androgens and anabolic steroids are contraindicated in children.

_____ 3. Drug therapy with androgens can be short or long term.

_____ 4. Androgens may decrease the effects of warfarin.

_____ 5. Dehydroepiandrosterone (DHEA) is contraindicated in men with prostate cancer or benign prostatic hypertrophy.

_____ 6. Androgens increase the effects of sulfonylurea antidiabetic drugs.

_____ 7. Danazol inhibits metabolism of carbamazepine and increases the risk of toxicity.

_____ 8. Androgens and anabolic steroids are widely abused in attempts to enhance muscle development.

_____ 9. Testosterone secretion levels remain relatively high until about 65 years of age.

_____ 10. Testosterone increases skin thickness.

SHORT ANSWER

Answer the following.

1. Name three organs of the body that secrete androgens.

2. List the three functions of testosterone.

3. Why are androgens and anabolic steroids classified as Schedule III drugs?

4. List 10 potentially serious side effects of anabolic steroids.

5. What happens when male sex hormones are given to women?

■ Applying Your Knowledge

You and your spouse are at a social gathering. Someone asks you what you think of the rumor going around town about the high school football team and anabolic steroids. How would you respond?

■ Practicing for NCLEX

MULTIPLE-CHOICE QUESTIONS

1. A client has acquired primary hypogonadism and is to begin testosterone therapy. Androderm has been prescribed. He is instructed to apply the patch to his
   a. scrotum   c. buttocks
   b. upper back   d. chest

2. A client is to start testosterone transdermal therapy. The health care provider instructs him to change the patch
   a. every 12 hours   c. every 3 days
   b. daily   d. weekly

3. A 62-year-old is on androgen therapy. The nurse will inform him of which of the following possible adverse effects?
   a. increased sperm count
   b. increased libido
   c. a high-pitched voice
   d. increased pubic hair

4. A 13-year-old client takes testosterone because his father had delayed puberty. The client will be assessed for which of the following every 6 months?
   a. migraine headaches
   b. altered long-bone growth
   c. hyperglycemia
   d. increased hair growth

5. A nurse works in a women's clinic and is aware that women who are unresponsive to conventional therapy for endometriosis are given which of the following?
   a. danazol (Danocrine)
   b. testosterone enanthate (Delatestryl)
   c. testosterone cypionate (Depo Testosterone)
   d. methyltestosterone (Methitest)

6. A client, age 48, is taking testosterone for hypogonadism caused by an androgen deficiency. Which of the following lab tests should be monitored during therapy?
   a. renal blood urea nitrogen (BUN) and creatinine levels
   b. cardiac enzymes
   c. sperm count levels
   d. hepatic function levels

7. A client, age 15, is taking testosterone. The nurse suspects he is concerned about his appearance. Which of the following nursing diagnoses would be appropriate for him?
   a. Disturbed Self-esteem
   b. Disturbed Personal Identity
   c. Knowledge Deficit
   d. Ineffective Sexuality Patterns

8. A client is prepubescent and has been taking testosterone for cryptorchidism. Follow-up care would include
   a. monthly tests for creatinine levels
   b. a radiograph of hands and wrists every 6 months
   c. weekly tests for blood glucose levels
   d. monthly tests for partial thromboplastin time levels

9. A client, 62 years old, who has been on warfarin (Coumadin) for some time, has recently been diagnosed with androgen deficiency and has been placed on testosterone (Androderm). Which of the following should be monitored?
   a. prothrombin time
   b. serum creatinine
   c. blood glucose level
   d. BUN level

10. A 56-year-old female has been placed on testolactone (Teslac) for breast cancer. Which of the following will likely be a concern for her?
    a. high blood pressure
    b. increase in appetite
    c. excessive growth of hair
    d. headaches

ALTERNATE FORMAT QUESTIONS

1. When instructing a client in the use of Androgel 1%, the nurse will include which of the following? (Select all that apply.)
   a. _____ Wait preferably 4 to 6 hours after application before showering.
   b. _____ Apply to the scrotal area.
   c. _____ Apply twice daily, once in the morning and once at bedtime.
   d. _____ Wash hands after application.
   e. _____ Allow application site to dry before dressing.

2. Adverse effects of androgens and anabolic steroids include which of the following? (Select all that apply.)
   a. _____ edema
   b. _____ masculinizing effects
   c. _____ itching
   d. _____ light-colored urine
   e. _____ yellow skin and sclera

CHAPTER 29

General Characteristics of Antimicrobial Drugs

■ Mastering the Information

MATCHING

Match the terms in Column I with a definition, example, or related statement from Column II.

COLUMN I

1. _____ anaerobic bacteria

2. _____ viruses

3. _____ *Escherichia coli*

4. _____ nosocomial infection

5. _____ streptococci

6. _____ aerobic bacteria

7. _____ pathogenic

8. _____ "opportunistic" microorganism

9. _____ bactericidal

10. _____ fungi

COLUMN II

a. intracellular parasites that survive only in living tissue

b. bacteria that require oxygen

c. normal endogenous or environmental flora

d. an infection acquired in a hospital

e. plantlike organisms that live as parasites on living tissue

f. a drug that kills a microorganism

g. normal microbial skin flora

h. disease producing

i. an organism that most often causes urinary tract infections

j. bacteria that cannot live in the presence of oxygen

TRUE OR FALSE

Indicate if the following statements are true or false.

_____ 1. Use of antimicrobial drugs may lead to serious infections caused by drug-resistant microorganisms.

_____ 2. In an infection, microorganisms initially attach to proteins, carbohydrates, or lipids.

_____ 3. Normal skin flora includes staphylococci, streptococci, diphtheroids, and transient environmental organisms.

_____ 4. *E. coli* is a normal resident of the vagina and intestinal tract.

_____ 5. Nosocomial infections are less severe and easier to treat than community-acquired infections.

_____ 6. Laboratory tests to identify causative organisms usually take 24 hours or longer.

_____ 7. Clients in critical care units are more at risk for antibiotic-resistant organisms.

_____ 8. The body protects damaged tissues from infections.

_____ 9. Antimicrobials are among the most frequently used drugs worldwide.

_____ 10. Antimicrobial drugs are effective in treating most viral infections.

SHORT ANSWER

Answer the following.

1. List the major defense mechanisms of the body.

   _____

   _____

   _____

2. List contributing factors for the increasing prevalence of antibiotic-resistant microorganisms.

   _____

   _____

   _____

3. List the mechanism of action for antimicrobial drugs.

   _____

   _____

   _____

4. Describe empiric therapy when treating infections.

   _____

   _____

   _____

5. Why are tetracyclines contraindicated in children younger than 8 years of age?

   _____

   _____

   _____

■ Practicing for NCLEX

MULTIPLE-CHOICE QUESTIONS

1. It is important to administer antimicrobial drugs at scheduled, evenly spaced intervals to ensure
   a. use of all packaged medication
   b. therapeutic blood levels
   c. minimal adverse effects
   d. client compliance

2. Which of the following outcomes would be appropriate for a client receiving antimicrobial therapy who has a wound infection?
   a. decrease in white blood cell count
   b. increase in malaise and lethargy
   c. increase in drainage
   d. decrease in appetite

3. Most intravenous (IV) administration of antimicrobial drugs should infuse over
   a. 5 to 10 minutes   c. 30 to 60 minutes
   b. 15 to 30 minutes   d. 60 to 90 minutes

4. Which of the following adverse effects will occur with most antimicrobial agents?
   a. diarrhea   c. headache
   b. nausea   d. hypersensitivity

5. The nurse has an order to mix an antibiotic with multivitamins in 50 cc of solution and administer intravenously over 1 hour. Which of the following nursing measures is most appropriate?
   a. Prepare and administer the order as written.
   b. Check with the head nurse before administration of the IV medications.
   c. Call the physician to clarify the order.
   d. Decrease the amount of solution used to mix the antibiotic powder because the multivitamins will be added to the antibiotics.

6. A client has been receiving antimicrobial therapy for 2 weeks. He has lost 7 lb during that time. When the nurse questions him concerning the weight loss, he tells her he doesn't feel like eating. The most appropriate nursing diagnosis for this client would be as follows:
   a. Fatigue Related to Infection
   b. Knowledge Deficit: Use of Antimicrobial Drugs
   c. Imbalanced Nutrition: Less Than Body Requirements Related to Adverse Effects of Drug Therapy
   d. Risk for Injury: Related to Adverse Drug Effects

7. The most effective method of preventing infections is
   a. accurate administration of antibiotics
   b. the use of isolation procedures
   c. keeping skin clean and dry
   d. hand washing

8. If severe adverse effects of antimicrobial therapy occur, clients should
   a. stop the drug immediately
   b. continue taking the medication until it is all gone
   c. report adverse effects to their health care provider
   d. decrease the dosage and continue therapy

9. Which of the following laboratory tests identifies infectious agents by measuring the titer in the serum of a diseased host?
   a. a Gram stain   c. serology
   b. a culture   d. detection of antigens

10. The duration of antimicrobial therapy is usually
    a. 3 to 5 days   c. 12 to 15 days
    b. 7 to 10 days   d. 14 to 21 days

ALTERNATE FORMAT QUESTIONS

1. A nurse is observing for therapeutic effects of an antimicrobial agent 48 hours after the client's first dose. The nurse will assess for which of the following? (Select all that apply.)
   a. _____ decreased fever
   b. _____ decreased appetite
   c. _____ decreased white blood count
   d. _____ verbal report from client of "feeling better"
   e. _____ decreased red blood cells

2. A client has been diagnosed with nephrotoxicity related to use of an aminoglycoside. The nurse will look for which of the following adverse effects? (Select all that apply.)
   a. _____ increased creatinine clearance
   b. _____ increased blood urea nitrogen
   c. _____ increased creatinine
   d. _____ decreased fluid and electrolyte imbalances
   e. _____ increased urine output

CHAPTER 30

Beta-Lactam Antibacterials: Penicillins, Cephalosporins, and Others

■ Mastering the Information

MATCHING

Match the terms in Column I with a definition, example, or related statement from Column II.

COLUMN I

1. _____ amoxicillin (Amoxil)

2. _____ nafcillin (Unipen)

3. _____ cephalosporins

4. _____ cefoxitin (Mefoxin)

5. _____ penicillin G

6. _____ aztreonam (Azactam)

7. _____ ampicillin

8. _____ imipenem/cilastatin (Primaxin)

9. _____ penicillin V

10. _____ carbenicillin

COLUMN II

a. an extended-spectrum/antipseudomonal penicillin used to treat urinary tract infections and prostatitis

b. active against *Bacteroides fragilis*, an anaerobic organism resistant of most drugs

c. administered only by the oral route

d. a monobactam active against gram-negative bacteria

e. a broad-spectrum, semisynthetic penicillin used for gram-negative and gram-positive bacterial infections

f. a carbapenum that requires lidocaine to be added for an intramuscular (IM) injection to decrease pain

g. a penicillinase-resistant penicillin

h. broad-spectrum antibacterial agents that come from fungus

i. a prototype for penicillins

j. an aminopenicillin that is converted to ampicillin in the body

TRUE OR FALSE

Indicate if the following statements are true or false.

_____ 1. Beta-lactam antibiotics are most effective when bacterial cells are dividing.

_____ 2. The most serious adverse effect of the penicillins is nephropathy.

_____ 3. Penicillins are more effective in infections caused by gram-negative bacteria.

_____ 4. An allergic reaction to one penicillin usually means a client will be allergic to all penicillins.

_____ 5. In general, cephalosporins are more active against gram-positive organisms.

_____ 6. Third-generation cephalosporins are used to treat meningeal infections.

_____ 7. Penicillins are more effective in most streptococcal infections.

_____ 8. Penicillin is the most common cause of drug-induced anaphylaxis.

_____ 9. Second-generation cephalosporins are often used for surgical prophylaxis with prosthetic implants.

_____ 10. In the hospital setting, the intramuscular route is always used for the administration of penicillin.

SHORT ANSWER

Answer the following.

1. List four groups of beta-lactam antibacterials.

   _____

   _____

   _____

2. Describe the mechanism of action for beta-lactam antibacterial drugs.

   _____

   _____

   _____

3. Explain how a beta-lactamase inhibitor, when combined with a penicillin, produces a therapeutic effect.

   _____

   _____

   _____

4. Why are some clients allergic to both penicillins and cephalosporins?

   _____

   _____

   _____

5. List the adverse effects of penicillins.

   _____

   _____

   _____

■ Applying Your Knowledge

Ellen Driver is admitted to the emergency department with cellulitis in her left leg. One gram of cefotetan (a second-generation cephalosporin) is given intravenously (IV) over 30 minutes. Before administering this medication, you note that she is allergic to penicillin, sulfa, and fish, but she denies any allergies to other antibiotics. Ten minutes after the IV cefotetan starts to infuse, Ms. Driver complains that she feels odd. She appears flushed and her throat feels tight and itchy. Her respiratory rate is slightly elevated at 24 breaths per minute, but you do not see any rash. How should you proceed?

_____

_____

_____

_____

_____

_____

_____

_____

■ Practicing for NCLEX

MULTIPLE-CHOICE QUESTIONS

1. A 28-year-old female has been given a prescription for 300 mg of cefdinir (Omnicef) every 12 hours for bronchitis. Which of the following statements indicates that she has an understanding of cefdinir therapy?

   a. "I take my medication on an empty stomach."

   b. "I take my medication every 4 hours."

   c. "I take my antibiotic right before breakfast and before my evening meal."

   d. "I will take this medication as long as my throat hurts."

2. A client is 73 years old and is taking a cephalosporin. There is a possibility that this client may develop

   a. nephrotoxicity   c. fibromyalgia

   b. pernicious anemia   d. endocarditis

3. When explaining to a client that he should not drink cranberry or orange juice while taking nafcillin, the nurse will advise him that

   a. if acidic juices are ingested, solid foods should be taken with penicillin

   b. oral penicillins are destroyed by acids

   c. acids increase the absorption rate of penicillins

   d. acids increase the blood level of penicillins

4. A priority assessment of a client who is to be started on imipenem (Primaxin) is determining if the client has

   a. anemia   c. diabetes mellitus

   b. hypertension   d. seizure disorders

5. While instructing new RN graduates about the use of penicillin and an aminoglycoside, the following should be included:

   a. When giving an IM injection, draw up the penicillin first and then the aminoglycoside.

   b. Give each drug in separate syringes if administering them IM.

   c. Never mix the two in a syringe or IV solution.

   d. The two are not prescribed to be given at the same time.

6. Which of the following electrolyte imbalances may occur with the use of large doses of IV penicillin G potassium?

   a. hypokalemia   c. hyponatremia

   b. hyperkalemia   d. hypernatremia

7. A client has cancer of both kidneys. Which of the following will be important in determining the correct dosage of a cephalosporin?

   a. urinary output

   b. creatinine clearance level

   c. 24-hour urine

   d. Urine pH

8. When teaching a young mother about administration of a penicillin, the home care nurse will advise her to

   a. shake the liquid suspension to resuspend the medication before giving it

   b. warm the medication prior to administration

   c. administer the medication with a fruit juice

   d. give it only when the child is awake

9. A nurse is responsible for medication administration for an 8-hour shift. She must give ampicillin IM. In planning for preparation of all the mediations to be given, the nurse is aware that reconstituted ampicillin must be given

   a. with breakfast

   b. within 15 minutes of preparation

   c. in the deltoid muscle

   d. within 1 hour of preparation

10. A client is taking a cephalosporin for a urinary tract infection. Which of the following drugs would the nurse inform the client that he should not take with the cephalosporin therapy?

    a. Lanoxin   c. erythromycin

    b. Mylanta   d. Valium

ALTERNATE FORMAT QUESTIONS

1. Drugs that alter the effects of cephalosporins include which of the following? (Select all that apply.)

   a. _____ furosemide (Lasix)

   b. _____ probenecid (Benemid)

   c. _____ Mylanta

   d. _____ cimetidine (Tagamet)

   e. _____ cyclosporine

CHAPTER 31

Aminoglycosides and Fluoroquinolones

■ Mastering the Information

MATCHING

Match the terms in Column I with a definition, example, or related statement from Column II.

COLUMN I

1. _____ gemifloxacin (Factive)

2. _____ tobramycin (Nebcin)

3. _____ moxifloxacin (Avelox)

4. _____ ciprofloxacin (Cipro)

5. _____ norloxacin (Noroxin)

6. _____ streptomycin

7. _____ lomefloxacin (Maxaquin)

8. _____ amikacin (Amikin)

9. _____ neomycin

10. _____ paramomycin (Humatin)

COLUMN II

a. approved for bronchitis, urinary infections, and transurethral surgical procedures

b. used topically to treat infections of the eye, ear, and skin

c. often used with other antibiotics for septicemia and infections of burn wounds

d. acts against bacteria and amoebae in the intestinal lumen

e. indicated for community-acquired pneumonia

f. can be taken without regard to meals

g. used only for urinary tract infections and uncomplicated gonorrhea

h. may be used in a four- to six-drug regimen for treatment of multidrug-resistant tuberculosis

i. has a broader spectrum of antibacterial activity than other aminoglycosides

j. do not take alone with dairy products or calcium-fortified juices

TRUE OR FALSE

Indicate if the following statements are true or false.

_____ 1. Nephrotoxicity occurs more often with fluoroquinolones than with aminoglycosides.

_____ 2. Many nosocomial infections are caused by gram-negative organisms.

_____ 3. Fluoroquinolones are contraindicated in children younger than 18 years of age.

_____ 4. Smaller doses of aminoglycosides are indicated for urinary tract infections.

_____ 5. Aminoglycosides should be given no longer than 14 days.

_____ 6. If nephrotoxicity occurs with aminoglycoside therapy, it is reversible when the drug is discontinued.

_____ 7. Hepatic impairment is not a factor in aminoglycoside therapy.

_____ 8. Trough blood levels should be drawn 30 to 60 minutes after administering a drug.

_____ 9. Ciprofloxacin (Cipro) must be taken 1 hour before or 2 hours after a meal.

_____ 10. Oral fluoroquinolones can cause dizziness or light-headedness.

SHORT ANSWER

Answer the following:

1. What is the mechanism of action for aminoglycosides?

_____

_____

_____

2. What is the major clinical use of parenteral aminoglycosides?

_____

_____

_____

3. Why are fluoroquinolones not recommended for use in children?

_____

_____

_____

4. What factors are considered when aminoglycoside dosages are calculated?

_____

_____

_____

5. What is the main goal in decreasing the incidence and severity of nephrotoxicity and ototoxicity from use of aminoglycosides?

_____

_____

_____

■ Applying Your Knowledge

William Howles, 82 years of age, has been receiving gentamicin for the last 3 days to treat a serious wound infection. Peak and trough blood levels have been drawn, and you receive the following results: peak: 7 mcg/mL and trough: 4 mcg/mL (normal peak: 5 to 8 mcg/mL and trough: <2 mcg/mL). How will you interpret these results, and what, if any, action will you take?

_____

_____

_____

_____

_____

_____

_____

_____

■ Practicing for NCLEX

MULTIPLE-CHOICE QUESTIONS

1. A client is to start on tobramycin (Nebcin) for a nosocomial infection. Which of the following would be the most helpful in determining the correct dosage of Nebcin?
   a. the client's blood pressure
   b. the client's weight
   c. the time the client eats breakfast
   d. other client medication

2. Clients who are on aminoglycoside therapy would be assessed for factors that could predispose them to
   a. cardiotoxicity and hepatotoxicity
   b. diabetes mellitus and nephrotoxicity
   c. ototoxicity and hypertension
   d. nephrotoxicity and ototoxicity

3. A client has been on moxifloxacin (Avelox) for acute sinusitis for 10 days. Which of the following laboratory tests should be initiated?
   a. complete blood count
   b. blood glucose level
   c. prothrombin time
   d. electrocardiogram (ECG)

4. A client is taking norfloxacin (Noroxin) for a urinary tract infection. The nurse will be sure to include the following when discussing norfloxacin therapy:

   a. Take it with meals.

   b. Sunscreen lotions do not prevent photosensitivity reactions.

   c. Limit fluid intake to 1 quart per day.

   d. Oral medication is taken once a day.

5. Gentamicin (Garamycin) is begun for a client. The most important laboratory value to be monitored is

   a. potassium level

   b. serum creatinine level

   c. serum albumin level

   d. prothrombin time

6. Neomycin has been ordered for a client. The nurse will administer this drug by which of the following routes?

   a. oral   c. intramuscular

   b. subcutaneous   d. intravenous

7. A client is taking gentamicin. A trough level should be obtained

   a. 15 to 30 minutes before the next dose

   b. 1 hour before the next dose

   c. 2 hours before the next dose

   d. 30 minutes after the next dose

8. A client, age 50, has been receiving gentamicin therapy for 3 days. Which of the following would be the most appropriate nursing action?

   a. monitoring blood pressure

   b. assessing for tinnitus

   c. monitoring weight

   d. assessing for gout

9. A client has completed a 7-day course of ciprofloxacin (Cipro). She tells the nurse she thinks she has a vaginal yeast infection. The nurse suspects that she has

   a. a suprainfection

   b. an allergic reaction

   c. a sexually transmitted disease

   d. a skin disease

10. A client has been taking gatifloxacin (Tequin) for 3 days for pneumonia. She calls the clinic and reports that she has an itchy rash all over her body. The nurse advises her to

    a. stop taking the drug immediately

    b. request a topical cream for the rash

    c. decrease the dosage of Tequin

    d. continue the drug as ordered

ALTERNATE FORMAT QUESTIONS

1. A nurse is caring for a client who is receiving an aminoglycoside. In order to reduce the potential for nephrotoxicity, the nurse is aware of which of the following? (Select all that apply.)

   a. _____ Lower dosages may be warranted.

   b. _____ Shorter intervals between doses may be needed.

   c. _____ Adequate hydration is important.

   d. _____ A low-salt diet is indicated.

   e. _____ Substances that alkalinize the urine should be avoided.

2. Which of the following are adverse effects of fluoroquinolones? (Select all that apply.)

   a. _____ urticaria

   b. _____ constipation

   c. _____ nausea and vomiting

   d. _____ tinnitus

   e. _____ abnormal liver enzymes

CHAPTER 32

Tetracyclines, Sulfonamides, and Urinary Agents

■ Mastering the Information

MATCHING

Match the terms in Column I with a definition, example, or related statement from Column II.

COLUMN I

1. _____ tetracycline (Achromycin)
2. _____ sulfasalazine (Azulfidine)
3. _____ fosfomycin (Monurol)
4. _____ demeclocycline (Declomycin)
5. _____ phenazopyridine (Pyridium)
6. _____ trimethoprim (Trimpex)
7. _____ doxycycline (Vibramycin)
8. _____ nitrofurantoin (Macrodantin)
9. _____ sulfisoxazole
10. _____ methenamine mandelate (Mandelamine)

COLUMN II

a. urine pH must be acidic to be effective
b. less likely to cause crystalluria than most other sulfonamides
c. a drug of choice for *Bacillus anthracis* (which causes anthrax)
d. an azo dye that acts as a urinary tract analgesic
e. the tetracycline most likely to cause photosensitivity
f. approved only for treatment of uncomplicated urinary tract infections (UTIs) in women due to susceptible strains
g. the most common side effects are rash and pruritus
h. a prototype drug for tetracyclines
i. used to treat ulcerative colitis and rheumatoid arthritis
j. used for short-term treatment of UTIs or long-term suppression of bacteria in chronic, recurrent UTIs

TRUE OR FALSE

Indicate if the following statements are true or false.

_____ 1. Tetracyclines may be substituted for penicillin in treating streptococcal pharyngitis.

_____ 2. Tetracyclines should not be substituted for penicillin in serious staphylococcal infections.

_____ 3. Once resistance to one sulfonamide develops, cross-resistance to others is common.

_____ 4. Urinary antiseptics can be used to treat UTIs and ulcerative colitis.

_____ 5. Doxycycline can be used in clients with renal failure.

_____ 6. The intramuscular route is preferred for tetracycline therapy.

_____ 7. With sulfonamide therapy, alkaline urine decreases drug solubility.

_____ 8. Urine pH must be acidic for Mandelamine therapy to be therapeutic.

_____ 9. Sulfonamides may be used to treat UTIs in children older than 2 months.

_____ 10. Nausea is an allergic response to Bactrim.

SHORT ANSWER

Answer the following.

1. List four clinical indications for tetracyclines.

_____

_____

_____

2. Describe the mechanism of action for tetracyclines.

_____

_____

_____

3. Describe the mechanism of action for sulfonamides.

_____

_____

_____

4. Why are tetracyclines contraindicated in pregnant women and children up to 8 years of age?

_____

_____

_____

5. Outline a teaching plan for a client who has a UTI.

_____

_____

_____

■ Applying Your Knowledge

You are working in a nursing home, caring for an elderly, incontinent client who has an indwelling urinary catheter. You notice her urine is cloudy with lots of sediment, and it has a strong, foul odor. The client is afebrile and is not complaining of any pain. Analyze these data and discuss how you will proceed.

_____

_____

_____

_____

_____

_____

_____

■ Practicing for NCLEX

MULTIPLE-CHOICE QUESTIONS

1. A client, age 19, has been on tetracycline therapy for 3 years. A priority nursing action will be to monitor
   a. blood pressure
   b. liver function
   c. blood glucose level
   d. renal function

2. A 58-year-old female is being started on sulfonamide therapy for ulcerative colitis. Which of the following would be an appropriate outcome for this client?
   a. urinary output of 100 to 250 mL daily
   b. urinary output of 250 to 500 mL daily
   c. urinary output of 600 to 1000 mL daily
   d. urinary output of 1200 to 1500 mL daily

3. Which of the following statements by a client indicates that she does not have an understanding of doxycycline (Vibramycin) therapy?
   a. "I will be spending my summer at the beach."
   b. "I will take my medication by mouth."
   c. "If I experience perineal itching, I will let my doctor know."
   d. "I will take my medication with saltine crackers."

4. When instructing a client concerning tetracycline therapy, which of the following should be included in your teaching plan?
   a. The intramuscular route is preferred.
   b. Avoid dairy product ingestion with tetracycline.
   c. Outdated tetracycline may be used for up to 1 year.
   d. Always take all tetracycline on an empty stomach.

5. Which of the following drugs is used as prophylaxis for recurrent UTIs?
   a. nitrofurantoin (Macrodantin)
   b. trimethoprim (Trimpex)
   c. fosfomycin (Monurol)
   d. mafenide (Sulfamylon)

6. A 30-year-old female comes to the clinic complaining of dysuria, burning, and frequency and urgency of urination. A urinalysis indicates she has a UTI. The physician prescribes sulfamethoxazole (Gantanol). Which of the following drugs may also be prescribed to relieve her discomfort?
   a. methenamine mandelate (Mandelamine)
   b. phenazopyridine (Pyridium)
   c. fosfomycin (Monurol)
   d. sulfamethizole (Thiosulfil)

7. A client is being treated for Rocky Mountain spotted fever. He is taking 2 g of tetracycline (Achromycin) per day in four equal doses. He complains of soreness and white patches in his mouth and states that his tongue has turned black. The nurse suspects that
   a. his condition has worsened
   b. he has a monilial superinfection
   c. he is having adverse effects from the Achromycin
   d. he is having an allergic reaction to a food substance

8. A client will be taking sulfamethoxazole/trimethoprim (Bactrim) for an extended period of time. Which of the following laboratory tests would be most important to include in periodic clinic visits?
   a. aspartate aminotransferase levels
   b. blood urea nitrogen
   c. pulmonary function
   d. complete blood count

9. A client is to be placed on sulfonamide therapy for a UTI. Which of the following drugs being taken by the client should be reported to the client's physician?
   a. Fosamax   c. Synthroid
   b. aspirin   d. Inderal

10. The client is taking fosfomycin (Monurol) for a UTI. The nurse is aware that administration of this drug is
   a. without food
   b. with a full glass of water
   c. immediately after the powder is mixed with water
   d. three times a day

ALTERNATE FORMAT QUESTIONS

1. A nurse is caring for a 72-year-old client admitted to the respiratory care unit with a diagnosis of acute exacerbation of chronic bronchitis. The client begins trimethoprim/sulfamethoxazole (Bactrim) therapy. The nurse is aware that the client is most at risk for which of the following? (Select all that apply.)
   a. _____ folic acid deficiency
   b. _____ severe skin reactions
   c. _____ hematologic disorders
   d. _____ superinfections
   e. _____ bone marrow depression

2. A 10 year-old child weighing 66 pounds is taking 2.2 mg/kg/d of Vibramycin. How many milligrams per day is the client receiving?

CHAPTER 33

Macrolides, Ketolides, and Miscellaneous Antibacterials

■ Mastering the Information

MATCHING

Match the terms in Column I with a definition, example, or related statement from Column II.

COLUMN I

1. _____ telithromycin (Ketek)

2. _____ chloramphenicol (Chloromycetin)

3. _____ azithromycin (Zithromax)

4. _____ clindamycin hydrochloride (Cleocin)

5. _____ metronidazole (Flagyl)

6. _____ quinupristin/dalfopristin (Synercid)

7. _____ spectinomycin (Trobicin)

8. _____ linezolid (Zyvox)

9. _____ erythromycin

10. _____ vancomycin

COLUMN II

a. used to treat urethritis and cervicitis

b. myelosuppression may result from use

c. macrolide prototype

d. effective against trichomoniasis

e. used to treat infections caused by *Bacteroides fragilis*

f. a streptogramin antimicrobial

g. used to treat severe infections

h. used to treat gonococcal exposure

i. a ketolide that will treat *Streptococcus pneumoniae* infection

j. used to treat serious infections for which no adequate substitute drug is available

TRUE OR FALSE

Indicate if the following statements are true or false.

_____ 1. The rapid infusion of vancomycin, which causes flushing, is referred to as the "red man effect."

_____ 2. Azithromycin (Zithromax) should be taken with food.

_____ 3. Clarithromycin (Biaxin) may be taken without regard to meals.

_____ 4. Macrolides should be taken with 6 to 8 oz of water.

_____ 5. Vancomycin should not be given to children under 18 years of age.

_____ 6. Ketolides have a greater affinity for ribosomal RNA, which expands their antimicrobial spectrum compared to macrolides.

_____ 7. Clarithromycin (Biaxin) decreases carbamazepine levels.

_____ 8. Therapeutic levels of chloramphenicol (Chloromycetin) are 10 to 20 mcg/mL.

_____ 9. Telithromycin (Ketek) can be used in people who have hypersensitivity reactions to macrolides.

_____ 10. Flagyl is effective against *Clostridium difficile*.

SHORT ANSWER

Answer the following.

1. Which lipopeptide is a bactericidal agent effective only for gram-positive infections caused by *Staphylococcus*?

_____

_____

_____

2. Which serious adverse effect can occur with prolonged use of linezolid (Zyvox)?

_____

_____

_____

3. Why should 6 to 8 oz of water be taken with oral erythromycin preparations?

_____

_____

_____

4. Why should caution be used while driving or operating machinery when taking telithromycin (Ketek)?

_____

_____

_____

5. How do macrolides and ketolides produce their therapeutic actions?

_____

_____

_____

■ Applying Your Knowledge

After gynecologic surgery, Susan Miller contracts a serious wound infection. She is treated with intravenous (IV) clindamycin and gentamicin. After 5 days of treatment, Ms. Miller develops severe diarrhea (12 watery, bloody stools per day) and feels dizzy and weak, especially when getting out of bed. She is afebrile. Based on these assessment data, how should you proceed?

_____

_____

_____

_____

_____

_____

_____

■ Practicing for NCLEX

MULTIPLE-CHOICE QUESTIONS

1. A client is to receive clindamycin (Cleocin). In order to promote therapeutic effects, the nurse will administer the drug
   a. with a fruit juice
   b. with a light snack
   c. when the client has an empty stomach
   d. with meals

2. Linezolid (Zyvox) is being given to a client for pneumonia. He has been told that he should decrease his salt intake. The priority nursing action will be to monitor the client's
   a. blood glucose level
   b. weight
   c. blood urea nitrogen level
   d. blood pressure

3. A client has *Haemophilus* meningitis. He is allergic to penicillin and has been placed on chloramphenicol. The nurse should assess for which of the following:
   a. diabetes mellitus   c. hepatic toxicity
   b. blood dyscrasia   d. ototoxicity

4. Erythromycin has been prescribed for a client. Which of the following may have been considered when selecting this drug?

   a. age
   b. diet
   c. activity level
   d. family history

5. Erythromycin can interfere with the elimination of other drugs. Which of the following explains why toxicity of the other drugs may occur?

   a. The affected drugs are eliminated more slowly, increasing their serum levels.
   b. The affected drugs are eliminated quickly, decreasing their serum levels.
   c. Erythromycin causes an increase in metabolism of the other drugs.
   d. Erythromycin can cause an antagonistic effect when given other drugs.

6. A client is receiving IV erythromycin lactobionate for bacterial endocarditis. After 6 hours of therapy, he complains of burning pain, and the IV infusion site is warm. Which of the following would be the nurse's initial action?

   a. Change the infusion site every 48 to 72 hours.
   b. Slow the rate of infusion.
   c. Apply an ice compress.
   d. Discontinue the IV.

7. A client is receiving linezolid (Zyvox). Which of the following foods should he avoid?

   a. green beans
   b. blue cheese
   c. beets
   d. red meat

8. A client is having colorectal surgery and is receiving metronidazole (Flagyl) for prevention of anaerobic bacterial infections. A priority assessment will be to observe for which of the following?

   a. jaundice
   b. seizures
   c. increased blood pressure
   d. confusion

9. In a client receiving clarithromycin (Biaxin), which of the following lab values should be monitored in relation to dosage?

   a. creatinine clearance
   b. prothrombin time
   c. liver enzymes
   d. urine specific gravity

10. A client has a severe systemic infection and is being treated with vancomycin IV. The nurse will monitor the client for

    a. decrease in blood pressure and flushing
    b. increase in fever and heart rate
    c. shortness in breath and dizziness
    d. increase in blood pressure and itching

ALTERNATE FORMAT QUESTIONS

1. A nurse is following a client who has been taking a macrolide. The nurse suspects hepatotoxicity. Which of the following would support this? (Select all that apply.)

   a. _____ abdominal cramps
   b. _____ leucopenia
   c. _____ jaundice
   d. _____ oliguria
   e. _____ fever

2. Which of the following drugs increase the effects of clarithromycin? (Select all that apply.)

   a. _____ fluconazole
   b. _____ efavirenz
   c. _____ nevirapine
   d. _____ omeprazole
   e. _____ ritonavir

CHAPTER 34

Drugs for Tuberculosis and *Mycobacterium Avium* Complex (MAC) Disease

■ Mastering the Information

MATCHING

Match the terms in Column I with a definition, example, or related statement from Column II.

COLUMN I

1. _____ rifampin (Rifadin)

2. _____ pyrazinamide

3. _____ capreomycin (Capastat)

4. _____ isoniazid (INH)

5. _____ ofloxacin

6. _____ streptomycin

7. _____ rifabutin (Mycobutin)

8. _____ ethambutol (Myambutol)

9. _____ rifapentine (Priftin)

10. _____ Riafter

COLUMN II

a. used to treat pulmonary tuberculosis (TB); less frequent administration than rifampin

b. an antitubercular drug that inhibits synthesis of ribonucleic acid and interferes with mycobacterial protein metabolism

c. used synergistically with isoniazid (INH) to kill TB bacilli

d. used with INH and rifampin for the first 2 months of active TB treatment

e. used in a combination of INH, rifampin, and pyrazinamide to promote compliance of drug therapy for TB

f. a fluoroquinolone that can be used to treat multidrug-resistant TB in adults

g. the most commonly used antitubercular drug

h. a drug that has tuberculostatic properties and may be used in combination with other drugs for treatment

i. an aminoglycoside antibiotic used in a medication regimen for TB

j. used in clients with human immunodeficiency virus (HIV) who have *Mycobacterium avium* complex and used as a substitute for rifampin

TRUE OR FALSE

Indicate if the following statements are true or false.

_____ 1. Older adults are more likely to have prominent signs and symptoms of TB than younger adults.

_____ 2. Initial signs and symptoms of TB in children may occur within a few weeks of exposure.

_____ 3. Pyrazinamide is contraindicated during pregnancy.

_____ 4. INH therapy should be once a week.

_____ 5. Screening for TB is done only at public health departments.

_____ 6. People with silicosis are more likely to have TB.

_____ 7. Hepatitis is more likely to occur during the first 8 weeks of INH therapy.

_____ 8. INH therapy is questioned in older adults because of the increased risk of drug-induced hepatotoxicity.

_____ 9. Rifampin increases blood levels and therapeutic effects of anti-HIV drugs.

_____ 10. INH increases blood levels of phenytoin.

SHORT ANSWER

Answer the following:

1. Describe the physiological action of isoniazid (INH).

_____

_____

_____

2. Differentiate latent tuberculosis infection (LTBI) from active TB.

_____

_____

_____

3. What is a major concern among public health care providers concerning TB?

_____

_____

_____

4. How can nurses help control the spread of TB?

_____

_____

_____

5. Name five primary drugs used to treat TB.

_____

_____

_____

■ Applying Your Knowledge

Christine Sommers, during chemotherapy of breast cancer, experienced symptoms of TB and had an abnormal chest x-ray. Sputum results are not yet available, but treatment with isoniazid and rifampin is started. Ms. Sommers voices anxiety about taking medications that are "toxic" and have so many side effects. How can you individualize your teaching for Ms. Sommers?

_____

_____

_____

_____

_____

_____

■ Practicing for NCLEX

MULTIPLE-CHOICE QUESTIONS

1. A client, age 43, has been diagnosed with active TB. He is taking multiple drug therapy, including INH and rifampin (Rifadin). Which of the following laboratory tests should be done at least once a month?

    a. serum alanine aminotransferase (ALT), aspartate aminotransferase (AST), and bilirubin

    b. red blood count, white blood count, and differential

    c. thyroid-stimulating hormone, thyroxine, and triiodothyronine levels

    d. a fasting blood sugar and 2-hour postprandial blood sugar

2. INH therapy has been started on a client. The nurse has completed a thorough assessment. Of the following prescribed drugs for the client, which one should be reported to the client's physician?

    a. acetaminophen (Tylenol)

    b. vitamin B_6

    c. diltiazem hydrochloride (Cardizem)

    d. folic acid

3. When teaching clients concerning the use of antituberculosis drugs, a nurse would advise which of the following?

   a. There is no need for concern of liver damage.

   b. Drug therapy for TB is a lifetime commitment.

   c. Drug therapy lasts only a couple of months.

   d. Hypersensitivity reactions are more likely to occur between the third and eighth week of drug therapy.

4. A 28-year-old female is being treated for active TB with INH and rifampin (Rifadin). She should be informed of the following:

   a. She should have her blood glucose levels checked at least every month while on drug therapy.

   b. She should use additional birth control if she is taking an oral contraceptive.

   c. She will probably gain weight while on TB drug therapy.

   d. She will most likely have to take the medication for 2 to 3 years.

5. A client who has active TB asks the nurse how long it will take the medication to make him feel better. An appropriate response would be the following:

   a. "Don't worry about that. You are going to feel better soon."

   b. "You will probably be on the medication for about a year."

   c. "You should begin to feel better within 2 to 3 weeks of starting the medication."

   d. "That's really hard to predict."

6. Which of the following groups of people who may be on INH therapy are more likely to have serious liver impairment?

   a. Asians   c. diabetics

   b. alcoholics   d. homeless people

7. Why should rifampin therapy not be used in people with HIV?

   a. Rifampin increases the severity of the anti-HIV drugs' adverse effects.

   b. Rifampin increases blood levels and therapeutic effects of anti-HIV drugs.

   c. Rifampin's therapeutic effects are decreased by the anti-HIV drugs.

   d. Rifampin decreases blood levels and therapeutic effects of anti-HIV drugs.

8. A client has recently been diagnosed with active TB and is taking INH and rifampin. Pyrazinamide is also added for the first 2 months of therapy. Which of the following laboratory tests should be done during the first 2 months of therapy in relation to pyrazinamide?

   a. blood urea nitrogen levels

   b. ALT and AST levels

   c. creatinine levels

   d. urine osmolality

9. A client is receiving ethambutol as part of a four-drug regimen for TB. Which of the following may be of concern for this client?

   a. driving his car in town

   b. eating a high protein, low-fat diet

   c. playing tennis every weekend

   d. smoking a pack of cigarettes per day

10. A client is taking rifampin (Rifadin) for active TB. When discussing this drug with the client, the nurse should stress that

   a. the drug does not cause gastrointestinal upset

   b. the drug can cause seizures

   c. a "butterfly rash" may appear across the face but will go away once therapy is concluded

   d. the red/orange discoloration of urine is a side effect but is harmless

ALTERNATE FORMAT QUESTIONS

1. Mark the spot with an X in the right lung where primary TB may be found.

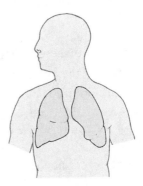

2. A client is receiving 5 mg/kg of INH daily. The client's weight is 100 lbs. How many milligrams will he receive daily?

CHAPTER 35

Antiviral Drugs

■ Mastering the Information

MATCHING

Match the terms in Column I with a definition,
example, or related statement from Column II.

COLUMN I

1. _____ trifluridine (Viroptic)

2. _____ ganciclovir (Cytovene)

3. _____ amantadine (Symmetrel)

4. _____ zidovudine (AZT)

5. _____ vidarabine (Vira-A)

6. _____ tenofovir (Viread)

7. _____ ribavirin (Virazole)

8. _____ acyclovir (Zovirax)

9. _____ ritonavir (Norvir)

10. _____ ganciclovir (Cytovene)

COLUMN II

a. used to treat genital herpes

b. used to treat encephalitis

c. nucleoside reverse transcriptase inhibitor
   prototype

d. applied topically to treat keratoconjunctivitis and
   corneal ulcers caused by herpes simplex virus

e. inhibits replication of the influenza A virus

f. used to treat bronchiolitis or pneumonia caused
   by respiratory syncytial virus (RSV)

g. a nucleotide reverse transcriptase inhibitor used to
   treat hepatitis B

h. used to prevent cytomegalovirus mainly in people
   with organ transplants or human
   immunodeficiency virus (HIV) infection

i. can cause thrombocytopenia

j. a protease inhibitor used in clients with HIV

TRUE OR FALSE

Indicate if the following statements are true or false.

_____ 1. Anticholinergics increase the effects of
amantadine.

_____ 2. Viruses are extracellular parasites that live
and produce by living outside other cells.

_____ 3. Amantadine dosage should be increased
for clients with renal impairment.

_____ 4. Rimantadine (Flumadine) dosage should
be increased for clients with renal
impairment.

_____ 5. Cidofovir (Vistide) can safely be used in
children.

_____ 6. There are approximately 100 types of
rhinovirus that cause the common cold.

_____ 7. Foscarnet (Foscavir) may cause hematuria.

_____ 8. Indinavir (Crixivan) is taken on an empty
stomach.

_____ 9. Zidovudine (AZT) may cause pancreatitis.

_____ 10. Most antiviral drugs inhibit viral
reproduction by eliminating viruses from
tissue.

SHORT ANSWER

Answer the following:

1. List symptoms associated with acute viral
   infections.

   _____

   _____

   _____

2. List the five classes of drugs used for HIV infection and acquired immunodeficiency syndrome (AIDS).

_____

_____

_____

3. List common side effects of drugs used to treat influenza A.

_____

_____

_____

4. Why are herbal products not recommended during use of antiretroviral medications?

_____

_____

_____

5. How do antiviral drugs produce a therapeutic action?

_____

_____

_____

■ Applying Your Knowledge

Nick, a 19-year-old college student, is diagnosed with genital herpes at the student health center. Two hundred mg of acyclovir q4h is prescribed for 10 days. In addition, 400 mg of acyclovir bid is ordered to control recurrence of symptoms when lesions appear. What client teaching will Nick need at this time?

_____

_____

_____

_____

_____

_____

■ Practicing for NCLEX

MULTIPLE-CHOICE QUESTIONS

1. A client is a 42-year-old male who was recently diagnosed with AIDS. He is to begin drug therapy with 300 mg of zidovudine (AZT) PO. The nurse will anticipate which of the following dosage schedules?

   a. every 4 hours   c. three times a day

   b. twice a day   d. four times a day

2. A client who takes abacavir (Ziagen) should avoid taking the drug with

   a. high-protein meals

   b. fatty foods

   c. acidic fruit juices

   d. high-carbohydrate foods

3. A client who has been taking stavudine (Zerit) for 3 weeks is complaining of numbness, burning, and pain in his hands and feet. The nurse suspects that his physician will

   a. continue therapy as prescribed

   b. decrease the dosage of stavudine

   c. add a therapeutic dose of acetaminophen

   d. discontinue the drug

4. A client is diagnosed with AIDS and has developed cytomegalovirus infections. He is place on ganciclovir (Cytovene) therapy. When discussing the drug therapy with the client, the nurse stresses that thrombocytopenia may occur

   a. during the first 2 weeks of therapy

   b. during the first month of therapy

   c. at the end of therapy

   d. years after the therapy has been stopped

5. A 70-year-old male has developed keratoconjunctivitis caused by herpes simplex virus. Trifluridine (Viroptic) has been prescribed. The health care provider is aware that the drug

   a. regimen will last at least 6 weeks

   b. is given orally

   c. should not be used longer than 21 days

   d. does not have adverse effects

6. Before clients are placed on amprenavir (Agenerase), they should be assessed for an allergic reaction to which of the following drugs?

   a. penicillin   c. benzodiazepines

   b. sulfonamides   d. acetaminophens

7. A client has been diagnosed with influenza A and amantadine (Symmetrel) has been prescribed for her. The nurse will inform her of which of the following side effects?

   a. nausea

   b. headache

   c. palpitations

   d. burning sensation in hands and feet

8. Which of the following drugs is given for prevention of influenza in children?

   a. amantadine (Symmetrel)

   b. zanamivir (Relenza)

   c. oseltamivir (Tamiflu)

   d. rimantadine (Flumadine)

9. A client who has AIDS is taking cidofovir (Vistide) for treatment of cytomegalovirus retinitis. Which of the following should be monitored?

   a. serum creatinine   c. uric acid

   b. hematocrit   d. blood glucose

10. A client is taking an antiretroviral drug. She calls the clinic and tells the nurse she missed her last dose. The nurse should tell her

    a. to double the next dose

    b. not to double the next dose

    c. to take half the dosage with the next dose

    d. to skip the next dose

ALTERNATE FORMAT QUESTIONS

1. A client is taking 400 mg of delavirinde (Rescriptor) PO three times a day. The drug comes in 100-mg tablets. How many milligrams and tablets will the client take daily?

2. A female HIV client is taking amprenavir (Agenerase). What should the nurse inform the client concerning this drug? (Select all that apply.)

   a. _____ You may need to use a second form of contraception if you're taking birth control pills.

   b. _____ Have your blood pressure monitored weekly by a health care provider.

   c. _____ Do not take vitamin E supplements.

   d. _____ Decrease salt intake in your diet.

   e. _____ If you're allergic to sulfa drugs, do not take the drug.

CHAPTER 36

Antifungal Drugs

■ Mastering the Information

MATCHING

Match the terms in Column I with a definition, example, or related statement from Column II.

COLUMN I

1. _____ nystatin (Mycostatin)
2. _____ terbinafine (Lamisil)
3. _____ naftifine (Naftin)
4. _____ griseofulvin (Fulvicin)
5. _____ miconazole (Monistat)
6. _____ amphotericin B (Fungizone)
7. _____ itraconazole (Sporanox)
8. _____ flucytosine (Ancobon)
9. _____ caspofungin (Cancidas)
10. _____ voriconazole (Vfend)

COLUMN II

a. an antifungal drug that should be taken with fatty meal
b. and oral antifungal drug used to treat onychomycosis
c. an antifungal drug used to treat serious systemic fungal infections
d. a popular antifungal agent used to treat vulvovaginal candidiasis
e. an antifungal drug used to treat athlete's foot and jock itch
f. a polyene agent used topically to treat oral, intestinal, or vaginal candidiasis
g. drug of choice for histoplasmosis
h. indicated for treatment of invasive aspergillosis in clients who cannot take amphotericin B or itraconazole
i. mainly used to treat yeast infections
j. a common adverse effect is transient visual disturbances

TRUE OR FALSE

Indicate if the following statements are true or false.

_____ 1. People may develop histoplasmosis years after the primary infection.

_____ 2. Fungi are smaller and less complex than bacteria.

_____ 3. Most invasive fungal infections are acquired by inhalation of airborne spores.

_____ 4. Drugs for superficial fungal infections are usually taken orally.

_____ 5. Amphotericin B is highly toxic to humans.

_____ 6. All azoles are contraindicated in pregnancy.

_____ 7. Multiple doses of fluconazole (Diflucan) are needed for vaginal candidiasis.

_____ 8. Adverse effects of caspofungin include fever, headache, skin rash, nausea, and vomiting.

_____ 9. Griseofulvin is contraindicated for clients with renal disease.

_____ 10. Therapeutic effects of terbinafine (Lamisil) may not be evident for several months after the drug is stopped.

SHORT ANSWER

Answer the following:

1. What is the most common opportunistic infection?

_____

_____

_____

2. How do antifungal drugs produce their therapeutic effects?

_____

_____

_____

3. List the four azoles available for systemic use.

_____

_____

_____

4. What is the main concern with use of amphotericin B?

_____

_____

_____

5. List two drugs that will decrease the effects of fluconazole.

_____

_____

_____

■ Applying Your Knowledge

Harold Johnson has oral candidiasis and is being treated with 5 cc of nystatin, swish and swallow, after meals and at bedtime. What nursing considerations are important to ensure a therapeutic effect?

_____

_____

_____

_____

■ Practicing for NCLEX

MULTIPLE-CHOICE QUESTIONS

1. Griseofulvin (Fulvicin) has been prescribed for a client who has a fingernail infection. When discussing the drug with her, she states that she is afraid of the adverse effects of the drug, especially an allergic reaction. An appropriate response would be as follows:

    a. "Adverse effects are very common with this drug. We will monitor you very closely for these effects."

    b. "This drug causes very serious adverse effects. You could die."

    c. "There is a very low incidence of serious reactions to this drug."

    d. "Don't worry about it. You probably won't experience any ill effects from the drug."

2. A client, age 50, is taking amphotericin B (Fungizone) intravenously (IV). For which of the following electrolyte imbalances will the nurse observe?

    a. hyperkalemia   c. hypernatremia

    b. hypokalemia   d. hyponatremia

3. The nurse is to administer nystatin suspension to a client who has thrush. Which of the following will the nurse include in instructions to the client regarding administration?

    a. Swish and swallow.

    b. Hold in the mouth for 2 minutes and then spit it out.

    c. Swallow it immediately.

    d. Use a cotton swab to apply medication to mouth lesions.

4. A client has a tinea infection of the scalp. Itraconazole (Sporanox) capsules have been ordered. What will the nurse tell her in regard to taking the capsules?

    a. "Take prior to meals."

    b. "Take after a full meal."

    c. "Take with a full glass of water."

    d. "Take with just enough water to swallow the capsule."

5. A client is taking amphotericin B for aspergillosis. Which of the following lab values would indicate that the medication should not be given?

   a. hematocrit of 45%

   b. blood urea nitrogen of 62 mg/dL

   c. bilirubin (total) of 0.8 mg/dL

   d. sodium 142 mEq/L

6. Fluconazole (Diflucan) 400 mg/d PO has been prescribed for a client who has human immunodeficiency virus (HIV). He should be instructed to notify his health care provider immediately if he experiences

   a. headaches and slight dizziness

   b. dryness and itching of skin

   c. nausea and constipation

   d. unusual fatigue and dark urine

7. A client has tinea pedis. Haloprogin (Halotex) 1% cream has been prescribed for daily use. Which of the following instructions should be given to the client?

   a. Wash hair before applying cream to scalp.

   b. Wash and dry feet before applying the cream.

   c. Do not wet area before application of cream.

   d. Apply cream and remove after 30 minutes.

8. Which of the following drugs should not be taken with oral ketoconazole (Nizoral)?

   a. Prilosec

   b. acetylsalicylic acid (ASA)

   c. folic acid

   d. digoxin

9. Which of the following is the most common and most serious adverse effect of amphotericin B?

   a. hepatotoxicity   c. nephrotoxicity

   b. cardiotoxicity   d. ototoxicity

10. A client has a diagnosis of oral candidiasis. On which of the following drugs does the nurse expect her to be placed?

   a. nystatin (Mycostatin)

   b. natamycin (Natacyn)

   c. naftifine (Naftin)

   d. ketoconazole (Nizoral)

ALTERNATE FORMAT QUESTIONS

1. A client has a vaginal yeast infection. In preparing the client for self-administration of a vaginal antifungal, the nurse will include which of the following instructions? (Select all that apply.)

   a. _____ Discontinue use during menstruation.

   b. _____ Insert high into the vagina.

   c. _____ Wear a minipad to avoid staining clothing.

   d. _____ Do not use a tampon.

   e. _____ Avoid sexual intercourse during use of the drug.

2. A nurse is instructing a client concerning the adverse effects of fluconazole (Diflucan). Which of the following should the nurse include? (Select all that apply.)

   a. _____ unusual fatigue

   b. _____ loss of appetite

   c. _____ nausea and vomiting

   d. _____ dark urine

   e. _____ pale stools

CHAPTER 37

Antiparasitics

■ Mastering the Information

MATCHING

Match the terms in Column I with a definition, example, or related statement from Column II.

COLUMN I

1. _____ mefloquine (Lariam)

2. _____ iodoquinol (Yodoxin)

3. _____ primaquine phosphate (Primaquine)

4. _____ tinidazole (Tindamax)

5. _____ nitazoxanide (Alinia)

6. _____ metronidazole (Flagyl)

7. _____ trimethoprim-sulfamethoxazole (Bactrim)

8. _____ thiabendazole (Mintezol)

9. _____ chloroquine (Aralen)

10. _____ pyrimethamine (Daraprim)

COLUMN II

a. drug of choice for all forms of amebiasis except asymptomatic intestinal amebiasis

b. can cause a metallic or bitter taste

c. acts against erythrocytic forms of plasmodial parasites to prevent or treat malarial attacks

d. used to prevent the initial occurrence of malaria

e. used to treat cryptosporidiosis in children 1 to 11 years

f. effective against threadworms and pinworms

g. an intestinal amebicide

h. used to prevent chloroquine-resistant strains of malaria

i. folic acid antagonist used to prevent malaria

j. drug of choice for prevention and treatment of pneumocystis pneumonia

TRUE OR FALSE

Indicate if the following statements are true or false.

_____ 1. Permethrin (Nix) is the drug of choice for pediculosis and scabies.

_____ 2. Many antiparasitic drugs are toxic.

_____ 3. Chloroquine should be used with caution in clients with hepatic disease.

_____ 4. Anthelmintics may be taken without regard to food.

_____ 5. Pyrantel (Pin-Rid) can be used in infants 3 to 6 months of age.

_____ 6. Malathion (Ovide) is a second-line drug for scabies and pediculosis.

_____ 7. Take chloroquine with or after meals.

_____ 8. Amebiasis is a common disease in the United States.

_____ 9. Phenytoin may alter the effects of metronidazole (Flagyl).

_____ 10. Pyrethrin can be obtained over the counter (OTC).

SHORT ANSWER

Answer the following:

1. Formulate a nursing diagnosis important to the management of a parasitic condition.

_____

_____

_____

2. How is malaria transmitted?

_____

_____

_____

3. Scabies and pediculosis are most likely to occur in what type of environments?

_____

_____

_____

4. List adverse effects of atovaquone (Mepron).

_____

_____

_____

5. Which anthelmintic is considered broad spectrum for use in the treatment of parasitic infections by hookworms, pinworms, roundworms, and whipworms?

_____

_____

_____

■ Applying Your Knowledge

You are a nurse in a travel clinic. Sally and Bill, college students, plan to spend part of their summer vacation traveling in Africa. You update their immunizations and then talk with them about malaria prevention. The physician has written a prescription for chloroquine phosphate and primaquine, one tablet every week. What information would you include in your teaching?

_____

_____

_____

_____

_____

_____

_____

■ Practicing for NCLEX

MULTIPLE-CHOICE QUESTIONS

1. A client is taking pyrimethamine (Daraprim) for the prevention of malaria. Because this drug interferes with folic acid metabolism, the nurse will observe for

   a. hypotension   c. depression

   b. anemia   d. diabetes mellitus

2. A sexually active 18-year-old female client is taking Flagyl for trichomoniasis. A primary concern for the health care provider would be

   a. the administration of the drug three times daily for 7 days

   b. the decrease in severity of symptoms

   c. the treatment of the client's sexual partner

   d. the adverse effects of the drug

3. The mother of a 5-year-old boy who is taking pyrantel (Antiminth) for pinworms asks the nurse when she can be sure that the drug has worked. The nurse's best response should be as follows:

   a. "After six weeks of therapy, we can assume the pinworms have been eradicated."

   b. "It will take 2 to 3 months after drug therapy to be sure there are no more pinworms."

   c. "One negative stool culture will indicate the pinworms are gone."

   d. "We will need three negative stool cultures before your son is considered free of the worms."

4. A nurse is taking care of a missionary who has spent a year in Asia. He is being treated with iodoquinol (Yodoxin) for intestinal amebiasis. Which of the following statements would the nurse expect from the client?

   a. "I'm not sure where I am."

   b. "I'm experiencing severe headaches."

   c. "I have heartburn."

   d. "I wish this nausea would go away."

5. A 28-year-old male was recently diagnosed with acquired immunodeficiency syndrome (AIDS). He is being treated through a private clinic specializing in immunosuppressed clients. He is taking trimethoprim-sulfamethoxazole (Bactrim) for pneumocystosis. A common adverse effect of this drug is

   a. skin rash
   b. increased blood pressure
   c. difficulty in swallowing
   d. dizziness

6. When teaching a young mother about treatment of pediculosis capitis for her 5-year-old, the nurse will stress the importance of

   a. following drug therapy, including measures to avoid reinfection or transmission to others
   b. keeping her child from playing in dirt
   c. keeping the child isolated from other children for at least 2 weeks
   d. avoiding raw fish and undercooked meat

7. When instructing a client who has malaria regarding administration of chloroquine (Aralen), the nurse should include the following instructions:

   a. Take medication with or after meals.
   b. Drink a full glass of water with each dose.
   c. Take the medication 2 hours before meals.
   d. Avoid dairy products when taking the medication.

8. The nurse is discussing the use of permethrin (Nix, supplied OTC) with a grandmother for treatment of head lice of a 6-year-old. Which of the following would be an appropriate statement to her?

   a. "Leave the medication on longer than the directions indicate."
   b. "Decrease the amount of the medication indicated in the directions."
   c. "Leaving the medication on longer than indicated can cause seizures."
   d. "Do not leave the medication on as long as the directions indicate."

9. How does phenobarbital alter the effects of metronidazole (Flagyl)?

   a. It increases the effects by decreasing hepatic metabolism of Flagyl.
   b. It decreases effects of Flagyl by increasing its rate of hepatic metabolism.
   c. It causes a decreased rate of urinary excretion.
   d. It increases the risk of Flagyl toxicity and retinal damage by inhibiting metabolism.

10. A client is taking quinine for malaria and is complaining of headaches, tinnitus, difficulty hearing, and blurred vision. The nurse suspects that he is experiencing

   a. vertigo   c. pruritus
   b. hypocalcemia   d. cinchonism

ALTERNATE FORMAT QUESTIONS

1. A client is taking 650 mg of Quinine (Quinamm) PO (orally) every 8 hours for 14 days. How many total milligrams will the client take in the treatment period?

2. The nurse is instructing a mother on how to use permethrin (Nix). Arrange the following steps in correct order starting with No. 1.

   a. _____ Dry hair with a towel.
   b. _____ Shampoo hair.
   c. _____ Apply medication.
   d. _____ Leave medication on hair for 10 minutes.
   e. _____ Rinse off medication with water.
   f. _____ Rinse off shampoo.
   g. _____ Wet hair.

CHAPTER 38

Physiology of the Hematopoietic and Immune Systems

■ Mastering the Information

MATCHING

Match the terms in Column I with a definition, example, or related statement from Column II.

COLUMN I

1. _____ chemotaxis

2. _____ antigens

3. _____ neutrophils

4. _____ cytokines

5. _____ eosinophils

6. _____ T lymphocytes

7. _____ interleukins

8. _____ basophils

9. _____ granulocytes

10. _____ interferons

COLUMN II

a. interfere with the ability of viruses to replicate in uninfected cells

b. the body's main defense against pathogenic bacteria

c. facilitate movement of leukocytes into injured tissue

d. the attraction of white blood cells to injured tissue areas

e. cells that release histamine

f. regulate blood cell activity by working as chemical messengers

g. cells that kill parasites

h. the main regulators of immune responses

i. foreign substances that initiate immune responses

j. contain inflammatory mediators or digestive enzymes

TRUE OR FALSE

Indicate if the following statements are true or false.

_____ 1. Hematopoietic and immune blood cells originate in pluripotent stem cells.

_____ 2. The body's main external defense mechanism is the histocompatibility complex.

_____ 3. Adaptive or acquired immunity is not produced by the immune system.

_____ 4. Passive immunity is a generalized response to tissue damage that helps in tissue repair.

_____ 5. The duration of active immunity may be short lived or may last a lifetime.

_____ 6. In neoplastic disease, immune cells lose their ability to recognize and destroy mutant or early malignant cells.

_____ 7. In autoimmune disorders, the body perceives normally harmless substances as antigens and produces an immune response.

_____ 8. The main function of dendritic cells is the presentation of antigens to T lymphocytes, which activates the T cells and initiates the adaptive immune response.

_____ 9. Drugs that modify the immune system can enhance or restrict immune responses to various disease processes.

_____ 10. In allergic disorders, the body perceives its own tissue as antigens and causes an immune response.

SHORT ANSWER

Answer the following.

1. List three methods of modifying immune functions.

   _____

   _____

   _____

2. How does nutrition contribute to immunodeficiency?

   _____

   _____

   _____

3. List autoimmune disorders.

   _____

   _____

   _____

4. Describe the neonatal immune system.

   _____

   _____

   _____

5. List the three types of lymphocytes.

   _____

   _____

   _____

■ Practicing for NCLEX

MULTIPLE-CHOICE QUESTIONS

1. The main function of interferons is to
   a. stimulate growth of bone marrow
   b. inhibit viral replication in uninfected cells
   c. promote growth of monocyte macrophages
   d. activate growth of T cells

2. Hematopoietic agents are used to prevent or treat
   a. symptoms of diseases and/or adverse side effects of their treatments
   b. neoplastic diseases
   c. allergic disorders
   d. adverse effects of drugs used to replace iron in the body

3. The process in which weak extracts of antigenic substances are prepared as a drug and administered in small, increasing amounts to develop a tolerance for the substance is called
   a. immunosuppression   c. activation
   b. detoxification   d. desensitization

4. An inadequate amount of which of the following minerals can depress the functions of T and B cells?
   a. magnesium   c. zinc
   b. iron   d. copper

5. The mother of a 3-month-old baby girl is concerned that the baby has been exposed to chickenpox. An appropriate response to her would be the following:
   a. "Let your pediatrician know as soon as you notice a rash on the baby."
   b. "The baby should be covered by maternal antibodies until approximately 6 months of age."
   c. "Don't worry; the baby will be okay."
   d. "The baby's immune system is still immature. She will probably contract the virus."

6. B lymphocytes that are capable of forming antibodies originate in
   a. stem cells in bone marrow
   b. lymph nodes
   c. neutrophils
   d. antigens

7. Which of the following immunoglobulins is stimulated in anaphylaxis?
   a. IgA   c. IgE
   b. IgM   d. IgG

8. Which of the following immunoglobulins is mainly found in mucous membranes and body secretions?
   a. IgG   c. IgM
   b. IgA   d. IgE

9. Which of the following lymphocytes do not need to interact with a specific antigen to become activated?

    a. R cells   c. B cells

    b. T cells   d. natural killer cells

10. Which of the following best describes acquired immunity?

    a. Antibodies are formed by the immune system of another person or animal and transferred to the host.

    b. It is a general, protective mechanism activated by a major histocompatibility complex.

    c. It is produced by a person's own immune system in response to a disease caused by a specific antigen from a source outside the body.

    d. Antibodies or B cells come in contact with antigens in the blood or other body fluids.

ALTERNATE FORMAT QUESTIONS

1. Neutrophils are the major white blood cells in the bloodstream and the body's main defense against pathogenic bacteria. Which of the following are characteristics of neutrophils? (Select all that apply.)

    a. _____ The cells arrive at the site of tissue injury within 90 seconds.

    b. _____ The cells phagocytize organisms by releasing digestive enzymes and oxidative metabolites that kill pathogens.

    c. _____ Neutrophils decrease during the inflammatory process.

    d. _____ The cells circulate in the bloodstream for about 10 minutes.

    e. _____ Neutrophils live for 1 to 3 days during the inflammatory process.

2. Antibodies in body fluids other than blood are produced by the mucosal immune system. B cells of this system travel through which of the following? (Select all that apply.)

    a. _____ tear ducts

    b. _____ salivary glands

    c. _____ breast

    d. _____ bronchi

    e. _____ intestines

CHAPTER 39

Immunizing Agents

■ Mastering the Information

MATCHING

Match the terms in Column I with a definition, example, or related statement from Column II.

COLUMN I

1. _____ DTaP
2. _____ Twinrix
3. _____ IPV
4. _____ Fluzone
5. _____ vaccines
6. _____ Hib
7. _____ Prevnar
8. _____ toxoids
9. _____ Varivax
10. _____ MMR

COLUMN II

a. bacterial toxins or products that have been modified to destroy toxicity while retaining antigenic properties

b. measles, mumps, rubella

c. hepatitis A, inactivated, and B, recombinant, vaccine

d. inactivated poliovirus vaccine

e. influenza vaccine

f. pneumococcal 7-valent conjugate vaccine

g. suspensions of microorganisms that have been killed or attenuated so that they can induce antibody formation while preventing or causing very mild forms of the disease

h. varicella virus vaccine

i. *Haemophilus influenzae* type b vaccine

j. diphtheria and tetanus toxoids and acellular pertussis vaccine

TRUE OR FALSE

Indicate if the following statements are true or false.

_____ 1. Antigens that activate the immune response can be microorganisms that cause infectious diseases.

_____ 2. It is recommended that only activated polio vaccine be used in the United States.

_____ 3. Immunization against diphtheria and tetanus is required one time only for life.

_____ 4. Vaccines should not be given together.

_____ 5. Immunization involves administration of an antibody to produce an antigen.

_____ 6. Attenuated vaccines are weakened or reduced in virulence, which can cause mild forms of the disease.

_____ 7. Most often, attenuated live vaccines produce lifelong immunity.

_____ 8. Toxoid immunity is not permanent, and repeated doses are needed.

_____ 9. The measles, mumps, rubella (MMR) vaccine should be stored away from light.

_____ 10. Health care workers should have a tetanus-diphtheria booster every 10 years.

SHORT ANSWER

Answer the following.

1. What is the main disadvantage of using inactivated poliovirus vaccine (IPV)?

_____

_____

_____

2. How often should a person be immunized against diphtheria and tetanus?

_____

_____

_____

3. When are vaccines and toxoids contraindicated?

_____

_____

_____

4. Where can you find the best source of information regarding current recommendations for immunizations?

_____

_____

_____

5. Why should clients with human immunodeficiency virus (HIV) infection not be given live bacterial or viral vaccines?

_____

_____

_____

■ Applying Your Knowledge

You are working in an urgent care clinic. A 53-year-old housewife sustains a laceration and puncture wound on a rusty nail while gardening. Prioritize the immunization history to obtain from this patient and explain why.

_____

_____

_____

_____

_____

_____

Practicing for NCLEX

MULTIPLE-CHOICE QUESTIONS

1. A mother has brought her 15-month-old daughter to the health department for diphtheria and tetanus toxoids and acellular pertussis (DTaP) and MMR vaccines. Which of the following drugs should be suggested for fever and soreness at the injection site?

    a. aspirin   c. Tylenol

    b. Advil   d. Motrin

2. A 20-year-old female is given a rubella immunization. Which of the following statements by the nurse is most important?

    a. "You may take Tylenol for the fever and pain."

    b. "You must use effective birth control for at least 3 months."

    c. "You may experience flulike symptoms."

    d. "You should take it easy for about 3 days."

3. A young mother has brought her 6-month-old baby into the clinic for immunizations. The nurse should assess for

    a. fever   c. anemia

    b. weight loss   d. slowed development

4. After a baby receives a DTaP vaccine, the nurse will teach the mother to watch for which of the following potential adverse effects?

    a. anorexia and nausea

    b. tremors and possible seizures

    c. difficulty swallowing and abdominal distention

    d. diarrhea and abdominal pain

5. Which of the following drugs decrease the overall effects of vaccines?

    a. acetaminophen (Tylenol)

    b. diazepam (Valium)

    c. furosemide (Lasix)

    d. phenytoin (Dilantin)

6. In assessing immunization needs for a client who will be leaving for Asia in several weeks, a nurse explains that he should receive a tetanus toxoid injection if she has not had one in the last

    a. 6–9 months   c. 4–5 years

    b. 1–2 years   d. 7–10 years

7. The hepatitis B vaccine is recommended as early as

   a. a few hours after birth   c. 1 year of age

   b. 6 months of age   d. 6 years of age

8. RhoGAM must be given to an Rh-negative client who just delivered an Rh-positive baby within

   a. 1 hour   c. 24 hours

   b. 6 hours   d. 72 hours

9. A nurse has just administered vaccines to three children. She explains to the mother that she must wait with the children in the clinic for at least

   a. 15 minutes   c. 1 hour

   b. 30 minutes   d. $1\frac{1}{2}$ hours

10. Which of the following drugs should be readily available when administering any immunizations?

   a. Tylenol   c. epinephrine

   b. Lasix   d. Lasix

ALTERNATE FORMAT QUESTIONS

1. A nurse is preparing to give the MMR vaccine. She is aware of which of the following concerning this vaccine? (Select all that apply.)

   a. _____ The vaccine will be administered subcutaneously.

   b. _____ Only the diluent provided by the manufacturer should be used.

   c. _____ The reconstituted preparation should be used within 12 hours.

   d. _____ Aspiration is not necessary when giving the injection.

   e. _____ An 18- to 20-gauge needle is used when administering the vaccine.

2. A nurse is instructing a young mother regarding common adverse effects of DTaP. Which of the following will she include? (Select all that apply.)

   a. _____ severe fever

   b. _____ anorexia

   c. _____ soreness, erythema, and edema at the injection site

   d. _____ nausea

   e. _____ seizures

CHAPTER 40

Hematopoietic and Immunostimulant Drugs

■ Mastering the Information

MATCHING

Match the terms in column I with a definition, example, or related statement from Column II.

COLUMN I

1. _____ darbepoetin alfa (Aranesp)
2. _____ aldesleukin (Proleukin)
3. _____ interferon alfa-2a (Roferon-A)
4. _____ filgrastim (Neupogen)
5. _____ interferon beta 1a (Avonex)
6. _____ interferon gamma 1b (Actimmune)
7. _____ bacillus Calmette-Guérin (BCG) vaccine
8. _____ interferon alfacon-1 (Infergen)
9. _____ oprelvekin (Neumega)
10. _____ levamisole (Ergamisol)

COLUMN II

a. used to stimulate blood cell production by the bone marrow
b. used to treat hairy cell leukemia
c. used to treat chronic hepatitis in adults
d. restores the function of macrophages and T cells and is used in the treatment of intestinal cancer
e. used to prevent severe thrombocytopenia in clients with cancer
f. used for multiple sclerosis
g. used to treat metastatic renal cell carcinoma and melanoma
h. used in serious infections associated with chronic granulomatous disease
i. used to treat bladder cancer
j. used to prevent or treat anemia

TRUE OR FALSE

Indicate if the following statements are true or false.

_____ 1. Epoetin alfa has a longer half-life than darbepoetin alfa in clients with renal failure.

_____ 2. Interferons can be given orally.

_____ 3. Aldesleukin (Proleukin) is contraindicated for initial use in clients with serious cardiovascular disease.

_____ 4. Most hematopoietic and immunostimulant drugs are synthetic versions of cytokines.

_____ 5. Interferons should be stored on a shelf away from bright light.

_____ 6. Filgrastim and sargramostim can be used in children.

_____ 7. Cytokines have a short half-life and require frequent administration.

_____ 8. Additional iron is not necessary when taking epoetin alfa.

_____ 9. Hematopoietic and immunostimulant drugs can be self-administered.

_____ 10. An adverse effect of interferons is depression and possible suicide.

SHORT ANSWER

Answer the following.

1. Why are hematopoietic and immunostimulant drugs given?

2. What are the disadvantages of using cytokines?

3. How do interferons weaken viruses?

4. How does BCG vaccine act against cancer of the urinary bladder?

5. Why are hematopoietic and immunostimulant drugs given subcutaneously or intravenously?

■ Applying Your Knowledge

John Miller is receiving monthly chemotherapy. The nadir is expected 10 days after treatment. Last month, the nadir lasted for 6 days, during which his neutrophil count was less than 1000/mm^3. This month he is given filgrastim (granulocyte colony-stimulating factor [G-CSF]). Why is the G-CSF given, and how will you evaluate its effectiveness?

■ Practicing for NCLEX

MULTIPLE-CHOICE QUESTIONS

1. The nurse should be aware that immunostimulant therapy
   a. should be administered by mouth
   b. involves shaking the medication vigorously before preparing the administration
   c. has very few minor adverse effects
   d. can cause anaphylactic or other allergic reactions to occur

2. A client is receiving darbepoetin alfa (Aranesp) for anemia associated with chronic renal failure. The nurse will omit a dose if the hemoglobin level is
   a. >2 g/dL   c. >8 g/dL
   b. >5 g/dL   d. >12 g/dL

3. A client is being treated with aldesleukin (Proleukin) for metastatic renal cell carcinoma. He has just experienced a severe reaction from the medication. The nurse suspects that his physician will
   a. decrease the dosage of the drug
   b. withhold one or more doses
   c. add a second drug to decrease adverse effects
   d. continue with the prescribed dosage and see whether a reaction occurs again

4. Which of the following should be monitored before and during treatment with darbepoetin alfa and epoetin alfa?
   a. transferring saturation and serum ferritin
   b. serum amylase and nucleotidase
   c. thrombin clotting time and prothrombin time
   d. complete blood count and platelet count

5. A client has neutropenia as a result of chemotherapy. In order to prevent infection, filgrastim (Neupogen) will be started
   a. immediately after the last dose of chemotherapy
   b. 24 hours after the last dose of chemotherapy
   c. in between chemotherapy doses
   d. 2 weeks after chemotherapy has ended

6. Aldesleukin is contraindicated in clients with preexisting
   a. diabetes mellitus
   b. Parkinson's disease
   c. spastic colon or diverticulitis
   d. cardiovascular or pulmonary disease

7. Oprelvekin (Neumega) is being given to a 7-year-old client who has thrombocytopenia. The nurse will observe for which of the following adverse effects?
   a. hypertension   c. tachycardia
   b. bradycardia   d. hypotension

8. The nurse is aware that a client had a preexisting renal impairment before she started sargramostim therapy. The nurse will monitor which of the following?
   a. serum creatinine levels
   b. electrolyte levels
   c. blood glucose levels
   d. aspartate transaminase levels

9. A 78-year-old client is taking oprelvekin (Neumega). Which of the following adverse effects is most likely to occur in the client?
   a. bone pain   c. increased uric acid
   b. atrial dysrhythmias d. arthralgia levels

10. A favorable outcome for a client who is on epoetin alfa therapy would be
   a. an increase in hematocrit
   b. a decrease in hemoglobin
   c. an increase in white blood cells
   d. a decrease in red blood cells

ALTERNATE FORMAT QUESTIONS

1. When assessing the medication history of his client who is taking aldesleukin (Proleukin), a nurse is aware of which of the following drugs increasing the effects of aldesleukin? (Select all that apply.)
   a. _____ gentamicin
   b. _____ methotrexate
   c. _____ lithium
   d. _____ ibuprofen
   e. _____ acetaminophen

2. When planning care for a client who is on immunostimulant therapy, the nurse will formulate which of the following client outcomes? (Select all that apply.)
   a. _____ Remain afebrile during therapy.
   b. _____ Decrease weight.
   c. _____ Experience increased white blood cell (WBC) count.
   d. _____ Avoid preventable infections.
   e. _____ Maintain adequate levels of nutrition and fluids.

CHAPTER 41

Immunosuppressants

■ Mastering the Information

MATCHING

Match the terms in column I with a definition, example, or related statement from Column II.

COLUMN I

1. _____ azathioprine (Imuran)

2. _____ mycophenolate mofetil (CellCept)

3. _____ lymphocyte immune globulin (Atgam)

4. _____ omalizumab (Xolair)

5. _____ leflunomide (Arava)

6. _____ etanercept (Enbrel)

7. _____ tacrolimus (Prograf)

8. _____ cyclosporine (Sandimmune)

9. _____ methotrexate (Rheumatrex)

10. _____ alefacept (Amevive)

COLUMN II

a. a folate antagonist that inhibits production and function of immune cells

b. insoluble in water and formulated in alcohol, olive oil, and castor oil

c. an antimetabolite that interferes with production of ribonucleic acid (RNA) and deoxyribonucleic acid (DNA)

d. obtained from the serum of horses immunized with human thymus tissue or lymphocytes

e. used to treat moderate to severe allergic asthma

f. has antiproliferative and anti-inflammatory activities and is used to treat rheumatoid arthritis

g. less toxic than azathioprine and has synergistic effects with corticosteroids

h. a tumor necrosis factor receptor used to treat rheumatoid arthritis when other treatments have failed

i. drugs used to treat moderate to severe psoriasis

j. children require higher doses to maintain plasma drug levels

TRUE OR FALSE

Indicate if the following statements are true or false.

_____ 1. The immune response is an important factor in the success or failure of an organ transplant.

_____ 2. In autoimmune disorders, a person's body can differentiate between self-antigens and foreign antigens.

_____ 3. Most autoantigens are protein in nature.

_____ 4. In organ and tissue transplantation, the goal is to rid the body of immunosuppression.

_____ 5. Immunosuppression can cause serious infections in the body.

_____ 6. A rejection reaction occurs when the host's immune system is activated to destroy the transplanted organ.

_____ 7. In a rejection reaction, the initial target of the recipient antibodies is the blood vessels surrounding the transplanted organ.

_____ 8. Chronic rejection reactions cause a gradual decrease in serum creatinine levels.

_____ 9. Chronic graft versus host disease occurs when symptoms last or occur 1 month after transplantation.

_____ 10. Long-term use of immunosuppressant drugs can cause cancer.

SHORT ANSWER

Answer the following.

1. List four conditions that may occur because of inappropriate activation of the immune response.

   _____

   _____

   _____

2. Describe the physiological action of corticosteroids when used to suppress the immune response.

   _____

   _____

   _____

3. What is the most important assessment of clients receiving or anticipating immunosuppressant drug therapy?

   _____

   _____

4. List adverse effects of infliximab (Remicade).

   _____

   _____

   _____

5. What is the therapeutic effect of a drug given to suppress the immune response to organ transplants?

   _____

   _____

■ Applying Your Knowledge

Jane Reily, a kidney transplant recipient taking corticosteroids and cyclosporine, comes to the clinic 6 months after transplantation. She complains of general malaise for the past week. Her temperature is 38°C (100.4°F). What additional information will you collect to differentiate between infection and organ rejection?

_____

_____

_____

_____

_____

_____

_____

_____

■ Practicing for NCLEX

MULTIPLE-CHOICE QUESTIONS

1. Clients on long-term immunosuppressant drug therapy with autoimmune disorders and organ transplantation are at increased risk for
   a. hypotension
   b. osteoporosis
   c. cancer
   d. chronic urinary tract infections

2. Before a client is put on cyclosporine (Sandimmune) to help prevent a rejection reaction from a liver transplant, the nurse should assess for which of the following?
   a. use of alcohol   c. blood glucose level
   b. weight loss   d. activity level

3. A client has had a heart transplant and is receiving cyclosporine (Sandimmune) as part of his postoperative treatment plan. A major adverse effect of this drug is
   a. hepatotoxicity
   b. hypersensitive reactions
   c. nephrotoxicity
   d. nausea and vomiting

4. Sirolimus (Rapamune) is given in combination with cyclosporine (Sandimmune) to prevent renal transplant rejection. The two drugs given 4 hours apart have a greater total effect than the sum of their individual effects. This drug action is

   a. synergism   c. potentiation

   b. simple summation   d. antagonism

5. A client is receiving an antibody preparation, lymphocyte immune globulin (Atgam). The nurse will administer the medication

   a. by mouth

   b. by the intradermal method

   c. subcutaneously

   d. intravenously

6. A nurse works in a rheumatology clinic where infliximab (Remicade) is administered. Which of the following drugs should be available for easy access if necessary?

   a. vitamin B_{12} c. Maalox

   b. Dramamine   d. epinephrine

7. A client is taking azathioprine (Imuran) to prevent renal transplant rejection. In order to assess for bone marrow depression, which of the following lab results should be monitored?

   a. white blood cell and platelet counts

   b. red blood cell and platelet counts

   c. complete blood cell and platelet counts

   d. white blood cell and plasma counts

8. Which of the following elevated lab results could indicate hepatotoxicity from the use of cyclosporine (Sandimmune)?

   a. serum aminotransferases and bilirubin

   b. blood glucose level and ketone count

   c. urine specific gravity and urine pH

   d. arterial blood gases and O_2 saturation

9. A client has been placed on methotrexate (Rheumatrex) therapy for rheumatoid arthritis. The nurse will monitor the client throughout therapy for

   a. peripheral neuropathy   c. nephrotoxicity

   b. hyperthyroidism   d. hepatotoxicity

10. A nurse is preparing an oral dose of cyclosporine (Sandimmune) for a client. The nurse will mix the medication with

   a. room-temperature apple juice

   b. cold orange juice

   c. lukewarm grapefruit juice

   d. cold milk

ALTERNATE FORMAT QUESTIONS

1. Which of the following nursing diagnoses would be appropriate for a client who is receiving immunosuppressant drug therapy? (Select all that apply.)

   a. _____ Social Isolation Related to Activities to Reduce Exposure to Infection

   b. _____ Anxiety Related to Need for Organ Transplant

   c. _____ Risk for Injury: Adverse Drug Effect

   d. _____ Risk for Injury: Infection and Cancer Related to Immunosuppression and Increased Susceptibility

   e. _____ Knowledge Deficit: Disease Process and Immunosuppressant drug therapy

2. When preparing and administering etanercept (Enbrel), which of the following actions will the nurse use? (Select all that apply.)

   a. _____ Slowly inject 1 mL of sterile bacteriostatic water for injection into the vial.

   b. _____ Shake vigorously to mix the solution.

   c. _____ Rotate sites so that a new dose is injected at least 1 inch from old injection site.

   d. _____ Do not inject into an area that is tender, bruised, red, or hard.

   e. _____ Use the Z-track method for injection.

CHAPTER 42

Drugs Used in Oncologic Disorders

■ Mastering the Information

MATCHING

Match the drugs in Column I with the disease process for which they are used from Column II.

COLUMN I

1. _____ etoposide (vePesid)

2. _____ topotecan (Hycamtin)

3. _____ doxorubicin liposomal (Doxil)

4. _____ oxaliplatin (Eloxatin)

5. _____ bleomycin (Blenoxane)

6. _____ methotrexate (Mexate)

7. _____ 5-fluorouracil (5-FU)

8. _____ cyclophosphamide (Cytoxan)

9. _____ vincristine (Oncovin)

10. _____ tamoxifen (Nolvadex)

COLUMN II

a. leukemias, non-Hodgkin's lymphomas

b. squamous cell carcinoma

c. colon, breast, stomach, and pancreatic cancer

d. small-cell lung cancer and advanced ovarian cancer

e. Wilms' tumor and neuroblastoma

f. Hodgkin's disease

g. acquired immunodeficiency syndrome (AIDS)-related Kaposi's sarcoma

h. colorectal cancer

i. prophylaxis and treatment of metastatic breast cancer

j. testicular cancer

TRUE OR FALSE

Indicate if the following statements are true or false.

_____ 1. For most cancer, it may take years to produce a detectable tumor.

_____ 2. Leukemias are cancers of lymphoid tissues.

_____ 3. Chemotherapy is the treatment of choice for colon cancer.

_____ 4. Antineoplastic drugs are sometimes used to treat rheumatoid arthritis.

_____ 5. Alkylating agents cause significant myelosuppression.

_____ 6. Taxanes are used for early stages of breast and ovarian cancers.

_____ 7. Cytotoxic chemotherapy is most effective when started before extensive tumor growth.

_____ 8. Most chemotherapy regimens use single-drug therapy.

_____ 9. Antineoplastic drugs are usually given in low doses on a cyclic schedule.

_____ 10. Normal cells repair themselves faster than malignant cells.

SHORT ANSWER

Answer the following.

1. Describe how most cytotoxic antineoplastic drugs produce their therapeutic actions.

_____

_____

_____

2. List common adverse effects of cytotoxic antineoplastic drugs.

_____

_____

_____

3. Describe tumor lysis syndrome.

_____

_____

_____

4. Describe the difference between tamoxifen (Nolvadex) and an aromatase inhibitor in treating breast tumors.

_____

_____

_____

5. List factors that are considered when determining a chemotherapy dosage.

_____

_____

_____

■ Applying Your Knowledge

Your client Sally Moore is receiving an antineoplastic drug that is known to cause bone marrow depression, with a nadir (lowest point) 12 days after administration. Discuss the effects of bone marrow depression and appropriate nursing assessments. What teaching would be appropriate for this client?

_____

_____

_____

_____

_____

_____

_____

■ Practicing for NCLEX

MULTIPLE-CHOICE QUESTIONS

1. A client is being treated with fluorouracil (5-FU) for breast cancer. The nurse's teaching plan will include

   a. an increase in activity

   b. avoidance of fat in the diet

   c. frequent oral hygiene

   d. restriction of fluid intake

2. A 52-year-old female is taking tamoxifen (Nolvadex). Which of the following will need monitoring during therapy?

   a. creatinine level   c. blood glucose

   b. liver enzymes   d. weight

3. Hospitalization is recommended for the first course of treatment for which of the following antineoplastic drugs?

   a. melphalan (Alkeran)

   b. procarbazine (Matulane)

   c. bleomycin (Blenoxane)

   d. gemcitabine (Gemzar)

4. Which of the following should the nurse not be concerned about in a client who is taking doxorubicin?

   a. excessive fatigue   c. shortness of breath

   b. edema   d. urine that is red

5. A client who is taking vincristine (Oncovin) complains to the nurse that she is constipated. Which of the following is the best response from the nurse?

   a. "A stool softener can be used daily for constipation."

   b. "If you are able, try eating high-fiber foods such as raw fruits and vegetables and whole grains."

   c. "Walking at least one mile a day can help prevent constipation."

   d. "Unfortunately constipation is a side effect of vincristine. Once you stop taking the drug, your normal elimination pattern should return."

6. A client is receiving cisplatin (Platinol) at 3–4 week intervals. The nurse will monitor which of the following laboratory tests prior to each course of therapy?

   a. serum creatinine, blood urea nitrogen (BUN), and serum electrolytes

   b. white blood cell count and red blood cell count

   c. serum aspartate aminotransferase, alanine aminotransferase, and alkaline phosphatase

   d. urine specific gravity and urine pH

7. A client who is 28-years-old is diagnosed with Hodgkin's disease. He is receiving vincristine (Oncovin) therapy. When planning care for the client, the nurse will plan to

   a. monitor blood glucose levels

   b. limit solid foods throughout therapy

   c. sedate him during the infusions

   d. observe for intravenous (IV) infiltration

8. A client is taking oral cyclophosphamide (Cytoxan) therapy. Because hemorrhagic urethritis is an adverse effect, the nurse will encourage

   a. drinking lots of fluids

   b. limiting fluid intake

   c. taking the medication at bedtime

   d. increasing protein in the diet

9. When taking methotrexate (Mexate), a client should avoid

   a. Tylenol   c. aspirin

   b. vitamin K   d. sodium

10. When caring for a client who is receiving antineoplastic agents, the nurse is aware that the most common threat to the client is

    a. bleeding   c. hyperuricemia

    b. extravasation   d. infection

ALTERNATE FORMAT QUESTIONS

1. A client is receiving 250 mg of fulvestrant (Faslodex) once a month. The drug is available in 50 mg/mL. How many milliliters will the client receive?

2. Which of the following nursing diagnoses would be appropriate for a client who is receiving chemotherapy? (Select all that apply.)

   a. _____ Deficient Knowledge about cancer chemotherapy

   b. _____ Ineffective Coping related to cancer diagnosis

   c. _____ Imbalanced Nutrition: Less than body requirements related to disease process

   d. _____ Nausea and Vomiting, Weakness, and Activity Intolerance related to chemotherapy

   e. _____ Risk for Injury: Infection related to drug-induced neutropenia

CHAPTER 43

Physiology of the Respiratory System

■ Mastering the Information

MATCHING

Match the terms in column I with a definition, example, or related statement from Column II.

COLUMN I

1. _____ diffusion
2. _____ ventilation
3. _____ cilia
4. _____ compliance
5. _____ lobule
6. _____ respiration
7. _____ nasopharynx
8. _____ pleura
9. _____ alveoli
10. _____ perfusion

COLUMN II

a. process of gas exchange by which oxygen is obtained and carbon dioxide is eliminated
b. tiny hairlike projections that move mucus toward the pharynx to be expectorated or swallowed
c. a grapelike cluster of air sacs
d. functions as a passageway and air "conditioner" that helps warm, humidify, and filter incoming air
e. the process by which oxygen and carbon dioxide are transferred between alveoli and blood and between blood and body cells
f. the ability of lungs to stretch or expand to accommodate incoming air
g. membranes that encase the lungs
h. the movement of air between the atmosphere and the alveoli of the lungs
i. blood flow through the lungs
j. the functional unit of the lung where gas exchange takes place

TRUE OR FALSE

Indicate if the following statements are true or false.

_____ 1. Normal respiration requires atmospheric air containing at least 15% O_2.

_____ 2. Normal breathing occurs 16 to 20 times per minute.

_____ 3. Approximately 100 mL of air is inspired and expired with a normal breath.

_____ 4. Exercise decreases respirations.

_____ 5. Sleep increases respirations.

_____ 6. Drug therapy for respiratory disorders is more effective in relieving respiratory symptoms than in curing the underlying cause of the symptoms.

_____ 7. The nervous system regulates the rate and depth of respiration by the respiratory center in the medulla oblongata.

_____ 8. Perfusion is the process by which O_2 and CO_2 are transferred between alveoli and blood and between blood and body cells.

_____ 9. Respiration is the process of gas exchange by which O_2 is obtained and CO_2 is eliminated.

_____ 10. Bronchioles are grapelike clusters of air sacs surrounded by capillaries.

SHORT ANSWER

Answer the following.

1. What percentage of oxygen is in atmospheric air?

_____

_____

_____

2. How many times per minute does normal breathing occur?

_____

_____

_____

3. How much air is inspired and expired with a normal breath?

_____

_____

_____

4. How many times an hour do deep breaths or sighs occur?

_____

_____

_____

5. List common signs and symptoms of respiratory disorders.

_____

_____

_____

■ Practicing for NCLEX

MULTIPLE-CHOICE QUESTIONS

1. Permanent brain damage from lack of oxygen occurs within
   a. 1 to 2 minutes   c. 10 to 15 minutes
   b. 4 to 6 minutes   d. 20 to 30 minutes

2. Carbon dioxide is considered a
   a. necessary component of cell metabolism
   b. nontoxic gas
   c. major waste product of cell metabolism
   d. liquid

3. Which of the following is not part of the respiratory tract?
   a. loop of Henle   c. pharynx
   b. nose   d. bronchi

4. Which of the following is considered an alternate airway?
   a. epiglottis   c. Purkinje fiber
   b. cochlear   d. mouth

5. Pharyngeal walls are composed of
   a. smooth muscle   c. vocal cords
   b. skeletal muscle   d. bronchi

6. Which of the following is the passageway between the larynx and main-stem bronchi?
   a. pharynx   c. trachea
   b. bronchioles   d. nose

7. Which of the following helps protect and defend the lungs?
   a. bronchi and bronchioles
   b. oxygen and carbon dioxide
   c. larynx and pharynx
   d. cilia and mucus

8. Blood enters the lungs through which of the following?
   a. pulmonary artery   c. aorta
   b. pulmonary vein   d. coronary arteries

9. Which of the following is a lipoprotein substance that decreases surface tension in the alveoli?
   a. glycerin   c. bile
   b. surfactant   d. interferon

10. Which of the following transports oxygen to body cells?
    a. alveoli   c. neutrophils
    b. B lymphocytes   d. hemoglobin

ALTERNATE FORMAT QUESTIONS

1. Which of the following are common signs and symptoms of respiratory disorders? (Select all that apply.)
   a. _____ cough
   b. _____ increased secretions
   c. _____ decreased blood pressure
   d. _____ bronchospasms
   e. _____ skin rash

2. Which of the following is/are part of the lungs? (Select all that apply.)
   a. _____ bronchi
   b. _____ bronchioles
   c. _____ alveoli
   d. _____ pleura
   e. _____ aorta

CHAPTER 44

Drugs for Asthma and Other Bronchoconstrictive Disorders

■ Mastering the Information

MATCHING

Match the terms in column I with a definition, example, or related statement from Column II.

COLUMN I

1. _____ isoproterenol (Isuprel)

2. _____ theophylline, aminophylline

3. _____ beclomethasone (Beclovent)

4. _____ omalizumab (Xolair)

5. _____ albuterol (Proventil)

6. _____ metaproterenol (Alupent)

7. _____ ipratropium bromide (Atrovent)

8. _____ epinephrine (Adrenalin)

9. _____ formoterol (Foradil)

10. _____ cromolyn (Intal)

COLUMN II

a. used only for prophylaxis of acute bronchoconstriction

b. an anticholinergic taken by inhalation for maintenance therapy of bronchoconstriction with chronic bronchitis and emphysema

c. used to prevent exercise-induced asthma

d. a second-line xanthine agent used in prevention and treatment of bronchoconstriction

e. a short-acting bronchodilator and cardiac stimulant

f. a topical corticosteroid for inhalation used to treat asthma

g. a mast cell stabilizer that prevents the release of bronchoconstrictive and inflammatory substances

h. the treatment of choice to relieve acute asthma

i. indicated in clients with allergic asthma whose symptoms do not respond adequately to inhaled steroids

j. an adrenergic agent that may be injected subcutaneously in an acute attack of bronchoconstriction

TRUE OR FALSE

Indicate if the following statements are true or false.

_____ 1. Hispanics have a higher death rate from asthma than do other ethnic groups.

_____ 2. Children who are exposed to tobacco smoke are at risk for the development of asthma.

_____ 3. A chronic cough can be the only symptom of asthma.

_____ 4. Asthma is a respiratory disorder characterized by bronchodilation.

_____ 5. Antiasthmatic medications can increase acid reflux.

_____ 6. Anti-inflammatory drugs reduce inflammation by increasing bronchoconstriction.

_____ 7. Adrenergic bronchodilators are contraindicated in clients with severe cardiac disease.

_____ 8. Epinephrine is the treatment of choice to relieve acute asthma.

_____ 9. Intravenous (IV) administration of a corticosteroid in acute severe asthma has a therapeutic advantage over oral administration.

_____ 10. Leukotriene modifiers and mast cell stabilizers cause serious adverse effects.

SHORT ANSWER

Answer the following.

1. What are the two major groups of drugs used to treat asthma, bronchitis, and emphysema?

   _____

   _____

   _____

2. How does reducing inflammation reduce bronchoconstriction?

   _____

   _____

   _____

   _____

3. List three drugs that decrease the effects of bronchodilators.

   _____

   _____

   _____

   _____

4. What is a common cause of acute asthma attacks?

   _____

   _____

   _____

5. List signs and symptoms of theophylline overdose.

   _____

   _____

   _____

■ Applying Your Knowledge

Gwen, a 7th grader, comes to the health center at the middle school in moderate respiratory distress. Her respiratory rate is 36, and you hear audible wheezing without a stethoscope. Her inhalers (albuterol and Vanceril) are kept in the health center for administration during school hours. Gwen has not been in to use her inhalers for the last week. What is most important to do now to treat Gwen's asthma attack? What assessment/interventions might be important to assist Gwen in long-term management of her asthma?

_____

_____

_____

_____

_____

_____

_____

_____

■ Practicing for NCLEX

MULTIPLE-CHOICE QUESTIONS

1. A 16-year-old enters the hospital emergency room with a severe asthma attack. Which of the following drugs will most likely be used?

   a. salmeterol (Serevent)

   b. epinephrine (Adrenalin)

   c. albuterol (Proventil)

   d. formoterol (Foradil)

2. An asthmatic client's medication has been changed to theophylline (Theo-Dur). Which of the following is most important to include in his client teaching?

   a. Take only on an empty stomach.

   b. Increase intake of fatty foods.

   c. Decrease intake of fluids.

   d. Limit intake of caffeine.

3. When teaching an asthma client the proper technique for administering a metered-dose inhaler, the nurse will emphasize

   a. not to eat or drink prior to or after administration

   b. to lie in semi-Fowler's position while administering the inhaler

   c. to hold his breath 10 seconds after inhaling the medication before exhaling

   d. to place his lips firmly around the inhaler's mouthpiece

4. A client has been diagnosed with asthma. The nurse has just finished explaining the use of a metered-dose inhaler. Which of the following responses indicates the need for further instruction?

   a. "I should inhale deeply before depressing the inhaler."

   b. "I will shake the inhaler well before each use."

   c. "I will wait about 5 minutes before I inhale for the second time."

   d. "I will not use more than one or two puffs per treatment."

5. A client has been using a beclomethasone (Beclovent) inhaler for several months. She is in the clinic complaining of a rash in her mouth. She is upset and states she knows it is from the inhaler she is using. Which of the following should the nurse do?

   a. Recommend that she stop using the Beclovent inhaler immediately.

   b. Instruct the client to decrease the dosage of Beclovent.

   c. Inform the client that she is having an allergic reaction to something she has eaten.

   d. Remind her that she must rinse her mouth after each treatment.

6. A client has been taking zafirlukast (Accolate) for asthma for 3 weeks. She is in the clinic for a follow-up visit. Which of the following findings would cause the nurse alarm?

   a. pulse rate of 84

   b. absence of wheezing

   c. pink nail beds

   d. whites of eyes are yellow in color

7. A client who is on theophylline (Theo-Dur) is in the clinic for a theophylline level test. The nurse knows that the optimal therapeutic range for this drug is

   a. 0.5 to 3 mcg/mL   c. 20 to 30 mcg/mL

   b. 5 to 15 mcg/mL   d. 50 to 65 mcg/mL

8. Which of the following drugs is used only for prophylaxis of bronchoconstriction?

   a. epinephrine (Adrenalin)

   b. salmeterol (Serevent)

   c. isoproterenol (Isuprel)

   d. albuterol (Proventil)

9. A client is taking a combination of ipratropium and albuterol (Combivent). Which of the following will the nurse stress as a common adverse effect?

   a. increased pulse rate   c. weight gain

   b. rhinorrhea   d. cough

10. A nurse is instructing a client on the administration of zafirlukast (Accolate). Which of the following should the nurse include in her instructions?

    a. Take 1 hour before or 2 hours after a meal.

    b. Take with fatty foods.

    c. Take medication once daily.

    d. It may be taken with or without food.

ALTERNATE FORMAT QUESTIONS

1. A nurse is explaining the proper use of an inhaler to a 15-year-old client. Arrange the following steps in the correct order for use of an inhaler (with number 1 being the first step).

    a. _____ Wait 3 to 5 minutes before taking a second inhalation of the drug.

    b. _____ Remove the cap from the mouthpiece.

    c. _____ While pressing down on the inhaler, take a slow, deep breath for 3 to 5 seconds. Hold the breath for approximately 10 seconds and exhale slowly.

    d. _____ Rinse the mouth with water.

    e. _____ Shake well.

    f. _____ Exhale to the end of a normal breath.

    g. _____ With the inhaler in the upright position, place the mouthpiece just inside the mouth and use the lips to form a tight seal.

    h. _____ Rinse the mouthpiece and store the inhaler away from heat.

2. Which of the following is an appropriate outcome for an asthmatic client taking a bronchodilator? (Select all that apply.)

    a. _____ increased respiratory rate

    b. _____ decreased dyspnea and wheezing

    c. _____ improved exercise tolerance

    d. _____ increased respiratory secretions

    e. _____ decreased anxiety and restlessness

CHAPTER 45

Antihistamines and Allergic Disorders

■ Mastering the Information

MATCHING

Match the terms in column I with a definition, example, or related statement from Column II.

COLUMN I

1. _____ type I allergic reaction

2. _____ urticaria

3. _____ epinephrine

4. _____ anaphylaxis

5. _____ hydroxyzine (Atarax)

6. _____ serum sickness

7. _____ allergic rhinitis

8. _____ antigens

9. _____ anaphylactoid reactions

10. _____ type II allergic reaction

COLUMN II

a. mediated by IgG and IgM

b. drug of choice for treating severe anaphylaxis

c. a vascular reaction of skin characterized by papules or wheals and severe itching

d. example of type I allergic reaction

e. foreign materials

f. prescribed for pruritus

g. a delayed hypersensitivity reaction most often caused by drugs

h. inflammation of nasal mucosa

i. may occur on first exposure to a foreign substance

j. mediated by IgE

TRUE OR FALSE

Indicate if the following statements are true or false.

_____ 1. Histamine is the first chemical mediator to be released in immune and inflammatory responses.

_____ 2. When H_1 receptors bind with histamine, there is a decrease in mucous gland secretions.

_____ 3. When H_2 receptors are stimulated, gastric acid secretion increases.

_____ 4. Any drug can induce an immunologic response in susceptible people.

_____ 5. First-generation H_1 receptor antagonists may cause central nervous system (CNS) stimulation in children.

_____ 6. Diphenhydramine (Benadryl) causes CNS stimulation in children.

_____ 7. Antihistamines prevent histamine release.

_____ 8. Diphenhydramine (Benadryl) should not be given to newborns.

_____ 9. More than one antihistamine may be taken at a time.

_____ 10. Loratadine (Claritin) should be taken on an empty stomach.

SHORT ANSWER

Answer the following.

1. Where is histamine mainly located in the body?

_____

_____

_____

2. What causes histamine to be discharged from mast cells and basophils?

_____

_____

_____

3. Where are H_1 receptors located?

_____

_____

_____

4. List six responses that may occur when histamine binds with H_1 receptors.

_____

_____

_____

5. List three responses that occur when H_2 receptors are stimulated.

_____

_____

_____

Applying Your Knowledge

Jane Morgan is admitted to the oncology unit for chemotherapy. Before administering a chemotherapeutic agent that is known to cause allergic symptoms in some clients, diphenhydramine (Benadryl) is ordered. Discuss the rationale for this order. If anaphylaxis were to develop in this client, would administering additional Benadryl help?

_____

_____

_____

_____

_____

_____

_____

Practicing for NCLEX

MULTIPLE-CHOICE QUESTIONS

1. A 25-year-old female calls the clinic at 3:00 P.M. and tells the nurse she forgot to take her morning dose of fexofenadine (Allegra). She wants to know what she should do. The nurse tells her to
   a. double her evening dose
   b. skip the evening dose and start back in the morning
   c. forget about the morning dose and take the evening dose early
   d. take the morning dose now and the evening dose at the scheduled time

2. A client has just been placed on an antihistamine for allergic rhinitis. Which of the following will the nurse be sure to include in the teaching plan regarding antihistamines?
   a. Use sunscreen outdoors.
   b. Weigh daily and note any change in weight.
   c. Reduce fat intake in your diet.
   d. Reduce intake of citrus juices.

3. A 32-year-old businessman is in the clinic for allergies. He has to make a major presentation in 3 days, and his allergies are worse. He asks whether the doctor can prescribe another antihistamine for him to use with the loratadine (Claritin) he is already taking. The nurse's best response to him would be as follows:
   a. "Sure, I'll ask right now."
   b. "If you take another antihistamine, you will have to decrease the Claritin dosage."
   c. "You should not take two antihistamines at the same time because of possible severe adverse effects."
   d. "Why do you think you need more medication?"

4. A 22-year-old male is in the clinic for seasonal allergies. He states that he works in construction and operates heavy equipment. Which of the following drugs will be prescribed for him?
   a. desloratadine (Clarinex)
   b. clemastine (Tavist)
   c. promethazine (Phenergan)
   d. chlorpheniramine (Chlor-Trimeton)

5. A client is going to start on antihistamines for seasonal allergies. Which of the following would the nurse assess for first?

    a. diabetes mellitus   c. Alzheimer's disease

    b. urinary retention   d. multiple sclerosis

6. A client is taking diphenhydramine (Benadryl) for allergic rhinitis. Which of the following nursing diagnoses would be appropriate, especially during the first few days of therapy?

    a. Knowledge Deficit: Safe and Accurate Drug Use

    b. Risk for Injury Related to Drowsiness

    c. Knowledge Deficit: Strategies for Minimizing Exposure to Allergens

    d. Risk for Activity Intolerance Related to Antihistamine Use

7. On a return visit to the clinic, a client, a 69-year-old male, complains of difficulty voiding. He was seen 1 week ago for pruritus. The nurse suspects he may have

    a. benign prostatic hypertrophy

    b. renal failure

    c. diabetes mellitus

    d. cardiac dysrhythmias

8. Which of the following antihistamines is not recommended for children with chickenpox or flulike infections?

    a. hydroxyzine (Atarax)

    b. clemastine (Tavist)

    c. chlorpheniramine (Chlor-Trimeton)

    d. diphenhydramine (Benadryl)

9. A client is to begin taking loratadine (Claritin). She asks you how long it will take to help her allergies. The nurse's response should be as follows:

    a. "You should feel better immediately."

    b. "You should see some effects within 1 to 3 hours of your first dose."

    c. "It will take about 3 weeks before you will see any effects."

    d. "In about 2 days, you should feel better."

10. When instructing your client in taking loratadine (Claritin), the nurse should include which of the following?

    a. Take it on an empty stomach.

    b. Chew the tablet and follow it with a glass of water.

    c. Take it with meals.

    d. Take it three times a day.

ALTERNATE FORMAT QUESTIONS

1. A client has just started loratadine (Claritin). Which of the following drugs would the nurse assess for? (Select all that apply.)

    a. _____ erythromycin

    b. _____ rifampin

    c. _____ cimetidine

    d. _____ monoamine oxidase inhibitors

    e. _____ fluconazole

2. A 5-year-old client hospitalized for severe conjunctivitis has an order for 6.25 mg of Benadryl orally (PO) every 4 hours. The bottle reads 25 mg/10 mL. How many milliliters will the client receive in each dose?

CHAPTER 46

Nasal Decongestants, Antitussives, and Cold Remedies

■ Mastering the Information

MATCHING

Match the terms in column I with a definition, example, or related statement from Column II.

COLUMN I

1. _____ pseudoephedrine (Sudafed)

2. _____ codeine

3. _____ ipratropium (Atrovent)

4. _____ phenylephrine (Neo-Synephrine)

5. _____ diphenhydramine

6. _____ rhinorrhea

7. _____ dextromethorphan (Benylin DM)

8. _____ rhinitis

9. _____ oxymetazoline (Afrin)

10. _____ acetylcysteine (Mucomyst)

COLUMN II

a. antihistamine used in treatment for allergic rhinitis

b. adrenergic nasal decongestant taken orally

c. a central-acting antitussive that is a narcotic

d. anticholinergic nasal spray used for the treatment of rhinorrhea

e. a mucolytic administered by inhalation to liquefy mucus in the respiratory tract

f. a nasal decongestant that can be used in infants

g. the antitussive drug of choice

h. secretions discharged from the nose

i. an adrenergic nasal spray

j. inflammation of nasal mucosa

TRUE OR FALSE

Indicate if the following statements are true or false.

_____ 1. Rebound nasal swelling can occur with excessive use of nasal sprays.

_____ 2. An antitussive suppresses coughing by depressing the cough center in the lungs.

_____ 3. The major clinical indication for use of antitussives is a wet, productive cough.

_____ 4. Guaifenesin is the most commonly used expectorant.

_____ 5. Acetylcysteine (Mucomyst) is effective within 5 minutes after inhalation.

_____ 6. Vitamin C is used to reduce the incidence and severity of colds and influenza.

_____ 7. Oral decongestive agents are used with clients who have cardiovascular disease.

_____ 8. Dextromethorphan (Benylin DM) is the antitussive drug of choice.

_____ 9. Antibiotics are given for most upper respiratory infections.

_____ 10. Adverse effects from oral decongestants are less likely than topical agents.

SHORT ANSWER

Answer the following.

1. Why is it recommended that two decongestants containing the same or similar active ingredients not be taken together?

_____

_____

_____

2. Why are nasal decongestants contraindicated in clients with severe hypertension?

_____

_____

_____

3. Name three types of drugs usually contained in a product used to treat the common cold.

_____

_____

_____

4. Why are oral decongestants preferred over topical preparations?

_____

_____

_____

5. List two nursing diagnoses appropriate for a client using a nasal decongestant.

_____

_____

_____

■ Applying Your Knowledge

Joan, a college student, comes to the health clinic with cold symptoms (productive cough, low-grade fever, continuous nasal discharge, and general malaise and discomfort). She states she went to the drugstore to buy some cold medicine, but there were so many different preparations that she was confused. Discuss your recommendations for Joan, with their underlying rationales.

_____

_____

_____

_____

_____

_____

_____

_____

_____

■ Practicing for NCLEX

MULTIPLE-CHOICE QUESTIONS

1. Your client is a 74-year-old female who is taking pseudoephedrine (Sudafed) for nasal congestion. Which of the following adverse effects will concern the nurse most?

   a. increased blood pressure   c. irritability

   b. diarrhea   d. constipation

2. Which of the following instructions would the nurse give to a client who is taking an antitussive with codeine?

   a. avoid coffee, tea, and caffeine drinks

   b. decrease fluid intake

   c. increase protein in your diet

   d. avoid alcohol

3. Which of the following instructions will a nurse give to a client who is taking pseudoephedrine (Dimetapp) in order to facilitate the therapeutic effect of the drug?

   a. Increase fluid intake.

   b. Decrease sodium in diet.

   c. Decrease physical activity.

   d. Take it with a glass of milk.

4. A 32-year-old male is in the clinic complaining of a chronic, nonproductive cough. Which of the following drugs will be prescribed for him?

   a. guaifenesin (Robitussin)

   b. dextromethorphan (Benylin DM)

   c. acetylcysteine (Mucomyst)

   d. naphazoline (Privine)

5. The nurse is instructing a 12-year-old boy on how to self-administer a nasal spray. Which of the following will be the nurse's initial instruction to him?

   a. "Sit with your neck hyperextended."

   b. "Squeeze the container twice before you spray in each nostril."

   c. "Blow your nose gently."

   d. "Cough up as much mucus as you can."

6. A nurse is instructing a mother on how to administer cough syrup to her 8-year-old. The nurse will include which of the following?

   a. Avoid eating or drinking 30 minutes after administration.

   b. Do not eat or drink 15 minutes prior to administration.

   c. Have the child lie down for 10 minutes after the dose.

   d. Avoid hot baths after taking the medication.

7. A middle-aged woman calls the clinic and states that she has a cold and that she has been using an over-the-counter (OTC) cold remedy for 3 days. She asks the nurse whether she should continue. An appropriate response would be the following:

   a. "No. You should come into the clinic for prescription medication."

   b. "If you are not better in 1 week, you should come to the clinic."

   c. "You should be okay in a couple of days."

   d. "Yes. You can take over-the-counter medication for up to 14 days."

8. A client, who has been diagnosed with congestive heart failure, is in the clinic for a cold. The physician orders a topical nasal decongestant. Oral agents are contraindicated in this client because these drugs

   a. increase heart rate and blood pressure

   b. increase heart rate and decrease blood pressure

   c. decrease heart rate and blood pressure

   d. decrease heart rate and increase blood pressure

9. A client is taking acetylcysteine (Mucomyst) by inhalation. An expected outcome for this client would be a therapeutic effect within

   a. 1 minute   c. 5 minutes

   b. 3 minutes   d. 10 minutes

10. The nurse suspects that a client is overusing her nasal spray. The nurse should remind the client that she can most likely expect

   a. sweaty palms   c. nosebleeds

   b. rebound nasal congestion   d. diarrhea

ALTERNATE FORMAT QUESTIONS

1. A nurse is teaching a 12-year-old how to instill nose drops. Which of the following would be included in her instructions? (Select all that apply.)

   a. _____ Blow the nose before instilling the drops.

   b. _____ Lie down or sit.

   c. _____ Hyperextend the neck.

   d. _____ Place the dropper to the side against the nostril.

   e. _____ Rinse the dropper after use.

2. A nurse is assessing a client with nasal congestion. Which of the following would be included in the assessment? (Select all that apply.)

   a. _____ ability of the client to breathe through the nose

   b. _____ amount, color, and thickness of drainage, if present

   c. _____ duration and extent of condition

   d. _____ factors that could have precipitated the symptoms

   e. _____ any prescribed or OTC drugs that relieve symptoms

CHAPTER 47

Physiology of the Cardiovascular System

■ Mastering the Information

MATCHING

Match the terms in Column I with a definition, example, or related statement from Column II.

COLUMN I

1. _____ blood
2. _____ left ventricle
3. _____ endocardium
4. _____ right ventricle
5. _____ myocardium
6. _____ right atrium
7. _____ sinoatrial (SA) node
8. _____ capacitance
9. _____ pericardium
10. _____ left atrium

COLUMN II

a. receives oxygenated blood from the lungs
b. the fibroserous sac that encloses the heart
c. functions to nourish and oxygenate body cells
d. receives deoxygenated blood through the pulmonary circulation
e. the normal pacemaker of the heart
f. sends deoxygenated blood through the pulmonary circulation
g. contracts against high pressure to pump oxygenated blood through the body
h. the membrane lining the heart chambers
i. veins and venules that assist blood flow against gravity
j. the muscular layer of the heart that provides the pumping action for blood circulation

TRUE OR FALSE

Indicate if the following statements are true or false.

_____ 1. The main function of the cardiovascular system is to remove waste products of cell metabolism.

_____ 2. The atria are the distributing chambers of the heart.

_____ 3. The right ventricle sends deoxygenated blood through the pulmonary circulation.

_____ 4. Heart valves function to maintain a two-way flow of blood.

_____ 5. The pulmonary valve separates the right ventricle and pulmonary artery.

_____ 6. The SA node is the normal pacemaker of the heart.

_____ 7. Coronary arteries fill during diastole.

_____ 8. Plasma constitutes approximately 45% of the total blood volume.

_____ 9. Erythrocytes transport oxygen.

_____ 10. Platelets are found in the bone marrow.

SHORT ANSWER

Answer the following.

1. List two general functions of the cardiovascular system.

_____

_____

_____

2. Describe the heart.

_____

_____

_____

3. What is the main function of the heart valves?

_____

_____

_____

4. Define collateral circulation.

_____

_____

_____

5. Describe the function of capillaries.

_____

_____

_____

■ Practicing for NCLEX

MULTIPLE-CHOICE QUESTIONS

1. Which of the following structures separates the right and left sides of the heart?
   a. mitral valve   c. septum
   b. epicardium   d. ventricles

2. If a client had a conduction malformation in his heart, the nurse would suspect a problem with the
   a. endocardium   c. collateral circulation
   b. SA node   d. aortic valve

3. Through the release of epinephrine and norepinephrine, sympathetic nerves
   a. increase heart rate
   b. decrease heart rate
   c. cause the myocardium to stop contracting
   d. cause collateral circulation

4. Which of the following vessels drains tissue fluid that has filtered through capillaries?
   a. arteries   c. veins
   b. lymphatic   d. venules

5. Platelets are necessary for
   a. defense against microorganisms
   b. blood coagulation
   c. blood cell replication
   d. oxygen transportation

6. Most leukocytes are produced in the
   a. bone marrow   c. liver
   b. spleen   d. lymph nodes

7. What percentage of the total blood volume is plasma?
   a. 10%   c. 55%
   b. 25%   d. 85%

8. The primary function of erythrocytes is to
   a. decrease peripheral vascular resistance
   b. alter the heart rhythm
   c. restore homeostasis
   d. transport oxygen

9. Which of the following valves separate the left atrium and left ventricle?
   a. mitral   c. pulmonic
   b. tricuspid   d. aortic

10. Which of the following blood cells produce antibodies?
    a. erythrocytes   c. platelets
    b. leukocytes   d. fibrinogen

ALTERNATE FORMAT QUESTIONS

1. Blood functions to nourish and oxygenate body cells. Which of the following are specific functions? (Select all that apply.)

   a. _____ transports oxygen from cells and carbon dioxide to cells

   b. _____ transports hormones from endocrine glands to other parts of the body

   c. _____ transports leukocytes and antibodies to sites of injury

   d. _____ assists in regulation of body temperature

   e. _____ transports platelets to bone marrow

2. Which of the following are the two functions of endothelial cells found in blood vessel walls? (Select two answers.)

   a. _____ act as a semipermeable membrane

   b. _____ act as a defense mechanism against microorganisms

   c. _____ act as a permeable barrier and regulate the passage of molecules and cells across the blood vessel wall

   d. _____ adhere to the vessel wall and prevent leakage of blood

   e. _____ secrete opposing mediators that maintain a balance between bleeding and clotting of blood

CHAPTER 48

Drug Therapy for Heart Failure

■ Mastering the Information

MATCHING

Match the terms in Column I with a definition, example, or related statement from Column II.

COLUMN I

1. _____ thrombocytopenia

2. _____ bosentan (Tracleer)

3. _____ captopril

4. _____ nesiritide

5. _____ digoxin

6. _____ milrinone (Primacor)

7. _____ photophobia

8. _____ furosemide

9. _____ inamrinone (Inocor)

10. _____ rennin

COLUMN II

a. a loop diuretic used in clients with heart failure who have impaired renal function

b. a phosphodiesterase inhibitor used for severe heart failure not controlled by digoxin

c. the drug of choice to treat clients who have chronic heart failure

d. the only commonly used digitalis glycoside

e. an adverse effect of prolonged use of inamrinone

f. an enzyme produced in the kidneys in response to impaired blood flow and tissue perfusion

g. an endothelin receptor antagonist used in the treatment of pulmonary hypertension

h. used in the management of acute heart failure to increase diuresis and secretion of sodium and decrease the secretion of neurohormones

i. an inotropic agent used alone or with dobutamine or nitroprusside

j. an adverse effect of digoxin

TRUE OR FALSE

Indicate if the following statements are true or false.

_____ 1. Clients with compensated heart failure exhibit dyspnea and fatigue at rest.

_____ 2. Digoxin toxicity develops more often and lasts longer in renal impairment.

_____ 3. Digoxin is the drug of choice for clients with acute myocardial infarction.

_____ 4. The onset of action for oral digoxin is 30 minutes to 2 hours.

_____ 5. Maximum drug effects of digoxin occur in about 1 week.

_____ 6. The drug of choice for acute heart failure is an angiotension-converting enzyme (ACE) inhibitor.

_____ 7. In chronic heart failure, there is a high risk for hypokalemia.

_____ 8. Digoxin dosage must be reduced by approximately half in clients with renal failure.

_____ 9. In the management of digoxin toxicity, potassium chloride may be given if the serum potassium level is low.

_____ 10. In children, there is a significant difference between a therapeutic dose and a toxic dose.

SHORT ANSWER

Answer the following.

1. Describe heart failure.

_____

_____

_____

2. What is endothelin?

_____

_____

_____

3. How does digitalization occur?

_____

_____

_____

4. What are the most common conditions leading to heart failure?

_____

_____

_____

5. Explain how the release of rennin into the bloodstream can cause heart failure.

_____

_____

_____

■ Applying Your Knowledge

Your assessment of Pamela Kindra reveals the following: blood pressure: 118/92, pulse: 110, and respirations: 32 and labored. Respiratory assessment reveals coarse rhonchi and wheezing bilaterally. Urine output has been less than 30 cc per hour, and she has gained 12 pounds over the last 2 days.

You place Ms. Kindra in a high-Fowler's position and call her health care provider. After examining her, he orders 0.5 mg of digoxin intravenously (IV) stat: repeat in 4 hours; then give 0.25 mg qd. Do you feel this is a safe dosage of digoxin to give? Discuss the rationale for your answer.

_____

_____

_____

_____

_____

_____

_____

■ Practicing for NCLEX

MULTIPLE-CHOICE QUESTIONS

1. A client who is in renal failure has been successfully digitalized. Serum levels of digoxin are within the therapeutic range. The nurse will monitor which of the following to determine the maintenance dose of digoxin?

   a. hepatic function   c. potassium levels

   b. creatinine clearance   d. magnesium levels

2. A 72-year-old male is admitted to the cardiac care unit with severe heart failure. He is to receive a bolus dose of inamrinone (Inocor). Which of the following adverse effects suggest that the nurse may need to recommend a change in the client's medication?

   a. dysrhythmias   c. disorientation

   b. headache   d. seizures

3. A client is to be discharged on 0.125 mg of Lanoxin daily. Which of the following statements by the client indicates successful client teaching by the nurse?

    a. "If I miss a dose, I should not take two tablets in 1 day."

    b. "I will have to take this drug 2 or 3 months."

    c. "This drug can cause a bitter taste in my mouth."

    d. "This drug may cause me to retain fluid."

4. The nurse is preparing to administer digoxin to a client. The most recent serum digoxin level is 2.5 ng/mL. Which nursing action is most appropriate?

    a. Administer the drug.

    b. Take the apical pulse. If it is 60 beats per minute, administer the drug.

    c. Withhold the drug and administer the regular dose the next day.

    d. Withhold the drug and notify the health care provider.

5. A priority nursing action related to the care of a client who is receiving digoxin includes

    a. administering the drug

    b. relying on client blood pressure readings for dosage

    c. reporting an apical heart rate below 60 to the client's physician

    d. discontinuing the medication if the serum digoxin level is within therapeutic range

6. A 58-year-old male is admitted to the emergency room. A diagnosis of severe digoxin toxicity is made. Which of the following drugs may be given immediately?

    a. digoxin immune fab   c. captopril

    b. furosemide   d. dopamine

7. A client is taking 0.125 mg of digoxin (Lanoxin) daily for heart failure. She reports that since she has been on the drug, she can breathe better and her heart rate has been around 74 beats per minute. The nurse notices that, according to the scales, she has lost 3 pounds since her last visit. The nurse suspects

    a. the drug dosage will be increased

    b. the drug dosage will stay the same

    c. the drug dosage will be decreased

    d. the drug will be discontinued

8. Which of the following should be emphasized when instructing a client who is to begin taking digoxin (Lanoxin)?

    a. Digoxin tablets may be crushed and taken with food.

    b. Digoxin should not be taken with an antacid.

    c. It doesn't matter what time of day digoxin is taken.

    d. If a daily dose is missed, it may be taken with the next dose.

9. Which of the following indicates a therapeutic effect of digoxin (Lanoxin) when given for an atrial dysrhythmia?

    a. increase in weight

    b. elimination of pulse deficit

    c. gradual increase in heart rate

    d. decrease in edema

10. A client is to receive nesiritide (Natrecor) for acute heart failure. It is important for the nurse to remember that

    a. the drug must be administered through a separate IV line

    b. a bolus injection of Natrecor must be given over a 10-minute period

    c. the drug cannot be diluted with sodium chloride

    d. it is not necessary to prime the infusion tubing prior to administration

ALTERNATE FORMAT QUESTIONS

1. A client is to receive a digitalizing dose of 0.75 mg of digoxin (Lanoxin) in three divided doses over 24 hours. How many milligrams per dose will the client receive?

2. A nurse is formulating nursing diagnoses for a client with congestive heart failure. Which of the following diagnoses would be appropriate for drug therapy for this client? (Select all that apply.)

    a. _____ Ineffective Tissue perfusion related to decreased cardiac output

    b. _____ Anxiety related to lifestyle changes

    c. _____ Imbalanced Nutrition: Less than body requirements related to drug-induced anorexia

    d. _____ Impaired Gas Exchange related to venous congestion and fluid accumulation in lungs

    e. _____ Knowledge Deficit: Appropriate nutrition associated with heart failure

CHAPTER 49

Antidysrhythmic Drugs

■ Mastering the Information

MATCHING

Match the terms in Column I with a definition, example, or related statement from Column II.

COLUMN I

1. _____ tocainide (Tonocard)

2. _____ flecainide (Tambocor)

3. _____ lidocaine (Xylocaine)

4. _____ moricizine (Ethmozine)

5. _____ ibutilide (Corvert)

6. _____ phenytoin (Dilantin)

7. _____ quinidine (Quinaglute)

8. _____ amiodarone (Cordarone)

9. _____ procainamide (Pronestyl)

10. _____ acebutolol (Sectral)

COLUMN II

a. when used long term, may increase the effects of anticoagulants

b. a prototype of class IB antidysrhythmics; must be given by injection

c. can cause new dysrhythmias or aggravate preexisting dysrhythmias

d. an anticonvulsant used to treat dysrhythmias

e. indicated for recent onset of atrial fibrillation or atrial flutter

f. adverse effects include a syndrome similar to lupus erythematosus

g. a prototype for class IA antidysrhythmics; its use is declining

h. used for chronic therapy to prevent ventricular dysrhythmias

i. recommended for use only in life-threatening ventricular dysrhythmias

j. an oral analog of lidocaine

TRUE OR FALSE

Indicate if the following statements are true or false.

_____ 1. Automaticity is the ability of cardiac tissue to transmit electrical impulses.

_____ 2. Electrical impulses in the heart originate in the SA node.

_____ 3. Cardiac dysrhythmias can only originate in the atrial or ventricular muscle.

_____ 4. Antidysrhythmic drugs can alter the heart's electrical conduction system.

_____ 5. Drugs used for rapid dysrhythmias mainly reduce automaticity, slow conduction of electrical impulses, and prolong the refractory period.

_____ 6. Class I sodium channel blockers block the movement of potassium into cells of the cardiac conducting system.

_____ 7. Class IA drugs are used for both supraventricular and ventricular dysrhythmias.

_____ 8. Class IB drugs decrease conductivity in the ventricles.

_____ 9. Atrial fibrillation is the most common dysrhythmia.

_____ 10. A beta blocker may be used as a first-line drug for symptomatic ventricular dysrhythmias.

SHORT ANSWER

Answer the following.

1. What are the two calcium channel blockers approved for management of dysrhythmias?

   _____

   _____

   _____

2. Why should renal function be assessed in clients receiving dofetilide?

   _____

   _____

   _____

3. Describe the physiological action of amiodarone.

   _____

   _____

   _____

4. List the adverse effects of lidocaine.

   _____

   _____

   _____

5. What is the therapeutic serum drug level of lidocaine?

   _____

   _____

   _____

■ Applying Your Knowledge

You are working on a telemetry unit. The monitor indicates that your patient, Mr. Sweeny, is experiencing paroxysmal supraventricular tachycardia. You have a standing order to treat this dysrhythmia with 20 mg of the calcium channel blocker diltiazem, administered by intravenous (IV) push. How will you proceed to administer this medication safely?

   _____

   _____

   _____

   _____

   _____

   _____

   _____

■ Practicing for NCLEX

MULTIPLE-CHOICE QUESTIONS

1. A client has been diagnosed with supraventricular tachycardia. He is started on disopyramide (Norpace). Which of the following will be a priority assessment for the nurse?
   a. headache
   b. diarrhea
   c. urinary retention
   d. dry mouth

2. During IV administration of an antidysrhythmic drug, the priority nursing action would be to
   a. check blood pressure every 5 minutes
   b. withhold all other medications
   c. turn the client on his or her left side
   d. check the serum potassium level

3. Which of the following should a nurse recognize as a desired response to an antidysrhythmic drug?
   a. increased cardiac output
   b. decreased cardiac output
   c. increased renal insufficiency
   d. decreased respiratory distress

4. A client is being discharged from the hospital on an antidysrhythmic drug. Which of the following would indicate that the medication is decreasing blood pressure?

    a. dizziness

    b. constipation

    c. increased appetite

    d. stiffness in joints

5. A priority nursing action before administering an antidysrhythmic drug would be to

    a. take the client's temperature

    b. assess the client's metal status

    c. check the apical and radial pulses

    d. place the client in the semi-Fowler's position

6. The initial nursing measure before intramuscular (IM) administration of lidocaine (Xylocaine) to a client with premature ventricular contractions would be to

    a. measure intake and output

    b. take the blood pressure

    c. check apical and radial pulses

    d. weigh the client

7. The heart monitor indicates that a client is experiencing supraventricular tachycardia. The nurse is to administer 20 mg of diltiazem (Cardizem) by IV push. An expected outcome for this client would be a/an

    a. decreased heart rate

    b. increased heart rate

    c. increased blood pressure

    d. increased body temperature

8. Sotalol (Betapace) is contraindicated in a client who has

    a. diabetes mellitus   c. asthma

    b. respiratory impairment   d. edema

9. Which statement by the client reflects a correct understanding of quinidine (Quinaglute)?

    a. "I should decrease my salt intake while taking quinidine."

    b. "I will take my medication with orange juice."

    c. " I need to decrease the fiber in my diet while taking this drug."

    d. "I should take this drug with meals."

10. A client is taking propranolol (Inderal) for a dysrhythmia. The client should be instructed to

    a. report a weight gain of more than 2 pounds

    b. increase caloric intake

    c. have her blood pressure checked every day

    d. observe for blood in her urine

ALTERNATE FORMAT QUESTIONS

1. Identify the dysrhythmia and appropriate drug used for treatment in the following electrocardiogram (ECG) strips. Choose from the following dysrhythmias and drugs.

Dysrhythmias	Drugs
Premature ventricular contractions	digoxin (Lanoxin)
Sinus bradycardia	lidocaine (Xylocaine)
Atrial fibrillation	atropine
Supraventricular tachycardia	verapamil (Calan)

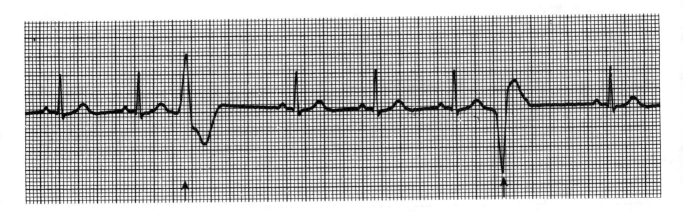

Dysrhythmia _____

Drug _____

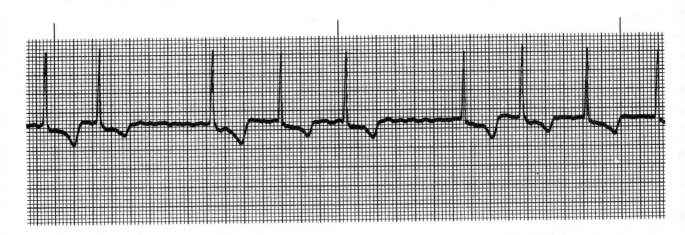

Dysrhythmia _____

Drug _____

2. Mark the location of the SA node in the following figure with an X.

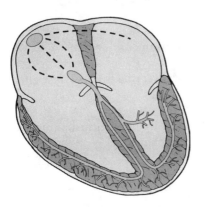

CHAPTER 50

Antianginal Drugs

■ Mastering the Information

MATCHING

Match the terms in Column I with a definition, example, or related statement from Column II.

COLUMN I

1. _____ beta-adrenergic blocking agents

2. _____ nifedipine (Procardia)

3. _____ nadolol (Corgard)

4. _____ aspirin

5. _____ nitroglycerin

6. _____ cimetidine

7. _____ isosorbide mononitrate (Ismo)

8. _____ carbamazepine (Tegretol)

9. _____ propranolol (Inderal)

10. _____ isosorbide dinitrate (Isordil)

COLUMN II

a. a prototype beta blocker

b. an organic nitrate prototype

c. used in long-term management of angina to decrease the frequency and severity of attacks

d. has become part of the standard of care in coronary heart disease

e. a beta-adrenergic blocker that can be given once daily

f. used only for prophylaxis of angina

g. the prototype of the dihydropyridine group of calcium channel-blocking agents

h. decreases the effects of calcium channel blockers

i. an effective oral dose, obtained by increasing the dose until a headache occurs

j. increases the beta-blocking effect of propranolol

TRUE OR FALSE

Indicate if the following statements are true or false.

_____ 1. The most common causes of angina are low blood pressure and an increased amount of blood and oxygen to the heart.

_____ 2. Long-acting medications for angina are not effective in relieving sudden anginal pain.

_____ 3. Clients may increase or decrease dosages of medication for angina according to the frequency and severity of attacks.

_____ 4. Nitroglycerin tablets should be replaced every 6 months.

_____ 5. Hypertension is an adverse effect of antianginal drugs.

_____ 6. A health care provider should always wear gloves when applying nitroglycerin ointment.

_____ 7. Nitroglycerin patches may be applied anywhere on the body.

_____ 8. It takes between 3 and 5 hours for transmucosal tablets to dissolve.

_____ 9. Bradycardia is an adverse effect of nitrates.

_____ 10. Nifedipine (Procardia) may cause hypotension.

SHORT ANSWER

Answer the following.

1. What causes angina pectoris to develop?

   _____

   _____

   _____

2. Describe the development of coronary artery disease.

   _____

   _____

   _____

3. List the three main types of angina.

   _____

   _____

   _____

4. Describe anginal pain.

   _____

   _____

   _____

5. How do nitrates relieve angina?

   _____

   _____

   _____

■ Applying Your Knowledge

Mrs. Sinatro, a patient with newly diagnosed coronary artery disease (CAD), has been started on a nitroglycerin patch that she is to apply in the morning and remove before going to bed at night. Sublingual (SL) nitroglycerin, PRN (to be taken as needed), is ordered for episodes of chest pain. Discuss appropriate teaching for Mrs. Sinatro.

_____

_____

_____

_____

_____

_____

_____

_____

■ Practicing for NCLEX

MULTIPLE-CHOICE QUESTIONS

1. A client is admitted to the hospital with a diagnosis of chest pain. He has an order for 0.3 mg of SL nitroglycerin PRN for chest pain. Which of the following actions should the nurse do first when he complains of chest pain?

   a. Call the physician.

   b. Place three nitroglycerin tablets under his tongue.

   c. Have the client swallow a tablet every 5 minutes for 20 minutes.

   d. Administer a tablet under his tongue; the nurse may need to repeat this action in 5 minutes and again in 5 more minutes.

2. A client with a history of severe anemia is admitted to the hospital with a diagnosis of angina. Which of the following medication orders would the nurse question?

   a. digoxin (Lanoxin) 0.25 mg PO daily

   b. metoprolol (Lopressor) 200 mg PO daily

   c. nitroglycerin (Nitro-Bid) 5-mg, immediate-release tablets, two or three times per day

   d. folic acid (Folvite) 1 mg daily

3. An expected outcome for a client who has just taken nitroglycerin should be

   a. increased pulse and decreased blood pressure

   b. decreased pulse and decreased blood pressure

   c. increased pulse and increased blood pressure

   d. decreased pulse and increased blood pressure

4. The nurse explains to the client that nitroglycerin patches should be applied in the morning and removed in the evening. This dosage schedule reduces the potential for

   a. nitrate tolerance   c. toxic effects

   b. adverse effects   d. nitrate dependence

5. The nurse is to administer 20 mg of isosorbide (Isordil) PO to a client complaining of chest pain. The client's blood pressure is 86/58. The nurse should

   a. Check the client's pulse if it is greater than 80 beats/minute.

   b. Administer 10 mg of the drug instead of 20 mg.

   c. Omit the dose and report to the client's physician.

   d. Administer the dose as ordered.

6. Which of the following conditions would a nurse assess for initially before starting nifedipine (Procardia) therapy?

   a. severe hepatic disease   c. diabetes mellitus

   b. Raynaud's syndrome   d. myasthenia gravis

7. A client complains of headaches and dizziness with nitrate therapy. Which of the following would be the most appropriate response to her?

   a. "Avoid strenuous activity and stand up slowly."

   b. "These effects are temporary and should subside with continuous use."

   c. "You will have these adverse effects as long as you use nitroglycerin."

   d. "You may reduce your dosage to help relieve the adverse effects."

8. A client has started nitrate antianginal therapy. When discussing dizziness, the nurse will instruct him to avoid

   a. a high-fat diet

   b. alcohol

   c. dairy products

   d. over-the-counter cold remedies

9. In regard to the administration of oral nitrates, the nurse will instruct the client to

   a. take them on an empty stomach

   b. take them with food

   c. place each tablet between the cheek and gum

   d. place each tablet under the tongue

10. A nurse is applying a topical preparation of nitroglycerin. Her initial action will be to

   a. place the ointment on a nonhairy part of the body

   b. wipe off the previous dose

   c. cover the area with a plastic wrap or tape

   d. put on a pair of gloves

ALTERNATE FORMAT QUESTIONS

1. When a nurse discusses the use of nitrates with a client for the first time, which of the following will be included in the instructions? (Select all that apply.)

   a. _____ Alcohol may be used in moderation.

   b. _____ Always sit when taking the medication.

   c. _____ Aspirin or acetaminophen may be taken with a nitrate if the headache is severe.

   d. _____ Over-the-counter medications for a "cold" can be used.

   e. _____ The times of administration of oral and topical nitrates should be staggered when they are used concurrently.

2. Which of the following are adverse effects of nitrates? (Select all that apply.)

   a. _____ bradycardia

   b. _____ lightheadedness

   c. _____ constipation

   d. _____ nausea

   e. _____ edema

CHAPTER 51

Drugs Used in Hypotension and Shock

■ Mastering the Information

MATCHING

Match the terms in column I with a definition, example, or related statement from Column II.

COLUMN I

1. _____ epinephrine (Adrenalin)

2. _____ metaraminol (Aramine)

3. _____ anaphylactic shock

4. _____ dopamine (Intropin)

5. _____ neurogenic shock

6. _____ isoproterenol (Isuprel)

7. _____ milrinone (Primacor)

8. _____ septic shock

9. _____ dobutamine (Dobutrex)

10. _____ norepinephrine (Levophed)

COLUMN II

a. most useful in shock that requires increased cardiac output without the need for blood pressure support

b. used to treat clients unresponsive to dopamine or dobutamine

c. used for hypotension associated with spinal anesthesia

d. results from hypersensitivity reaction to drugs or other substances

e. results from any organism that gains access to the bloodstream; associated with bacterial infections and fungi

f. the drug of choice for management of anaphylactic shock

g. increases renal blood flow and glomerular filtration rate

h. results from inadequate sympathetic nervous system stimulation

i. used in shock associated with slow heart rates and myocardial depression

j. a drug used to treat heart failure that is also useful in managing cardiogenic shock

TRUE OR FALSE

Indicate if the following statements are true or false.

_____ 1. All people in shock are hypotensive.

_____ 2. Beta-adrenergic drugs are used to increase myocardial contractility and heart rate, which increases blood pressure

_____ 3. Shock is characterized by an increased blood supply to body tissues.

_____ 4. Acidosis increases the effectiveness of dopamine.

_____ 5. Dobutamine is less likely to cause tachycardia than dopamine.

_____ 6. Adrenergic drugs can cause renal failure.

_____ 7. Adrenergic drugs with beta activity may be contraindicated in shock complicated by cardiac dysrhythmias.

_____ 8. A blood pressure of less than 90/60 may indicate hypotension and shock.

_____ 9. Dobutamine is recommended for long-term use.

_____ 10. Adrenergic blocking drugs are primarily used in the management of shock.

SHORT ANSWER

Answer the following.

1. Describe the three categories of shock.

   _____

   _____

   _____

2. List common signs and symptoms of shock.

   _____

   _____

   _____

3. Why is it important to know the etiology of shock?

   _____

   _____

   _____

4. Differentiate between alpha-adrenergic and beta-adrenergic drugs in the treatment of hypotension and shock.

   _____

   _____

   _____

5. Why are beta-adrenergic drugs used cautiously in cardiogenic shock after a myocardial infarction?

   _____

   _____

   _____

■ Applying Your Knowledge

Brent Williams, a 24-year-old, comes to the emergency department following a reaction to a bee sting that involved swelling, pain, dyspnea, and throat tightness. He is treated with subcutaneous epinephrine, corticosteroids, fluids, and nebulized albuterol. Discharge medications include Benadryl and an EpiPen (a syringe prefilled with epinephrine). What discharge teaching will you provide for Brent?

_____

_____

_____

_____

_____

_____

_____

_____

■ Practicing for NCLEX

MULTIPLE-CHOICE QUESTIONS

1. A nurse is starting an IV on a client who is to receive dopamine (Intropin) intravenously (IV). To decrease the risk of extravasation, the nurse will first

   a. administer a concentrated solution of dopamine

   b. dilute the dopamine in 50 mL of IV fluids

   c. use a large vein for the venipuncture

   d. mix the dopamine with other drugs to be administered

2. IV dobutamine (Dobutrex) as been started on a client. The flow rate will be titrated according to

   a. the client's response to the drug

   b. the manufacturer's directions

   c. the weight of the client

   d. the type of shock the client is experiencing

3. A client has been receiving dopamine (Intropin) for the management of hypovolemia. The physician has discontinued the drug. The nurse will taper the drug dose gradually in order to prevent
   a. hypertension   c. dysrhythmia
   b. hypotension   d. tachycardia

4. An expected client outcome of drug therapy for hypotension associated with shock is
   a. systolic blood pressure of 180 and heart rate of 40
   b. systolic blood pressure of 80 and heart rate of 120
   c. systolic blood pressure of 98 and heart rate of 70
   d. systolic blood pressure of 130 and heart rate of 50

5. Extravasation of metaraminol (Aramine) has occurred with a client. Which of the following drugs will the nurse administer?
   a. diltiazem (Cardizem)
   b. phentolamine (Regitine)
   c. cinoxacin (Cinobac)
   d. betamethasone (Celestone)

6. Which of the following is the most important nursing measure when caring for a client who is being managed for shock?
   a. Monitor blood pressure frequently.
   b. Take an apical pulse prior to medication administration.
   c. Weigh daily.
   d. Decrease fluid intake.

7. A nurse is caring for a critically ill client who is receiving epinephrine. The nurse is aware that the recommended infusion rate will be between
   a. 0.002 to 0.01 mcg/kg/min
   b. 0.01 to 0.15 mcg/kg/min
   c. 0.02 to 0.2 mcg/kg/min
   d. 0.1 to 1.0 mcg/kg/min

8. Milrinone (Primacor) is being given to a client who is experiencing cardiogenic shock. Which of the following is necessary for the maximum therapeutic effect of the drug?
   a. administration of a cardiac glycoside
   b. a heart rate above 50
   c. an infusion rate of 100 μg/kg/min
   d. adequate fluid therapy

9. Which of the following decreases the effectiveness of dopamine (Intropin)?
   a. acidosis   c. benign prostatic hypertrophy
   b. alkalosis   d. hypokalemia

10. A nurse is to administer an IV infusion of metaraminol (Aramine) to treat hypotension caused by spinal anesthesia. Which nursing action is most appropriate?
    a. Add the medication to the existing IV bag of fluids.
    b. Add medication to 500 mL of IV fluid and use a separate line to infuse the dose.
    c. Administer the medication through direct injection at the IV injection site.
    d. Dilute the mediation in 100 mL of D5W and add it to the existing IV fluids.

ALTERNATE FORMAT QUESTIONS

1. Which of the following assessment data could indicate a need for a drug to treat shock? (Select all that apply.)
   a. _____ blood pressure: 78/42 mm Hg
   b. _____ pulse: 140 beats/min
   c. _____ urine output: 15 mL/h
   d. _____ respirations: 20 breaths/min
   e. _____ cool, clammy skin

2. A client is admitted to the emergency room in hypovolemic shock. Dopamine (Intropin) 10 mcg/kg/min is ordered stat. Is this order within therapeutic range?

CHAPTER 52

Antihypertensive Drugs

■ Mastering the Information

MATCHING

Match the terms in column I with a definition, example, or related statement from Column II.

COLUMN I

1. _____ prazosin (Minipress)

2. _____ verapamil (Calan)

3. _____ nifedipine (Procardia)

4. _____ losartan (Cozaar)

5. _____ clonidine (Catapres)

6. _____ fenoldopam (Corlopam)

7. _____ hydrochlorothiazide

8. _____ captopril (Capoten)

9. _____ sodium nitroprusside (Nipride)

10. _____ propranolol (Inderal)

COLUMN II

a. decreases rennin release from the kidneys to decrease blood pressure

b. a first-line agent for treating hypertension in diabetic clients

c. a short-acting calcium channel blocker used to treat hypertensive emergencies or urgencies

d. the first angiotensin II receptor blocker that may be used in combination with hydrochlorothiazide

e. a thiazide diuretic commonly used to treat hypertension

f. a vasodilator that acts on arterioles and venules to decrease blood pressure

g. an initial dose may be taken at bedtime to prevent acute hypotension

h. a fast-acting drug indicated for short-term use in hypertensive emergencies

i. chronic use may result in sodium and fluid retention

j. a calcium channel blocker that dilates peripheral arteries and decreases peripheral vascular resistance to decrease blood pressure

TRUE OR FALSE

Indicate if the following statements are true or false.

_____ 1. Hypertension is defined as a systolic pressure above 160 mm Hg or a diastolic pressure above 100 mm Hg on more than one blood pressure measurement.

_____ 2. It is best to lower blood pressure gradually.

_____ 3. Captopril (Capoten) is recommended as a first-line agent for treating hypertension in diabetic clients.

_____ 4. Angiotensin II receptor blockers are more likely to cause hyperkalemia than are angiotension-converting enzyme (ACE) inhibitors.

_____ 5. Vasodilator antihypertensive drugs directly relax smooth muscle in blood vessels to decrease peripheral vascular resistance.

_____ 6. Children have a greater incidence of secondary hypertension than adults do.

_____ 7. Captopril (Capoten) is the preferred agent for children with hypertension.

_____ 8. A diuretic is the drug of first choice in older adults who are hypertensive.

_____ 9. ACE inhibitors are used to help diabetic clients with renal impairment.

_____ 10. Nonprescription medication may decrease the effectiveness of antihypertensive drugs.

SHORT ANSWER

Answer the following.

1. Describe the three mechanisms that regulate blood pressure.

_____

_____

_____

2. List nonpharmacologic measures to control hypertension.

_____

_____

_____

3. List conditions that may cause a person to be at risk for hypertension.

_____

_____

_____

4. Differentiate between stage 1 and stage 2 hypertension.

_____

_____

_____

5. How does diuretic therapy lower blood pressure?

_____

_____

_____

▪ Applying Your Knowledge

Your client, Tom Betts, age 69, is admitted to the intensive care unit in hypertensive crisis. His blood pressure at time of admission is 225/160 mm Hg. He is to receive sodium nitroprusside (Nipride) intravenously (IV). At what rate will you infuse the medication? What is the expected outcome of the Nipride therapy? After a day of therapy, Mr. Betts develops slurred speech and muscle twitching and has a seizure. What should you do regarding the Nipride therapy and why?

_____

_____

_____

_____

_____

_____

_____

_____

▪ Practicing for NCLEX

MULTIPLE-CHOICE QUESTIONS

1. A client has been placed on 25 mg of captopril (Capoten) to take orally (PO) bid. The nurse should instruct the client to
   a. avoid citric juices with administration of the drug
   b. take the medication with a full glass of water
   c. take the medication on an empty stomach
   d. take the medication with food

2. How often should a nurse instruct a client to apply clonidine (Catapres) skin patches to a hairless area on the upper arm or torso?
   a. every day   c. every 3 days
   b. every other day   d. every 7 days

3. The physician has prescribed 1 mg of prazosin (Minipress) PO daily. When teaching the client about his drug, the most important instruction from the nurse will be to

   a. take the first dose at bedtime to prevent dizziness

   b. limit fluid intake to 1000 mL per day to decrease urinary output

   c. take the drug early in the day to prevent sleepiness

   d. take the drug on an empty stomach to promote absorption

4. The nurse is planning follow-up care for a client who has been taking hydrochlorothiazide (Hydrodiuril) for hypertension. An additional antihypertensive agent has been added to her treatment regimen. The nurse is aware that

   a. most clients on multidrug therapy follow the treatment plan

   b. most clients understand the importance of taking their medication as prescribed

   c. clients who are actively involved in their therapy are usually more compliant

   d. it is unusual for more than one medication to be prescribed for hypertension

5. In determining whether a client can be started on metoprolol (Lopressor), a priority assessment of the nurse will be concerning

   a. renal disease   c. diabetes mellitus

   b. hepatic disease   d. peptic ulcer disease

6. A client has a prescription for ramipril (Altace). She asks the nurse how long it will take to lower her blood pressure. The most appropriate response to her would be as follows:

   a. "That's a question you should really ask your doctor."

   b. "It will probably take 3 to 4 weeks before you feel better."

   c. "This drug usually produces effects within 1 hour after you take a dose."

   d. "It will take 6 months before you feel any effects of the drug."

7. A client is diabetic and has been diagnosed with hypertension. An ACE inhibitor has been prescribed for her. A priority assessment will be for

   a. hypocalcemia   c. hypokalemia

   b. hypercalcemia   d. hyperkalemia

8. A 62-year-old female is taking losartan (Cozaar) for hypertension. It has been determined that the drug therapy is not controlling her blood pressure. Which of the following drugs may be added to her treatment plan?

   a. hydrochlorothiazide   c. fenoldopam

   b. omeprazole   d. sodium nitroprusside

9. A hypertensive client has been taking clonidine (Catapres) for 6 weeks. The nurse will assess for

   a. increased energy level

   b. increased heart rate to 90 beats/minute

   c. constipation

   d. weight gain of 5 pounds

10. A 42-year-old African American male has been diagnosed with hypertension. Initial drug therapy will be

    a. a calcium channel blocker

    b. a diuretic

    c. a beta-blocker

    d. an ACE inhibitor

ALTERNATE FORMAT QUESTIONS

1. Which of the following drugs would most likely be prescribed for African Americans with hypertension? (Select all that apply.)

   a. _____ diltiazem (Cardizem Sr)

   b. _____ losartan (Cozaar)

   c. _____ labetalol (Trandate)

   d. _____ enalapril (Vasotec)

   e. _____ prazosin (Minipress)

2. A client has 30-mg tablets of diltiazem (Cardizem). He is to take 120 mg daily in two doses. How many tablets will he take per dose?

CHAPTER 53

Diuretics

■ Mastering the Information

MATCHING

Match the terms in column I with a definition, example, or related statement from Column II.

COLUMN I

1. _____ spironolactone (Aldactone)

2. _____ hyperkalemia

3. _____ amiloride (Midamor)

4. _____ hydrochlorothiazide (Hydrodiuril)

5. _____ mannitol (Osmitrol)

6. _____ ototoxicity

7. _____ hyperkalemia

8. _____ chlorothiazide (Diuril)

9. _____ pulmonary edema

10. _____ furosemide (Lasix)

COLUMN II

a. an osmotic agent

b. a prototype for loop diuretics

c. may occur with potassium-sparing diuretics

d. an adverse effect that is likely to occur with furosemide (Lasix)

e. the only thiazide diuretic that can be given intravenously (IV)

f. an adverse effect that occurs with osmotic diuretics

g. may be taken without regard to meals

h. blocks the sodium-retaining effects of aldosterone

i. a major adverse effect of potassium-sparing diuretics

j. the most commonly used thiazide diuretic

TRUE OR FALSE

Indicate if the following statements are true or false.

_____ 1. Diuretics decrease renal excretion of water, sodium, and other electrolytes.

_____ 2. Each kidney contains approximately 100 nephrons.

_____ 3. Sodium is reabsorbed in the ascending limb of Henle's loop.

_____ 4. Edema interferes with blood flow to tissues.

_____ 5. Initially, diuretics increase blood volume and cardiac output.

_____ 6. Furosemide (Lasix) is contraindicated in a client who is allergic to sulfonamide drugs.

_____ 7. Dietary sodium is restricted in loop diuretic therapy.

_____ 8. Loop diuretics are the drugs of choice when rapid diuresis is required.

_____ 9. Furosemide (Lasix) is the loop diuretic most often used in children.

_____ 10. Bumetanide (Bumex) produces less ototoxicity than does furosemide (Lasix).

SHORT ANSWER

Answer the following.

1. What is the primary function of the kidneys?

_____

_____

_____

2. Describe the functional unit of the kidney.

_____

_____

_____

3. What is the general physiological action of diuretics?

_____

_____

_____

4. List three major clinical indications for diuretics.

_____

_____

_____

5. Which group of diuretics produces significant diuresis?

_____

_____

_____

■ Applying Your Knowledge

You are caring for a client with severe heart disease who is being treated for hypertension and heart failure. Medications include 10 mg of enalapril (Vasotec) qd and 40 mg of Lasix bid. What assessment data are important to collect before administering these medications?

_____

_____

_____

_____

_____

_____

_____

■ Practicing for NCLEX

MULTIPLE-CHOICE QUESTIONS

1. A client is being treated for hypertension with 500 mg of furosemide (Lasix) to be taken orally (PO) daily. The nurse will teach her about which of the following adverse effects?
   a. muscle cramps   c. muscle weakness
   b. drowsiness   d. dry mouth

2. A 48-year-old female is diabetic and has been on oral hypoglycemics for several years. She has recently been diagnosed with hypertension and started on a thiazide diuretic. The nurse will be most concerned about which of the following?
   a. hypoglycemia   c. hypokalemia
   b. hyperglycemia   d. hyperkalemia

3. The most appropriate nursing intervention for a client who is hospitalized and has just begun diuretic therapy would be to
   a. record blood pressure readings two to four times daily
   b. weigh the client every other day
   c. record fluid intake and output every 36 hours
   d. enforce strict bed rest

4. To avoid increased risks of adverse effects, the nurse will administer an IV injection of furosemide (Lasix) over
   a. 1 to 2 minutes   c. 2 to 5 minutes
   b. 2 to 3 minutes   d. 5 minutes

5. For clients at home, oral diuretics should be taken
   a. early in the morning
   b. at noon
   c. during the afternoon hours
   d. at bedtime

6. A client is taking an antihypertensive agent and a diuretic. A priority nursing action would be to teach the client to
   a. take both drugs on an empty stomach
   b. suck on hard candy
   c. change positions
   d. increase daily exercise

7. A client is taking a potassium-sparing diuretic. Which of the following instructions should the nurse give to her?

   a. "Decrease salt in your diet."

   b. "Limit your intake of foods high in potassium."

   c. "Drink two glasses of orange juice and eat a banana every day."

   d. "Decrease fat in your diet."

8. A 16-year-old boy is admitted to the intensive care unit with increased intracranial pressure from a head injury. Which of the following diuretics will be administered to him?

   a. furosemide (Lasix)

   b. chlorothiazide (Diuril)

   c. spironolactone (Aldactone)

   d. mannitol (Osmitrol)

9. A client is taking hydrochlorothiazide (Hydrodiuril) for ankle edema. On a follow-up visit to the clinic, she states that she has taken her medication as prescribed but continues to have swelling. The nurse should question the client about

   a. alcohol intake

   b. sodium intake in her diet

   c. activity level

   d. possible drug–drug interactions

10. A client has been on chlorothiazide (Diuril) therapy for 3 weeks. She has a serum potassium level of 2.8 mEq/L. This indicates the client is

    a. experiencing hypokalemia

    b. receiving the correct dose

    c. skipping doses frequently

    d. including too much salt in her diet

ALTERNATE FORMAT QUESTIONS

1. Place an X in the area of the nephrons in the following figure where loop diuretics act to produce therapeutic effects.

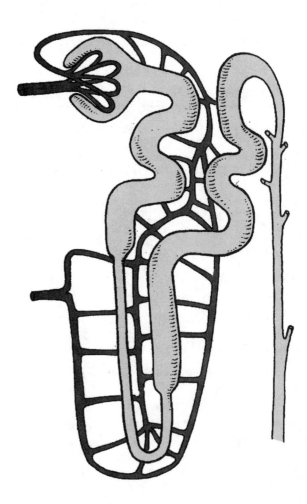

2. The nurse is caring for a client who is on furosemide (Lasix). A diagnosis of dehydration has been made. Which of the following would indicate a correct diagnosis? (Select all that apply.)

   a. _____ heart rate of 50 beats/minute

   b. _____ poor skin turgor

   c. _____ blood pressure of 92/48

   d. _____ urine output of 200 mL/day

   e. _____ moist mucous membranes

CHAPTER 54

Drugs That Affect Blood Coagulation

■ Mastering the Information

MATCHING

Match the terms in column I with a definition, example, or related statement from Column II.

COLUMN I

1. _____ aspirin

2. _____ warfarin (Coumadin)

3. _____ clopidogrel (Plavix)

4. _____ abciximab (ReoPro)

5. _____ bivalirudin (Angiomax)

6. _____ streptokinase (Streptase)

7. _____ aminocaproic acid (Amicar)

8. _____ fondaparinux (Arixtra)

9. _____ heparin

10. _____ ticlopidine (Ticlid)

COLUMN II

a. most commonly used oral anticoagulant

b. a commonly used analgesic, antipyretic, anti-inflammatory drug with antiplatelet effects

c. a thrombolytic agent that breaks down fibrin

d. an anticoagulant used to prevent deep vein thrombosis in clients having surgery for hip fracture or joint replacement

e. indicated for reduction of myocardial infarction and stroke

f. a monoclonal antibody that prevents the binding of fibrinogen

g. a direct thrombin inhibitor used as a heparin substitute

h. a second-line platelet aggregation inhibitor for clients who cannot take aspirin

i. used to stop bleeding caused by overdoses of thrombolytic agents

j. combines with antithrombin III to inactivate clotting factors IX, X, XI, and XII; inhibits the conversion of prothrombin to thrombin

TRUE OR FALSE

Indicate if the following statements are true or false.

_____ 1. Blood clotting is a normal body defense mechanism.

_____ 2. Anticoagulants are more effective in preventing thrombosis than venous thrombosis.

_____ 3. Anticoagulant drugs dissolve formed clots.

_____ 4. Heparin does not cross the placental barrier.

_____ 5. Heparin is the most commonly used oral anticoagulant.

_____ 6. Warfarin is contraindicated during pregnancy.

_____ 7. Lepirudin is used as a heparin substitute.

_____ 8. Heparin and warfarin are given during thrombolytic therapy.

_____ 9. Protamine sulfate is an antidote for heparin.

_____ 10. Ginkgo can decrease the effects of warfarin.

SHORT ANSWER

Answer the following.

1. List three types of drugs used in the prevention and management of thrombotic and thromboembolic disorders.

2. Explain how thrombogenesis may be lifesaving and life threatening.

3. Why is aspirin classified as an antiplatelet?

4. Describe the physiological action of warfarin.

5. What are the disadvantages of heparin?

■ Applying Your Knowledge

You are caring for a client who is in traction. He is receiving 5000 units of subcutaneous heparin bid. Discuss the reason why this client is receiving heparin and how you will safely administer the medication.

■ Practicing for NCLEX

MULTIPLE-CHOICE QUESTIONS

1. A client is receiving intermittent intravenous (IV) doses of heparin. A priority nursing action related to heparin administration would be to
   a. massage the back and legs
   b. observe for signs and symptoms of hemorrhage
   c. ambulate the client three times a day
   d. protect the IV bag and tubing from the light

2. A nurse is caring for a client admitted to the hospital with deep vein thrombosis. Admission orders include 30 units/kg of heparin. The nurse will have which of the following drugs available?
   a. vitamin K
   b. aminocaproic acid (Amicar)
   c. protamine sulfate
   d. tranexamic acid

3. Heparin is contraindicated in a client with
   a. deep vein thrombosis
   b. cirrhosis
   c. peptic ulcer disease
   d. acute myocardial infarction

4. A client has started warfarin (Coumadin) therapy. She asks the nurse how long it will be before the drug starts breaking up the clots. The nurse's response should be

   a. "I'm not sure, but I'll ask your doctor."

   b. "It will take about 3 to 5 days for the anticoagulant effects to occur."

   c. "We should be able to see positive results in 24 hours."

   d. "Anticoagulant effects will start immediately."

5. Which of the following statements by a client who is on warfarin (Coumadin) would indicate that he needs further teaching?

   a. "I take aspirin for my arthritis."

   b. "I love to eat fresh corn in the summer."

   c. "I walk a mile every other day."

   d. "I take an antacid when I have heartburn."

6. A client has intermittent claudication from peripheral vascular disease in both legs. She is taking cilostazol. Which of the following would be a desired outcome of drug therapy for her?

   a. decreased shortness of breath

   b. walking a quarter mile without leg pain

   c. decreased blood pressure

   d. participation in a 2-mile heart walk

7. A client is receiving warfarin (Coumadin). She should be scheduled for which of the following laboratory tests to monitor drug effectiveness?

   a. prothrombin time (PT) only

   b. international normalized ratio (INR) and PT

   c. activated partial thromboplastin time and PT

   d. INR only

8. A client is to receive 5000 units of heparin subcutaneously (SC). When administering this medication, the nurse should

   a. pull the skin tight with the thumb and forefinger before injecting the medication

   b. aspirate the syringe for possible blood return

   c. massage the area for 1 minute once the medication is administered and the needle removed

   d. avoid aspirating the syringe and massaging the injection site

9. A client in the cardiac care unit is receiving an IV of streptokinase infusion for a suspected acute myocardial infarction. During the administration of this drug, the nurse will monitor the client for

   a. headache   c. dry mouth

   b. skin rash   d. increased blood pressure

10. A client is taking warfarin (Coumadin) for continued therapy for myocardial infarction. The nurse observes that she has hematuria and gingival bleeding. You will plan to administer

   a. vitamin K   c. aspirin

   b. protamine sulfate   d. alterplase

ALTERNATE FORMAT QUESTIONS

1. A nurse is aware that drugs given to prevent a heart attack or stroke include the following. (Select all that apply.)

   a. _____ heparin

   b. _____ lepirudin (Refludan)

   c. _____ aspirin

   d. _____ clopidogrel (Plavix)

   e. _____ warfarin (Coumadin)

2. A nurse is instructing a client concerning warfarin (Coumadin) therapy. Which of the following will the nurse include? (Select all that apply.)

   a. _____ Avoid eating large amounts of broccoli, lettuce, and tomatoes.

   b. _____ Avoid walking barefoot.

   c. _____ Avoid injections when possible.

   d. _____ Use an electric razor.

   e. _____ Avoid contact sports.

CHAPTER 55

Drugs for Dyslipidemia

■ Mastering the Information

MATCHING

Match the terms in Column I with a definition, example, or related statement from Column II.

COLUMN I

1. _____ fenofibrate (Tricor)

2. _____ pravastatin (Pravachol)

3. _____ lovastatin (Mevacor)

4. _____ colestipol

5. _____ cholestyramine (Questran)

6. _____ fluvastatin (Lescol)

7. _____ gemfibrozil (Lopid)

8. _____ ezetimibe (Zetia)

9. _____ niacin (nicotinic acid)

10. _____ atorvastatin (Lipitor)

COLUMN II

a. used in clients who have had a transplant or are receiving immunosuppressants

b. most effective for reducing serum triglycerides

c. a fibrate that should be administered with food

d. acts in the small intestine to inhibit absorption of cholesterol

e. a statin that should be administered with food

f. mix granules with water or other liquid for administration

g. the most widely used statin to decrease cholesterol

h. used in clients who are already taking a statin drug

i. has a high rate of absorption

j. decreases both cholesterol and triglycerides

TRUE OR FALSE

Indicate if the following statements are true or false.

_____ 1. Drugs for dyslipidemia should be taken in the morning because more cholesterol is produced in the morning hours.

_____ 2. Statin-type dyslipidemics may increase sensitivity to sunlight.

_____ 3. Cholesterol is necessary for normal body functioning.

_____ 4. High-density lipoproteins (HDLs) transport cholesterol away from arteries and back to the liver, where it is broken down.

_____ 5. Type III dyslipidemia is characterized by lipid deposits in the feet, knees, and elbows.

_____ 6. Low-density lipoprotein (LDL) cholesterol has protective effects against coronary heart disease.

_____ 7. Fibrate agents may cause gallstones.

_____ 8. Estrogen replacement therapy increases HDL cholesterol.

_____ 9. Dyslipidemic drugs may be given to children younger than 10 years of age.

_____ 10. Statins are contraindicated in clients with active liver disease.

SHORT ANSWER

Answer the following.

1. List the three types of blood lipids.

_____

_____

_____

2. How are blood lipids transported in plasma?

_____

_____

_____

3. How do drugs used for dyslipidemia work in the body to decrease lipids?

_____

_____

_____

_____

4. List adverse effects of statins.

_____

_____

_____

5. Which statin is approved for use in children 10 to 17 years of age?

_____

_____

_____

■ Applying Your Knowledge

John Dwyer, 55 years of age, visits his primary health care provider. His cholesterol level (306 mg/dL) has been elevated for the last two visits. His health care provider prescribes niacin (nicotinic acid) to reduce his cholesterol level. Describe the data you will collect and how you will use it to individualize a teaching plan.

_____

_____

_____

_____

_____

_____

_____

_____

■ Practicing for NCLEX

MULTIPLE-CHOICE QUESTIONS

1. Which of the following clients receiving gemfibrozil (Lopid) needs special instruction?
   a. a 52-year-old male bus driver
   b. a 25-year-old housewife
   c. a 73-year-old retired female teacher
   d. a 42-year-old sales associate

2. A client who has hyperlipidemia and is taking lovastatin (Mevacor) should be instructed to take the medication
   a. with the evening meal
   b. at noon with lunch
   c. 2 hours after breakfast
   d. At 9 P.M. before bedtime

3. A client has high cholesterol and triglycerides. Her health care provider has prescribed niacin (nicotinic acid). During a follow-up visit, she complains of skin flushing. An appropriate response to her would be the following:
   a. "This is an adverse effect that will continue as long as you take the medication."
   b. "Don't worry about it. It's really not that noticeable."
   c. "Take 325 mg of aspirin 30 minutes prior to the niacin dose. This should decrease the flushing."
   d. "You need to stop the medication immediately. I will notify your physician."

4. Which of the following may be responsible for noncompliance with statin therapy in older adults?
   a. severe adverse effects
   b. cost of the medication
   c. bitter taste of the medication
   d. frequency of dosage

5. A client who is taking cholestyramine (Questran) will most likely experience which of the following adverse effects?
   a. headache   c. diarrhea
   b. rash   d. constipation

6. A client taking lovastatin (Mevacor) is in the clinic for a follow-up visit. Blood levels of total and LDL cholesterol are slightly decreased from initial levels at start of therapy. The nurse will question the client about use of which of the following?

   a. antacids   c. erythromycin

   b. alcohol   d. niacin

7. The serum drug level of atorvastatin (Lipitor) is increased in a client. The nurse suspects that the client is ingesting

   a. sweet potatoes   c. peanuts

   b. grapefruit juice d. canned tuna

8. A client has been diagnosed with type IV dyslipidemia. Which of the following laboratory tests should be performed prior to and during therapy?

   a. creatinine clearance and specific gravity

   b. blood glucose level

   c. serum aspartate and alanine aminotransferase

   d. complete blood count

9. Assessment by the nurse of which of the following will indicate if a client can take fenofibrate (Tricor)?

   a. hepatotoxicity

   b. severe renal impairment

   c. diabetes mellitus

   d. peptic ulcer disease

10. A diabetic client is to start dyslipidemic therapy. Which of the following drugs will most likely be prescribed for the client?

    a. niacin (nicotinic acid)

    b. gemfibrozil (Lopid)

    c. glycerin (glycerol)

    d. triamterene (Dyrenium)

ALTERNATE FORMAT QUESTIONS

1. Which of the following drugs used to lower body lipids may be taken with or without food? (Select all that apply.)

   a. _____ atorvastatin (Lipitor)

   b. _____ fluvastatin (Lescol)

   c. _____ lovastatin (Mevacor)

   d. _____ pravastatin (Pravachol)

   e. _____ gemfibrozil (Lopid)

2. A client is to take 15 mg of rosuvastatin (Crestor) a day. Each tablet contains 5 mg of rosuvastatin. How many tablets will the client take per day?

CHAPTER 56

Physiology of the Digestive System

■ Mastering the Information

MATCHING

Match the terms in Column I with a definition, example, or related statement from Column II.

COLUMN I

1. _____ esophagus
2. _____ gallbladder
3. _____ duodenum
4. _____ liver
5. _____ alimentary canal
6. _____ saliva
7. _____ stomach
8. _____ pancreas
9. _____ pepsin
10. _____ peristalsis

COLUMN II

a. propels food through the gastrointestinal tract and mixes food with digestive juices

b. a tube extending from the mouth to the anus

c. secretes insulin and glucagons

d. a small pouch on underside of the liver that stores and concentrates bile

e. stores fat-soluble vitamins

f. a 10-inch tube that conveys food from the pharynx to the stomach

g. lubricates the food bolus and starts starch digestion

h. a major digestive enzyme in gastric juice

i. the first 10 to 12 inches of the small intestine

j. serves as a reservoir for food

TRUE OR FALSE

Indicate if the following statements are true or false.

_____ 1. Drugs used in digestive disorders act only systemically.

_____ 2. Stimulation of the parasympathetic nervous system decreases gastrointestinal motility and secretions.

_____ 3. Blood flow increases during digestion.

_____ 4. Most drugs are absorbed from the stomach.

_____ 5. The stomach normally holds approximately 2000 mL.

_____ 6. Fatty foods cause the stomach to empty quickly.

_____ 7. Saliva consists of mucus, ptyalin, and salivary amylase.

_____ 8. The large intestine consists of the cecum, colon, rectum, and anus.

_____ 9. The gallbladder releases bile when fats are present in the duodenum.

_____ 10. The liver receives approximately 500 mL of blood per minute.

SHORT ANSWER

Answer the following.

1. What is the main function of the digestive system?

_____

_____

_____

2. How long is the small intestine?

_____

_____

_____

3. What stimulates the secretion of gastric juices?

_____

_____

_____

4. How much saliva is produced daily?

_____

_____

_____

5. What is the function of each end of the esophagus?

_____

_____

_____

■ Practicing for NCLEX

MULTIPLE-CHOICE QUESTIONS

1. The stomach normally empties in about
   a. 1 hour
   b. 2 hours
   c. 4 hours
   d. 6 hours

2. Excess glucose that cannot be converted to glycogen is converted to
   a. amino acids
   b. proteins
   c. carbohydrates
   d. fat

3. When the liver is damaged, which of the following may accumulate in body fluids?
   a. hormones
   b. bile
   c. glucose
   d. fat

4. The formation of which of the following removes ammonia from body fluids?
   a. glycogen
   b. urea
   c. bile
   d. galactose

5. Which body organ produces about 20% of total body heat?
   a. stomach
   b. pancreas
   c. gallbladder
   d. liver

6. The major digestive enzyme in gastric juice is
   a. trypsin
   b. pepsin
   c. amylase
   d. lipase

7. Which of the following stimulates secretion of pancreatic juices?
   a. gastrin
   b. chymotrypsin
   c. amino acids
   d. cholecystokinin

8. When fats are present in the stomach, the duodenal mucosa produces
   a. pepsin
   b. enterogastrone
   c. insulin
   d. phospholipids

9. The substance that initiates the digestion of starch is
   a. saliva
   b. mucus
   c. insulin
   d. bile

10. Most digestion and absorption occur in the
   a. liver
   b. stomach
   c. small intestine
   d. large intestine

ALTERNATE FORMAT QUESTION

Identify the stomach in the following figure by placing an X on the organ.

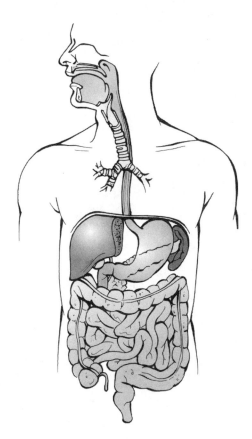

CHAPTER 57

Nutritional Support Products, Vitamins, and Mineral–Electrolytes

■ Mastering the Information

MATCHING

Match the terms in column I with a definition, example, or related statement from Column II.

COLUMN I

1. _____ vitamin E

2. _____ folic acid (folate)

3. _____ Ensure

4. _____ cyanocobalamin (vitamin B$_{12}$)

5. _____ sodium polystyrene sulfonate (Kayexalate)

6. _____ vitamin A

7. _____ thiamine (vitamin B$_1$)

8. _____ deferoxamine (Desferal)

9. _____ ascorbic acid (vitamin C)

10. _____ ferrous sulfate (Feosol)

COLUMN II

a. functions as an antioxidant

b. a liquid enteral formula

c. a prototype for iron preparations

d. an agent used to treat hyperkalemia

e. essential for normal metabolism of all body cells, red blood cells, and growth

f. necessary for collagen formation

g. required for normal vision, growth, and bone development

h. an agent used to remove excess iron from the body

i. essential for normal metabolism of all body cells

j. essential for energy production

TRUE OR FALSE

Indicate if the following statements are true or false.

_____ 1. Vitamins are required for absorption of carbohydrates, protein, and fat.

_____ 2. Vitamin A is water soluble.

_____ 3. There are 22 minerals considered necessary for human nutrition.

_____ 4. Most minerals are supplied by a well-balanced diet.

_____ 5. Succimer (Chemet) is used to treat lead poisoning in children.

_____ 6. Excessive intake of vitamins may cause harmful effects.

_____ 7. Magnesium preparations can be safely used in clients with impaired renal function.

_____ 8. Parenteral nutritional solutions can be administered through central or peripheral intravenous (IV) lines.

_____ 9. B-complex vitamins have cardioprotective effects.

_____ 10. Women of childbearing age should take folic acid to prevent severe birth defects in infants.

SHORT ANSWER

Answer the following.

1. List the adverse effects of niacin.

_____

_____

_____

2. Why do alcoholics usually have a thiamine deficiency?

_____

_____

_____

3. What is the drug of choice to prevent or treat hypokalemia?

_____

_____

_____

4. How does deferoxamine (Desferal) remove excess iron from the body?

_____

_____

_____

5. List signs and symptoms of nutritional deficiencies.

_____

_____

_____

■ Applying Your Knowledge

You receive the following order for Mrs. Leader's tube feedings: 2000 mL of half-strength Ensure daily. The Ensure is supplied in 240-cc cans. How will you dilute this formula, and at what rate will you set the infusion pump?

_____

_____

_____

_____

_____

_____

_____

■ Practicing for NCLEX

MULTIPLE-CHOICE QUESTIONS

1. A client is receiving an intravenous fat emulsion. Which of the following lab values should be checked before administration?

   a. blood glucose levels   c. triglyceride levels

   b. serum sodium levels   d. potassium levels

2. A client is to begin taking pancrelipase (Viokase). Instructions regarding administration should include taking the medication

   a. at least 2 hours prior to eating

   b. immediately before or with meals

   c. with a full glass of water

   d. at bedtime

3. A nurse is caring for an 18-year-old client who has a seizure disorder and takes carbamazepine. In preparation for the future, the nurse suggests she take which of the following vitamins to prevent birth defects?

   a. folic acid   c. niacin

   b. retinol   d. riboflavin

4. A nurse works in an emergency room in a large hospital in a major city. A client presents with erythematous skin sore, gastrointestinal (GI) complaints, headaches, and dizziness. The physician suspects pellagra. The nurse will administer which of the following?

   a. pyridoxine (B_6)

   b. pantothenic acid (B_5)

   c. thiamine (B_1)

   d. niacin (B_3)

5. A 53-year-old client has been diagnosed with pernicious anemia. The nurse has just given him his first injection of vitamin B_{12}. He asks the nurse why he can't take pills instead of injections. The nurse's best response should be as follows:

   a. "The oral form of vitamin B_{12} is more costly than the injectable form."

   b. "You would have to sit upright for 30 minutes after an oral dose of B_{12} to decrease esophageal irritation."

   c. "The oral form of B_{12} is too irritating to the lining of the stomach."

   d. "Oral forms of vitamin B_{12} are not absorbed from the GI tract."

6. A nurse is discussing healthy lifestyles with a group of residents at a retirement complex. One resident asks the nurse which vitamin can help prevent cancer. The nurse's response should be as follows:

   a. "Vitamin B_{12} helps prevent all types of cancer."

   b. "Vitamins A and C help prevent certain types of cancer."

   c. "Folic acid is helpful in the prevention of cancer."

   d. "Vitamins don't help prevent cancer."

7. A client has hemochromatosis. The physician prescribes deferoxamine (Desferal). It is important for the client to understand that

   a. he must increase fluids while taking the medication

   b. he should take the medication on an empty stomach

   c. his urine will be reddish brown

   d. his blood pressure may increase slightly

8. A client is receiving magnesium sulfate for eclampsia. Which of the following IV preparations would the nurse have on hand if the client began to experience lethargy, skeletal muscle weakness, decreased blood pressure, and respiratory distress?

   a. Narcan   c. KCL

   b. calcium gluconate   d. Magnesium oxide

9. A client is admitted to the hospital with dehydration. According to the following lab values, which electrolyte imbalance is she experiencing (serum sodium 115 mEq/L, serum chloride 100 mEq/L, and serum potassium 3.5 mEq/L)?

   a. hyperchloremia   c. hyponatremia

   b. hyperkalemia   d. hypokalemia

10. A 42-year-old client has been started on ferrous sulfate (Feosol) for iron deficiency anemia. Which of the following instructions should be given to her?

    a. "Ferrous sulfate should be taken at night."

    b. "You will need to take the iron preparation for about 2 months."

    c. "You may take a drug holiday once a week."

    d. "Take the medication on an empty stomach if you can tolerate the gastric irritation."

ALTERNATE FORMAT QUESTIONS

1. Arrange the following steps for administration of a tube feeding in the proper order.

   a. _____ Give feeding by gravity flow.

   b. _____ Position the client in a sitting or lying position.

   c. _____ Prepare the solution at room temperature.

   d. _____ Check the placement of the tube.

   e. _____ Rinse the nasogastric tube with at least 50 to 100 mL of water.

2. Which of the following drugs decreases the action of fat-soluble vitamins? (Select all that apply.)

   a. _____ bile salts

   b. _____ laxatives

   c. _____ isoniazid or INH

   d. _____ antibiotics

   e. _____ alcohol

CHAPTER 58

Drugs to Aid Weight Management

■ Mastering the Information

MATCHING

Match the terms in Column I with a definition, example, or related statement from Column II.

COLUMN I

1. _____ orlistat (Xenical)

2. _____ glucomannan

3. _____ kilocalories

4. _____ phentermine (Adipex)

5. _____ guarana

6. _____ epinephrine

7. _____ guar gum

8. _____ alcohol

9. _____ sibutramine (Meridia)

10. _____ LipoKinetix

COLUMN II

a. a source of commercial caffeine found in weight-loss products

b. a combination dietary supplement associated with severe hepatotoxicity

c. the most frequently prescribed adrenergic anorexiant

d. decreases absorption of dietary fat from the intestine

e. a measurement of energy

f. produces a feeling of stomach fullness, causing a person to eat less

g. increases the effects of phentermine and sibutramine

h. decreases the effects of phentermine and sibutramine

i. the most commonly prescribed antiobesity drug

j. dietary fiber found in weight-loss products

TRUE OR FALSE

Indicate if the following statements are true or false.

_____ 1. Diseases are a major cause of obesity.

_____ 2. A deficiency of fats in human nutrition can impair health.

_____ 3. Clients taking orlistat (Xenical) must take a vitamin C supplement.

_____ 4. Sibutramine (Meridia) is approved by the U.S. Food and Drug Administration (FDA) for long-term use.

_____ 5. Drug therapy for obesity can cause serious adverse effects.

_____ 6. Carbamazepine (Tegretol) can cause weight gain.

_____ 7. Obesity is more likely to occur in men.

_____ 8. When drug therapy is indicated for weight loss, combination drugs in the lowest effective dose are recommended.

_____ 9. Treatment of childhood obesity should focus on eating healthy and increasing physical activity rather than drug therapy.

_____ 10. Obesity usually leads to diabetes mellitus.

SHORT ANSWER

Answer the following.

1. Why is obesity considered a major public health problem?

_____

_____

_____

2. Define overweight and obesity.

_____

_____

_____

3. What is the desirable range for body mass index (BMI)?

_____

_____

_____

4. What is the recommended rate of weight loss when using phentermine and sibutramine?

_____

_____

_____

5. List the adverse effects of orlistat (Xenical).

_____

_____

_____

■ Applying Your Knowledge

Joan Croft, age 30, has just been diagnosed with hypertension. She is 5' 4" and weighs 160 pounds. Her physician has told her she needs to lose weight. She asks you what her weight has to do with her blood pressure. Discuss how you will answer her question.

_____

_____

_____

_____

_____

_____

_____

■ Practicing for NCLEX

MULTIPLE-CHOICE QUESTIONS

1. Phentermine (Ionamin), an adrenergic anorexiant, has been prescribed for a client. Which of the following conditions is a contraindication to the use of this drug?
   a. diabetes mellitus
   b. cardiovascular disease
   c. chronic fatigue syndrome
   d. confusion

2. Which of the following statements by a client would lead the nurse to believe that the client has a good understanding of the drug orlistat (Xenical)?
   a. "I hate having to take the medication three times a day."
   b. "I no longer have a lot of gas."
   c. "I take a multivitamin with my morning dose of Xenical."
   d. "I shouldn't have as many bowel movements as I have been having."

3. A client is concerned about long-term use of drug therapy for weight management. An appropriate response by the nurse should be the following:
   a. "I'm sure your doctor will discuss this with you."
   b. "There has been no indication that long-term use of drugs for obesity is harmful."
   c. "It is true that drug safety and efficacy beyond 1 to 2 years has not been established."
   d. "You shouldn't worry about that at this time."

4. When discussing weight gain associated with the use of oral contraceptives, the nurse will include which of the following?
   a. Weight gain is related to retention of fluid and sodium.
   b. Weight gain is a common reason for noncompliance with oral contraceptives.
   c. Weight gain is associated with the blockade of the estrogen and progesterone receptors.
   d. Oral contraceptives cause an increase in appetite.

5. Drug therapy for clients wanting to lose weight will most likely be prescribed for a person who has a BMI of
   a. 28 and has cardiovascular disease
   b. 24 and wants to lose 15 pounds
   c. 25 and has no known health problems
   d. 29.5 and is physically fit

6. Additional instructions to a client taking orlistat (Xenical) would include which of the following?
   a. Constipation is a long-term adverse effect.
   b. Milk will help the absorption of the drug.
   c. Decrease the amount of fatty foods in the diet.
   d. Take one capsule with each meal even if the meal does not contain fat.

7. Which of the following adverse effects of phentermine (Ionamin) would concern a nurse?
   a. hypertension   c. insomnia
   b. nervousness   d. constipation

8. When caring for a client taking sibutramine (Meridia), the nurse should include which of the following as a priority in a teaching plan?
   a. Weigh and record weight daily.
   b. Keep a record of the amount of food eaten.
   c. Have blood pressure and heart rate checked regularly.
   d. Increase fluids daily.

9. Which of the following outcomes would a nurse expect from a client who is taking sibutramine (Meridia)?
   a. increased food intake   c. increased hunger
   b. faster metabolism rate   d. decreased satiety

10. A nurse is working with an obese client who tells her that she does not like to leave her house, even to go to the grocery store. She states that she has had her groceries delivered to her home for the past 2 years. Which of the following would be an appropriate nursing diagnosis for her?
    a. Chronic Low Self-esteem Related to Body Image
    b. Fluid Volume: Excess Related to Excessive Intake
    c. Imbalanced Nutrition, More Than Body Requirements
    d. Activity Intolerance Related to Weight

ALTERNATE FORMAT QUESTIONS

1. A client has been taking orlistat (Xenical). The nurse should inform the client that he should be taking a multivitamin. The multivitamin should contain which of the following vitamins? (Select all that apply.)
   a. _____ A
   b. _____ B complex
   c. _____ C
   d. _____ D
   e. _____ E
   f. _____ K

2. Which of the following are potential serious adverse effects of appetite suppressant drugs? (Select all that apply.)
   a. _____ increased blood pressure
   b. _____ fast heart rate
   c. _____ heart attack
   d. _____ stroke
   e. _____ dizziness
   f. _____ mental confusion

CHAPTER 59

Drugs Used for Peptic Ulcer and Acid Reflux Disorders

■ Mastering the Information

MATCHING

Match the terms in Column I with a definition, example, or related statement from Column II.

COLUMN I

1. _____ pepsin

2. _____ gastric ulcers

3. _____ GERD

4. _____ proton pump inhibitors

5. _____ pyrosis

6. _____ gastritis

7. _____ gastropathy

8. _____ antacid

9. _____ *H. pylori*

10. _____ duodenal ulcers

COLUMN II

a. associated with stress, ingestion of nonsteroidal anti-inflammatory drugs (NSAIDs), and *H. pylori* infection; manifested by painless bleeding

b. a gram-negative bacterium found in the gastric mucosa

c. the strongest gastric acid suppressants

d. a proteolytic enzyme that helps digest protein foods

e. acute gastritis resulting from irritation of the gastric mucosa

f. caused by *H. pylori* infection and NSAID ingestion; associated with abdominal pain

g. an acute or chronic inflammatory reaction of the gastric mucosa

h. regurgitation of gastric contents into the esophagus

i. heartburn from gastroesophageal reflux disease (GERD)

j. an alkaline substance that neutralizes acids

TRUE OR FALSE

Indicate if the following statements are true or false.

_____ 1. Gastric and duodenal ulcers are less common than esophageal ulcers.

_____ 2. Pepsinogen is converted to pepsin when the pH of gastric juices is 3 or less.

_____ 3. Smokers are more likely to develop duodenal ulcers.

_____ 4. GERD is common in people older than 40 years of age.

_____ 5. Antacids act primarily in the small intestine.

_____ 6. Calcium compounds are used to treat peptic ulcer disease.

_____ 7. Magnesium-based antacids are contraindicated in clients with renal failure.

_____ 8. Cimetidine (Tagamet) is administered by the oral route only.

_____ 9. Proton pump inhibitors are the drugs of first choice in most gastric and duodenal ulcers.

_____ 10. Most cases of peptic ulcer disease are caused by a *Helicobacter pylori* infection.

SHORT ANSWER

Answer the following.

1. What is pepsin's role in the digestion process?

_____

_____

_____

2. What is Zollinger-Ellison syndrome?

_____

_____

_____

_____

3. How do antacids produce their therapeutic effect?

_____

_____

_____

4. List clinical indications for histamine$_2$ receptor antagonists.

_____

_____

_____

5. What is the advantage of a proton pump inhibitor over a histamine$_2$ receptor antagonist?

_____

_____

_____

■ Applying Your Knowledge

Ellen Jones, a 54-year old homemaker with a seizure disorder that has been well controlled on carbamazepine (Tegretol) comes to the clinic complaining of ataxia, slurred speech, and lethargy. You obtain a history, and the only significant change for Ellen over the last few weeks is an episode of severe heartburn. She has been self-medicating with over-the-counter cimetidine (Tagamet) with good results. What do you think is causing Mrs. Jones's symptoms, and what action is indicated?

_____

_____

_____

_____

_____

_____

_____

_____

_____

■ Practicing for NCLEX

MULTIPLE-CHOICE QUESTIONS

1. When teaching a client about taking antacids, the nurse will include which of the following statements?
   a. Antacid tablets are not equal to the liquid form.
   b. Take antacids with food.
   c. Antacids absorb pepsin in the stomach.
   d. Do not take antacids with other medications.

2. A client is taking sucralfate (Carafate). A potential nursing diagnosis for her would be the following:
   a. Risk for Constipation
   b. Impaired Urinary Elimination
   c. Activity Intolerance
   d. Deficient Fluid Volume

3. A 42-year-old male is being treated for a peptic ulcer with 159 mg of ranitidine (Zantac) taken orally (PO) at bedtime. Even though few adverse effects have been associated with ranitidine, the nurse will inform the client of which of the following common adverse effects?

   a. headache   c. dry mouth
   b. irritability   d. fever

4. A client is receiving drugs to prevent hyperacidity. An appropriate outcome for him would be the following:

   a. two formed stools per day
   b. a loss of 2 pounds per week
   c. stools negative for occult blood
   d. increased appetite

5. Which of the following instructions would be given to a client in regard to administration of sucralfate (Carafate)?

   a. Take it with meals.
   b. Take the medication at least 1 hour before meals.
   c. Take it after each meal.
   d. Take the medication with a full glass of milk.

6. When evaluating a client on ranitidine therapy, which of the following laboratory tests should be performed?

   a. red blood cell count   c. hepatic enzymes
   b. potassium level   d. serum creatinine level

7. A client is taking aluminum hydroxide. The nurse expects the client to complain of

   a. diarrhea   c. nausea
   b. constipation   d. headache

8. A client is taking omeprazole (Prilosec). The nurse will know that the client is being treated for

   a. constipation   c. diarrhea
   b. GERD   d. asthma

9. A client has GERD and is taking ranitidine (Zantac). She continues to have gastric discomfort and asks whether she can take an antacid. The nurse's response should be as follows:

   a. "Sure, you may take an antacid with Zantac."
   b. "No, the two drugs will work against each other."
   c. "Yes, but be sure to wait at least 1 hour to take the antacid after you take the Zantac."
   d. "I wouldn't advise it. You may experience severe constipation."

10. Which of the following drugs would be indicated for a client who is taking NSAIDs for arthritis and is at high risk for gastrointestinal ulceration and bleeding?

    a. misoprostol (Cytotec)
    b. sucralfate (Carafate)
    c. lansoprazole (Prevacid)
    d. cimetidine (Tagamet)

ALTERNATE FORMAT QUESTIONS

1. A nurse is discussing the use of a histamine$_2$ receptor antagonist (H$_2$RA) with his client who has an acute gastrointestinal ulcer. Which of the following will he include in his discussion? (Select all that apply.)

   a. _____ An antacid may be given concurrently with the H$_2$RA to help relieve the pain.

   b. _____ H$_2$RA therapy is usually short term.

   c. _____ Full dosage may be prescribed for 8 weeks.

   d. _____ The drug is usually taken as a single dose at bedtime.

   e. _____ Multiple daily doses may be required for adequate symptom control.

   f. _____ H$_2$RAs usually relieve pain after 1 week of administration.

2. A nurse suspects that her client, age 70, is overusing Mylanta. Which of the following should she tell the client concerning use of a magnesium antacid? (Select all that apply.)

   a. _____ These drugs are contraindicated in a client with impaired renal function.

   b. _____ They can cause alkalosis.

   c. _____ Magnesium antacids bind with phosphate in the gastrointestinal tract to prevent phosphate absorption and hyperphosphatemia.

   d. _____ Five to 10 percent of the magnesium can be absorbed and accumulate to cause hypermagnesemia.

   e. _____ These drugs inhibit hepatic metabolism of other drugs.

CHAPTER 60

Laxatives and Cathartics

■ Mastering the Information

MATCHING

Match the terms in Column I with a definition, example, or related statement from Column II. Some terms may be used more than once.

COLUMN I

1. _____ bulk-forming laxatives

2. _____ surfactant laxatives

3. _____ saline cathartics

4. _____ stimulant cathartics

5. _____ lubricant laxatives

COLUMN II

a. act as a detergent to help mix fat and water in stools

b. increase osmotic pressure in the intestinal lumen and cause water to be retained

c. the strongest and most abused laxative product

d. the most physiologic laxative

e. used with caution in clients with congestive heart failure

f. when water is added, these substances swell and become gel-like

g. irritate the gastrointestinal (GI) mucosa and pull water into the bowel lumen

h. used when rapid bowel evacuation is needed

i. the therapeutic effect is to prevent straining while expelling stool

j. lubricate fecal mass and slow colonic absorption of water

TRUE OR FALSE

Indicate if the following statements are true or false.

_____ 1. Defecation is stimulated by movements and reflexes in the GI tract.

_____ 2. The cerebral cortex normally controls the defecation reflex.

_____ 3. Involuntary control inhibits the external anal sphincter to allow defecation or prevents the sphincter to prevent defecation.

_____ 4. Bulk-forming laxatives usually produce a therapeutic effect within 12 to 24 hours.

_____ 5. Surfactant laxatives should be taken every other day.

_____ 6. Saline laxatives are well absorbed from the intestine.

_____ 7. Stimulant cathartics are the most abused laxative products.

_____ 8. Lubricant laxatives produce effects usually within 1 to 2 hours.

_____ 9. Laxatives and cathartics should not be used in the presence of undiagnosed abdominal pain.

_____ 10. Stool softeners may be given to small children.

SHORT ANSWER

Answer the following.

1. List adverse effects of saline cathartics.

_____

_____

_____

2. Why are bulk-forming laxatives taken with at least 8 oz of water or other fluid?

_____

_____

_____

3. Why should clients not take bisacodyl tablets within an hour after ingesting milk or taking cimetidine?

_____

_____

_____

4. List two groups of drugs that decrease the effects of laxatives and cathartics.

_____

_____

_____

5. List indications for use of laxatives and cathartics.

_____

_____

_____

■ Applying Your Knowledge

You are a home health nurse visiting Gina Simboli, a 36-year-old client with cancer. Her disease has progressed to a point where she is taking large amounts of narcotics to control the pain, and she spends most of the day in a recliner chair. Your assessment reveals complaints of feeling full and bloated. For over a week, Ms. Simboli has been incontinent of small amounts of liquid stool two to three times a day. What will you recommend to promote normal bowel function?

_____

_____

_____

_____

_____

■ Practicing for NCLEX

MULTIPLE-CHOICE QUESTIONS

1. A client has recently had a myocardial infarction. He is complaining of constipation. Which of the following drugs will be prescribed for him?
   a. methylcellulose (Citrucel)
   b. bisacodyl (Dulcolax)
   c. docusate sodium (Colace)
   d. castor oil (Neoloid)

2. A nurse is caring for a 79-year-old male who has been in an extended care facility for 2 years. He has not had a bowel movement in 5 days. Before administering a laxative, the nurse will check the client for
   a. anxiety   c. fever
   b. fecal impaction   d. urinary incontinence

3. A client is to receive bisacodyl (Dulcolax) orally. The nurse will administer this drug with
   a. food   c. milk
   b. water   d. an antacid

4. A nurse is instructing a client on the use of psyllium hydrophilic mucilloid. She asks the nurse how long it will take to work. The nurse will tell her
   a. within 1 hour   c. as long as 2 to 3 days
   b. within 8 hours   d. as long as 4 to 5 days

5. Which of the following clients should not take a saline laxative?
   a. a 32-year-old diabetic
   b. a 55-year-old woman with breast cancer
   c. a 67-year-old male in congestive heart failure
   d. a 22-year-old who has acquired immunodeficiency syndrome (AIDS)

6. Which of the following laxatives would be used for rapid bowel movement?
   a. Metamucil   c. Dulcolax
   b. milk of magnesia d. castor oil

7. A client is taking a bulk-forming laxative. The nurse will observe for which of the following adverse effects?
   a. fecal impaction   c. fluid retention
   b. diarrhea   d. edema

8. Which of the following drugs decrease the effects of laxatives and cathartics?

   a. Demerol
   b. Synthroid
   c. Inderal
   d. Dilantin

9. Instructions regarding administration of lactulose should include the following:

   a. Take it with food.
   b. Take it every other day.
   c. Take it without food or liquid.
   d. Mix it with fruit juice to improve the taste.

10. A laxative is contraindicated in which of the following clients?

    a. a client who is to have a colonoscopy
    b. a client who is taking a narcotic for pain control
    c. a client who has undiagnosed abdominal pain
    d. a client complaining of frequent headaches

ALTERNATE FORMAT QUESTIONS

1. A nurse is caring for a 65-year-old client who is constipated. Which of the following drugs would be safe to administer to the client? (Select all that apply.)

   a. _____ docusate sodium
   b. _____ Metamucil
   c. _____ Neoloid
   d. _____ Effersyllium
   e. _____ Dulcolax

2. Which of the following are appropriate actions for a client who is constipated? (Select all that apply.)

   a. _____ Decrease activity and exercise.
   b. _____ Drink at least 2000 mL of fluid daily.
   c. _____ Decrease intake of grains in the diet.
   d. _____ Establish a routine time for bowel elimination.
   e. _____ Increase intake of vegetables in the diet.

CHAPTER 61

Antidiarrheals

■ Mastering the Information

MATCHING

Match the terms in Column I with a definition, example, or related statement from Column II.

COLUMN I

1. _____ loperamide (Imodium)

2. _____ naloxone hydrochloride (Narcan)

3. _____ octreotide (Sandostatin)

4. _____ diphenoxylate (Lomotil)

5. _____ cholestyramine (Questran)

6. _____ polycarbophil (FiberCon)

7. _____ acute diarrhea

8. _____ tannin

9. _____ bismuth subsalicylate (Pepto-Bismol)

10. _____ chronic diarrhea

COLUMN II

a. mechanism by which the body tries to rid itself of irritants, toxins, and infectious agents

b. occasionally used when diarrhea occurs to decrease fluidity of stools

c. can cause malnutrition and anemia

d. an opiate derivative for diarrhea that requires a prescription

e. used to treat diarrhea by binding and inactivating bile salts

f. used to treat diarrhea associated with carcinoid syndrome

g. a substance found in berry plants that reduces intestinal inflammation and secretions and is used to treat diarrhea

h. an antidote for overdose of loperamide (Imodium)

i. over-the-counter bismuth salt

j. a nonprescription antidiarrheal drug

TRUE OR FALSE

Indicate if the following statements are true or false.

_____ 1. Difenoxin (Motofen) is contraindicated in children younger than 2 years of age.

_____ 2. Loperamide (Imodium) is the drug of choice for ulcerative colitis.

_____ 3. Diarrhea is more common in older adults than constipation.

_____ 4. Taking medication to stop diarrhea is not always desirable.

_____ 5. Long-term use of antidiarrheal drugs can cause constipation.

_____ 6. An adverse effect of octreotide (Sandostatin) is abdominal distention.

_____ 7. Alcohol can decrease the effects of antidiarrheal agents.

_____ 8. Many oral drugs irritate the gastrointestinal tract and cause diarrhea.

_____ 9. Acute diarrhea may cause malnutrition and anemia.

_____ 10. Opiates and opiate derivatives are the most effective agents for symptomatic treatment of diarrhea.

SHORT ANSWER

Answer the following.

1. Define diarrhea.

_____

_____

_____

2. List two causes of diarrhea.

_____

_____

_____

3. List three indications for use of antidiarrheal drugs.

_____

_____

_____

4. What is the indicated use of rifaximin (Xifaxan)?

_____

_____

_____

5. Why should caution be used when administering nitazoxanide (Alinia) concurrently with warfarin?

_____

_____

_____

■ Applying Your Knowledge

Mrs. Greta Riley, a 72-year-old resident of the retirement center where you work as the nurse, comes in to see you. She states, "My bowels have been in an uproar for over 3 weeks. First I had terrible constipation and had to use all sorts of laxatives to get cleaned out. Now I seem to be having just the opposite problem. What kind of medication can I take for the diarrhea?" How will you respond?

_____

_____

_____

_____

_____

_____

_____

_____

■ Practicing for NCLEX

MULTIPLE-CHOICE QUESTIONS

1. A client, age 3, is admitted to the hospital with an overdose of loperamide (Imodium). Which of the following medications would be administered to him?
   a. meclizine hydrochloride (Antivert)
   b. naloxone (Narcan)
   c. diphenhydramine (Benadryl)
   d. hydroxyzine hydrochloride (Atarax)

2. A client is diagnosed with ulcerative colitis. Which of the following drugs would be prescribed for him?
   a. tacrine (Cognex)
   b. bethanechol (Urecholine)
   c. balsalazide (Colazal)
   d. furosemide (Lasix)

3. A client experiences traveler's diarrhea caused by a noninvasive strain of _Escherichia coli_. Which of the following drugs will be prescribed for him?
   a. colestipol (Colestid)
   b. psyllium preparation (Metamucil)
   c. loperamide (Imodium)
   d. rifaximin (Xifaxan)

4. A client develops diarrhea secondary to antibiotic therapy. He is to receive two tablets of diphenoxylate (Lomotil) orally (PO) as needed (PRN) for each diarrheal stool. The nurse should inform him that he may experience
   a. dizziness
   b. hypersensitivity reaction
   c. muscle aches
   d. increase in appetite

5. A client has carcinoid syndrome. Which of the following drugs would be most effective in treating the diarrhea?
   a. loperamide (Imodium)
   b. octreotide (Sandostatin)
   c. difenoxin (Motofen)
   d. colestipol (Colestid)

6. The goal of drug therapy for diarrhea is to
   a. prevent severe fluid and electrolyte loss
   b. increase weight by 2 to 5 pounds
   c. eliminate the bacterial organism
   d. decrease anal discomfort

7. A client has chronic diarrhea. Which of the following drugs would be contraindicated for this client?
   a. antibacterial agents
   b. bismuth preparations
   c. psyllium preparations
   d. opiates

8. A home health nurse is caring for a client who has human immunodeficiency virus (HIV) and acquired immunodeficiency syndrome (AIDS). The client has diarrhea and will be taking octreotide (Sandostatin). The client will self-administer the medication
   a. by mouth   c. in the deltoid muscle
   b. subcutaneously   d. under the tongue

9. Instructions regarding the administration of paregoric should include the following:
   a. Add at least 30 mL of water to each dose.
   b. Take with 4 oz of water.
   c. Take after every meal.
   d. You may include up to eight doses daily.

10. A client is taking colestipol (Colestid). Which of the following is an important instruction to give to the client?
    a. Take with at least 4 oz of water.
    b. Take within 1 hour of taking other drugs.
    c. Avoid driving while taking the medication.
    d. Eliminate salt intake while taking the drug.

ALTERNATE FORMAT QUESTIONS

1. A nurse is discussing the use of rifaximin (Xifaxan). Which of the following will she include as adverse effects of the drug? (Select all that apply.)
   a. flatulence
   b. headache
   c. urgent bowel movement
   d. fever
   e. dizziness

2. Which of the following antidiarrheals may cause dizziness or drowsiness during use? (Select all that apply.)
   a. cholestyramine (Questran)
   b. difenoxin (Motofen)
   c. bismuth subsalicylate (Pepto-Bismol)
   d. diphenoxylate (Lomotil)
   e. loperamide (Imodium)

CHAPTER 62

Antiemetics

■ Mastering the Information

MATCHING

Match the terms in column I with a definition, example, or related statement from Column II.

COLUMN I

1. _____ antihistamines

2. _____ dronabinol (Marinol)

3. _____ ondansetron (Zofran)

4. _____ metoclopramide (Reglan)

5. _____ scopolamine

6. _____ promethazine (Phenergan)

7. _____ meclizine (Antivert)

8. _____ phosphorated carbohydrate solution (Emetrol)

9. _____ dexamethasone

10. _____ palonosetron

COLUMN II

a. used in the management of chemotherapy-induced vomiting

b. a prokinetic agent used to decrease nausea and vomiting associated with gastroparesis

c. a 5-hydroxytryptamine$_3$ (5-HT$_3$) receptor antagonist that is only administered intravenously (IV)

d. a cannabinoid used in the management of nausea and vomiting associated with anticancer drugs

e. a phenothiazine used for nausea and vomiting, which also causes sedation

f. a hyperosmolar solution with phosphoric acid thought to reduce smooth muscle contraction in the gastrointestinal tract

g. an anticholinergic drug effective in relieving nausea and vomiting associated with motion sickness, which is used to prevent seasickness

h. thought to relieve nauseas and vomiting by blocking the action of acetylcholine

i. used to manage nausea associated with vertigo

j. antagonizes serotonin receptors, preventing their activation by the effects of emetogenic drugs and toxins

TRUE OR FALSE

Indicate if the following statements are true or false.

_____ 1. Most antiemetic drugs should be used cautiously in clients with liver disease.

_____ 2. Older adults are usually more sensitive to dronabinol's psychoactive effects than younger adults.

_____ 3. Nausea must occur prior to vomiting.

_____ 4. All antihistamines are effective as antiemetics.

_____ 5. Benzodiazepines are considered antiemetics.

_____ 6. Phenothiazines block dopamine from receptor sites in the brain and chemoreceptive trigger zone (CTZ) to exert antiemetic effects.

_____ 7. Dronabinol (Marinol) has a high potential for abuse.

_____ 8. Metoclopramide (Reglan) is contraindicated in Parkinson's disease.

_____ 9. The 5-HT$_3$ receptor antagonists are the first choice for clients with chemotherapy-induced nausea and vomiting.

_____ 10. Large doses of phenothiazines are needed to produce antiemetic effects.

SHORT ANSWER

Answer the following.

1. Where is the vomiting center located?

   _____

   _____

   _____

2. Describe how chemotherapy causes vomiting.

   _____

   _____

   _____

3. List common adverse effects of 5-HT$_3$ receptor antagonists.

   _____

   _____

   _____

4. Which drugs are preferred for motion sickness?

   _____

   _____

   _____

5. Why is lorazepam (Ativan) commonly used for clients who experience anticipatory nausea and vomiting before administration of chemotherapy?

   _____

   _____

   _____

■ Applying Your Knowledge

Sally Roberts is being treated in an outpatient chemotherapy unit. She will be receiving cisplatin, a very emetogenic chemotherapeutic drug. The following drugs have been ordered IV 30 minutes before her treatment: ondansetron (Zofran), metoclopramide (Reglan), and lorazepam (Ativan). Explain the rationale for these orders.

   _____

   _____

   _____

   _____

   _____

   _____

   _____

   _____

   _____

■ Practicing for NCLEX

MULTIPLE-CHOICE QUESTIONS

1. A 50-year-old is receiving promethazine (Phenergan) for chemotherapy-induced emesis. The nurse will encourage

   a. frequent oral care   c. a low-fat diet

   b. increased fluid intake   d. ambulation

2. A client is receiving metoclopramide (Reglan) for severe nausea. The nurse will monitor the client for which of the following adverse effects?

   a. hypoglycemia

   b. dystonia

   c. gastroesophageal reflux disease (GERD)

   d. photosensitivity

3. A client has been on antiemetic therapy. Which of the following statements indicates a need for further instruction?

   a. "I should avoid driving my car while taking my medication."

   b. "If I start losing weight, I should let you know."

   c. "I enjoy drinking a glass of red wine every night."

   d. "I have stopped going to my exercise class since I have been on medication."

4. A client is taking dronabinol (Marinol) for nausea and vomiting associated with chemotherapy. A possible concern for this client when the drug is discontinued is

   a. urinary frequency   c. joint pain and stiffness

   b. sleep disturbance   d. decreased appetite

5. Which of the following clients would not be a candidate for metoclopramide (Reglan) therapy?

   a. a 65-year-old male with congestive heart failure

   b. a 42-year-old female with breast cancer

   c. a 33-year-old female with diabetic gastroparesis

   d. a 50-year-old male with esophageal reflux

6. Which of the following antiemetic drugs should not be given to a child under the age of 12?

   a. promethazine (Phenergan)

   b. ondansetron (Zofran)

   c. dronabinol (Marinol)

   d. scopolamine (Transderm Scop)

7. In older adults, a positive outcome of antiemetic therapy is

   a. a decrease in blood pressure

   b. a weight gain of 2 pounds per week

   c. increased activity level

   d. electrolyte balance

8. A client is taking an antiemetic. Which of the following nursing diagnoses could be appropriate for her?

   a. Noncompliance: Failure to Take Medication as Prescribed

   b. Risk for Injury

   c. Disturbed Sleep Pattern

   d. Imbalanced Nutrition, More Than Body Requirements

9. A 28-year-old female is in the clinic for antiemetic therapy. She is going on an ocean cruise and expects to experience motion sickness. Instructions regarding this medication will include the following:

   a. Take medication at the first sign of nausea.

   b. Take the medication 30 minutes prior to getting on the ship and then every 4 to 6 hours as needed.

   c. Take the medication with food.

   d. Take the medication 10 minutes before getting on the ship and then once a day throughout the cruise.

10. A client, age 40, is receiving chemotherapy for ovarian cancer. To decrease the adverse effects of the chemotherapy, the nurse will administer metoclopramide (Reglan)

    a. immediately after the chemotherapy treatment

    b. every 4 hours orally (PO) during the treatment

    c. by IV 30 to 60 minutes prior to the chemotherapy treatment

    d. intramuscularly (IM), just prior to chemotherapy treatment

ALTERNATE FORMAT QUESTIONS

1. Which of the following drugs increase the effects of antiemetic agents? (Select all that apply.)

   a. _____ antianxiety agents

   b. _____ anticholinergic agents

   c. _____ antihypertensive agents

   d. _____ antipsychotic agents

   e. _____ antidiarrheal agents

2. When caring for clients receiving antiemetics for prevention of vomiting with cancer therapy, the nurse is aware of which of the following? (Select all that apply.)

   a. _____ Parenteral antiemetics in a syringe can be mixed with other drugs.

   b. _____ Intramuscular antiemetics are injected deeply into the gluteal area.

   c. _____ Drugs should be administered 15–30 minutes prior to the treatment.

   d. _____ If a client is excessively drowsy, omit the antiemetic drug and notify the physician.

   e. _____ Antiemetic drugs should not be given if the client's blood pressure is low.

CHAPTER 63

Drugs Used in Ophthalmic Conditions

■ Mastering the Information

MATCHING

Match the terms in column I with a definition, example, or related statement from Column II.

COLUMN I

1. _____ conjunctiva
2. _____ hyperopia
3. _____ miosis
4. _____ aqueous humor
5. _____ keratitis
6. _____ blepharitis
7. _____ glaucoma
8. _____ myopia
9. _____ conjunctivitis
10. _____ mydriasis

COLUMN II

a. the mucous membrane lining of the eyelids
b. inflammation of the cornea
c. nearsightedness
d. chronic infection of glands and lash follicles in the margins of the eyelids
e. pupil constriction
f. a common eye disorder characterized by redness, tearing, itching, edema, and a burning sensation
g. farsightedness
h. pupil dilation
i. clear fluid produced by capillaries in the ciliary body
j. a disease characterized by optic nerve damage, changes in visual fields, and increased intraocular pressure

TRUE OR FALSE

Indicate if the following statements are true or false.

_____ 1. Eye ointments should be administered more often than eyedrops.

_____ 2. Systemic administration is the most common route for ophthalmic drugs.

_____ 3. When administering multiple eyedrops, there should be intervals of 5 to 10 minutes between applications.

_____ 4. Topical ophthalmic medications should be discarded after the expiration date.

_____ 5. Topical ophthalmic medications can be safely applied while wearing soft contact lenses.

_____ 6. Ocular infections are often treated with broad-spectrum antibacterial agents.

_____ 7. Nonprescription eyedrops should never be used longer than 72 hours.

_____ 8. Most ophthalmic drops contain sulfites, which can cause allergic reactions.

_____ 9. Normal intraocular pressure is less than 12 mm Hg.

_____ 10. Glaucoma is a common, preventable cause of blindness.

SHORT ANSWER

Answer the following.

1. What is the most common and preferred method of ophthalmic drug therapy?

_____

_____

_____

2. List therapeutic classifications of drugs used to diagnose and treat ophthalmic disorders.

_____

_____

_____

3. Why should long-term use of corticosteroids to treat inflammatory conditions of the eye be avoided?

_____

_____

_____

4. Which drug is the drug of choice for fungal eye infections?

_____

_____

_____

5. Why are accurate dosage and occlusion of the nasolacrimal duct in the inner canthus of the eye important when administering ophthalmic drug therapy in older adults?

_____

_____

_____

_____

■ Applying Your Knowledge

Sylvia Jetson, an 82-year-old widow, is diagnosed in your clinic with open-angle glaucoma. She is given a prescription of timolol maleate (Timoptic) eyedrops to decrease her intraocular pressure. Discuss teaching that is important before Mrs. Jetson leaves the clinic.

_____

_____

_____

_____

_____

_____

_____

_____

■ Practicing for NCLEX

MULTIPLE-CHOICE QUESTIONS

1. A client has recently been diagnosed with open-angle glaucoma. She is to begin treatment with pilocarpine (Pilocar) 0.25%, administering two drops every 6 hours. The nurse will caution her that the most common adverse effects are
   a. irritability and mood swings
   b. increased pulse and heart palpitations
   c. itching and burning
   d. anorexia and weight loss

2. A 48-year-old client is to begin timolol maleate (Timoptic), administering one drop in both eyes twice a day. Prior to beginning therapy, the nurse will evaluate the client for
   a. diabetes mellitus
   b. renal impairment
   c. liver disease
   d. respiratory and cardiac problems

3. While a nurse is administering a mydriatic into a client's eyes, the client asks how long it will take for the pupils to dilate. The nurse should respond,
   a. "Not long."
   b. "About 30 minutes."
   c. "Between 5 and 15 minutes."
   d. "No longer than a couple of minutes."

4. When assessing a client's eyes after the administration of pilocarpine (Pilocar), the nurse will anticipate
   a. dilated pupils
   b. constricted pupils
   c. increased visual acuity
   d. a decrease in the aqueous humor

5. A diagnosis of conjunctivitis is made for a client. One drop of gentamicin (Garamycin) every 4 hours in both eyes is prescribed. It would be important for the nurse to determine whether the client has a history of
   a. drug abuse   c. diabetes mellitus
   b. allergic reactions   d. mental illness

6. Before the administration of eyedrops, the nurse's initial action should be to
   a. warm the medication
   b. take the blood pressure
   c. ask the client to lie down
   d. wash his or her hands

7. After the administration of a miotic drug in both eyes, a client may complain of
   a. halos around lights
   b decreased vision in dim light
   c. pain in both eyes
   d. nausea and vomiting

8. Systemic absorption from ophthalmic administration can be prevented by
   a. applying pressure to the inner canthus after administration of the medication
   b. administering the drug at bedtime
   c. placing a warm, moist towel over the eyes after administration of the medication
   d. rinsing the eyes with sterile water after administering the medication

9. A client is taking a prostaglandin analog for glaucoma. The nurse suspects which of the following adverse effects?
   a. nausea and vomiting
   b. dehydration
   c. upper-respiratory and flulike symptoms
   d. dry mouth

10. A client complains of ocular itching caused by seasonal allergies. The nurse is aware that the physician will most likely prescribe which of the following for the client?
    a. diclofenac (Voltaren)
    b. flurbiprofen (Ocufen)
    c. ketorolac (Acular)
    d. suprofen (Profenal)

ALTERNATE FORMAT QUESTIONS

1. Which of the following drugs are used to decrease redness and itching associated with allergic conjunctivitis? (Select all that apply.)
   a. _____ acetazolamide (Diamox)
   b. _____ cromolyn (Crolom)
   c. _____ timolol maleate (Timoptic)
   d. _____ loteprednol (Lotemax)
   e. _____ mannitol (Osmitrol)

2. A nurse is instructing a client how to administer eyedrops. Arrange the following steps in correct order of self-administration.
   a. _____ Apply drops and look down for several seconds after application.
   b. _____ Wash hands thoroughly.
   c. _____ Pull the lower eyelid down to expose the conjunctiva.
   d. _____ Place the dropper directly over the eye.
   e. _____ Tilt head back or lie down and look up.
   f. _____ Release the eyelid, close the eyes, and press on the inside corner of the eye with a finger for 3 to 5 minutes.

CHAPTER 64

Drugs Used in Dermatologic Conditions

■ Mastering the Information

Match the terms in Column I with a definition, example, or related statement from Column II.

COLUMN I

1. _____ psoriasis

2. _____ *Candida albicans*

3. _____ keratolytic agents

4. _____ astringent

5. _____ benzoyl peroxide

6. _____ retinoids

7. _____ aloe

8. _____ oral candidiasis

9. _____ urticaria

10. _____ rosacea

COLUMN II

a. characterized by erythema; flushing; fine, red, superficial blood vessels; and acne-like lesions of the face

b. a fungal infection that usually occurs after the use of a broad-spectrum systemic antibiotic

c. vitamin A derivatives used to treat acne, psoriasis, and aging and wrinkling of the skin

d. skin lesions called wheals, "hives"

e. causes most fungal infections of the skin

f. a skin disorder characterized by erythematous, dry, scaling lesions

g. a topical substance used for minor burns and wounds

h. used to remove warts, corns, and calluses

i. a topical bactericidal agent

j. a drying agent

TRUE OR FALSE

Indicate if the following statements are true or false.

_____ 1. The skin is the smallest organ of the body.

_____ 2. The skin's pH is acidic.

_____ 3. Scratching can damage skin and cause secondary infections.

_____ 4. Hyperplasia of the nose (rhinophyma) can develop from intertrigo.

_____ 5. Tinea capitis is the most common type of ringworm infection.

_____ 6. Increased secretion of androgens at puberty in both sexes may contribute to acne.

_____ 7. Chocolate and fatty foods increase the severity of acne.

_____ 8. External otitis is most often caused by beta-hemolytic streptococci.

_____ 9. Tacrolimus (Protopic) ointment can be used in children as young as 2 years of age.

_____ 10. Most dermatologic medications are applied topically.

SHORT ANSWER

Answer the following.

1. List six functions of the skin.

_____

_____

_____

2. What is the most common mediator of urticaria?

_____

_____

_____

3. Describe a topical drug-induced skin reaction.

_____

_____

_____

4. How long does it take for oral antibiotics to produce therapeutic effects in treating inflammatory acne?

_____

_____

_____

5. List adverse effects that commonly occur with oral retinoid preparations.

_____

_____

_____

■ Applying Your Knowledge

You are making a home visit to young parents of a 6-month-old baby. The teenage mother is home alone with the baby when you visit. You ask if she has any concerns. She states that the baby has had a severe diaper rash for the last 2 weeks. What assessment data do you need to collect? What general principles should you include in your teaching about diaper rash?

_____

_____

_____

_____

_____

■ Practicing for NCLEX

MULTIPLE-CHOICE QUESTIONS

1. Before topical application of a medication, the nurse should
   a. rinse the area with cold water
   b. scrub the skin area and rub it dry
   c. expose the skin area to a heat lamp
   d. wash the skin and pat it dry

2. A client has been taking isotretinoin (Accutane) for 2 months. A priority assessment by the nurse will be which of the following during a follow-up clinic visit?
   a. increased blood pressure   c. irritability
   b. depression   d. dry mouth

3. A 10-year-old client has started taking an oral retinoid. It will be most important for her to avoid
   a. dairy products
   b. carbonated drinks
   c. extremely cold air
   d. vitamin A supplements

4. A client is taking an oral antihistamine to relieve itching associated with contact dermatitis. Instructions should include the following:
   a. "Take oral medication on a regular schedule, around the clock."
   b. "Take the medication only when the itching is worse."
   c. "Use it in combination with a topical medication to decrease itching."
   d. "You may increase the dosage as the itching severity warrants."

5. A 22-year-old female has been diagnosed with acne vulgaris. Tetracycline has been ordered. Which of the following would be an appropriate question to ask her before therapy is started?
   a. "How long have you had the cystlike nodules on your face?"
   b. "When was your last menstrual period?"
   c. "How many times a day do you scrub your face?"
   d. "Have you been taking any oral medication for the acne?"

6. A nurse is caring for a 28-year-old male who has second-degree burns on his hands and arms. Treatment includes application of silver sulfadiazine (Silvadene) to the burn area twice a day. A priority nursing intervention should include

   a. washing the burn area with warm water before application of Silvadene

   b. applying salve after Silvadene to seal the medication over the skin area

   c. applying the medication using sterile technique

   d. applying the medication at bedtime

7. A client has used a topical corticosteroid for several days to treat psoriasis. Which of the following adverse effects may occur?

   a. an increase in blood pressure

   b. atrophy of the skin

   c. anorexia

   d. a burning sensation in the area of application

8. A client presents with chronic dry, scaly lesions. The nurse is aware that the lesions will be best treated with

   a. aerosol sprays   c. ointments

   b. gels   d. lotions

9. A client, a 15-year-old male, is beginning drug therapy for acne. Instructions concerning benzoyl peroxide should include the following:

   a. Overuse can cause extreme dryness of skin.

   b. Use caution when driving or operating machinery.

   c. Adverse effects are nausea and vomiting.

   d. A decrease in appetite may occur.

10. A client is taking clobetasol (Temovate). The nurse is aware that systemic effects of this drug include

    a. hypotension

    b. suppression of adrenal function

    c. muscle spasms

    d. stimulation of hepatic enzymes

ALTERNATE FORMAT QUESTIONS

1. The nurse is preparing to administer a topical application to a skin lesion. Which of the following actions will she take? (Select all that apply.)

   a. _____ Wash the skin and rub it dry.

   b. _____ Apply a small amount of the drug preparation and rub it in thoroughly.

   c. _____ Wash the area after the medication has been applied.

   d. _____ Wash her hands before and after the application of medication.

   e. _____ Apply the medication using sterile gloves or sterile cotton-tipped applicators.

2. A client is taking isotretinoin (Accutane) for severe cystic acne. The prescribed dosage is 2 mg/kg/day in two divided doses for 20 weeks. The client weighs 140 lb. How many milligrams will she take in one dose?

CHAPTER 65

Drugs Used During Pregnancy and Lactation

■ Mastering the Information

MATCHING

Match the terms in column I with a definition, example, or related statement from Column II.

COLUMN I

1. _____ ferrous sulfate

2. _____ magnesium sulfate

3. _____ meclizine (Antivert)

4. _____ aspirin

5. _____ ritodrine (Yutopar)

6. _____ oxytocin (Pitocin)

7. _____ folic acid

8. _____ methylergonovine (Methergine)

9. _____ meperidine (Demerol)

10. _____ Metamucil

COLUMN II

a. used to treat anemia during pregnancy

b. may be used for prophylaxis in women at risk of developing preeclampsia

c. used to treat nausea and vomiting during pregnancy

d. the drug of choice for preventing or treating seizures during preeclampsia and eclampsia

e. stimulates uterine contractions to initiate labor

f. opioid analgesic used during labor and delivery

g. may be used during pregnancy for constipation

h. used in the management of postpartum hemorrhage

i. relaxes uterine smooth muscle, which will slow or stop uterine contractions

j. necessary to prevent neural tube birth defects

TRUE OR FALSE

Indicate if the following statements are true or false.

_____ 1. Many drugs are considered safe during pregnancy.

_____ 2. Drug effects are more predictable during pregnancy than in the nonpregnant state.

_____ 3. In the fetus, a large proportion of a drug dose is active because the fetus has low levels of serum albumin and low levels of drug binding.

_____ 4. Drug teratogenicity is most likely to occur during the first trimester of pregnancy.

_____ 5. Small amounts of alcohol during pregnancy are considered safe.

_____ 6. Caffeine is the most commonly ingested drug during pregnancy.

_____ 7. Cigarette smoking during pregnancy can cause fetal and infant death.

_____ 8. Marijuana can cause third-trimester bleeding.

_____ 9. Abruptio placentae can occur from ingestion of cocaine during the third semester of pregnancy.

_____ 10. Herbal supplements are recommended during pregnancy.

SHORT ANSWER

Answer the following.

1. Why should large amounts of caffeine be avoided by mothers who are breast-feeding?

   _____

   _____

   _____

2. Why should marijuana not be used during pregnancy?

   _____

   _____

   _____

3. Why is aspirin considered a category-D risk and contraindicated during pregnancy?

   _____

   _____

   _____

4. Which antiepileptic drugs are known teratogens and are rated risk category D by the U.S. Food and Drug Administration (FDA)?

   _____

   _____

   _____

5. Which drug is the only antidiabetic drug recommended for use during pregnancy?

   _____

   _____

   _____

■ Applying Your Knowledge

Rosa Sanchez is breast-feeding her 6-month-old son when she develops a cold. After she has started taking over-the-counter cold remedies, she calls the consulting nurse to see if these medications will affect her ability to breast-feed her son. If you were the consulting nurse, how would you respond?

_____

_____

_____

_____

_____

_____

_____

_____

■ Practicing for NCLEX

MULTIPLE-CHOICE QUESTIONS

1. A client is 20 weeks pregnant, and fetal heart tones can no longer be heard. It is determined that the pregnancy is to be terminated. Which of the following drugs will be given after mifepristone to ensure full expulsion of the conceptus?
   a. ritodrine   c. methylergonovine
   a. prostaglandin   d. oxytocin

2. A client is receiving a tocolytic. Which of the following may indicate hypermagnesemia?
   a. blood pressure of 170/90
   b. heart rate of 60
   c. respiratory rate of 8
   d. body temperature of 102°F

3. Which of the following indicates an appropriate dose of vitamin K for a neonate at delivery?
   a. 0.25 to 0.5 mg   c. 1 to 1.5 mg
   b. 0.5 to 1 mg   d. 2.5 to 5 mg

4. A nurse is counseling a group of pregnant women at the health department concerning use of immunizations during pregnancy. The nurse should stress that which of the following immunizations should not be taken during pregnancy?

   a. influenza
   b. rubella
   c. hepatitis B
   d. tetanus

5. Oxytocin is the drug of choice for prevention and control of postpartum uterine hemorrhage because it is unlikely to cause

   a. hypotension
   b. hypertension
   c. tachycardia
   d. bradycardia

6. A new mother who is breast-feeding questions a nurse concerning use of antihistamines for her allergies. An appropriate response would be as follows:

   a. "An antihistamine may cause you to be drowsy."
   b. "As long as you take only one a day, it should be all right."
   c. "Antihistamines can cause a decrease in milk production."
   d. "Antihistamines may cause your baby's heart rate to increase."

7. Which of the following drugs should be completely avoided during pregnancy?

   a. nicotine
   b. caffeine
   c. acetaminophen
   d. alcohol

8. Tetracyclines are contraindicated during pregnancy because they

   a. decrease the white blood cell count in the mother
   b. interfere with the development of teeth and bone in the fetus
   c. interfere with folic acid metabolism in the fetus
   d. cause long-bone growth retardation in the fetus

9. A 40-year-old has just been told she is pregnant by her health care provider. She has a history of mild hypertension and is concerned about taking medication during pregnancy. An appropriate response should include the following:

   a. "Hydralazine is considered safe to use during pregnancy."
   b. "Guanfacine can be used in reduced dosages."
   c. "All antihypertensive drugs are unsafe to use during pregnancy."
   d. "Clonidine can be used."

10. Which of the following drugs is used to promote fetal production of surfactant?

    a. furosemide
    b. ergotamine
    c. nifedipine
    d. betamethasone

ALTERNATE FORMAT QUESTIONS

1. A nurse has just given a tocolytic drug. She will observe for which of the following therapeutic effects? (Select all that apply.)

   a. _____ absence of seizures
   b. _____ cessation of uterine contractions
   c. _____ a firm uterus
   d. _____ minimal vaginal bleeding
   e. _____ decreased uterine contractions

2. When preparing to administer magnesium sulfate intravenously (IV), the nurse should include which of the following actions? (Select all that apply.)

   a. _____ Have a second nurse check all preparations before medication administration.
   b. _____ Read the medication label correctly for correct preparation.
   c. _____ Give the initial bolus dose over a 5- to 10-minute period.
   d. _____ Have IV calcium gluconate readily available.
   e. _____ If available, use a premixed IV bag of 20 g of magnesium sulfate in 1000 mL of IV fluid.

Answers

Chapter 1 Introduction to Pharmacology

MASTERING THE INFORMATION

MATCHING

1. c   2. j   3. e   4. b   5. h   6. d   7. f   8. a   9. g
10. i

TRUE OR FALSE

1. f   2. t   3. t   4. f   5. f   6. t   7. t   8. f   9. t
10. f

SHORT ANSWER

1. Synthetic drugs are more standardized in chemical characteristics, more consistent in effects, and less likely to produce allergic reactions.
2. Pharmacoeconomics involves the costs of drug therapy, including purchasing, dispensing, storing, administering, and conducting laboratory and other tests used to monitor client responses and losses from expiration dates on drugs.
3. The two routes are by prescription or order form by a licensed health care provider and by over-the-counter purchase of drugs that do not require a prescription.
4. Trade names are capitalized; generic names are lowercase—usually.
5. Drugs are classified according to their effects on certain body systems, their therapeutic uses, and chemical characteristics.

APPLYING YOUR KNOWLEDGE

Meperidine (Demerol) is an opioid analgesic that is used to manage severe pain. Its abuse potential is high, and it is therefore given a Schedule II classification. Diazepam (Valium) is an antianxiety agent that has some potential for abuse so it is listed as a Schedule IV drug. Different references give you different information and are organized differently. A nursing textbook of pharmacology is comprehensive and gives you enough information to understand how drugs work. It is the best resource to use when you are first learning about drugs. Drug handbooks are helpful when you are trying to research specific information about a drug. They are arranged alphabetically and assume you have a basic understanding of pharmacology. The *Physicians' Desk Reference* (PDR) is available in many health care facilities. It provides the reader with the drug insert from the manufacturer and color photographs of many medications. It is published annually so it is a good resource for new drugs. Much information is provided but without prioritization (eg, any reported side effect is given rather than identifying the most common or most serious side effects), which can make it difficult for a beginning student to use effectively.

PRACTICING FOR NCLEX

MULTIPLE-CHOICE QUESTIONS

1. b   2. a   3. c   4. d   5. b   6. c   7. b   8. c   9. d
10. a

ALTERNATE FORMAT QUESTIONS

1. a b c d
2. a b c d

Chapter 2 Basic Concepts and Processes

MASTERING THE INFORMATION

MATCHING

1. b   2. f   3. h   4. c   5. d   6. i   7. j   8. e   9. a
10. g

TRUE OR FALSE

1. f   2. t   3. f   4. t   5. t   6. f   7. t   8. t   9. t
10. f

SHORT ANSWER

1. Age, body weight, genetic and ethnic characteristics, gender, pathologic conditions, and psychological considerations influence the drug action.
2. Allergic reactions, damaging body tissues, increasing body heat, interference with dissipation of body heat, and action on the temperature regulating center in the brain can cause drug fever.
3. Goals of treatment are supporting and stabilizing vital functions, preventing further damage from the toxic agent, and administering specific antidotes.
4. When a drug is displaced by a second drug from plasma protein-binding sites, the effect of the displaced drug is increased. This occurs because the displaced drug is freed from its bound form and becomes pharmacologically active.
5. Drug tolerance occurs when the body becomes accustomed to a certain drug over a period of time so that larger doses must be given to produce the same effects. When a person develops a drug tolerance, a larger-than-usual dose of another pharmacologically related drug may be required to produce a therapeutic effect.

APPLYING YOUR KNOWLEDGE

Half-life is the time required for the serum concentration of a drug to decrease by 50%. After 1 hour, the serum concentration would be 50 units/mL (100/2). After 2 hours, the serum concentration would be 25 units/mL (50/2) and reach the nontoxic range.

PRACTICING FOR NCLEX

MULTIPLE-CHOICE QUESTIONS

1. c   2. b   3. d   4. c   5. d   6. c   7. a   8. c   9. c
10. c

ALTERNATE FORMAT QUESTIONS

1. a b e f

2. a. 3   b. 2   c. 4   d. 1

Chapter 3   Administering Medications

MASTERING THE INFORMATION

MATCHING

1. g   2. h   3. c   4. f   5. d   6. i   7. a   8. b   9. j
10. e

MATCHING

1. g   2. m   3. j   4. e   5. o   6. i   7. b   8. c
9. d   10. f   11. a   12. k   13. l   14. h   15. n

TRUE OR FALSE

1. f   2. t   3. f   4. f   5. t   6. t   7. t   8. t   9. f
10. f

SHORT ANSWER

1. The seven rights are right drug, dose, client, route, time, documentation, and right to refuse.
2. The nurse is liable for his or her actions and is expected to have knowledge concerning all medications he or she is responsible for administering.
3. A medication order consists of the name of the client; the generic or trade name of the drug; the dose; the route and frequency of administration; and the date, time, and signature of the prescriber.
4. The order means 30 mL of Mylanta by mouth before meals and at bedtime.
5. They should never be broken or crushed because they contain high amounts of a drug intended to be absorbed slowly and act over an extended period of time.

APPROXIMATE EQUIVALENTS

1. 2.2   2. 1000   3. 1   4. 1   5. 15 or 16
6. 250   7. 1000   8. 1   9. 4 or 5   10. 1

CONVERSIONS

1. 30   2. 22.73   3. 8 or 10   4. 3.5   5. 10 or 12.5
6. 15   7. 2000   8. 2   9. 2   10. 2500

CALCULATE THE DOSAGE

1. 4 tablets   2. 10 mL   3. 60 mL   4. 1.5 mL
5. 2 tablets   6. 11.25   7. 2 capsules   8. 0.5 mL
9. 2 mL   10. 15 cc

APPLYING YOUR KNOWLEDGE

First check tube placement by aspirating gastric content or instilling air into the stomach (listen with a stethoscope for a swishing sound over the gastric area). Use liquid preparations when possible. When a liquid formulation is not available, crush a tablet or empty a capsule into 15 to 30 mL of warm water and mix well. Note: Do **not** crush enteric-coated or sustained-release products because this alters their rate of absorption and could be dangerous to the client.

To administer, flush the feeding tube with tap water, draw medication into a syringe and slowly instill the medication into the tube; then flush the tube again. Preferably give each medication separately and rinse the tube between medications. When all medications are given, flush the tube with 50 mL of water unless the client is on a fluid restriction. Small feeding tubes occlude easily and must be rinsed well to prevent clogging.

PRACTICING FOR NCLEX

MULTIPLE-CHOICE QUESTIONS

1. b   2. c   3. d   4. b   5. d   6. d   7. d   8. d   9. a
10. c

ALTERNATE FORMAT QUESTIONS

1. b d e f g

2.

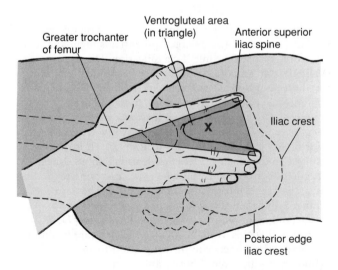

Chapter 4 Nursing Process in Drug Therapy

MASTERING THE INFORMATION

MATCHING

1. i   2. j   3. d   4. g   5. h   6. a   7. c   8. e   9. f
10. b

TRUE OR FALSE

1. f   2. f   3. t   4. t   5. t   6. t   7. f   8. t   9. t
10. f

SHORT ANSWER

1. Areas of nursing intervention are assessment, drug administration, teaching, problem solving related to drug therapy, promotion of compliance with prescribed drug therapy and identification of barriers to compliance, and identification of resources for obtaining medications.
2. Client teaching is important because most medications are self-administered and clients need information and assistance to use drugs safely and effectively.
3. Nurses have difficulties because of emphasis on outpatient treatments, short hospitalization periods, and clients' reluctance to admit to noncompliance.
4. Major components are the medical diagnosis, aspects of care related to the medical diagnosis, desired client outcomes, and time frames for desired outcomes.
5. Use of supplements may keep the client from seeking treatment from a health care provider when indicated, and the products may interact with prescription drugs to decrease therapeutic effects or increase adverse effects.

APPLYING YOUR KNOWLEDGE

With infants, especially low-birth-weight infants, the danger of potential drug toxicity is high. This is especially true for a drug like digoxin that has a narrow therapeutic range. Decreased protein binding may result in higher blood levels of digoxin, causing toxicity. Also, excretion is reduced because the liver and kidneys are often immature in the low-birth-weight infant. It is prudent, especially with the very young and the very old, to start drug doses low and increase if necessary. It is never wrong to discuss your concerns with the physician, especially if your assessment reveals that therapeutic effects have not occurred (eg, worsening congestive heart failure.)

PRACTICING FOR NCLEX

MULTIPLE-CHOICE QUESTIONS

1. d   2. b   3. b   4. b   5. b   6. a   7. c   8. d   9. b
10. b

ALTERNATE FORMAT QUESTIONS

1. a. 5   b. 3   c. 2   d. 1   e. 4   f. 6
2. b c e

Chapter 5 Physiology of the Central Nervous System

MASTERING THE INFORMATION

MATCHING

1. f   2. a   3. i   4. g   5. c   6. h   7. d   8. j   9. e   10. b

TRUE OR FALSE

1. f   2. f   3. t   4. f   5. t   6. t   7. f   8. t   9. t   10. f

SHORT ANSWER

1. drowsiness, sleep, decreased muscle tone, decreased ability to move, and decreased perception of sensations
2. wakefulness, decreased fatigue, mental alertness, hyperactivity, excessive talking, nervousness, and insomnia
3. the ability to produce an action potential or be stimulated (excitability) and the ability to convey electrical impulses (conductivity)
4. transportation back into the presynaptic nerve terminal for reuse, diffusion into surrounding body fluids, and destruction by enzymes
5. the availability of precursor proteins and enzymes required to synthesize neurotransmitters, the number and binding capacity of receptors in the cell membranes of presynaptic and postsynaptic nerve endings, acid-base imbalances, and drugs

PRACTICING FOR NCLEX

MULTIPLE-CHOICE QUESTIONS

1. d   2. a   3. a   4. c   5. b   6. a   7. c   8. d   9. b   10. a

ALTERNATE FORMAT QUESTIONS

1. Synapse
2. Release site
3. Postsynaptic nerve terminal
4. Receptor sites
5. Postsynaptic nerve cell membrane
6. Presynaptic nerve cell membrane
7. Neurotransmitters
8. Presynaptic nerve terminal

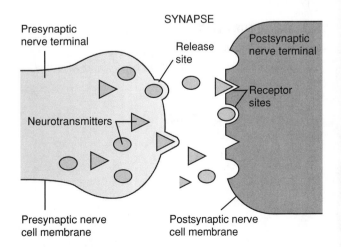

Chapter 6   Opioid Analgesics and Opioid Antagonists

MASTERING THE INFORMATION

MATCHING

1. d   2. j   3. h   4. b   5. g   6. c   7. a   8. e   9. f
10. i

TRUE OR FALSE

1. f   2. t   3. f   4. t   5. t   6. f   7. f   8. t   9. t
10. t

SHORT ANSWER

1. It binds with opioid receptors to relieve pain by inhibiting the release of substance P in central and peripheral nerves, decreasing the perception of pain sensation in the brain.
2. Effects include analgesia, drowsiness to sleep to unconsciousness, decreased mental and physical activity, respiratory depression, nausea and vomiting, and pupil constriction.
3. It further depresses respirations.
4. Opioid antagonists reverse or block analgesia and central nervous system (CNS) respiratory functions.
5. Oral doses go through extensive metabolism on their first pass through the liver.

APPLYING YOUR KNOWLEDGE

Mr. Reyes' decreased level of consciousness and decreased respiratory rate and depth suggest that he is receiving too much morphine. Call the doctor and suggest that the continuous infusion of morphine be discontinued and the patient-controlled modality be used instead. Giving continuous infusions of morphine to opiate-naive individuals (clients who have not been receiving opiates) can cause respiratory depression and ultimately respiratory arrest. Naloxone, an opioid antagonist, can reverse these effects. Because his respiratory rate is not yet below 8, try getting him up and moving around. If the respiratory rate continues to drop, naloxone may need to be administered. Naloxone has a shorter half-life than morphine so repeat doses may be required to prevent recurrent respiratory depression.

PRACTICING FOR NCLEX

MULTIPLE-CHOICE QUESTIONS

1. b   2. b   3. d   4. d   5. a   6. b   7. b   8. a   9. a
10. b

ALTERNATE FORMAT QUESTIONS

1. 67.5 mg
2. a. 4   b. 3   c. 1   d. 5   e. 2

Chapter 7   Analgesic–Antipyretic–Anti-Inflammatory and Related Drugs

MASTERING THE INFORMATION

MATCHING

1. i   2. c   3. e   4. d   5. f   6. g   7. h   8. j   9. a
10. b

TRUE OR FALSE

1. t   2. f   3. t   4. t   5. t   6. f   7. t   8. t   9. f
10. t

SHORT ANSWER

1. Conditions include mild to moderate pain associated with musculoskeletal disorders (osteoarthritis, tendonitis, gout), headache, dysmenorrhea, minor trauma, and minor surgery.
2. Signs and symptoms include nausea, vomiting, fever, fluid and electrolyte deficiencies, tinnitus, decreased hearing, visual changes, drowsiness, confusion, and hyperventilation. Severe signs and symptoms include delirium, stupor, coma, and seizure.
3. Acetaminophen does not cause gastric irritation and does not increase risk of bleeding.
4. Aspirin should be avoided because of increased risk of bleeding—anticoagulant properties.
5. COX-2 inhibitors block production of prostaglandins associated with pain and inflammation without blocking those associated with protective effects on gastric mucosa.

APPLYING YOUR KNOWLEDGE

The symptoms may be related to her medications, but you need to collect more information before you can be sure. A common side effect of aspirin (and all nonsteroidal anti-inflammatory drugs) is gastric irritation that can cause gastrointestinal ulceration and bleeding. Blood loss is often gradual so clients get used to the fatigue. When clients become volume depleted secondary to the blood loss, they can exhibit signs of dizziness and syncope. Take Mrs. Whynn's postural blood pressure. Refer her to her physician, who will do some diagnostic tests. Most important, to prevent falls and accidental injury, make sure Mrs. Whynn seeks care promptly.

PRACTICING FOR NCLEX

MULTIPLE-CHOICE QUESTIONS

1. a   2. b   3. c   4. d   5. d   6. b   7. b   8. d   9. b
10. d

ALTERNATE FORMAT QUESTIONS

1. d a b c
2. a c e f

Chapter 8 Antianxiety and Sedative-Hypnotic Drugs

MASTERING THE INFORMATION
MATCHING

1. h 2. j 3. a 4. i 5. d 6. e 7. b 8. f 9. c
10. g

TRUE OR FALSE

1. t 2. f 3. f 4. t 5. t 6. f 7. t 8. t 9. t
10. t

SHORT ANSWER

1. Major clinical uses include antianxiety, hypnotic effects, and anticonvulsant effects.
2. Benzodiazepines are highly lipid soluble, allowing drugs to enter the CNS and perform their actions. Drugs are redistributed to peripheral tissues and then slowly eliminated.
3. Contraindications include severe respiratory disease, severe liver or kidney disease, hypersensitivity reactions, history of alcohol, and other drug abuse.
4. Buspirone lacks muscle relaxant and anticonvulsant effects, does not cause sedation or physical or psychological dependence, does not cause increased CNS depression with alcohol and other drugs, and is not a controlled substance.
5. The goal is to find the lowest effective dose that does not cause excessive daytime drowsiness or impaired mobility.

APPLYING YOUR KNOWLEDGE

Xanax, a benzodiazepine, is used for short-term treatment of anxiety. The length of time and high dose of Xanax indicates that Ms. Summers has developed tolerance to this drug. Alcohol works synergistically with benzodiazepines to increase effects such as CNS depression and sedation. The nurse should consult with the surgeon and anesthesiologist concerning Ms. Summers' use of Xanax and alcohol. Abruptly stopping these medications before surgery could result in withdrawal. A long-term plan that avoids dependence on benzodiazepines should be developed to assist Ms. Summers with her anxiety.

PRACTICING FOR NCLEX
MULTIPLE-CHOICE QUESTIONS

1. c 2. d 3. a 4. b 5. a 6. c 7. c 8. b 9. a
10. b

ALTERNATE FORMAT QUESTIONS

1. a b c d
2. a d e f

Chapter 9 Antipsychotic Drugs

MASTERING THE INFORMATION
MATCHING

1. c 2. e 3. h 4. d 5. j 6. g 7. b 8. i 9. a
10. f

TRUE OR FALSE

1. f 2. t 3. t 4. t 5. f 6. f 7. t 8. f 9. t
10. t

SHORT ANSWER

1. agitation, behavioral disturbances, delusions, disorganized speech, hallucinations, insomnia, and paranoia
2. lack of pleasure, motivation, a blunted affect, poor grooming and hygiene, poor social skills, poor speech, and social withdrawal
3. typical—older, have more adverse effects, act mainly on positive symptoms of schizophrenia than the atypical antipsychotic agents
4. nausea, vomiting, and intractable hiccups
5. causes agranulocytosis, a life-threatening blood disease, which occurs in first 3 weeks of therapy

APPLYING YOUR KNOWLEDGE

Although these symptoms may accompany some psychiatric disorders, it is important to consider that John may be experiencing extrapyramidal side effects from the antipsychotic medication (Prolixin) he is taking. Notify the physician of the new symptoms. The dose of Prolixin may be lowered, or an antiparkinson agent may be ordered to treat the extrapyramidal symptoms.

PRACTICING FOR NCLEX
MULTIPLE-CHOICE QUESTIONS

1. b 2. a 3. c 4. d 5. d 6. a 7. d 8. b 9. c
10. a

ALTERNATE FORMAT QUESTIONS

1. b d e c a
2. a c e f

Chapter 10 Antidepressants and Mood Stabilizers

MASTERING THE INFORMATION
MATCHING

1. c 2. a 3. f 4. b 5. g 6. e 7. h 8. d 9. j
10. i

TRUE OR FALSE

1. t 2. f 3. t 4. t 5. f 6. f 7. t 8. t 9. t
10. f

SHORT ANSWER

1. Depression is thought to result from a deficiency of norepinephrine and/or serotonin. It is thought that antidepressant drugs increase the amounts of one or both of these in the CNS synapse.
2. Antidepressants normalize abnormal neurotransmission systems in the brain by altering the amount of neurotransmitters and the number of receptors.
3. They are effective and produce fewer and milder adverse effects.
4. Supplies are limited to prevent suicide.
5. Such overdoses occur 1 to 4 hours after drug ingestion and cause nystagmus, tremors, restlessness, seizures, hypotension, dysrhythmias, and myocardial depression.

APPLYING YOUR KNOWLEDGE

Prozac has a long half-life (24 to 72 hours) so it takes longer than a week to reach a steady state. The dosage is usually not increased for 3 to 4 weeks. It is important to teach all clients beginning therapy with antidepressants that they may not see significant improvement in their depression for a number of weeks. Ms. Jordon's sleeping difficulty could be a symptom of her depression or a side effect of the Prozac. If it is a drug side effect, it might help to take the drug in the morning.

PRACTICING FOR NCLEX

MULTIPLE-CHOICE QUESTIONS

1. c   2. c   3. c   4. b   5. b   6. c   7. d   8. a   9. c
10. b

ALTERNATE FORMAT QUESTIONS

1. a c e f
2. a c d e

Chapter 11   Antiseizure Drugs

MASTERING THE INFORMATION

MATCHING

1. c   2. j   3. f   4. i   5. h   6. d   7. g   8. b   9. a
10. e

TRUE OR FALSE

1. f   2. f   3. t   4. t   5. t   6. f   7. t   8. f   9. t
10. f

SHORT ANSWER

1. The most common adverse effects are ataxia, drowsiness, lethargy, nausea and vomiting, and gingival hyperplasia in children.
2. It can cause a skin rash that can progress to the severe form of Stevens-Johnson syndrome.
3. It produces significant somnolence and dizziness.
4. The drug is not metabolized by the liver and does not affect the hepatic metabolism.
5. Because of differences in absorption and bioavailability, there is a risk of lower serum phenytoin levels, loss of therapeutic effectiveness, and seizures.

APPLYING YOUR KNOWLEDGE

Although Mr. Eng's Dilantin level falls within the high end of normal (10–20 mcg/mL), his symptoms indicate phenytoin toxicity. Laboratory values are guides for appropriate dosing, but it is important that treatment be based on clinical data. Mr. Eng should be referred to his physician for evaluation of Dilantin toxicity and adjustment of Dilantin dosage.

PRACTICING FOR NCLEX

MULTIPLE-CHOICE QUESTIONS

1. b   2. a   3. d   4. b   5. c   6. b   7. c   8. b   9. c
10. c

ALTERNATE FORMAT QUESTIONS

1. 60 mg
2. b c e

Chapter 12   Antiparkinson Drugs

MASTERING THE INFORMATION

MATCHING

1. h   2. e   3. g   4. a   5. b   6. c   7. f   8. d   9. i
10. j

TRUE OR FALSE

1. t   2. f   3. t   4. t   5. f   6. t   7. f   8. t   9. f
10. t

SHORT ANSWER

1. destruction or degenerative changes in dopamine-producing nerve cells
2. control symptoms, maintain functional ability in activities of daily living, minimize adverse drug effects, and slow disease progression
3. better control of symptoms and reduced dosage of individual drugs
4. increase the effects of the anticholinergic drug
5. anorexia, nausea and vomiting, orthostatic hypotension, cardiac dysrhythmias, dyskinesia, CNS stimulation (restlessness, agitation, confusion, and delirium), and abrupt swings in motor function

APPLYING YOUR KNOWLEDGE

Yes. Both Sinemet and tricyclic antidepressants have anticholinergic side effects, including urinary retention and constipation. When the medications are given together, enhanced anticholinergic effects are seen. Tachycardia and palpitations can also occur. Refer Mr. Simmons to his physician to see if another antidepressant with fewer anticholinergic side effects could be used.

PRACTICING FOR NCLEX

MULTIPLE-CHOICE QUESTIONS

1. b 2. a 3. c 4. b 5. a 6. a 7. b 8. d 9. c
10. a

ALTERNATE FORMAT QUESTIONS

1. a c e

2. 600 mg

Chapter 13   Skeletal Muscle Relaxants

MASTERING THE INFORMATION

MATCHING

1. f 2. c 3. g 4. a 5. k 6. j 7. h 8. b 9. e
10. d 11. i

TRUE OR FALSE

1. f 2. f 3. t 4. f 5. t 6. f 7. t 8. t 9. f
10. f

SHORT ANSWER

1. neurological and musculoskeletal disorders, muscle spasms and cramps, spinal cord injury, and multiple sclerosis
2. cause CNS depression; use cautiously in clients with impaired renal function, hepatic or respiratory depression, and those who must be alert for performing basic functions
3. to relieve pain, muscle spasms, and spasticity without impairing the ability to perform self-care activities of daily living
4. anticholinergic effects (eg, dry mouth, constipation, urinary retention, and tachycardia), drowsiness and dizziness
5. Deficient Knowledge: Safe use of skeletal muscle relaxants (SMRs); Risk of Injury: Sedation and dizziness related to SMRs

APPLYING YOUR KNOWLEDGE

Check this order with the physician. Normal IV Valium dosage is 5–10 mg every 3–4 hours. A 50-mg dose is unsafe and should not be given. Anytime you have to administer 10 cc by IV push you should question whether the dose is appropriate.

PRACTICING FOR NCLEX

MULTIPLE-CHOICE QUESTIONS

1. c 2. a 3. b 4. a 5. c 6. b 7. a 8. b 9. b
10. c

ALTERNATE FORMAT QUESTIONS

1. 60 mg

2. a b c d e

Chapter 14   Substance Abuse Disorders

MASTERING THE INFORMATION

MATCHING

1. j 2. f 3. i 4. g 5. a 6. h 7. c 8. e 9. d
10. b

TRUE OR FALSE

1. t 2. f 3. t 4. t 5. f 6. t 7. f 8. t 9. t
10. t

SHORT ANSWER

1. self-administration of a drug for prolonged periods, producing physical or psychological dependence
2. a craving for a drug with unsuccessful attempts to decrease its use; compulsive drug-seeking behavior
3. feelings of satisfaction and pleasure from taking a drug
4. physiologic adaptation to chronic use of a drug so that unpleasant symptoms occur when the drug is stopped
5. when the body adjusts to drugs so that higher doses are needed to achieve feelings of pleasure

APPLYING YOUR KNOWLEDGE

Although you are not in a formal professional relationship with this young woman, it is important to support her efforts in smoking cessation. Tell her how proud you are that she is trying to quit and that research shows that it usually takes many attempts before success is obtained. It is also important to tell her she must apply only one patch at a time and avoid concurrent use of nicotine gum to prevent nicotine toxicity. Refer her back to her health care provider if she has additional questions or concerns.

PRACTICING FOR NCLEX

MULTIPLE-CHOICE QUESTIONS

1. c 2. a 3. b 4. b 5. d 6. a 7. d 8. d 9. a
10. c

ALTERNATE FORMAT QUESTIONS

1. b c d

2. a b d e

Chapter 15   Central Nervous System Stimulants

MASTERING THE INFORMATION

MATCHING

1. d 2. e 3. f 4. b 5. a 6. c 7. j 8. g 9. h
10. i

TRUE OR FALSE

1. t 2. f 3. t 4. f 5. t 6. t 7. f 8. t 9. t
10. f

SHORT ANSWER

1. It destroys the extended-release feature and allows the drug to be absorbed faster.
2. CNS stimulants result in fewer "sleep attacks" with narcolepsy, improved behavior and performance of cognitive and psychomotor tasks with attention deficit hyperactivity disorder (ADHD), improved mental alertness, and decreased fatigue.
3. This time frame minimizes the drug's appetite-suppressing effects and risks of interference with nutrition and growth.
4. They have a high potential for abuse; the risks of drug dependence are lessened if they are taken as prescribed.
5. Drug holidays increase beneficial effects and help prevent drug dependence and stunted growth.

PRACTICING FOR NCLEX

MULTIPLE-CHOICE QUESTIONS

1. a   2. b   3. b   4. c   5. a   6. d   7. a   8. b   9. a
10. d

ALTERNATE FORMAT QUESTIONS

1. 100 mg
2. a. 2   b. 5   c. 3   d. 4   e. 1

Chapter 16   Physiology of the Autonomic Nervous System

MASTERING THE INFORMATION

MATCHING

1. j   2. i   3. g   4. c   5. d   6. h   7. f   8. b   9. e
10. a

TRUE OR FALSE

1. f   2. t   3. t   4. f   5. f   6. t   7. t   8. f   9. f
10. t

SHORT ANSWER

1. afferent
2. parasympathetic
3. alpha$_1$
4. efferent
5. sympathetic

PRACTICING FOR NCLEX

MULTIPLE-CHOICE QUESTIONS

1. b   2. c   3. b   4. c   5. d   6. b   7. d   8. a   9. c
10. a

ALTERNATE FORMAT QUESTIONS

1. a d e
2. b c d

Chapter 17   Adrenergic Drugs

MASTERING THE INFORMATION

MATCHING

1. e   2. g   3. g   4. e   5. j, c   6. e, f, g   7. g
8. c, e, j   9. e   10. a

TRUE OR FALSE

1. f   2. t   3. f   4. t   5. t   6. f   7. t   8. f   9. t
10. t

SHORT ANSWER

1. Direct-acting adrenergic drugs include isoproterenol, epinephrine, and norepinephrine.
2. Cardiac stimulation is the predominant effect.
3. Bronchodilation is the predominant effect of the activation of beta$_2$ receptors.
4. These drugs are used in the treatment of acute cardiovascular, respiratory, and allergic disorders.
5. Cardiac dysrhythmias, angina pectoris, hypertension, hyperthyroidism, and narrow-angle glaucoma are contraindications to using adrenergic drugs.

APPLYING YOUR KNOWLEDGE

As an adrenergic agent, ephedrine stimulates both alpha and beta receptors. Stimulation of alpha receptors causes vasoconstriction of vessels in the nasal passage, thus decreasing nasal congestion. Side effects are produced when beta receptors are stimulated, increasing heart rate and blood pressure. When high doses of the medications are taken, or normal doses are used by people with cardiovascular problems, the side effects can be serious.

PRACTICING FOR NCLEX

MULTIPLE-CHOICE QUESTIONS

1. a   2. c   3. b   4. a   5. c   6. d   7. b   8. b   9. c
10. c

ALTERNATE FORMAT QUESTIONS

1. b c d e
2. a b c d

Chapter 18   Antiadrenergic Drugs

MASTERING THE INFORMATION

MATCHING

1. b   2. i   3. g   4. d   5. f   6. c   7. a   8. h   9. j
10. e

TRUE OR FALSE

1. t   2. f   3. t   4. t   5. t   6. f   7. f   8. t   9. t
10. t

SHORT ANSWER

1. They decrease urinary retention and improve urine flow by inhibiting contraction of muscles in the prostate and urinary bladder.
2. Beta-adrenergic blocking agents decrease heart rate, cardiac output, blood pressure, and aqueous humor in the eye, and they provide bronchoconstriction.
3. The goal is to suppress pathologic stimulation, not the normal physiologic response to activity, stress, and other stimuli.
4. The drugs combine with alpha$_1$ and beta$_1$ and beta$_2$ receptors in peripheral tissues and prevent adrenergic effects.
5. Alpha$_2$ agonist drugs inhibit release of norepinephrine in the brain, decreasing effects of the sympathetic nervous system, which leads to a decrease in blood pressure.

APPLYING YOUR KNOWLEDGE

Although she is probably not allergic to the Inderal, this new medication is responsible for her breathing difficulties. Inderal is a nonselective beta-blocker, which means that it blocks beta$_1$ and beta$_2$ receptors. Blocking the beta$_2$ receptor causes bronchial constriction. Clients with asthma are likely to become symptomatic when this occurs. Selective beta-blockers, which primarily block beta$_1$ receptors, should be used for any clients with a history of asthma or chronic obstructive pulmonary disease. In high doses, even selective beta-blockers can cause bronchoconstriction in high-risk clients.

PRACTICING FOR NCLEX

MULTIPLE-CHOICE QUESTIONS

1. b   2. b   3. a   4. c   5. a   6. d   7. b   8. a   9. c
10. a

ALTERNATE FORMAT QUESTIONS

1.

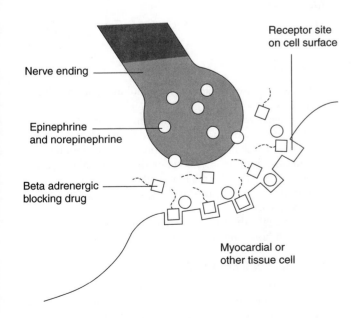

2. a b d e

Chapter 19   Cholinergic Drugs

MASTERING THE INFORMATION

MATCHING

1. c   2. d   3. b   4. f   5. g   6. h   7. e   8. j   9. a
10. i

TRUE OR FALSE

1. t   2. f   3. t   4. f   5. t   6. f   7. t   8. t   9. f
10. t

SHORT ANSWER

1. Reactions include abdominal cramps, diarrhea, excessive oral secretions, difficulty breathing, and muscle weakness.
2. Reversible inhibitors have a moderate duration of action and have therapeutic use. Irreversible inhibitors produce prolonged effects and are highly toxic.
3. The antidote is atropine.
4. Indicators of therapeutic effects include bowel sounds, passage of flatus through the rectum, and bowel movements.
5. These drugs prevent the breakdown of acetylcholine; therefore, acetylcholine remains in the synapse and continues to interact with receptors, producing a cholinergic response.

APPLYING YOUR KNOWLEDGE

Excessive stimulation of the parasympathetic nervous system causes decreased heart rate and cardiac contractility, hypotension, bronchial constriction, excessive saliva and mucus production, nausea, vomiting, diarrhea, and abdominal cramping. Because these symptoms are a result of excessive stimulation of cholinergic receptors, treatment includes administration of an anticholinergic drug such as atropine.

PRACTICING FOR NCLEX

MULTIPLE-CHOICE QUESTIONS

1. b   2. d   3. d   4. a   5. c   6. a   7. d   8. b   9. a
10. c

ALTERNATE FORMAT QUESTIONS

1. 2 mg

2. b c e

Chapter 20   Anticholinergic Drugs

MASTERING THE INFORMATION

MATCHING

1. d   2. a   3. g   4. h   5. f   6. e   7. c   8. b   9. i
10. j

TRUE OR FALSE

1. t   2. f   3. t   4. f   5. t   6. f   7. f   8. t   9. t
10. t

SHORT ANSWER

1. stimulation followed by depression of the CNS, decreased cardiovascular response, bronchodilation and decreased respiratory tract secretions, antispasmodic effects in the gastrointestinal tract (decreased muscle tone and motility), and mydriasis in the eye
2. to prevent vagal stimulation and potential bradycardia, hypotension, and cardiac arrest
3. hyperthermia—hot, dry, flushed skin; dry mouth; mydriasis; delirium; tachycardia; and ileus and urinary retention
4. have been associated with behavioral disturbances and psychotic reactions
5. blurred vision, confusion, heat stroke, constipation, urinary retention, and hallucinations

APPLYING YOUR KNOWLEDGE

Although anticholinergic medications are no longer used routinely as preoperative medication, they are still used in some preoperative situations when decreased secretions in the respiratory tract are important. Also, anticholinergic agents block excessive vagal stimulation by the parasympathetic nervous system, which can occur after administration of some anesthetics or muscle relaxants (eg, succinylcholine) or after manipulation of the pharynx or trachea. Vagal stimulation causes bradycardia and hypotension, and in severe cases, it can result in cardiac arrest.

PRACTICING FOR NCLEX

MULTIPLE-CHOICE QUESTIONS

1. c   2. a   3. b   4. a   5. c   6. d   7. a   8. b   9. c
10. d

ALTERNATE FORMAT QUESTIONS

1. a b d e
2. a c d e b

Chapter 21   Physiology of the Endocrine System

MASTERING THE INFORMATION

MATCHING

1. d   2. a   3. b   4. c   5. j   6. f   7. i   8. e   9. g
10. h

TRUE OR FALSE

1. f   2. f   3. t   4. t   5. f   6. t   7. f   8. t   9. t
10. t

SHORT ANSWER

1. Major organs include the hypothalamus, pituitary, thyroid, parathyroids, pancreas, adrenals, ovaries, and testes.
2. Body activities include metabolism of nutrients and water, reproduction, growth and development, and adaptation to changes in the internal and external environment.

3. Ovarian estrogen promotes maturation of ovarian follicles, stimulates growth and cyclic changes on the endometrial lining of the uterus, and stimulates the hypothalamic-pituitary system to regulate its own secretions.
4. Water-soluble, protein-derived hormones are inactivated by enzymes mainly in the liver and kidneys and excreted in bile or urine. Lipid-soluble steroid and thyroid hormones are conjugated in the liver to inactive forms and then excreted in bile or urine.
5. Physiologic use involves giving small doses as a replacement or substitute for the amount secreted by a normally functioning endocrine gland, such as insulin for diabetes mellitus. Pharmacologic use involves large doses for effects greater than physiologic effects as in use of anti–inflammatory effects in disorders.

PRACTICING FOR NCLEX

MULTIPLE-CHOICE QUESTIONS

1. d   2. a   3. b   4. c   5. c   6. b   7. a   8. b   9. d
10. a

ALTERNATE FORMAT QUESTIONS

1. a b c d
2. a b d f

Chapter 22   Hypothalamic and Pituitary Hormones

MASTERING THE INFORMATION

MATCHING

1. g   2. c   3. j   4. b   5. d   6. f   7. e   8. i   9. a
10. h

TRUE OR FALSE

1. t   2. f   3. t   4. f   5. t   6. f   7. t   8. f   9. t
10. t

SHORT ANSWER

1. use of drug by athletes for bodybuilding and to enhance athletic performance
2. by a negative feedback mechanism in proportion to metabolic needs and by increased thyroid hormones in body fluids that inhibit secretion of thyrotropin by the anterior pituitary and secretion of thyrotropin-releasing hormone (TRH) by the hypothalamus
3. stimulates Leydig's cells to secrete the androgen and testosterone
4. acromegaly, diabetes, hypertension, and heart failure
5. growth hormone and prolactin

APPLYING YOUR KNOWLEDGE

Lypressin replaces the antidiuretic hormone that acts to decrease urine output. The urine will have a higher specific gravity and appear less dilute. (It may be pale yellow rather than clear.) Keep accurate intake and output records on Mr. Willis, record daily weights, and monitor specific gravity.

PRACTICING FOR NCLEX

MULTIPLE-CHOICE QUESTIONS

1. a   2. b   3. c   4. d   5. a   6. a   7. b   8. c   9. b   10. c

ALTERNATE FORMAT QUESTIONS

1.

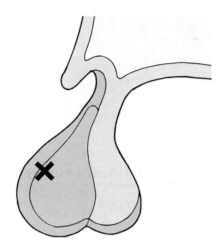

2. b c d e

Chapter 23   Corticosteroids

MASTERING THE INFORMATION

MATCHING

1. f   2. g   3. j   4. e   5. c   6. a   7. d   8. b   9. h
10. i

TRUE OR FALSE

1. t   2. t   3. f   4. f   5. t   6. f   7. t   8. t   9. f
10. f

SHORT ANSWER

1. Stimuli causes the hypothalamus to secrete corticotropin, which in turn stimulates the adrenal cortex to secrete corticosteroids.
2. They cause growth retardation even when used in small doses and administered by inhalation.
3. Decreasing salt intake may help decrease swelling; eating foods high in potassium may help prevent potassium loss; taking vitamin D (meats and dairy products) may help or prevent osteoporosis; and taking vitamin C may help prevent excessive bruising.
4. An example is betamethasone or dexamethasone.
5. A double dose is taken every other morning to allow rest periods so that adverse effects are decreased while anti-inflammatory effects continue.

APPLYING YOUR KNOWLEDGE

Kim's prednisone should not be stopped before surgery. In fact, the dose may be increased because of the physiologic stress of the surgery. Check with the surgeon to clarify preoperative and postoperative steroid orders. Side effects of steroid use are significant for the postoperative client. Wound healing is delayed because the inflammatory response is impaired. Carefully inspect the incision for dehiscence and know that staples or sutures may remain in place for a longer period of time. Signs of infection (fever, elevated white blood cell count, purulent drainage) may be absent or diminished even when an infection is present. Assess for fluid and electrolyte imbalances (sodium and fluid retention) during the postoperative period, as well as gastrointestinal irritation.

PRACTICING FOR NCLEX

MULTIPLE-CHOICE QUESTIONS

1. b   2. c   3. b   4. c   5. c   6. b   7. a   8. d   9. b
10. a

ALTERNATE FORMAT QUESTIONS

1. a. 5   b. 3   c. 8   d. 1   e. 4   f. 2   g. 6   h. 7
2. 12.5 mg

Chapter 24   Thyroid and Antithyroid Drugs

MASTERING THE INFORMATION

MATCHING

1. f   2. j   3. a   4. d   5. h   6. i   7. g   8. c   9. e
10. b

TRUE OR FALSE

1. f   2. t   3. t   4. f   5. t   6. f   7. f   8. t   9. f
10. t

SHORT ANSWER

1. antacids, iron, antihypertensives, estrogen, and phenytoin
2. to restore euthyroidism and normal metabolism
3. to reduce the size and vascularity of the thyroid gland to reduce the risk of excessive bleeding prior to a thyroidectomy
4. because thyroid hormone is essential for normal growth and development
5. can cause cancer and chromosome damage

APPLYING YOUR KNOWLEDGE

For most drugs, substituting generic brands is safe and economical. For some drugs, the bioavailability (amount of the drug absorbed into the bloodstream) differs for generic brands. This sometimes occurs with thyroid preparations. Mrs. Sanchez is experiencing signs of hypothyroidism because her blood levels have fallen below the therapeutic range since she started taking generic thyroid medication. In this situation, the cost benefit of taking generic drugs may be offset by the higher dose required to achieve therapeutic levels.

PRACTICING FOR NCLEX

MULTIPLE-CHOICE QUESTIONS

1. b   2. a   3. c   4. c   5. c   6. c   7. a   8. b   9. d
10. a

ALTERNATE FORMAT QUESTIONS

1. b c d
2. a b c d e

Chapter 25   Hormones that Regulate Calcium and Bone Metabolism

MASTERING THE INFORMATION

MATCHING

1. d   2. c   3. b   4. j   5. a   6. i   7. e   8. g   9. f
10. h

TRUE OR FALSE

1. f   2. f   3. f   4. t   5. t   6. t   7. f   8. t   9. f
10. f

SHORT ANSWER

1. Disorders include hypocalcemia, hypercalcemia, osteoporosis, Paget's disease, bone breakdown associated with breast cancer, and multiple myeloma
2. Bisphosphonates are poorly absorbed from the intestinal tract and must be taken on an empty stomach with water at least 30 minutes before any other fluid, food, or medication. The drugs are not metabolized. The drug bound to bone is slowly released into the bloodstream. Most of the drug that is not bound to bone is excreted in the urine.
3. Calcitonin inhibits bone reabsorption.
4. Calcium is responsible for cell membrane permeability and function; nerve cell excitability and transmission of impulses; contraction of cardiac, skeletal, and smooth muscle; conduction of electrical impulses in the heart; hormone secretion; and enzyme activity.
5. It is required for cell reproduction and body growth. It combines with fatty acids to form phospholipids, which are components of all cell membranes. Phosphorus also helps maintain acid-base balance and is necessary for cellular use of glucose, cellular production of energy, and proper function of several B vitamins.

APPLYING YOUR KNOWLEDGE

Tingling may be a symptom of hypocalcemia. Hypocalcemia can occur in Ms. Evans because during her thyroid surgery, the parathyroid glands that maintain calcium balance could have been damaged or inadvertently removed. Assess Chvostek's sign by tapping on Ms. Evans' face just above the temple, observing for twitching, which indicates hypocalcemia. Trousseau's sign can be assessed by constricting circulation in the arm by inflating a blood pressure cuff and observing for spasms of the lower arm and hand. Serum calcium levels should be obtained and compared with previous readings. Normal values are 8.5 to 10.5 mg/dL and must be adjusted when albumin levels are low. Report hypocalcemia or signs of tetany to the physician so that calcium replacement can be promptly administered.

PRACTICING FOR NCLEX

MULTIPLE-CHOICE QUESTIONS

1. b   2. d   3. c   4. b   5. b   6. c   7. a   8. d   9. a
10. c

ALTERNATE FORMAT QUESTIONS

1. a b e
2. a c

Chapter 26   Antidiabetic Drugs

MASTERING THE INFORMATION

MATCHING

1. a   2. f   3. e   4. i   5. g   6. d   7. j   8. b   9. c
10. h

TRUE OR FALSE

1. f.   2. f   3. t   4. t   5. f   6. f   7. t   8. t   9. f
10. t

SHORT ANSWER

1. In the liver, insulin acts to decrease breakdown of glycogen, formation of new glucose from fatty acids and amino acids, and formation of ketone bodies. At the same time, it acts to increase synthesis and storage of glycogen and fatty acids.
   In adipose tissue, insulin acts to decrease breakdown of fat and to increase production of glycerol and fatty acids.
   In muscle tissue, insulin acts to decrease protein breakdown and amino acid output and to increase amino acid uptake, protein synthesis, and glycogen synthesis.
2. Glucose or food in the digestive tract stimulates vagal activity and induces the release of gastrointestinal (GI) hormones called incretins.
3. Type 1 diabetes is a common chronic disorder of childhood that results from an autoimmune disorder that destroys pancreatic beta cells. It may occur at any age but usually starts between 4 and 20 years. The onset is sudden and produces severe symptoms; is difficult to control; produces a high incidence of complications, such as diabetic ketoacidosis (DKA) and renal failure; and requires administration of exogenous insulin.
   Type 2 diabetes is characterized by hyperglycemia and insulin resistance. The hyperglycemia results from increased production of glucose by the liver and decreased uptake of glucose in liver, muscle, and fat cells. Insulin resistance means that higher-than-usual concentrations of insulin required. The insulin is present but unable to work effectively. It usually occurs after 40 years of age, and obesity is the major cause.

4. Hypoglycemia is a contraindication.

5. For most clients, the goals of treatment are to maintain blood glucose at normal or near normal levels; promote normal metabolism of carbohydrates, fats, and proteins; prevent acute and long-term complications; and prevent hypoglycemic episodes.

APPLYING YOUR KNOWLEDGE

NPH is an intermediate-acting insulin that usually peaks 8 to 12 hours after administration. Hypoglycemia is most likely to occur before meals. The morning NPH is most likely to cause hypoglycemia before dinner, and the evening NPH is likely to cause hypoglycemia after midnight—so diabetics need to eat an evening snack.

PRACTICING FOR NCLEX

MULTIPLE-CHOICE QUESTIONS

1. c   2. a   3. b   4. d   5. b   6. d   7. b   8. d   9. b
10. a

ALTERNATE FORMAT QUESTIONS

1. a d e

2. a b d

Chapter 27   Estrogens, Progestins, and Hormonal Contraceptives

MASTERING THE INFORMATION

MATCHING

1. g   2. j   3. d   4. c   5. i   6. a   7. e   8. f   9. h
10. b

TRUE OR FALSE

1. t   2. t   3. f   4. f   5. f   6. t   7. t   8. t   9. f
10. f

SHORT ANSWER

1. promotes growth in tissues related to reproduction and sexual characteristics

2. to prevent endometrial cancer

3. pregnancy, thromboembolic disorders, suspected breast or genital tissues cancer, undiagnosed vaginal or uterine bleeding, fibroid tumors of the uterus, stroke victims, heart disease, and family history of breast cancer

4. inhibits hypothalamic secretion of gonadotropin-releasing hormone, which inhibits pituitary secretion of follicle-stimulating hormone (FSH) and luteinizing hormone (LH), which stops ovulation; produces mucus that resists penetration of sperm into the upper reproductive tract; and interferes with endometrial maturation and reception of ova that are released and fertilized

5. has been associated with vaginal cancer in female offspring and possible harmful effects in the male

APPLYING YOUR KNOWLEDGE

Factors such as the number of doses omitted and the time of the month such omission occurred may affect whether skipped doses could alter therapeutic drug levels. If Jane remembers a skipped dose within hours, instruct her to just take the pill late. If a longer period of time elapses (eg, more than 48 hours), instruct Jane not to take all of the missed doses at once and to check with her health care provider. Alternative forms of birth control may be required for the rest of the cycle.

Teach Jane to take her birth control pills at the same time each day, in association with a daily task or ritual (eg, after breakfast, after brushing teeth before bed). Advise her to notify any health care provider that she is taking birth control pills when other medications are prescribed. Drug interactions can occur with some other drugs. Antibiotics, which women of childbearing age may often require, can decrease the effectiveness of oral contraceptives.

PRACTICING FOR NCLEX

MULTIPLE-CHOICE QUESTIONS

1. c   2. b   3. d   4. a   5. a   6. d   7. b   8. b   9. d
10. b

ALTERNATE FORMAT QUESTIONS

1. 42 mg

2. a b c d e

Chapter 28   Androgens and Anabolic Steroids

MASTERING THE INFORMATION

MATCHING

1. e   2. b   3. a   4. h   5. d   6. g   7. i   8. c   9. j
10. f

TRUE OR FALSE

1. t   2. f   3. t   4. f   5. t   6. t   7. t   8. t   9. f
10. t

SHORT ANSWER

1. Testes, ovaries, and adrenal cortices secrete androgens.

2. Testosterone is responsible for development of male sexual characteristics, reproduction, and metabolism.

3. They are classified as Schedule III drugs because of abuse potential.

4. Potentially serious side effects include hypertension, decreased high-density lipoproteins (HDLs), increased low-density lipoproteins (LDLs), benign and malignant neoplasms, aggression, hostility, combativeness, decreased testicular function, amenorrhea, and acne.

5. They antagonize or reduce effects of female sex hormones. They suppress menstruation and cause atrophy of the endometrial lining of the uterus.

APPLYING YOUR KNOWLEDGE

Tell them that you would be very worried if the rumor were true because anabolic steroids are often abused, and nonprescription sales are illegal. However, they are easily obtained off the streets. They can stop bone growth and damage the heart, kidneys, and liver. Cardiac disorders, reproductive disorders, and changes in behavior can occur.

PRACTICING FOR NCLEX

MULTIPLE-CHOICE QUESTIONS

1. b   2. b   3. b   4. b   5. a   6. d   7. a   8. b   9. a
10. c

ALTERNATE FORMAT QUESTIONS

1. a d e
2. a b d e

Chapter 29   General Characteristics of Antimicrobial Drugs

MASTERING THE INFORMATION

MATCHING

1. j   2. a   3. i   4. d   5. g   6. b   7. h   8. c   9. f
10. e

TRUE OR FALSE

1. t   2. t   3. t   4. f   5. f   6. t   7. t   8. f   9. t
10. f

SHORT ANSWER

1. Major defenses include intact skin and mucous membranes, anti-infective secretions, mechanical movements, phagocytic cells, and immune and inflammatory processes.
2. Contributing factors include widespread use of antimicrobials, interrupted or inadequate treatment, type of bacteria, type of infection, condition of host, and location or setting.
3. The mechanism of action is inhibition of bacterial wall synthesis, inhibition of protein synthesis, disruption of microbial cell membranes, inhibition of organism reproduction by interfering with nucleic acid, and inhibition of cell metabolism and growth.
4. Because it takes 48–72 hours to determine susceptibility to antibiotics, physicians usually prescribe a drug that is likely to be effective. This therapy is based on an informed estimate of the most likely pathogens given the client, signs and symptoms, and apparent site of infection.
5. Tetracyclines may affect teeth and bones.

PRACTICING FOR NCLEX

MULTIPLE-CHOICE QUESTIONS

1. b   2. a   3. c   4. d   5. c   6. c   7. d   8. c   9. c
10. b

ALTERNATE FORMAT QUESTIONS

1. a c d
2. b c e

Chapter 30   Beta-Lactam Antibacterials: Penicillins, Cephalosporins, and Others

MASTERING THE INFORMATION

MATCHING

1. j   2. g   3. h   4. b   5. i   6. d   7. e   8. f   9. c
10. a

TRUE OR FALSE

1. t   2. f   3. f   4. t   5. f   6. t   7. t   8. t   9. f
10. f

SHORT ANSWER

1. penicillins, cephalosporins, carbapenums, and monobactams
2. inhibit synthesis of bacterial cell walls by binding to proteins that produce defective cell walls, which causes intracellular contents to leak, destroying microorganisms
3. protects the penicillin from destruction by the enzymes and extends the penicillin's antimicrobial activity
4. because the drugs are chemically similar
5. rash, hives, itching, severe diarrhea, shortness of breath, fever, sore throat, black tongue, and bleeding

APPLYING YOUR KNOWLEDGE

Ms. Driver may be experiencing anaphylaxis. Although she did not state an allergy to cephalosporin antibiotics, 5% to 10% of people allergic to penicillin may have a cross-sensitivity to cephalosporins because structurally all beta-lactams are similar. Stop infusing the cefotetan, but keep the IV line open because you may need to give emergency drugs IV if her condition worsens. Take her vital signs, administer oxygen, and have someone stay with her while you contact the physician. Make sure that you have epinephrine on hand.

PRACTICING FOR NCLEX

MULTIPLE-CHOICE QUESTIONS

1. c   2. a   3. b   4. d   5. c   6. b   7. b   8. a   9. d
10. b

ALTERNATE FORMAT QUESTIONS

1. a b c d

Chapter 31   Aminoglycosides and Fluoroquinolones

MASTERING THE INFORMATION

MATCHING

1. f   2. c   3. e   4. j   5. g   6. h   7. a   8. i   9. b
10. d

TRUE OR FALSE

1. f   2. t   3. t   4. t   5. f   6. t   7. t   8. f   9. f
10. t

SHORT ANSWER

1. Aminoglycosides penetrate the cell walls of susceptible bacteria and bind to intracellular structures that synthesize proteins. The bacteria cannot synthesize the proteins necessary for their function and replication.
2. Their major clinical use is to treat serious systemic infection caused by susceptible aerobic gram-negative organisms.
3. They have been associated with permanent damage in cartilage and joints in some animal studies.
4. Age, weight, renal function, and serum drug levels are factors that should be considered.
5. Adequate fluid intake is the main goal.

APPLYING YOUR KNOWLEDGE

Peak and trough gentamicin levels are obtained to assess whether the proper dosage is being administered and to avoid toxicity that can cause permanent damage to renal function and hearing. Peak (highest) blood levels should be drawn 30 to 60 minutes after administering the drug, and trough (lowest) blood levels should be drawn just before the dose is administered. The laboratory results indicate that the peak level is normal but the trough level is high (4 mc/mL rather than less than 2 mcg/mL). Dosage will need to be decreased to avoid renal damage. Considering Mr. Howles' age, he may have some renal impairment already that has decreased the rate of gentamicin excretion. Check to see if Mr. Howles' creatinine and blood urea nitrogen levels are elevated, which would indicate renal insufficiency. Notify the physician of the test results so that the gentamicin dose can be adjusted.

PRACTICING FOR NCLEX

MULTIPLE-CHOICE QUESTIONS

1. b 2. d 3. a 4. b 5. b 6. a 7. a 8. b 9. a
10. a

ALTERNATE FORMAT QUESTIONS

1. a c e
2. a c e

Chapter 32   Tetracyclines, Sulfonamides, and Urinary Agents

MASTERING THE INFORMATION

MATCHING

1. h 2. i 3. f 4. e 5. d 6. g 7. c 8. j 9. b
10. a

TRUE OR FALSE

1. f 2. t 3. t 4. f 5. t 6. f 7. f 8. t 9. t
10. f

SHORT ANSWER

1. Clinical indications include treatment of uncomplicated urethral, endocervical, or rectal infections; adjunctive therapy for pelvic inflammatory disease (PID) and sexually transmitted diseases (STDs); long-term acne; substitution for penicillin for traveler's diarrhea; and inhibition of antidiuretic hormone.
2. Tetracyclines inhibit microbial protein synthesis.
3. Sulfonamides act as antimetabolites of para-aminobenzoic acid (PABA) required to produce folic acid; cause formation of nonfunctional derivatives of folic acid; and halt multiplication of new bacteria but do not kill mature, fully formed bacteria.
4. Tetracyclines are contraindicated because they deposit in bones and teeth along with calcium and can cause permanent brown coloring of tooth enamel.
5. The treatment plan should include gathering assessment data, forcing fluids, cleansing appropriately after sexual intercourse, taking all medication, and taking it as directed.

APPLYING YOUR KNOWLEDGE

An indwelling catheter significantly increases the incidence of urinary tract infections (UTIs). Cloudy, foul-smelling urine with lots of sediment also supports the presence of a UTI. Because of their depressed immune function, elderly clients do not always experience common symptoms of UTI such as fever or pain. Obtain an order for a urine culture and sensitivity so appropriate antibiotics can be prescribed. Encourage fluids, at least 8 glasses per day, unless contraindicated. Work on a long-term plan for bladder retraining or intermittent catheterization to decrease risk of chronic, recurrent UTIs.

PRACTICING FOR NCLEX

MULTIPLE-CHOICE QUESTIONS

1. d 2. d 3. a 4. b 5. a 6. b 7. b 8. b 9. b
10. c

ALTERNATE FORMAT QUESTIONS

1. a b e
2. 66 mg

Chapter 33   Macrolides, Ketolides, and Miscellaneous Antibacterials

MASTERING THE INFORMATION

MATCHING

1. i 2. j 3. a 4. e 5. d 6. f 7. h 8. b 9. c
10. g

TRUE OR FALSE

1. t 2. f 3. t 4. t 5. f 6. t 7. f 8. t 9. f
10. t

SHORT ANSWER

1. daptomycin (Cubicin)
2. myelosuppression (anemia, leucopenia, pancytopenia, thrombocytopenia)
3. aids in absorption of the drug
4. can interfere with accommodation, resulting in blurred vision, difficulty focusing, and diplopia
5. inhibit microbial protein synthesis

APPLYING YOUR KNOWLEDGE

Diarrhea is a side effect of many antibiotics. When diarrhea is severe, it is important to determine if the cause is pseudomembranous colitis, which is caused when antibiotics suppress the growth of normal flora and allow the overgrowth of *Clostridium difficile*. This organism produces a toxin that kills mucosal cells and creates ulcerations. Pseudomembranous colitis is often associated with the use of clindamycin. Contact the physician for an order for a *C. difficile* stool toxin assay. Treatment includes metronidazole (Flagyl) or oral vancomycin. Mrs. Miller's dizziness maybe caused by volume depletion. Adequate fluids must be restored to prevent shock.

PRACTICING FOR NCLEX

MULTIPLE-CHOICE QUESTIONS

1. c   2. d   3. b   4. b   5. a   6. b   7. b   8. b   9. a
10. a

ALTERNATE FORMAT QUESTIONS

1. a c e

2. a d e

Chapter 34   Drugs for Tuberculosis and *Mycobacterium Avium* Complex (MAC) Disease

MASTERING THE INFORMATION

MATCHING

1. c   2. d   3. h   4. g   5. f   6. i   7. j   8. b   9. a
10. e

TRUE OR FALSE

1. f   2. t   3. t   4. f   5. f   6. t   7. t   8. t   9. f
10. t

SHORT ANSWER

1. Isoniazid (INH) penetrates body cells and mycobacteria, kills actively growing intracellular and extracellular organisms, and inhibits growth of dormant organisms in macrophages and tuberculous lesions.

2. With latent tuberculosis infection (LTBI), mycobacteria are inactive but remain alive in the body. There are no symptoms, and the infection does not spread to others. Patients will have a positive tuberculosis (TB) skin test and can develop active TB later. Active TB usually results from reactivation of a latent infection. Patients will have a persistent cough and productive sputum, chest pains, chills, fever, hemoptysis, night sweats, weight loss, weakness, and lack of appetite. They will have a positive skin test and abnormal chest x-rays.
3. A major TB-related concern is an increase in drug-resistant infections.
4. Nurses can help control TB by performing and reading TB skin tests; tracking contacts; assessing clients, their homes, etc.; educating clients and families; administering prescribed drugs; and maintaining records.
5. Drugs include isoniazid, rifampin, pyrazinamide, ethambutol, and streptomycin.

APPLYING YOUR KNOWLEDGE

First, it is important that you hear Ms. Sommers' concerns and acknowledge them. To comply with treatment, Ms. Sommers needs to see that the benefits are greater than the risks. Provide Ms. Sommers with specific information concerning side effects and how they will be monitored. Peripheral neuropathy and hepatotoxicity are significant side effects. Tell Ms. Summers to alert you about tingling in her feet or hands. Vitamin B_6 tablets can be given to decrease this side effect. Liver function is monitored by watching for symptoms such as jaundice and fatigue and by assessing laboratory results (liver enzymes, bilirubin levels.) Warn Ms. Sommers that her urine and other body fluids may turn red, but this is not harmful in any way. Ms. Sommers should also check with her doctor before taking over-the-counter medications because drug interactions with TB medications are common. Provide Ms. Sommers with written material and encourage her to call if she has any questions.

PRACTICING FOR NCLEX

MULTIPLE-CHOICE QUESTIONS

1. a   2. a   3. d   4. b   5. c   6. b   7. d   8. b   9. a
10. d

ALTERNATE FORMAT QUESTIONS

1.

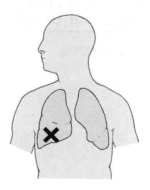

2. 22.5 mg

Chapter 35   Antiviral Drugs

MASTERING THE INFORMATION
MATCHING
1. d   2. h   3. e   4. c   5. b   6. g   7. f   8. a   9. j
10. i

TRUE OR FALSE
1. t   2. f   3. f   4. t   5. f   6. t   7. f   8. t   9. t
10. f

SHORT ANSWER
1. fever, headache, cough, malaise, muscle pain, nausea, vomiting, insomnia, photophobia, and normal white blood cells (WBCs)
2. nucleoside and nonnucleoside reverse transcriptase inhibitors, nucleotide reverse transcriptase inhibitors, protease inhibitors, and fusion inhibitors
3. gastrointestinal upset, anorexia and nausea, CNS symptoms, nervousness, light-headedness, and difficulty concentrating
4. because they decrease the serum level of antiviral agents
5. inhibit viral reproduction but do not eliminate viruses from tissues

APPLYING YOUR KNOWLEDGE
Nick may feel embarrassed or ashamed about this diagnosis and reluctant to ask questions. If his stress level is high, he may not comprehend everything that is said. Provide written information for his future reference. Stress that genital herpes is a sexually transmitted disease that can be controlled but not cured with the acyclovir. He should complete the entire 10-day prescription, and then take 400 mg bid for recurrences. Factors such as illness, emotional stress, or intense sunlight can increase recurrence. Because genital herpes is not cured, it is important to use a condom to prevent transmission of herpes to a sexual partner. The diagnosis of herpes is stressful and affects future life decisions. Listen to Nick's concerns and offer counseling.

PRACTICING FOR NCLEX
MULTIPLE-CHOICE QUESTIONS
1. b   2. b   3. d   4. a   5. c   6. b   7. a   8. d   9. a
10. b

ALTERNATE FORMAT QUESTIONS
1. 1200 mg, 12 tablets
2. a c e

Chapter 36   Antifungal Drugs

MASTERING THE INFORMATION
MATCHING
1. f   2. b   3. e   4. a   5. d   6. c   7. g   8. i   9. h
10. j

TRUE OR FALSE
1. t   2. f   3. t   4. f   5. t   6. t   7. f   8. t   9. f
10. t

SHORT ANSWER
1. candidiasis
2. by disrupting the structure and function of fungal cell components
3. ketoconazole, fluconazole, itraconazole, and voriconazole
4. nephrotoxicity
5. cimetidine and rifampin

APPLYING YOUR KNOWLEDGE
Nystatin works topically to treat fungal infestation in the oral cavity. "S & S" means "swish and swallow." To ensure that nystatin remains in contact with the oral mucosa for as long as possible, it should be administered after meals and all other medications. Instruct the client not to drink anything for 30 minutes.

PRACTICING FOR NCLEX
MULTIPLE-CHOICE QUESTIONS
1. c   2. b   3. a   4. b   5. b   6. d   7. b   8. a   9. c
10. a

ALTERNATE FORMAT QUESTIONS
1. b c d e
2. a b c d e

Chapter 37   Antiparasitics

MASTERING THE INFORMATION
MATCHING
1. h   2. g   3. d   4. b   5. e   6. a   7. j   8. f   9. c
10. i

TRUE OR FALSE
1. t   2. t   3. t   4. t   5. f   6. f   7. t   8. f   9. t
10. t

SHORT ANSWER
1. Deficient Knowledge: Management of disease process and prevention of recurrence
2. the anopheles mosquito
3. areas of poverty, overcrowding, and poor sanitation (any geographic area and any socioeconomic group)
4. nausea, vomiting, diarrhea, fever, insomnia, and increased hepatic enzymes
5. mebendazole (Vermox)

APPLYING YOUR KNOWLEDGE
Explain that malaria is transmitted by mosquito bites, and thus it is important to limit exposure to mosquitoes (by using insect repellent, wearing long pants and long-sleeve shirts, and sleeping in screened or well-netted areas).

Mosquitoes are most active at dusk and dawn so prevention is especially important at these times. Prophylactic medications must be started 2 weeks before entering infested areas and continued for 8 weeks after returning. The medication should be taken on the same day of the week at approximately the same time. If acute symptoms appear (headache, malaise, fever, chills), additional medication can be taken to treat the infection. Clear, written instructions regarding the dosage should be provided.

PRACTICING FOR NCLEX

MULTIPLE-CHOICE QUESTIONS

1. b   2. c   3. d   4. a   5. a   6. a   7. a   8. c   9. b
10. d

ALTERNATE FORMAT QUESTIONS

1. 1950 mg

2. a. 4   b. 2   c. 5   d. 6   e. 7   f. 3   g. 1

Chapter 38   Physiology of the Hematopoietic and Immune Systems

MASTERING THE INFORMATION

MATCHING

1. d   2. i   3. b   4. f   5. g   6. h   7. c   8. e   9. j
10. a

TRUE OR FALSE

1. t   2. f   3. t   4. f   5. t   6. t   7. f   8. t   9. t
10. f

SHORT ANSWER

1. Modification methods are immunizations and desensitization procedures, strengthening of antigens, and suppression of the normal response to an antigen.
2. A lack of calories or protein decreases numbers and functions of T cells, complement activity, neutrophil chemotaxis, and phagocytosis.
3. Autoimmune disorders include Hashimoto's thyroiditis, multiple sclerosis, myasthenia gravis, rheumatoid arthritis, systemic lupus erythematosus, and type I diabetes mellitus.
4. This system is very immature at birth; however, immunoglobulin G (IgG) levels from maternal blood are near adult levels. At birth, the source of maternal antibodies is severed. Antibody titers in infants decrease over 6 months as maternal antibodies are catabolized. The infant does start producing IgG at a rate lower than the rate of breakdown of maternal antibodies.
5. Natural killer cells, T cells and B cells

PRACTICING FOR NCLEX

MULTIPLE-CHOICE QUESTIONS

1. b   2. a   3. d   4. c   5. b   6. a   7. c   8. b   9. d
10. c

ALTERNATE FORMAT QUESTIONS

1. b d e
2. a b c d e

Chapter 39   Immunizing Agents

MASTERING THE INFORMATION

MATCHING

1. j   2. c   3. d   4. e   5. g   6. i   7. f   8. a   9. h
10. b

TRUE OR FALSE

1. t   2. f   3. f   4. f   5. f   6. t   7. t   8. t   9. t
10. t

SHORT ANSWER

1. It must be injected and is more expensive.
2. A person must be immunized every 7 to 10 years of life.
3. They are contraindicated under the following conditions: febrile illnesses, immunosuppressive drug therapy, immunodeficiency states, leukemia, lymphoma or generalized malignancy, and pregnancy.
4. The Centers for Disease Control and Prevention (CDC) in Atlanta, Georgia, provides the best source of information.
5. Clients with HIV should not be given live bacterial or viral vaccines because the disease produces major defects in cell-mediated and humoral immunity.

APPLYING YOUR KNOWLEDGE

Ask the patient how long ago she received a tetanus booster. Lifelong immunity is not provided for tetanus, necessitating booster injections every 10 years. Adults often do not keep good immunization records. If the patient is not absolutely sure she has had a recent booster injection, a tetanus immunization should be given. Tetanus is common with puncture wounds and can be lethal.

PRACTICING FOR NCLEX

MULTIPLE-CHOICE QUESTIONS

1. c   2. b   3. a   4. a   5. d   6. d   7. a   8. d   9. b
10. c

ALTERNATE FORMAT QUESTIONS

1. a b
2. b c d

Chapter 40   Hematopoietic and Immunostimulant Drugs

MASTERING THE INFORMATION

MATCHING

1. j   2. g   3. b   4. a   5. f   6. h   7. i   8. c   9. e
10. d

TRUE OR FALSE

1. f   2. f   3. t   4. t   5. f   6. t   7. t   8. f   9. t
10. t

SHORT ANSWER

1. They are given to restore normal function or increase the ability of the immune system to eliminate harmful invaders.
2. Cytokines create difficulty in maintaining effective dose levels over treatment periods of weeks or months; some of the drugs have a short half-life and require frequent administration. Some are very powerful and cause adverse effects.
3. Interferons produce enzymes that inhibit protein synthesis and degrade viral ribonucleic acid (RNA).
4. It stimulates the immune system and elicits a local inflammatory response.
5. They are proteins that will be destroyed by digestive enzymes.

APPLYING YOUR KNOWLEDGE

Granulocyte colony-stimulating factor (G-CSF) is given to decrease the length and severity of bone marrow suppression after chemotherapy. Laboratory values (WBC count and differential) evaluate the degree of bone marrow suppression and whether G-CSF is effective. In this situation, the nadir (lowest neutrophil count) should be above 1000/mm^3 and should last for less than 6 days. Although bone marrow suppression can affect red blood cells (RBCs) and platelets, WBCs (neutrophils) are most significant because a low neutrophil count increases infection risk. Infection in a neutropenic client can be life threatening.

PRACTICING FOR NCLEX

MULTIPLE-CHOICE QUESTIONS

1. d   2. d   3. b   4. a   5. b   6. d   7. c   8. a   9. b   10. a

ALTERNATE FORMAT QUESTIONS

1. a b d
2. a c d e

Chapter 41   Immunosuppressants

MASTERING THE INFORMATION

MATCHING

1. c   2. g   3. d   4. e   5. f   6. h   7. j   8. b   9. a
10. i

TRUE OR FALSE

1. t   2. f   3. t   4. f   5. t   6. t   7. t   8. f   9. f
10. t

SHORT ANSWER

1. rheumatoid arthritis, Crohn's disease, psoriasis, and psoriatic arthritis
2. decrease accumulation of lymphocytes and macrophages and the production of cell-damaging cytokines at sites of inflammatory actions

3. current infection or factors predisposing them to potential infection
4. fever, chills, pruritus, urticaria, chest pain, nausea, vomiting, abdominal pain, bronchitis, chest pain, coughing, and dyspnea
5. absence of signs and symptoms indicating rejection of the transplanted tissue

APPLYING YOUR KNOWLEDGE

Complete a total body assessment, looking for signs of infection. It is important to note that clients taking immunosuppressive drugs do not mount an effective immune response in the presence of infection. Ms. Reily's temperature, even though it is a low-grade fever, is significant and supports the possibility that an infection might be present. Signs of organ rejection include fever, flank pain, and poor kidney functioning (increased creatinine and blood urea nitrogen [BUN], decreased urine output, and weight gain). Provide Ms. Reily's transplant surgeon with the data you have collected. He or she will order laboratory tests, including WBC count and differential, creatinine, BUN, and a cyclosporine level.

PRACTICING FOR NCLEX

MULTIPLE-CHOICE QUESTIONS

1. c   2. a   3. c   4. a   5. d   6. d   7. c   8. a   9. d   10. a

ALTERNATE FORMAT QUESTIONS

1. a b c d e
2. a c d

Chapter 42   Drugs Used in Oncologic Disorders

MASTERING THE INFORMATION

MATCHING

1. j   2. d   3. g   4. h   5. b   6. a   7. c   8. f   9. e
10. i

TRUE OR FALSE

1. t   2. f   3. f   4. t   5. t   6. f   7. t   8. f   9. f
10. t

SHORT ANSWER

1. They kill malignant cells by interfering with cell replication by affecting the supply and use of nutrients (amino acids, purines, pyrimidines) or with genetic materials in the cell nucleus (deoxyribonucleic acid [DNA] or RNA).
2. Common effects include alopecia, anemia, bleeding, fatigue, mucositis, nausea and vomiting, neutropenia, and thrombocytopenia.
3. Tumor lysis syndrome occurs when large numbers of cancer cells are killed or damaged and release their contents into the bloodstream. Hyperkalemia, hyperphosphatemia, hyperuricemia, hypomagnesemia, hypocalcemia, and acidosis may develop.

4. Tamoxifen inhibits the ability of breast cancer cells to use estrogen for growth, whereas an aromatase inhibitor inhibits the production of estrogen in fat, muscle, and other tissue.
5. Age, nutritional status, blood count, kidney and liver function, and previous chemotherapy or radiation therapy are considered when determining a chemotherapy dosage.

APPLYING YOUR KNOWLEDGE

Platelets, RBCs, and WBCs are produced in the bone marrow. The production of any of these cells can decrease when an antineoplastic agent is given with a side effect of bone marrow depression . The impact is greatest at nadir. When platelets decrease below 50,000/mm^3, there is an increased risk of bleeding, which may manifest as increased bruising, blood in the stool, dark urine, or even seizures and confusion if the bleeding is intracranial. When RBCs decrease, as evidenced by a hemoglobin of less than 9 g/dL, the client will experience anemia and fatigue. WBC count is a measure of the body's ability to fight infection. Neutrophils are WBCs that are especially helpful in fighting infection; thus when the WBC count is low, a neutrophil count is done. A client with neutrophil counts of less than 500/mm^3 is at significant risk for infection. Common signs of infection are often medicated by neutrophils. So the signs and symptoms of infection may be low in the neutropenic client.

Client teaching should focus on avoiding infection (washing hands, avoiding contact with infected individuals), especially if the neutrophil count is low. The client should report any fever, even low-grade fever. Fatigue can be managed with frequent rest, energy conservation measures, and good nutrition. When platelets are low, clients should be taught to avoid trauma. The importance of keeping appointments for monitoring should be stressed so that blood products can be given if values are critically low.

PRACTICING FOR NCLEX

MULTIPLE-CHOICE QUESTIONS

1. c   2. b   3. b   4. d   5. b   6. a   7. d   8. a   9. c   10. d

ALTERNATE FORMAT QUESTIONS

1. 5 mL

2. a d e

Chapter 43   Physiology of the Respiratory System

MASTERING THE INFORMATION

MATCHING

1. e   2. h   3. b   4. f   5. j   6. a   7. d   8. g   9. c   10. i

TRUE OR FALSE

1. f   2. t   3. f   4. f   5. f   6. t   7. t   8. f   9. t   10. f

SHORT ANSWER

1. 21%
2. 16 to 20 times/min
3. 500 mL
4. 6 to 10 times/hr
5. cough, increased secretions, mucosal congestion, and bronchospasms

PRACTICING FOR NCLEX

MULTIPLE-CHOICE QUESTIONS

1. b   2. c   3. a   4. d   5. b   6. c   7. d   8. a   9. b   10. d

ALTERNATE FORMAT QUESTIONS

1. a b d

2. a b c d

Chapter 44   Drugs for Asthma and Other Bronchoconstrictive Disorders

MASTERING THE INFORMATION

MATCHING

1. e   2. d   3. f   4. i   5. h   6. c   7. b   8. j   9. a   10. g

TRUE OR FALSE

1. f   2. t   3. t   4. f   5. t   6. f   7. t   8. f   9. f   10. f

SHORT ANSWER

1. bronchodilators and anti-inflammatory drugs
2. by decreasing mucosal edema and mucus secretion that narrow airways and by decreasing airway hyperreactivity to various stimuli
3. lithium, phenobarbital, and propranolol
4. not taking the medication correctly
5. anorexia, nausea and vomiting, nervousness, insomnia, and tachycardia

APPLYING YOUR KNOWLEDGE

First, have Gwen sit in a private area. An asthma attack can be very embarrassing for a middle schooler, and stress can increase her respiratory distress. Gwen needs to use her rescue inhaler now. Albuterol, a beta$_2$ agonist, will work quickly to dilate constricted bronchioles. Repeat if necessary. If Gwen's respiratory distress is not reversed by using the inhaler, the nurse should call 911 for emergency backup. Asthma can be lethal.

Plan follow-up with Gwen and her family at a later time to determine factors that may have contributed to Gwen's asthma attack. Have Gwen demonstrate using her inhalers so you can assess her technique. Question her regarding compliance with the medication regimen. Ask to see her peak flow log to assess whether she has been consistently monitoring her asthma control. Assess potential triggers that may have contributed to this attack (new pets, exposure to other allergens) and individualize teaching.

PRACTICING FOR NCLEX

MULTIPLE-CHOICE QUESTIONS

1. c   2. d   3. c   4. a   5. d   6. d   7. b   8. b   9. d
10. a

ALTERNATE FORMAT QUESTIONS

1. a. 6   b. 2   c. 5   d. 7   e. 1   f. 3   g. 4   h. 8
2. b c e

Chapter 45   Antihistamines and Allergic Disorders

MASTERING THE INFORMATION

MATCHING

1. j   2. c   3. b   4. d   5. f   6. g   7. h   8. e   9. i
10. a

TRUE OR FALSE

1. t   2. f   3. t   4. t   5. t   6. f   7. f   8. t   9. f
10. t

SHORT ANSWER

1. in secretory granules of mast and basophils cells—mostly tissue of skin and mucosal surfaces of eye, nose, lungs, and GI tract
2. response to certain stimuli (allergic reactions, cellular injury, and extreme cold)
3. mainly on smooth muscle cells in blood vessels and the respiratory and GI tract
4. contraction of smooth muscle in bronchi and bronchioles; simulation of vagus nerve endings to produce reflex bronchoconstriction and cough; increase in permeability of veins and capillaries, which causes fluid to flow into subcutaneous tissues and form edema; increased secretions of mucous glands; stimulation of sensory peripheral nerve endings to cause pain and pruritus; and dilation of capillaries in the skin to cause flushing
5. increased secretion of gastric acid and pepsin, increased rate and force of myocardial contraction, and decreased immunologic and inflammatory reactions

APPLYING YOUR KNOWLEDGE

Benadryl, an antihistamine, blocks histamine$_1$ receptors, thus decreasing histamine-induced symptoms such as rash, pruritus, cough, and swelling. If an allergic, histamine-related response occurs, the symptoms will be less severe if Benadryl has been previously administered. If a severe allergic reaction occurs, involving bronchospasm and hypotension, epinephrine should be administered to reverse these potentially life-threatening symptoms.

PRACTICING FOR NCLEX

MULTIPLE-CHOICE QUESTIONS

1. c   2. a   3. c   4. a   5. b   6. b   7. a   8. d   9. b
10. a

ALTERNATE FORMAT QUESTIONS

1. a c e
2. 2.5 mL

Chapter 46   Nasal Decongestants, Antitussives, and Cold Remedies

MASTERING THE INFORMATION

MATCHING

1. b   2. c   3. d   4. f   5. a   6. h   7. g   8. j   9. i
10. e

TRUE OR FALSE

1. t   2. f   3. f   4. t   5. f   6. t   7. f   8. t   9. f
10. f

SHORT ANSWER

1. It can increase dosage to toxic levels and cause irregular heart beats and extreme nervousness.
2. Nasal decongestants have stimulating and vasoconstricting effects.
3. Products that treat the common cold may contain an antihistamine, a nasal decongestant, and an analgesic.
4. Topical preparations may produce rebound nasal congestion.
5. Diagnoses may include Risk for Injury Related to Cardiac Dysrhythmias and Hypertension, and Noncompliance: Overuse of Nasal Decongestant.

APPLYING YOUR KNOWLEDGE

Joan has the symptoms of a cold. Tell her to avoid combination products that may include medications she does not need and are generally more expensive. Because her cough is productive, an antitussive agent (cough suppressant) is contraindicated because expectorating retained secretions promotes recovery and prevents pneumonia and other respiratory complications. An expectorant, such as guaifenesin, may help liquefy respiratory secretions and aid their removal. A nasal decongestant could be used to decrease nasal stuffiness and discharge. Acetaminophen can be taken to reduce generalized discomfort. In addition to discussing medications, stress the importance of getting adequate rest and drinking lots of fluids.

PRACTICING FOR NCLEX

MULTIPLE-CHOICE QUESTIONS

1. a   2. d   3. a   4. b   5. c   6. a   7. b   8. a   9. a
10. b

ALTERNATE FORMAT QUESTIONS

1. a c d e
2. a b c d e

Chapter 47 Physiology of the Cardiovascular System

MASTERING THE INFORMATION

MATCHING

1. c   2. g   3. h   4. f   5. j   6. d   7. e   8. i   9. b
10. a

TRUE OR FALSE

1. f   2. f   3. t   4. f   5. t   6. t   7. t   8. f   9. t
10. t

SHORT ANSWER

1. carry oxygen, nutrients, hormones, antibodies, and other substances to all body cells; remove waste products of cell metabolism (carbon dioxide and others)
2. a muscular organ that functions as a two-sided pump and circulates 5 to 6 liters of blood through the body every minute
3. maintain one-way flow of blood and prevent backflow
4. artery to artery anastomoses, which dilate to supply blood to the heart when a major artery is occluded
5. connect the arterial and venous portions of the circulation

PRACTICING FOR NCLEX

MULTIPLE-CHOICE QUESTIONS

1. c   2. b   3. a   4. b   5. b   6. a   7. c   8. d   9. a
10. b

ALTERNATE FORMAT QUESTIONS

1. b c d
2. c e

Chapter 48 Drug Therapy of Heart Failure

MASTERING THE INFORMATION

MATCHING

1. e   2. g   3. c   4. h   5. d   6. i   7. j   8. a   9. b
10. f

TRUE OR FALSE

1. f   2. t   3. f   4. t   5. t   6. f   7. f   8. t   9. t
10. f

SHORT ANSWER

1. Heart failure occurs when the heart cannot pump enough blood to meet tissue needs for oxygen.
2. Endothelin is a neurohormone that acts as a vasoconstrictor and may exert toxic effects on the heart, resulting in myocardial cell proliferation.
3. Digitalization occurs when a sufficient amount of digitalis is administered to produce therapeutic effects.

4. The most common conditions are blood clot formation and vasoconstriction that narrow the blood vessel lumen, which causes coronary artery disease and hypertension.
5. The kidney produces an enzyme that stimulates production of angiotensin II, a vasoconstrictor. This increases resistance, which causes increased pressure inside the heart, increasing stress on the myocardial wall and causing ischemia.

APPLYING YOUR KNOWLEDGE

Ms. Kindra's symptoms are consistent with acute heart failure and may indicate she is experiencing pulmonary edema. Administering digoxin is appropriate in the situation. The dose is a loading dose rather than a maintenance dose. The digoxin is given IV, and a loading dosage is used to achieve a therapeutic level more quickly so that adequate cardiac output can be restored. A loading dose should not exceed 1 mg/24 hours. Maintenance doses for digoxin are 0.125 to 0.5 mg/day, with the most common daily maintenance dose being 0.25 mg.

PRACTICING FOR NCLEX

MULTIPLE-CHOICE QUESTIONS

1. b   2. a   3. a   4. c   5. c   6. a   7. b   8. b   9. b
10. a

ALTERNATE FORMAT QUESTIONS

1. 25 mg/dose
2. c

Chapter 49 Antidysrhythmic Drugs

MASTERING THE INFORMATION

MATCHING

1. j   2. i   3. b   4. c   5. e   6. d   7. g   8. a   9. f
10. h

TRUE OR FALSE

1. f   2. t   3. f   4. t   5. t   6. f   7. t   8. f   9. t
10. t

SHORT ANSWER

1. The two calcium channel blockers are diltiazem and verapamil.
2. Adverse effects of the drug increase with decreasing creatinine clearance levels.
3. It decreases systemic vascular resistance, prolongs conduction in cardiac tissue and decreases heart rate. It also decreases contractility of the left ventricle.
4. Adverse effects include drowsiness, paresthesias, muscle twitching, convulsions, changes in mental status, and hypersensitivity reactions.
5. The therapeutic serum drug level of lidocaine is 1.5–6 mcg/mL.

APPLYING YOUR KNOWLEDGE

Research the correct administration time and time it carefully with the secondhand of your watch. It is usually given over 2 minutes. An injection given too rapidly can result in serious side effects. Make sure the client is monitored during administration so that you can quickly detect severe bradycardia or heart block. Because severe hypotension can occur, monitor blood pressure before administration and at 5-minute intervals after administration. Observe the client for improved heart rate and rhythm.

PRACTICING FOR NCLEX

MULTIPLE-CHOICE QUESTIONS

1. c   2. a   3. a   4. a   5. c   6. c   7. a   8. c   9. d   10. a

1. Identify the dysrhythmia and appropriate drug used for treatment in the following electrocardiogram (ECG) strips. Choose from the following:

Dysrhythmias	Drugs
Premature ventricular contractions	digoxin (Lanoxin)
Sinus bradycardia	lidocaine (Xylocaine)
Atrial fibrillation	atropine
Supraventricular tachycardia	verapamil (Calan)

a.

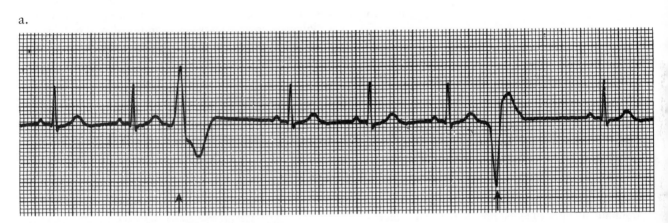

Dysrhythmia: Premature ventricular contractions
Drug: Lidocaine (Xylocaine)

b.

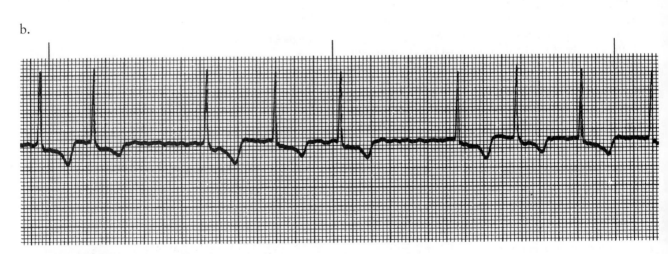

Dysrhythmia: Atrial fibrillation
Drug: Verapamil (Calan)

2.

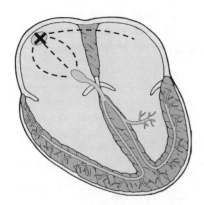

Chapter 50   Antianginal Drugs

MASTERING THE INFORMATION

MATCHING

 1. c   2. g   3. e   4. d   5. b   6. j   7. f   8. h   9. a
10. i

TRUE OR FALSE

 1. f   2. t   3. f   4. t   5. f   6. t   7. f   8. t   9. f
10. t

SHORT ANSWER

1. Atherosclerotic plaque in coronary arteries and coronary vasospasms cause angina pectoris to develop.
2. Atherosclerotic plaque narrows the lumen, decreases elasticity, and impairs dilation of coronary arteries, resulting in impaired blood flow to the myocardium.
3. The three main types of angina are classic, variant, and unstable.
4. Anginal pain is substernal chest pain that is constricting, squeezing, or suffocating in nature. It radiates to the jaw, neck, and shoulder; down the left or both arms; or to back. It lasts about 5 minutes or less.
5. Nitrates relax smooth muscle in blood vessel walls. This produces vasodilation, which relieves pain by reducing venous pressure and venous return to the heart. This decreases blood volume and pressure within the heart, which decreases cardiac workload and oxygen demand; dilates coronary arteries at higher doses and increases blood flow to ischemic areas; and dilates arterioles, which lowers peripheral vascular resistance, which decreases blood pressure and reduces cardiac workload.

APPLYING YOUR KNOWLEDGE

Assess Mrs. Sinatro's knowledge about coronary artery disease (CAD) and her readiness to learn about her new medications and other methods to manage this problem. Give Mrs. Sinatro written handouts about CAD and written information about her antianginal medications. Demonstrate how to apply the patch, stressing to rotate sites and not use hairy or scarred areas because they may decrease drug absorption. The patch is removed at night because the oxygen demand of the heart is usually less at rest, and continuous application can increase the development of drug tolerance. Discuss side effects, including headache and hypotension, that can cause dizziness and falls.

Teaching must include how to manage an episode of chest pain. First stress the importance of never ignoring chest pain. Some clients may deny they are experiencing chest pain and delay treatment. Tell her to rest if chest pain occurs. If pain does not subside, instruct her to place a nitroglycerin tablet under the tongue to dissolve and avoid swallowing the tablet. This can be repeated every 5 minutes, up to three nitroglycerin tablets. If the pain has not subsided with rest and nitroglycerin, the client or family should call 911. The client should not drive or be driven by family to the hospital or clinic because she may be having a heart attack (myocardial infarction). The nurse should also stress the importance of keeping nitroglycerin with her at all times and making sure the prescription is refilled before it reaches the expiration date. The tablets should be kept in the original amber bottle to protect them from sunlight and stored away from moisture and excessive heat.

PRACTICING FOR NCLEX

MULTIPLE-CHOICE QUESTIONS

1. d   2. c   3. a   4. a   5. b   6. a   7. b   8. b   9. a   10. d

ALTERNATE FORMAT QUESTIONS

1. b c e
2. b

Chapter 51   Drugs Used in Hypotension and Shock

MASTERING THE INFORMATION

MATCHING

 1. f   2. c   3. d   4. g   5. h   6. i   7. j   8. e   9. a
10. b

TRUE OR FALSE

 1. f   2. t   3. f   4. f   5. t   6. t   7. t   8. t   9. f
10. f

SHORT ANSWER

1. The three categories of shock include hypovolemic, cardiogenic, and distributive or vasogenic shock. Hypovolemic shock occurs when there is loss of intravascular fluid volume because of actual loss of blood or blood loss from shifts within the body. Cardiogenic shock occurs when the myocardium has lost its ability to contract efficiently and maintain an adequate cardiac output. Distributive or vasogenic shock is characterized by severe generalized vasodilation, causing severe hypotension and impaired blood flow.

2. Common signs and symptoms of shock are oliguria, heart failure, mental confusion, cool extremities, and coma.

3. It is important to know the etiology of shock because management and drug selection vary among the different types of shock.

4. Alpha-adrenergic drugs increase peripheral vascular resistance and raise blood pressure. Beta-adrenergic drugs increase myocardial contractility and heart rate and thus increase blood pressure.

5. They are used cautiously because increased contractility and heart rate will increase myocardial oxygen consumption and extend the area of infarction.

APPLYING YOUR KNOWLEDGE

First, it is important to impress on Brent that anaphylactic shock is life threatening. Explain that his allergic reaction when stung by a bee is severe and it can happen very quickly. The histamine released in the reaction affects his circulation and his breathing. When he experiences a bee sting, he should immediately take the Benadryl to decrease the amount of histamine that is released and decrease the severity of the reaction. If he experiences breathing difficulty or feels dizzy, he may need to use the EpiPen. Instruct him to take off the cap, push the needle right through his pants into his thigh, and inject the medication. (If he has an EpiPen Auto-Injector, the medication will be dispensed automatically after the needle is inserted into the thigh.) He then needs to have someone drive him to the nearest emergency department.

It is important to instruct Brent to keep an EpiPen with him at all times (home, car, office) and especially when outdoors (eg, in his backpack when hiking). Family may also need to be instructed because anaphylaxis occurs quickly, and as the patient becomes hypoxic, judgment and ability to use the EpiPen may be impaired.

PRACTICING FOR NCLEX

MULTIPLE-CHOICE QUESTIONS

1. c 2. a 3. b 4. c 5. b 6. a 7. b 8. d 9. a 10. b

ALTERNATE FORMAT QUESTIONS

1. a b c e

2. no

Chapter 52 Antihypertensive Drugs

MASTERING THE INFORMATION

MATCHING

1. g 2. j 3. c 4. d 5. i 6. h 7. e 8. b 9. f
10. a

TRUE OR FALSE

1. f 2. t 3. t 4. f 5. t 6. t 7. f 8. t 9. t
10. t

SHORT ANSWER

1. Three mechanisms that regulate blood pressure are neural, hormonal, and vascular. Neural involves the sympathetic nervous system (SNS); SNS neurons control the heart rate and force of contraction, as well as muscle tone of blood vessels. When blood pressure is decreased, the SNS produces secretions or epinephrine and norepinephrine, which causes constriction of blood vessels and increases the rate and force of contraction, resulting in a blood pressure increase.

Hormonal involves the rennin-angiotensin-aldosterone (RAA) system, which is activated in response to decreased blood pressure that releases rennin. Rennin converts angiotensinogen to angiotensin I. Angiotensin-converting enzyme (ACE) acts on angiotensin I to produce angiotensin II. Angiotensin II strongly constricts blood vessels, increases peripheral resistance, and increases blood pressure. Vasopressin, the antidiuretic hormone, is released in response to the decreased blood pressure. It causes retention of body fluids and vasoconstriction, which increases blood pressure.

Vascular consists of endothelial cells that line blood vessels and secrete substances that maintain a balance between vasoconstriction and vasodilation. The vasodilators (nitric oxide and prostacyclin) decrease vascular tone and blood pressure.

2. Nonpharmacologic measures include decreasing salt in the diet, controlling weight and fat intake, exercising, and avoiding smoking.

3. Obesity, increased serum cholesterol and triglycerides, cigarette smoking, sedentary lifestyle, family history, African-American race, adrenal disease, cardiovascular disorders, diabetes mellitus, oral contraceptives, and neurologic disorders may cause a person to be at risk for hypertension.

4. Stage 1 hypertension has a systolic blood pressure between 140 and159 or the diastolic is 90–99; in stage 2, the systolic is greater than 160 or the diastolic is 100 or more.

5. Diuretic therapy causes blood volume and cardiac output to decrease. There is a decrease in peripheral vascular resistance.

APPLYING YOUR KNOWLEDGE

The Nipride should infuse between 0.5 and 10 mcg/kg/min and you should expect that the blood pressure will decrease. These symptoms may indicate thiocyanate toxicity. The thiocyanate level should be checked. If the level is more than 12 mg/dL, the medication should be stopped and another drug should be ordered.

PRACTICING FOR NCLEX

MULTIPLE-CHOICE QUESTIONS

1. c 2. d 3. a 4. c 5. b 6. c 7. d 8. a 9. d 10. b

ALTERNATE FORMAT QUESTIONS

1. a c e

2. 2 tablets per dose

Chapter 53   Diuretics

MASTERING THE INFORMATION

MATCHING
1. h   2. i   3. g   4. j   5. a   6. d   7. c   8. e   9. f
10. b

SHORT ANSWER
1. f   2. f   3. t   4. t   5. f   6. f   7. t   8. t   9. t
10. t

APPLYING YOUR KNOWLEDGE

1. The kidneys regulate the volume, composition, and pH of body fluids.
2. The kidney contains 1 million nephrons, each of which is composed of a glomerulus and a tubule. The glomerulus is a network of capillaries that receive blood from the renal artery. The tubule is divided into the proximal tubule, loop of Henle, and distal tubule.
3. Diuretics decrease absorption of sodium, chloride, water, and other substances.
4. Clinical indications include edema, heart failure, and hypertension.
5. Loop diuretics produce significant diuresis.

APPLYING YOUR KNOWLEDGE

Assess blood pressure and compare this value with baseline blood pressure readings over the last few days. If blood pressure is significantly different from baseline (very high or greater than 180/90; very low or less than 100/60), notify the prescriber because adjustment of medications may be indicated. Postural blood pressure should be monitored because orthostatic hypotension is likely for clients on these medications. When orthostatic hypotension is present, instruct the client to rise slowly, sitting until dizziness has passed. Daily weight and intake and output records should also be assessed to evaluate whether drug therapy is effective. Check for signs of hypokalemia and serum potassium levels. This is especially important because the client is on a high dose (80 mg/day) of a potassium-wasting diuretic without potassium supplementation. Hypokalemia can increase the risk of cardiac dysrhythmias.

PRACTICING FOR NCLEX

MULTIPLE-CHOICE QUESTIONS
1. c   2. b   3. a   4. a   5. a   6. c   7. b   8. d   9. b
10. a

ALTERNATE FORMAT QUESTIONS
1.

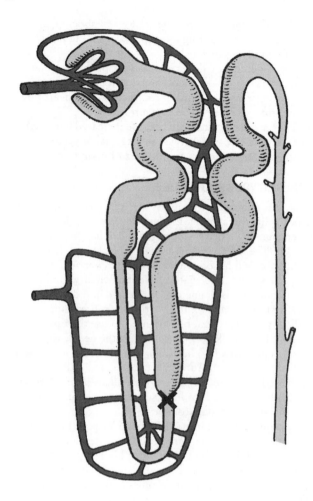

2. b c d

Chapter 54   Drugs that Affect Blood Coagulation

MASTERING THE INFORMATION

MATCHING
1. b   2. a   3. e   4. f   5. g   6. c   7. i   8. d   9. j
10. h

TRUE OR FALSE
1. t   2. f   3. f   4. t   5. f   6. t   7. t   8. f   9. t
10. f

SHORT ANSWER
1. Anticoagulants, antiplatelets, and thrombolytic drugs are used for thrombotic and thromboembolic disorders.
2. Thrombogenesis is life saving as a response to hemorrhage and life threatening when it obstructs a blood vessel and blocks the blood flow to tissues beyond the clot.

2. It inhibits synthesis of prostaglandins and interferes with platelet aggregation.
3. It acts in the liver to prevent synthesis of vitamin K-dependent clotting factors—II, VII, IX, and X.
4. Heparin has a short duration of action and need for frequent administration, the necessity of parenteral injection, local tissue reactions at the injection site, and a possibility of heparin-induced thrombocytopenia.

APPLYING YOUR KNOWLEDGE

Low-dose subcutaneous heparin is administered prophylactically to prevent deep vein thrombosis, which is associated with prolonged immobility. Activated partial thromboplastin time (aPTT) levels may be assessed before beginning therapy, but routine aPTT assessment and dosage adjustments are not required for low-dose heparin therapy. When giving the injection, take care to prevent trauma and subsequent bruising. A small, 26-gauge, ½ -inch needle is used. Leave a small air bubble in the syringe to follow the dose and lock the heparin into the subcutaneous space. The area is cleansed and grasped firmly, and the needle is inserted at a 90-degree angle. Do not aspirate or rub the area because this fosters bruising. Avoid injections within 2 inches of incisions or the umbilicus and any areas that are scarred or abnormal. Although research indicates that various sites (abdomen, arms, and legs) can be used, the preferred site is the abdomen. Observe and report any signs of bleeding.

PRACTICING FOR NCLEX

MULTIPLE-CHOICE QUESTIONS

1. b 2. c 3. c 4. b 5. a 6. b 7. b 8. d 9. b 10. a

ALTERNATE FORMAT QUESTIONS

1. a b c d e
2. a b c d e

Chapter 55 Drugs for Dyslipidemia

MASTERING THE INFORMATION

MATCHING

1. c 2. a 3. e 4. f 5. h 6. i 7. b 8. d 9. j
10. g

TRUE OR FALSE

1. f 2. t 3. t 4. t 5. f 6. f 7. t 8. t 9. f
10. t

SHORT ANSWER

1. cholesterol, phospholipids, and triglycerides
2. by specific proteins called lipoproteins
3. by altering the production, absorption, metabolism, or removal of lipids and lipoproteins
4. nausea, constipation, diarrhea, abdominal cramps or pain, headache, and skin rash
5. lovastatin (Mevacor)

APPLYING YOUR KNOWLEDGE

Mr. Dwyer will need teaching regarding lifestyle modifications to reduce his cholesterol level as well as information on the niacin that has been prescribed. First, ask what he knows about high cholesterol levels. Make sure you include a dietary assessment, especially his knowledge of foods high in cholesterol or fat. Explore together possible ways to reduce cholesterol and fat in the diet. If he is overweight, also talk about calorie reduction. Often, people have the correct knowledge about necessary changes, but compliance with lifestyle modification is difficult. Explore his supports and provide a list of referrals for long-term follow-up. Assess his exercise pattern. Provide positive reinforcement for any exercise that he does and together develop a reasonable exercise plan.

Mr. Dwyer also needs teaching about niacin to prevent unpleasant side effects. Gradually increasing the dose can possibly limit the unpleasant side effects of flushing and pruritus, as can premedicating with aspirin. Niacin should be taken with meals. Because niacin is a vitamin, many clients may feel it is safe to increase the dose. If side effects limit compliance, discuss this with the prescriber. Many newer, more expensive antilipid agents with fewer side effects can be prescribed to lower cholesterol. It is important to stress the importance of ongoing follow-up for clients with dyslipidemia.

PRACTICING FOR NCLEX

MULTIPLE-CHOICE QUESTIONS

1. a 2. a 3. c 4. b 5. d 6. a 7. b 8. c 9. b 10. b

ALTERNATE FORMAT QUESTIONS

1. a b d
2. 3 tablets/day

Chapter 56 Physiology of the Digestive System

MASTERING THE INFORMATION

MATCHING

1. f 2. d 3. i 4. e 5. b 6. g 7. j 8. c 9. h
10. a

TRUE OR FALSE

1. f 2. f 3. t 4. f 5. f 6. f 7. t 8. t 9. t
10. f

SHORT ANSWER

1. The digestive system provides the body with fluids, nutrients, and electrolytes in a form that can be used at the cellular level. It also disposes of waste products.
2. The small intestine is 20 feet long.
3. The parasympathetic nervous system—by the vagus nerve; the hormone gastrin; the presence of food in the mouth; and seeing, smelling, and thinking about food stimulate the secretion of gastric juices.

4. About 1000 mL of saliva is produced daily.
5. The upper sphincter prevents air from entering the esophagus during inspiration, and the lower sphincter prevents reflux of acidic gastric contents into the esophagus.

PRACTICING FOR NCLEX

MULTIPLE-CHOICE QUESTIONS

1. c   2. d   3. a   4. b   5. d   6. b   7. d   8. b   9. a   10. c

ALTERNATE FORMAT QUESTIONS

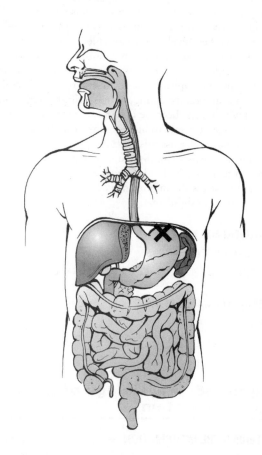

Chapter 57   Nutritional Support Products, Vitamins, and Mineral–Electrolytes

MASTERING THE INFORMATION

MATCHING

1. a   2. i   3. b   4. e   5. d   6. g   7. j   8. h   9. f
10. c

TRUE OR FALSE

1. f   2. f   3. t   4. t   5. t   6. t   7. f   8. t   9. f
10. t

SHORT ANSWER

1. Niacin can cause anorexia, nausea, vomiting, diarrhea, and postural hypotension.

2. They usually have a deficiency because of inadequate dietary intake and use of large amounts of thiamine to metabolize ethanol.
3. The drug of choice is potassium chloride (KCl).
4. It combines with iron to prevent its absorption. It can remove iron from storage sites and combine with iron to produce a water-soluble compound that can be excreted by the kidneys.
5. Signs and symptoms include unintended weight loss, increased susceptibility to infection, weakness and fatigability, impaired wound healing, impaired growth and development in children, edema, and decreased hemoglobin.

APPLYING YOUR KNOWLEDGE

To obtain a half-strength solution, the formula has to be diluted with an equal amount of water so you will add 240 cc of tap water to one can of Ensure. The infusion rate is for 2000 mL per 24 hours, which calculates to an hourly rate of 83 mL/hour. Set the infusion pump to deliver 83 mL/hour.

PRACTICING FOR NCLEX

MULTIPLE-CHOICE QUESTIONS

1. c   2. b   3. a   4. d   5. d   6. b   7. c   8. b   9. c   10. d

ALTERNATE FORMAT QUESTIONS

1. a. 4 b. 2 c. 1 d. 3 e. 5
2. b d

Chapter 58   Drugs to Aid Weight Management

MASTERING THE INFORMATION

MATCHING

1. d   2. f   3. e   4. c   5. a   6. g   7. j   8. h   9. i
10. b

TRUE OR FALSE

1. f   2. t   3. f   4. t   5. t   6. t   7. f   8. f   9. t
10. t

SHORT ANSWER

1. because of its association with high rates of morbidity and mortality
2. overweight—body mass index (BMI) of 25 to 29.9 kg/m^2; obesity—BMI of 30 kg/m^2 or more
3. 18.5 to 24.9 kg/m^2; values below 18.5 indicate underweight, and any values of 25 or above indicate excessive weight
4. 1 to 2 lb/wk
5. abdominal cramping, gas pains, diarrhea, and fatty stools

APPLYING YOUR KNOWLEDGE

Explain to Joan that according to your calculation of BMI, she is overweight by 15 pounds. Given her age and weight, she is at risk for cardiovascular disease. The combination of obesity and hypertension is associated with cardiac changes such as thickening of the ventricular wall, ischemia, and increased heart volume that can lead to heart failure more rapidly. Weight loss of as little as 4.5 kg (10 lb) can decrease blood pressure and cardiovascular risk.

PRACTICING FOR NCLEX

MULTIPLE-CHOICE QUESTIONS

1. b 2. a 3. c 4. a 5. a 6. c 7. a 8. c 9. b 10. a

ALTERNATE FORMAT QUESTIONS

1. a d e f
2. a b c d e f

Chapter 59 Drugs Used for Peptic Ulcer and Acid Reflux Disorders

MASTERING THE INFORMATION

MATCHING

1. d 2. a 3. h 4. c 5. i 6. g 7. e 8. j 9. b
10. f

TRUE OR FALSE

1. f 2. t 3. t 4. t 5. f 6. f 7. t 8. f 9. t
10. t

SHORT ANSWER

1. Pepsin is a proteolytic enzyme that helps digest protein foods. It is derived from pepsinogen, which is secreted by chief cells in the gastric mucosa. Pepsinogen is converted to pepsin only in highly acidic environments.
2. This is a rare condition characterized by excessive secretion of gastric acid and a high incidence of ulcers. It is caused by gastrin-secreting tumors in the pancreas, stomach, or duodenum. About two-thirds of the gastrinomas are malignant.
3. They react with hydrochloric acid in the stomach to produce neutral, less acidic, or poorly absorbed salts and to raise pH (alkalinity) of gastric secretions. Raising the pH inhibits the conversion of pepsinogen to pepsin.
4. Clinical indications include peptic ulcer disease, gastroesophageal reflux disease, esophagitis, GI bleeding caused by acute stress ulcers, and Zollinger-Ellison syndrome.
5. A proton pump inhibitor suppresses gastric acid more effectively and for a longer period of time.

APPLYING YOUR KNOWLEDGE

You should suspect that Ellen's carbamazepine levels are above the therapeutic range and causing toxic effects. The most likely reason for this is the concurrent use of cimetidine because both cimetidine and carbamazepine are metabolized by the cytochrome P450 system in the liver. The physician will probably want to draw a blood level to confirm this is the cause of Ellen's symptoms. Ellen needs to be cautioned to check with her health care provider before using over-the-counter medications because drug interactions can occur. The provider may switch Ellen to a proton pump inhibitor or a different histamine–receptor antagonist, such as famotidine (Pepcid) or ranitidine (Zantac) because these drugs are not metabolized through the P450 system and will not interact with her antiseizure medication.

PRACTICING FOR NCLEX

MULTIPLE-CHOICE QUESTIONS

1. d 2. a 3. a 4. c 5. b 6. b 7. b 8. b 9. c 10. a

ALTERNATE FORMAT QUESTIONS

1. a c d f
2. a d

Chapter 60 Laxatives and Cathartics

MASTERING THE INFORMATION

MATCHING

1. b 2. c 3. d 4. a 5. c 6. a 7. d 8. c 9. b
10. e

TRUE OR FALSE

1. t 2. t 3. f 4. t 5. f 6. f 7. t 8. f 9. t
10. f

SHORT ANSWER

1. Saline cathartics may cause hypermagnesemia, hyperkalemia, fluid retention, and edema.
2. They are taken with fluids to prevent thickening and expansion in the GI tract with possible obstruction. These substances absorb water rapidly and solidify into a gelatinous mass.
3. Milk and cimetidine can cause premature dissolution and gastric irritation and result in abdominal cramping and vomiting.
4. Two groups of drugs that decrease the effects of laxatives and cathartics are anticholinergics and CNS depressants.
5. Laxatives and cathartics are used to relieve constipation in pregnant women, elderly clients whose abdominal and perineal muscles have become weak and atrophied, children with megacolon, and clients that have decreased intestinal motility.

APPLYING YOUR KNOWLEDGE

Abdominal fullness, bloating, and seepage of liquid stool are all symptoms of fecal impaction. Fecal impaction is likely in this patient because she is taking large amounts of narcotics and is inactive. To treat the impacted stool, oil retention enemas are helpful to soften the hardened stool. Oral laxatives are usually ineffective in moving the hardened plug of feces. Frequently, manual removal of the impaction is required, especially if the patient is weak. It is important to institute an aggressive bowel program for any patient receiving long-term narcotics for pain control. Tolerance is never developed for the constipating side effect of opioids. Bulk-forming laxatives and stool softeners should be used on a daily basis. Saline or stimulant cathartics can be administered when 2 to 3 days elapse without a bowel movement. Because impaction can occur, enemas are also used. Teaching regarding increasing fluids, fiber, and activity, all within individual limitations, is also important.

PRACTICING FOR NCLEX

MULTIPLE-CHOICE QUESTIONS

1. c   2. b   3. b   4. c   5. c   6. b   7. a   8. a   9. d   10. c

ALTERNATE FORMAT QUESTIONS

1. a b d
2. b d e

Chapter 61   Antidiarrheals

MASTERING THE INFORMATION

MATCHING

1. j   2. h   3. f   4. d   5. e   6. b   7. a   8. g   9. i
10. c

TRUE OR FALSE

1. t   2. f   3. f   4. t   5. t   6. f   7. f   8. t   9. f
10. t

SHORT ANSWER

1. Diarrhea is a symptom of many conditions that increase bowel motility. Bowel contents are rapidly propelled toward the rectum, and absorption of fluids and electrolytes is limited.
2. Diarrhea is caused by excessive use or abuse of laxatives and intestinal infections.
3. Severe or prolonged diarrhea, ulcerative colitis and Crohn's disease, and ileostomies or surgical excision of portions of the ileum are indications for use of antidiarrheal drugs.
4. Rifaximin is used to treat traveler's diarrhea caused by noninvasive strains of *Escherichia coli*.
5. The active metabolite of nitazoxanide is highly bound to plasma proteins and may result in competitive drug interactions.

APPLYING YOUR KNOWLEDGE

First ask Mrs. Riley about her normal bowel pattern and her usual management strategies. Sometimes people think it is important to have a bowel movement every day; thus, they take laxatives when they perceive they are constipated, creating a cycle of bowel dysfunction. Try education first,

explaining the importance of exercise and fiber in the diet. A bulk-forming laxative can be helpful in reestablishing a regular bowel pattern. Unless the diarrhea is severe, causing significant fluid loss and impaired ability to carry on daily activities, antidiarrheal medications should be avoided.

PRACTICING FOR NCLEX

MULTIPLE-CHOICE QUESTIONS

1. b   2. c   3. d   4. a   5. b   6. a   7. d   8. b   9. a   10. a

ALTERNATE FORMAT QUESTIONS

1. a b c d e
2. b d e

Chapter 62   Antiemetics

MASTERING THE INFORMATION

MATCHING

1. h   2. d   3. j   4. b   5. g   6. e   7. i   8. f   9. a
10. c

TRUE OR FALSE

1. t   2. t   3. f   4. f   5. f   6. t   7. t   8. t   9. t
10. f

SHORT ANSWER

1. The vomiting center is located in the medulla oblongata.
2. The drugs are thought to stimulate the release of serotonin from the enterochromaffin cells of the small intestine, and this releases serotonin and then activates 5-HT$_3$ receptors located on vagal afferent nerves in the chemoreceptive trigger zone (CTZ) to initiate the vomiting reflex.
3. Diarrhea, headache, dizziness, constipation, muscle aches, and transient elevations of liver enzymes are common adverse effects.
4. Anticholinergics and antihistamines are preferred for motion sickness.
5. It produces relaxation and inhibits cerebral cortex input to the vomiting center.

APPLYING YOUR KNOWLEDGE

When giving very emetogenic drugs, it is important to use antiemetics preventively. The drugs are most effective when given before the onset of nausea. Because gastrointestinal absorption is often variable, the IV route is preferred in this situation to obtain adequate effects before treatment is started. The antiemetics work in different ways so they can be used in combination to treat chemotherapy-induced nausea and vomiting.

PRACTICING FOR NCLEX

MULTIPLE-CHOICE QUESTIONS

1. a   2. b   3. c   4. b   5. a   6. d   7. d   8. a   9. b   10. c

ALTERNATE FORMAT QUESTIONS
1. a b c d e
2. b d e

ALTERNATE FORMAT QUESTIONS
1. b
2. a. 5 b. 1 c. 3 d. 4 e. 2 f. 6

Chapter 63   Drugs Used in Ophthalmic Conditions

MASTERING THE INFORMATION

MATCHING

  1. a 2. g 3. e 4. i 5. b 6. d 7. j 8. c 9. f
10. h

TRUE OR FALSE

  1. f 2. f 3. t 4. t 5. f 6. t 7. t 8. t 9. f
10. t

SHORT ANSWER

1. The most common method is topical application or suspensions (eye drops) to the conjunctiva.
2. Local anesthetics, antihistamines, mast cell stabilizers, antimicrobials, autonomic drugs, corticosteroids, nonsteroidal anti-inflammatory drugs, prostaglandin analogs, carbonic anhydrase inhibitors, osmotic agents, and fluorescein are used to diagnose and treat ophthalmic disorders.
3. Corticosteroids can cause glaucoma, increase intraocular pressure, nerve damage, defects in visual acuity and fields of vision, cataracts, or secondary ocular infections.
4. Natamycin (Natacyn) is the drug of choice for fungal eye infections.
5. Older adults are more likely to have cardiovascular disorders that can be aggravated by systemic absorption of topical eye medication. Possible adverse drug effects include hypertension, tachycardia, or dysrhythmias with adrenergic drugs and bradycardia, heart block, or bronchoconstriction with beta blockers.

APPLYING YOUR KNOWLEDGE

Start by assessing what Mrs. Jetson knows about glaucoma and providing basic information about the condition. Review and write down the order for eyedrops. Sometimes the small print on the mediation container is difficult to read. Ask Mrs. Jetson if she has taken eyedrops before. If so, watch her demonstrate this procedure, reinforcing proper technique (tilt head back, pull down lower lid, drop medication into sac, close eyes, and occlude tear duct). Good aseptic techniques should be stressed (wash hands, keep container clean, do not let dropper touch eye). Also caution Mrs. Jetson to notify her doctor before taking any medications or remedies.

PRACTICING FOR NCLEX

MULTIPLE-CHOICE QUESTIONS

1. c 2. d 3. c 4. b 5. b 6. d 7. b 8. a 9. c. 10. c

Chapter 64   Drugs Used in Dermatologic Conditions

MASTERING THE INFORMATION

MATCHING

  1. f 2. e 3. h 4. j 5. i 6. c 7. g 8. b 9. d
10. a

TRUE OR FALSE

  1. f 2. t 3. t 4. f 5. f 6. t 7. f 8. f 9. t
10. t

SHORT ANSWER

1. Skin functions include (1) serving as a physical barrier against loss of fluids and electrolytes and against entry of microorganisms, foreign bodies and other potentially harmful substances; (2) detecting sensations of pain, pressure, touch, and temperature through sensory nerve endings; (3) assisting in regulating body temperature through production and elimination of sweat; (4) serving as a source of vitamin D when exposed to sunlight or other sources of UV light; (5) serving as an excretory organ (water, sodium, chloride, lactate, and urea are excreted in sweat); and (6) inhibiting growth of many microorganisms by its acidic pH (4.5 to 6.5).
2. The most common mediator of urticaria is histamine.
3. A localized, contact dermatitis type of reaction would exhibit erythema, facial edema, pain, blisters, necrosis, and urticaria.
4. It takes 6–8 weeks for oral antibiotics to produce therapeutic effects in treating inflammatory acne.
5. Nausea and vomiting, headache, blurred vision, eye irritation, conjunctivitis, skin disorders, abnormal liver function, musculoskeletal pain, increased plasma triglycerides, depression, and suicidal ideation commonly occur with oral retinoid preparations.

APPLYING YOUR KNOWLEDGE

Ask the mother to describe when the rash appeared and if its occurrence corresponded with diarrhea or new foods being introduced in the diet. Question the mother regarding the types of diapers she uses and how often the baby is changed. Inspect the baby's skin for the severity of diaper rash and other skin irritation. Observe for any sign of fungal infection.

    Stress the importance of keeping the baby clean and dry by changing the diaper frequently and washing with gentle soap and water. If the area is excoriated, a protective barrier can be achieved by applying a thin coat of many commercially available products such as petroleum jelly (Vaseline) or Desitin.

PRACTICING FOR NCLEX
MULTIPLE-CHOICE QUESTIONS

1. d 2. b 3. d 4. a 5. b 6. c 7. b 8. c 9. a 10. b

ALTERNATE FORMAT QUESTIONS

1. b d e

2. 8 mg per dose

Chapter 65   Drugs Used During Pregnancy and Lactation

MASTERING THE INFORMATION
MATCHING

1. a 2. d 3. c 4. b 5. i 6. e 7. j 8. h 9. f
10. g

TRUE OR FALSE

1. f 2. f 3. t 4. t 5. f 6. t 7. t 8. f 9. t
10. f

SHORT ANSWER

1. Caffeine can cause infants to be jittery and have difficulty sleeping.
2. Marijuana impairs formation of DNA and RNA and decreases oxygen supply to the mother and fetus.
3. Aspirin causes prolonged gestation, prolonged labor, and antepartum and postpartum hemorrhage. Fetal effects include constriction of the ductus arteriosus, low birth weight, and increased incidence of stillbirth and neonatal death.
4. Carbamazepine, phenytoin, and valproate are known teratogens and are rated risk category D.
5. Insulin is the only antidiabetic drug recommended for use during pregnancy.

APPLYING YOUR KNOWLEDGE

Many drugs given to the mother are excreted into breast milk. An increasing number of studies are being conducted to try to quantify drug effects during lactation so use current resources to get the most up-to-date information. To determine possible effects on her son, the mother should consult her pediatrician regarding any medications she is taking. At times, it is best for the mother to pump her breast and discard the milk until she in no longer taking medication. Antihistamines, which often are found in cold remedies, may dry up milk production and cause drowsiness in the infant.

PRACTICING FOR NCLEX
MULTIPLE-CHOICE QUESTIONS

1. b 2. c 3. b 4. b 5. b 6. c 7. d 8. b 9. a 10. d

ALTERNATE FORMAT QUESTIONS

1. b e

2. a b d